The Stritonoly Chronicles

William Kroupa

sci-fi-cafe.com

Introduction

The three books you are about to read in this collection were written quite a few years ago. I do hope you enjoy them.

I would like to dedicate these book to two people.

As a working musician and songwriter I draw much of my inspiration from music. There is one man who I consider my best friend even though we have never met. This man has written the most amazing music and lives on the same island I do in New York. We have never crossed paths personally but I have found significant guidance and inspiration from his music throughout the years. In fact, many times when I am writing I have his music on in the background. This man of course is Billy Joel. I would like to dedicate these books to him in the hope that one day he might read them himself. I know that's a long shot but that would be quite cool!

The second man I'd like to dedicate these books to is a man I have also never met face-to-face but have been friends with for almost a decade. He stood by me even when my books were not selling and he was making peanuts off of them. That man is my publisher Mr. Andy Severn. Thank you Andy for everything. You are an amazing man and I hope one day we can in fact meet face-to-face!

God is great indeed!!!

William Kroupa Jr.

The Eye of the Storm

PROLOGUE

BECKI SCREAMED. HER fingernails dug tight into the bark of the tree she held. With quick and uneven shots of breath, she gasped for air to fill her ever tightening lungs.

Clouds of black fog filled the rain soaked skies. Twirling, rolling furiously, like volcanic ash vomiting from the heavens. Then a lightning bolt pierced the back side of the tree. Becki was thrown backwards. She flew into the murky abyss, finally crashing down, slamming onto the rocky ground below. Oozing from her open mouth, blood dripped down her chin.

With the wind howling, dust shifting and debris flying, she could barely make out his form. Caught in this universal rage, The Czar of Stritonoly was alive for now. Becki could only lie there, almost lifeless, no energy left to fight anymore—her long, dirty blonde hair whipping around her pale and innocent face, almond green eyes blinking furiously.

The Czar felt the storm continue to yank his small frame back and forth. His body rocked violently from the tiny pieces of rubble smashing into him. His velvet cape torn— flapping wildly in the relentless wind. The Imperial logo, an embroidered row of serpents, ripped away from his chest. His mind started to erupt thought... *I'm losing it all... How did this happen?*

If she didn't know him so well, he would have been invisible to her now. Her eyes narrowed, squinting to see him more clearly. She knew instinctively how he walked, moved, breathed. He was still there, but only as a blurry apparition. He tried in vain to move towards her, throwing his body in her direction. Leaping for her with full force, the attempt only threw him away. The giant hands kept holding him back.

Hands! Are they human hands? Becki asked herself. *Or are they claws? I cannot tell!*

What she saw was real, but the creature that held the Czar was not human at all. The creature began to cling to him like a giant string of teeth ready to bite down. He felt the creature rip into his flesh, every fiber of his being sensing the agony in super slow-motion.

Beep... Beep... Beep!!!

Becki spun her head quickly around, searching for the sound. This constant beeping sound. Suddenly, every action and movement screeched to a violent halt. All was silent now... except for the beeping... the steady beeping. Then, she sensed the real pain growing inside her. Becki stopped breathing as she entered the darkness.

Chapter 1
The Morning

DMITRI SAT BACK in his well-cushioned green recliner and peered through the large northwest window. He was alone, sitting just off the main parlor on the first floor of the Imperial Citadel.

It was early morning and the sun of the north was beginning to rise. A light drizzle fell gently across the window pane. The rains had greatly diminished from the storm of the night before.

Dmitri sat in his light brown royal uniform, watching the rain subside and the sun grow. He could not help but admire its purity, its simplicity, an innocence he once treasured.

This place—ah this place; home to so many. The Imperial Citadel sat atop the largest mountaintop on Stritonoly. The people called it Mount Crito. Fat black cement columns, monstrous in density and depth, stood side by side and spread out all around the outskirts. The citadel itself was enormous, reaching up some twelve stories. Spires thrust defiantly towards the sky, while graceful arches and curves swept outwards, blending into the forests and rock of the mountain beneath.

The octagonal orange bricks used in the design of the citadel were shipped from factories very near the outermost edges of the galaxy—places no mortal man would ever go. Slave workers from a nearby moon were sent to retrieve these bricks almost five hundred years ago. The slave workers, commonly known as the acidel, were capable of withstanding the rigors of space flight at speeds no human could ever endure.

Acidel slaves were flexible creatures with beige wrinkled skin, much like a rubber band. The acidel were also very, very small. In fact, so small that a normal sized human could easily walk over them without even knowing. And that did happen from time to time. Dmitri had stepped over, and sometimes stepped *on* them a few times himself.

Acidel babies were born no bigger than the tip of a human finger. By the time they were teenagers most had achieved their full stature The tallest of the acidel would grow no higher than the waistline of an adult human, the large majority only reached up to about knee level. And although they did not have great height, their weight was a different story. A typical acidel weighed in excess of a hundred pounds. For a creature so small, they were, well... they were fat!

The most curious thing about the acidel was that their faces were identical. They all had the same large bald heads, sullen, droopy cheeks and wide circular eyes. They also dressed in the same white robes, black belts and brown sandals. There were times when it was virtually impossible to tell them apart.

As Dmitri pushed away the long red hair from his forehead, he sat up straight and reached for a piece of white cloth he had in his pants pocket. He brushed his hair into a tight knot behind his head and wrapped it with the cloth making a neat ponytail. Seeing his reflection in the window, he took note of the white cloth wrapped around such straight cherry red hair. He thought it made for a look of remarkable nobility. He wished his features were more mature. He still had the look of a child, a look he despised.

His blue eyes began to burn as he forced himself not to blink at the emerging light from the sunrise. This magnificent sunrise reminded Dmitri of his youth. He was born on this planet nineteen years ago, and was born into nobility. He had achieved great knowledge and learned everything there was to know about this planet; a world of extreme wealth and fortune. It was not a large planet but there were many small towns and outlying communities that stretched out in sparse patches across the many mountains and valleys.

Stritonoly was called the purple mountain planet and it was home to many creatures of the universe. The population of the entire planet never grew much larger than two-hundred thousand—half of that number being of human descent.

From space, an observer could clearly see high mountains and vast areas of purple land covering Stritonoly. There were very few water basins. But they did have one of the largest rivers in this sector of the galaxy. The River Frehenly flowed through several towns on the southern side of the planet. The citadel sat on the northern side so it was necessary for laborers to deliver water from the river to the citadel several times a week. The river itself spanned some forty miles as it swept past the citadel above. It was the main sightseeing attraction of the planet for visitors and residents alike.

Stritonoly's massive wealth came exclusively from the beautiful purple rocky surface that covered almost all the planet. This rocky surface was called purock. The majority of the population of Stritonoly were employed by the citadel as artists and designers. The purock, once it was detached from the ground, became a sight of extreme splendor. The purock was then sculpted by trained artists into works of stunning beauty. The practice of sculpting purock into artistic designs began nearly four hundred years ago. The artworks quickly became popular and were sought after by every significant empire in the galaxy. The rocky artwork was sold to planets all over the universe for incredibly large sums of currency. As the demand increased, so did the price. There seemed to be an unquenchable lust for owning the finest purock art Stritonoly could produce.

All human children on Stritonoly, who were not of nobility, were schooled in only two subjects: religious doctrine and art. They were provided the very best instruction in mixed media, layering and texture painting, beginning through advanced pastel interpretation, sculpting, etching, realist painting in oils and acrylic, dyeing, watercolor and of course the specific art of using these techniques on the purock itself.

The best part about the purock was that as soon as it was cut away from the surface, it would grow back just as fast. So there was always an endless supply of the material from which Stritonoly drew its finances.

Dmitri stood slowly, never taking his eye from the sun. He raised an arm and snapped his fingers.

Three acidel scampered into the room. Two immediately went for Dmitri's shoelaces and tied them quickly. The third acidel was Barok, leader of the slave workers.

The acidel maintained a very busy schedule as it was their job to cut away the purple rocky surface daily and prepare it for artists to render the material into a work worthy of selling at an enormous profit. This profit was due in large part to the fact that the acidel were slaves bound to this planet. They received no payment for their work assignments, only a home, residency in the rear of the citadel was their only reward for their tireless labor. They knew how to do their job well. Failure to do so would result in severe beatings and public humiliation.

"Master Dmitri," Barok said, "Will your sister be joining us?"

Barok spoke in a husky baritone growl, not at all befitting his tiny size. All the acidel had the same mono-tonality in their speech patterns. Dmitri had long since grown accustomed to this uniquely low sound, but if you were to hear them for the first time, it was a most annoying noise indeed.

"I love the morning," Dmitri replied. His soft voice completely ignoring the question Barok asked. "The morning here has such a peacefulness," Dmitri breathed. "I have not been able to find this peace anywhere… except here. This moment is a gift, I suppose."

Barok adjusted his robe collar, somewhat uncomfortable and fearful to respond. "Yes, Master Dmitri, it seems to be a beautiful morning."

Dmitri turned from the window and faced Barok: "I have no idea what my sister will be doing this morning. But I will be seeing her tonight. Oh yes, I will definitely be seeing her tonight."

"I understand," Barok said, as he flashed the customary acidel hand signal - one stubby finger placed upon his rubbery brow. This hand signal sent the two other workers scurrying away.

"With your permission," Barok continued, "I was wondering if I may be so bold as to ask a question, Master."

"Ask me your question, my dear Barok." Dmitri said. His voice was always so soothing, too soothing, as if he were hiding something of great importance. It reminded Barok of the rolling rapids on The River Frehenly in the springtime. No doubt an amazing wonder to observe from afar, but get too close and you risk falling victim to its deceptive splendor. Then you will most certainly be swept away by its force.

Taking several mechanical steps toward Dmitri, Barok continued, "I have heard strange things, Master. I have heard rumblings that our position here is… well, not what it appears to be. I know of our assignment for later this morning and I have a terrible concern things are not in order."

Dmitri smiled slowly. "Is anything what it appears to be at first glance? I have found that situations usually appear to be something they are not. When you gaze at a star, do you actually see a star? No, you see but a memory of what used to be."

"I am not sure. What does my master mean?" Barok swallowed. "I… do not understand. Does my master have a point? I seem to be missing it entirely."

"I would not waste even a second of time worrying about such nonsense." Dmitri turned sharply away from the window, and said: "I never worry about anything. There is no reason to." He made his way unhurriedly toward the door. Barok followed close behind.

Strolling casually from the room, the two entered the main parlor. This was the center of the citadel, and it offered a sumptuous display of all the finer things this planet had to offer. Narrow stalks of the yellow pipetu plant trailed up the side of every wall, their sweet fragrance filling the room. Several triangular windows allowed the north sun to shine through, splashing light upon the row of peculiar black serpents etched upon the freshly scrubbed white marble floor.

A gong hung atop a stony ledge just above the foyer. With the acidel hand signal, Barok summoned the workers to activate the sound. A moment later the gong sounded, although no one touched it. This was just one of the many tasks the acidel could perform using simple telepathic powers.

While they did not possess the mind bending characteristics or skills of most outer galaxy tribes, they were able to perform simple acts of labor when conditioned properly. This type of work could be accomplished only if taught to them by a human presence, preferably someone of considerable intelligence. The higher the level of intelligence a human possessed, the greater the task the acidel could perform, within reason, of course. The more confidence a human had in his own actions, the better the acidel could perform.

The front gates opened seconds after the gong sounded. As Dmitri slowly made his way past the gates, he paused to observe the morning dew. As he did, Barok clumsily smashed the top of his bald rubbery head into Dmitri's buttocks.

Embarrassed by this lack of concentration, Barok quickly retreated and repositioned himself directly behind his master. Dmitri suppressed a chuckle as best he could.

Over a thousand acidel waited outside the front gates. They stretched out in several straight lines just outside the entryway.

"Welcome to your day," a scratchy tenor voice said. It was the unmistakable articulation of Ethan Educai, the royal instructor and protection supervisor for the royal kindred. He always greeted Dmitri with these words, no matter what his mood.

Ethan had spent his whole life in the pursuit of knowledge. He was not a big man and had the look of an exhausted elder warrior after battle. The robe he wore today was navy blue. His eyes of steel peered out from beneath a floppy hood. The long flowing white beard complemented an educated but tired demeanor.

Ethan had seen the horrors of what his knowledge might bring.

Great knowledge eventually falls prey to even greater consequences, Ethan thought. *There are things no human need ever know in this lifetime.*

Dmitri continued to smile as Ethan nodded his head. No words were necessary to convey what appeared to be a simple hello between two men so close.

"It's a nice morning," Ethan said flatly, not a hint of excitement in his tone. The icy, matter-of-fact manner in which Ethan delivered his welcome left Dmitri angered.

Dmitri specifically told Ethan how he wished to be greeted on this morning. Ethan was not being as friendly or cooperative as Dmitri had hoped.

"Is it a nice morning?" Dmitri said rhetorically before answering himself, "Yes... now that you mention it, I suppose it is." And with a sudden turn away from his mentor, he withdrew his smile.

Barok sensed the disturbance immediately. This would not be a nice morning at all. His perception suggested that a storm unlike any other approached, one that he may even be able to stop, but would not. The storm of the night before was nothing compared to what was in store for this planet today.

Suddenly, a commotion from inside the citadel.

An abrupt roar was followed by a woman screaming, sounds of distress and confusion.

With a flurry of movement, Ethan grabbed Dmitri and flung him to the ground.

"You'll not see the end of this!" Ethan howled, standing over Dmitri.

Two imperial soldiers ran toward the conflict, unsure of whom to protect.

Hordes of acidel streamed out the front gates, yelling wildly in their deep growl.

As he drew his knife, Ethan locked his stare on Dmitri, ever more aware of the wailing cries emerging from just inside the gates.

Dozens of soldiers in battle fatigues quickly descended from all directions. They wore green and black masks, solid black riot gear with serpents shining on their shields and weaponry. Steel blades upon their jagged swords caught the glare of sunlight, and they glistened with a powerful brilliance.

"Get away from here at once!" Dmitri shouted, standing and simultaneously shoving the two imperial soldiers away. Adjusting his uniform, he focused all his energies onto Ethan. "All of you soldiers, be gone! This is not your concern!"

"Master Dmitri," Barok implored, "Please, do not be foolish!"

With an overly-confidant arrogance, Dmitri drew his royal sword. "This is my home, I took a vow to protect it!"

"That is true," Ethan said. "And I took a vow to protect you!"

"Do you still intend to keep your vow?" Dmitri snickered.

"It is a solemn vow...But...I..." Ethan staggered for a moment. Losing his balance, he felt suddenly short of breath. Clutching his chest, he crumbled to the ground.

Ah yes, Dmitri smiled. *The poison... The poison is finally working.*

Chapter 2

Subject: Re: Rebecca Brown
Date: 10/2/2014 3:31:17 P.M. EDT
From: Mrs. Raddick
To: Mr. Brown
CC: District Administration, Guidance
Department, Principal Dr. Danton

Mr. Brown,
Could you please contact me as soon as
possible. Rebecca seems to having a great
deal of difficulty staying on task. I would
like to schedule a conference at your
earliest convenience to discuss this matter.
Mrs. Raddick

Chapter 3
The night before

THE DAY HAD been long for Ethan. Weary but still alert, he ran his wrinkled fingers through his long white beard, lost in thought.

It was the end of the twelfth day of the New Year and darkness descended upon the forest. Tomorrow morning he'd get up early, meditate, exercise, and then meet his pupil Dmitri.

Presently however, his feelings were elsewhere.

Sitting down on a tree stump, he stared at the distant skies. So many moons, so many planets and galaxies. Far too many for one man to ever absorb in a single lifetime. The complexity of the universe unnerved his consciousness. *What is really out there?* He thought. *Will anyone ever know for certain?*

The puzzle of the universe was both a fascination and a horror for Ethan. He was full of joy and wonderment at times, despair and misery at others.

For a man of such intellect, he often found himself caught in doubt and inner turmoil, constantly pursuing the unknown, that which he could never firmly grasp. This uneasiness left Ethan depressed, hopelessly searching for an answer. And for all that he knew to be true, the only certainty he felt at this moment was that a cosmic truth about the universe, an answer to what it all really meant, would never be found in his lifetime.

Blump!...Blumb! It was the sound of drums, methodically striking. The beat signified the end of daylight hours here on Stritonoly. Then: *Clang!* The gong sound that meant curfew for residents of the citadel.

Ethan stood, walked onto a small patch of yellow grass and glanced again at the stars. Dim starlight illuminated his face, casting a gentle glow upon his tired deep-set eyes.

Then, a whispered conversation approached. Ethan detected voices in the distance. Two voices headed his way. Not wanting to be bothered with a confrontation of any sort, he looked for a place where he would not be seen. The conversation that approached did not sound kind.

Instinctively, and with catlike reflexes not befitting his age, Ethan went for cover behind the closest tree. *This is silly,* He thought. *What I am so leery of that I hide like a child? I am getting too old and nervous for my own good.*

As he ducked behind the tree, Ethan saw two figures approach, a young man and a woman of royalty, his pupils no doubt.

He thought to greet them, but the clear tension in their voices held him back.

"Yes, I am quite serious!" Dmitri said, bitterness in his tone. He trudged along sloppily, holding a bottle of plum wine in his hand. "This is exactly what I have feared from the start. The demise of our planet will surely come about if he is not stopped."

"He is only doing what he thinks to be right," his sister retorted, a strong sense of conviction in her dignified yet childlike response. She was still a teenager but acted the part of an adult. Her full lips, clear complexion and long blonde hair coupled with a natural genetic beauty were features that made many young ladies quite jealous. The bejeweled white night-robe she wore gently swayed in the soft breeze and she moved with the elegance and grace suitable for a royal princess.

"I am next in line to the throne," Dmitri barked. "I have not even been consulted on this matter, and I promise you, this will end the peace here." He belched, took a long gulp from his bottle of wine and wiped his mouth with the backside of his hand. "All that we have worked so hard to accomplish will be gone by this time tomorrow."

What is this about? Ethan thought.

"I do believe you may be overreacting," his sister said, trying to relay a measure of calm.

"Overreacting!" Dmitri shot back, spinning around to stare directly into her eyes. "I expect support and loyalty from you, nothing short of that will do. Especially...if I am to do what I must."

"Dmitri, you will have the throne one day, but Father is the Czar right now. Do not take sides against your own blood! You told me that many times."

Dmitri felt a rage churning up inside him, but he suppressed it. It was imperative that his sister not be a part of this treachery.

"Becki," Dmitri said, doing his best to appear comforting. "My dear sweet sister," he breathed. "I know in my heart you mean well, but this is politics. The acidel cannot be made to leave here. It is completely out of the question! They provide us our greatest need!"

"Labor?"

"Yes, of course labor! But much more than that. If used properly they will provide us with powers we could never attain on our own."

A clap of thunder roared above. Ethan swallowed hard, disturbed by the thunder but absorbed by the dialogue. *What if I am to be caught eavesdropping?* He worried.

"At least accept this proposition," Dmitri continued. "What if he is wrong? What if they are not the demon creatures he believes them to be?"

"I don't know," Becki said. "I don't have the answers you seek. I wish I could tell you differently."

She paused a long while, disturbed by the volatility her younger brother possessed.

"Is it really worth the risk?" Becki asked.

Dmitri burst into loud, obnoxious laughter. "You must be playing with me now. Don't be such a child, there is no risk whatsoever. Are you truly afraid of the silly little acidel? They are completely controllable."

"And what if Father is right? What if they mean us harm?"

"What if they do? So what! They have no power over us! They are but cursed creatures. We control them."

Doubt entered Becki's mind for the first time. She did not want to disobey her Father, but the thought of losing the prosperity the acidel labor provided frightened her. On the surface, Becki was innocent and sweet. But she was also a young and impressionable princess, very much used to living a life filled with extravagance. Not a thing she intended to ever give up.

"I am afraid," Becki said.

The wind hastened with another clap of thunder. Becki's long blonde hair swayed like a ballet in the breeze.

"Do not disobey me!" Dmitri stated with authority. "It is simple. You are with me...or...you are my enemy."

"You are frightening me," Becki said, a chill coming over her.

"Do not fear me. You are my only sister, I would never harm you... so long as you know your place."

I have never seen this side of Dmitri, Ethan thought. *How could I have been so blind?*

"There is something else," Dmitri said, "something that will ease your mind. It is a secret I have been holding for some time. I put trust in you as my sister that you will not reveal this secret to anyone."

Becki became attentive but unnerved. She found herself suddenly excited by the adrenaline rush such a secret could provide. Sitting down upon the damp yellow grass, her attractive features twisted into a look of morbid curiosity.

Dmitri knelt beside her and whispered: "You must swear to me that what I tell you is for your ears alone."

Becki swallowed, "I swear it."

Ethan peered out a fraction from behind the tree. Remaining still, he bent forward to hear every word clearly.

"I discovered something of vast importance in my youth," Dmitri paused, deliberate with his words. "You know that when the acidel work long hours, they perspire a great deal. And you know of the stories we have been told about this perspiration."

"Of course," Becki said, "it is deadly if ingested. It must be washed away immediately or it will harden and become toxic. It is written in our imperial scriptures. Even small children are taught this the moment they learn to read. No human under any circumstances can ever be exposed to their perspiration."

Ethan knew this scripture by heart. He remembered it as it appeared on the cover of his very first sacred course book:

> *IMPERIAL SCRIPTURES: chapter 14, verses 1-3. Acidel are to be treated with kindness for they provide us with a most valuable service. But be wary the virus they carry within their veins. The Lord Of All declares the acidel toxin seeping from their pores is an evil substance never to be touched by man. It is a crime for anyone to deliberately come into contact with any substance discharged from the acidel. It will be the responsibility of the imperial regime to discard any such substance so as to cause no man undue harm. It shall also be written into law that penalty for disobedience of this scripture edict will be a slow and painful death.*

Dmitri grinned. "That is a myth, and I know it for certain."

"How could you possibly know that for certain?"

"Because I have tasted it!"

Becki became cold. "What have you done?" she questioned, her head turned sideways.

"I have long been amazed by these creatures," Dmitri said quietly. "Amazed and repulsed! But their ability to harness mental capabilities, to perform tasks no human could ever hope to accomplish, this fascination led me from speculation to experimentation."

Dmitri leaned in, hissed: "For many years now...I have secretly saved it."

"Saved what?"

"Saved their sweat! Anywhere the flabby little mongrels worked, I would go after their day was done and wipe clean their filthy stench."

"But how were you able to do this?" Becki questioned. "We have imperial personnel trained in safe ways to clean the acidel work areas several times a day."

"Have you forgotten Becki? I am the royal heir. Imperial personnel will quickly look the other way for a promise of a lovely lady or a trinket or two of gold. That along with many promises I made to workers in exchange for their silence. Promises I will of course never keep."

"So what did you do then?" Becki asked.

"For many a sunrise I kept the liquid in my chambers. Like an alchemist I squeezed it from dirty rags...and then...I waited."

Becki appeared confounded, lost in confusion. "Dmitri! Why?"

He took a long gulp of wine, said: "I have eaten it after it hardens! Yes...Yes, I have...it is a euphoria you cannot begin to imagine!" Dmitri laughed, a sound full of lunacy and dementia.

This is a madness, Ethan thought. *How did I not see this before? Dmitri had pulled off a magic act in keeping this from me. I must learn more!*

The royal siblings shared a long moment of silence after Dmitri stopped laughing. Ethan closed his eyes as darkness crept further into the forest.

Maybe this is a dream from which I will soon wake? Ethan thought.

He opened his eyes slowly, realizing this was no dream at all, feeling as if he were trapped inside a frenetic nightmare. He leaned in, tried to hear more...he heard nothing. Then...he saw nothing.

The siblings had vanished from his sight.

Where did they go? He wondered. *They were just here!*

Smash! A blow to Ethan's head. He fell forward, shards of shattered glass exploded about him.

Dmitri stood over him, only the neck of the wine bottle left in his hand. "Hello Ethan, I believe you now owe me a bottle of plum wine!"

Becki watched in horror.

Ethan bled from the open gash on the back of his head. Crimson blood oozed into his silvery hair, a patch of color forming ever so slowly.

Beep...beep...beep!

The sound came from far beyond the night skies, resonating everywhere. It was constant, pounding into Becki's brain like a drum.

"Make it stop!" Becki screamed.

Dmitri only smiled as the beeping began to fade.

Chapter 4

"Have you ever seen The River Frehenly?" Gunther asked.

"Yes sir, in fact just last summer," the boy courier responded quietly, standing in the corner of an extremely plain, small room inside the citadel.

Gunther Sticks was standing also. Hands upon his hips, he was dressed as usual in his formal military uniform with medals adorning his brown jacket. Gunther was the commander of all military personnel employed by the citadel. General Sticks was his formal title but he found that to sound quite boring and even a little silly. Almost everyone, including the soldiers under his command, addressed him as Sir Gunther. He was a brash, large, menacing figure. His stubbly, tan and well-worn face bore the marks of several jagged scars. His shoulders and trapezium muscles were so massive that it appeared as if he had no neck.

Sir Gunther was also a ruthless killer but an equally faithful servant. This combination was unique and The Czar recognized the importance of having such a man on his side many years ago.

The Czar and Gunther met as young boys more than fifty years ago. They were trained as warriors and fought side by side in many a battle. They started their relationship as friends, but since that time they had formed an even stronger bond. Gunther considered them to be much more than just friends. He felt they had formed a strong bond of brotherhood and The Czar felt the same.

"The river is still quite a sight," Gunther said. "Is it not?" he asked the boy courier.

The courier was not sure if he was allowed to respond. He was only there to receive paperwork. He nervously shifted his eyes left to right.

"You may speak young lad," Gunther smiled.

"I found the rapids to be most lovely indeed," the courier said.

Gunther burst into laughter. "Are you a man or a child? Most lovely indeed! That is how you speak to me. You sound like a little girl! Go fetch yourself a pair of panties and a skirt!"

The other man in the room, Unic Heldar, tried to repress a smile but could not. Unic was the eldest of the noblemen who provided council. He wore a long glistening white robe with a burly hood that covered most of his face. When you looked at him, you could barely see a hint of a glow from his blue eyes, the rest was all in shadows.

"So, you really think you will make a good soldier one day," Gunther asked the boy.

"Um...Yes sir," the boy answered.

"Um...Yes sir!" Gunther mimicked him, "And you expect me to believe that a young lad with such obvious feminine qualities has the ability to kill?"

The boy was furious inside but he could not show it for fear of severe punishment. The boy felt he would make a remarkable soldier one day.

"Get out of my sight," Gunther ordered the boy, "Go to the study."

Embarrassed, the courier cowered away and quickly exited the room.

"What a numskull!" Gunther continued. "These boys they bring to us for training these days, they had better start to appear a bit more manly. They start these boys off as couriers and then expect us to make soldiers of them in short order. I will have my hands full trying to make a soldier out of that little prissy!"

Unic did not respond. He moved casually to a wooden chair that sat around a small circular table. Gunther took up a seat next to him.

They sat in a small conference room on the second floor of the citadel. A thin purple candle sat on the table and gave off just enough light to see about the bare room. The room itself was hardly ever used. It was empty except for the rounded table and the three chairs surrounding it.

"Good Evening," The Czar of Stritonoly said as he made his entrance into the room. He turned quickly and slammed the door behind him. He looked at Gunther and Unic sitting at the table. "I presume that third chair is for me?"

"You presume correct, old friend," Gunther said.

The Czar's velvet cape fluttered behind him as his thick black boots clicked across the floor. "Hmmm... Do I really need to sit for this?" The Czar asked.

"Only if you so desire," Unic said softly.

The Czar's old wrinkled face smiled. He pulled the wooden chair away from the table and sat down. Lifting the golden crown from his head and placing it on the table, it exposed his white hair which was currently combed up and bound into a tight bun.. Service medals of different shapes stretched out in lines upon the white lapels on the Czar's shirt. A small row of black serpents were stenciled onto his left shirt sleeve.

"So...I am here to finalize the paperwork?" The Czar asked.

"Yes," Gunther exclaimed.

"...and no," Unic answered back.

Gunther stretched out his mighty forearms unto the table, clenched his hands into two fists and pounded them down. "Not this again!"

"Gunther," The Czar said, "Be calm, I respect Unic even if I disagree with his position on this matter."

"I have the final draft ready for your signature, My Lord," Unic said with reverence. He reached inside the inner lining of his robe and produced the document.

"I hold in my hands the final draft of the order," Unic said. "Once you sign it my lord, there will be no reversing this action. The plan will be carried out to its completion."

Gunther's temper flared. "We have been over this in council! Just give The Czar the document Unic. Enough is enough! The time for discussion is at an end. Now is the time for action."

The Czar sat back in his chair. "Gunther," The Czar said with great compassion, "I love you my friend, you are truly my brother. But please, control your temper for just a while longer."

Gunther removed his fists from the table. Crossing his arms, he sat back and listened. His admiration for The Czar was apparent. He would lay down his life for him without a moment of hesitation.

The Czar fixed his attention upon Unic, "You obviously have something to say."

"I do," Unic replied, a morbid stillness in his voice.

"Then say it!" The Czar barked. He was through playing games now as well. He was tired and wanted this matter behind him. His frustration level had peaked. "Tell me Unic, tell me what I do not already know!"

"I feel an obligation to say this once more to you," Unic said, clearing his throat as he leaned forward, arms resting on the table. "I want for you to be aware of how history will judge us."

"Do you not think I have thought about this time and time again! I am well aware of the implications of what we are about to do."

"So then, there is no changing your mind, even if I were to offer a suggestion."

The Czar swallowed, gathered himself and looked straight at Unic, "Time is now of the essence. The execution of this plan awaits only my signature. If you have a suggestion, you should have told me many moons ago."

"My suggestion is a simple one...and I have suggested it before. I feel compelled to mention it one last time."

"Do not delay then," The Czar said, "Tell me what you need me to hear."

"Please, My Lord, wait just a few more days. Give the council more time to consider alternatives. We are about to join the long list of crimes against humanity. If it must be so, then I will someday come to understand. All I ask for is more time."

Gunther stood from his seat, pounded his fist again on the table. "Unic, you are not a warrior. You are very wise, of that I am sure. But these are matters of life and death for this entire planet."

"I agree with Sir Gunther," The Czar said, "I am struggling to see any other way to solve our problem."

"History will not be kind to your legacy," Unic warned.

"I do not care about history, I do not care about my legacy...I care about my son."

"Personal emotions can easily get in the way of prudent wisdom my lord," Unic said.

"This does not just concern the Czar's son," Gunther said. "We only know for certain about Dmitri's addiction. How do we know that others on this planet have not been contaminated as well."

"We do not," Unic admitted.

"So there it is," The Czar said, "give me the final document."

Hesitantly, Unic held the document in his hand but did not hand it over.

"Give the document to your Czar!" Gunther howled.

"May I be permitted to make one small request?" Unic asked respectfully.

The Czar let out a long sigh, "What is your request, my friend?"

"Do not sign it right now. I do not wish to be selfish, but I cannot bare to see you sign this in my presence. Go back to your study and pray on this matter. Meditate once more and call upon all your wisdom and knowledge. Be absolutely certain that what you do is the right course of action. If after you do this and you still choose to sign the final order, I will stand by you. I will take this burden on with you. But please, take the little time left before sunrise to think about it one more time. If only for another hour."

"Where is the boy courier?" The Czar asked Gunther.

"I sent him to the study."

The Czar turned to face Unic, "Out of respect for your council and your obvious wisdom, I will delay putting my signature to this document. I will retreat to my study to pray upon this matter once more. I must warn you however, do not hope for a change in my decision."

"I thank you for at least listening to my council."

"I have always listened to your council," The Czar said, standing, "and long after this is behind us, I will continue to do so.

The Czar paused a moment, then turned to face Unic, "I am sorry if I offended you with my tone earlier. I know you possess a strong and kind heart. But this is my decision to make. And it will be made before morning. I will allow only my own soul to bear the burden of this crime. That is the cost of leadership. My mirror stares back at me and sees an old and tired man. But still, I am a man with a purpose and a choice. This choice will be made before the north sun rises."

The Czar walked to the door, opened it, "Gunther, Where will you be this evening?"

"I will be awaiting your written orders at battle command headquarters."

"The courier will deliver this paperwork to you before morning. Thank you both for your council and your friendship...try to get some rest if you can," with that, The Czar left the room.

Using a thick vine he pulled from a dense patch, Dmitri tied Ethan to a tree. He stared blankly right through him. A devilish grin washed across his face.

"So, what are we to do with you now!" Dmitri sneered, striking the tree next to Ethan's head, forcefully driving his fist into the thick bark, a show of power that Ethan thought most absurd.

"It would befit you...to... put a halt to this," Ethan said, glistening in a cold sweat, drops of blood on his neck and robe.

"I don't recall asking for your counsel!"

"Maybe, you need to consider it."

Dmitri shot a glare at Becki, "What do you think?

Becki wet her lips and spoke cautiously: "It is not for me to decide. I know my place."

"As you should!" Dmitri said.

Ethan was sick, clammy with sweat. A thick vein in his forehead throbbed like a wild scherzo.

He tried to remember his training in therapeutic circumstances when a pupil was acting irrationally.

No matter what hand you are dealt, he told himself, *it is imperative to remain calm and objective at all times.*

But this was of little help now that the situation had seized control over his mind. Chaotic thoughts raced through his consciousness like a machete slashing its way through a rotten melon.

"I have long despised you," Dmitri hissed. "You think you know everything there is to know…You do not! There are no Gods to deliver you from torment, and you will never find the answers you seek. You are doomed to ignorance like the rest of humanity. You will rot in the ground upon your demise and all your knowledge will be for naught. For all you think you know…you eventually will be stripped naked. You will know nothing!"

"I have never professed to know all the answers to everything. No man can say such a thing."

"We will see about that!" Dmitri walked over to Becki "You know what must be done…Tell me you understand?"

It appeared she did not understand at all, but she felt the need to appease him, for now.

"Yes, I understand," Becki said. "You must do what you feel is right."

"And so I shall," Dmitri grinned.

Swinging back toward Ethan, he said: "I am not going to kill you, Ethan. There is no need for that presently. But there are a few things we need to discuss."

Ethan nodded his head. *Let me hear this out, Ethan thought. Maybe there is hope yet to talk some sense into him.*

Dmitri bent at his waist, seemed to be considering the options. "Bloodshed is sometimes necessary, but your disappearance would be cause for concern and attention I need not be bothered with. You do realize I hold your fate in my hand?"

"Yes." Ethan said hesitantly. "But I am a servant of the Czar. You are his son, if nothing else I have sworn my allegiance to the royal family. I shall not betray my solemn vow…I would never turn on you for any cause." But Ethan was lying, and Dmitri knew it.

"You are tied to a tree!" Dmitri said. "What else would you say to me! Am I to believe you simply on your word?" He laughed, a ferocious sound that froze both Ethan and Becki. Dmitri had assumed command, held a strangle hold on the conflict, and he loved every second of it.

Possibly beyond salvaging, the situation had rapidly lost any chance of order. It was Dmitri's game now. He was the ringleader, and a demon spirit continued to fester into his psyche. His red hair looked like an inferno of rage with the starlight bouncing off it.

The wind shifted its strength and began to swirl in uneven gusts about them. A sprinkle of rain was falling from the night skies.

"Do you believe?" Dmitri asked Ethan.

Somewhat bewildered by the question, Ethan politely requested: "Believe in what?"

"Do you believe in finality? The very end of all things?" Dmitri was clearly possessed by some other force, but his question had an eerie sensitivity to it, as if he really did seek an answer.

What is he talking about? Ethan thought. *Is he suicidal? He is not making sense. None of this is making sense!*

"I believe in hope," Ethan said, choosing his words carefully. "I believe that where there is hope, there is life."

"And what if we have lost our hope?" Becki asked.

Dmitri looked at Becki, head cocked.

Ethan detected an opening.

"Whatever the dilemma, the sickness, the storm...hope will always bring life," Ethan said, allowing his words some time to settle. "I have never encountered any condition that cannot be transformed by a state of hope."

"You speak of the desperate!" Dmitri shouted, his voice reverberating beyond the forest. "You must think me a fool, old man!"

"I think no such thing."

"Keep your voice down," Becki pleaded with her brother.

"Hope does not stop the inevitable," Dmitri whispered. "It is time for all to know this truth, and they will know it soon enough."

Ethan could not help but fear the worst.

I could be witnessing the beginning of the end, Ethan thought. The final moments of our lives may be at hand. Happiness and contentment are but a distant memory now.

As the rain began to gather pace, Ethan could no longer avoid the blackness that surrounded him.

The end was near.

Chapter 5

Young boy struck by vehicle at 8:00 am this morning after high speed pursuit on Route I-80. Rebecca Brown, 17, taken into custody at scene for reckless endangerment and driving while under the influence. She suffered a massive seizure at crime scene, taken to St. Paul's Hospital and declared dead on arrival. Condition and identity of the boy remains unknown.

Chapter 6

A SUDDEN CRASH of thunder lifted Barok from his slumber.

Jolted loose from his dreams, he jumped to his feet.

There was shouting coming from outside his room. He sensed the presence of humans just behind his chambers somewhere in the forest.

The acidel antechamber was located at the rear of the citadel in what used to be a greenhouse for exotic plants. It was attached to the citadel, but unlike the main structure, the walls were not solid. Every sound could be heard from the forest, including the thunder and the shouting that shook Barok from his deep sleep.

He scurried to the rear window, jumped atop a ledge and peered out into the darkness. Rain was falling and the trees swayed in the wind.

Barok's mate, an acidel female named Shroomy, turned sideways in their tiny bed and saw him on the ledge.

"What's wrong?" Shroomy asked. She had a slightly higher voice than her mate, but it had the unmistakable acidel quality, monotone and deep.

"It is past curfew and there are humans in the forest," Barok growled.

"It is not your concern," Shroomy yawned. "Come back to bed."

"I thought I heard Master Dmitri's voice. He was yelling, sounding most upset."

Barok continued to peer out the window. Through the rain it was difficult to see clearly, but he could make out a sliver of movement, no doubt human.

"Someone is out there," Barok said. "I sense it to be the royal kindred. I also sense a disturbance."

"Possibly," Shroomy said, sitting up on the side of the bed, her stubby feet barely reaching the floor. "And if it is a disturbance, you best not make yourself a part of it."

Barok knew her words to be true.

Whatever the dilemma, it would suit him best not to gain knowledge of it, lest he become involved.

"I am worried about other matters as well," Barok said, his back now to the window. He let out a long sigh, crossed his legs and sat on the ledge.

Shroomy lay belly down on the bed, faced Barok, put her tiny hands under her chin and stared at her mate. "You want to talk?" she asked.

"Yes, I do," Barok said. "But we have a very busy day tomorrow. We should sleep."

"What time will the freighter arrive for us?" Shroomy asked.

"It will be here shortly after morning. The acidel are to board no later than midday."

"It is just another mission and it will go according to plan."

Barok rubbed his temples with his stumpy fingers "I may be wrong about this entirely...but I fear the worst about this mission."

"We are slave workers. Who are we to question orders?"

"We have never had an assignment that required the use of every acidel slave worker on this planet."

"This mission is most complex. The Czar explained it is of the utmost importance that every acidel be aboard that freighter."

Barok looked down, nodded his head. He was conditioned to be a servant of the royal family. No matter what he feared, in the end, he would always obey his Czar.

Jumping down from the ledge, he shuffled to the bed and lay down face up next to Shroomy. He stared at the ceiling, abundant moss covering it. The room itself was small and thick with moisture. Nothing was on the thin brown walls except a few dirty pieces of dried up artwork sketched out by the acidel children Shroomy watched on occasion.

"I should not be so concerned," Barok acknowledged. "But I do feel uneasy, and this I cannot help."

"Konig shall protect us," Shroomy whispered quietly. "Remember, he never sleeps in the forest. He is our protector and our guide while we serve Stritonoly."

"Yes, I know he watches us always. I have not lost my faith in Konig. My only fear is that the humans will find out about him one day."

Shroomy smiled. "Let them find him. They do not know of the power he wields."

Barok felt a peace come over him. *What Shroomy speaks is true*, he thought. *They do not know...but they will...and in the end, there will be no chance for redemption.*

He rolled away from Shroomy, dropped to the floor and reached for a tiny case underneath the bed.

"Time for some music," Barok smiled.

Shroomy returned the smile. She really wanted to sleep but loved to hear him play.

Barok placed the case on the bed, opened it, and took out his violuna.

The violuna was the preferred musical instrument of the acidel. Seven strings sat atop a shiny yellow box-type frame. The strings were played with a bow fashioned from vine and leather.

"Play me a lullaby," Shroomy requested.

Barok lifted the violuna up under his chin, placed the bow carefully on the lowest pitched string and began to play tenderly.

The quiet richness of the melody soon filled the room.

Shroomy closed her eyes, still smiling. The melodic texture of the sound brought serenity to their chambers, a much deserved escape from the labors of the day.

With her eyes closed, Shroomy allowed the music to lift her spirit. Her mind danced with images of children playing, doves flying high into a clear blue sky, a majestic sun casting down a glorious beam of welcoming light.

Barok also became lost in the peaceful melody of the lullaby he played. His rubbery face widened with a glow of happiness as he bowed each note delicately.

Let us leave this place one day, he thought. *Let us find true peace when our slave labor has finally come to an end. May all things be as one, united forever.*

Chapter 7

Konig sat on a large mound of yellow grass and dirt.

From his perch high in the mountains, he looked down and saw three human figures, one tied to a tree just behind the Imperial Citadel.

A conflict brewed below, something he knew would come to fruition in due course.

Rain poured evenly onto his greenish-brown large hairy body. Presently, he identified the storm as only a precursor to the travesty that would arrive in the morning.

No flesh could be seen on Konig, only wet matted hair pressed against an extremely muscular frame. His face was droopy with acidel features, only much greater in size. His eyes were aglow, an awe-inspiring red beam of light jetting out from his two egg-shaped eyeballs. His hands were at least ten times the size of human hands. Long red nails stuck out from one thumb and two fingers that were actually claws. The fingernails formed into a perfect triangle at the end, so beautiful, so sharp, so deadly. Even though his two fingers were claws, his thumb was human-like and he had a clear palm with no hair on it. He'd describe them as claw-like hands and they were his most distinguishing feature.

He breathed with a subtle peace, harnessing his energies for the morning ahead. Konig was indeed the true ruler of this planet, not the Czar. Konig ruled from afar, using the multitude of clairvoyant talents he had gathered from years upon years of trolling the cosmos.

The Czar could hold the meaningless title if he desired. But unbeknownst to all humans on the planet, nothing happened here without Konig's approval. He was the one true master of all with telepathic powers humans only read about in wild stories of fantasy. Konig always existed. He was never born and would never die, he just was. While he could not predict every single universal event, he knew more than enough to forecast the immediate future, especially when it came to the planet he served at any particular time. His mission was to ensure that the universal plan was executed.

The universal plan was written before time began, and for the whole of the galaxy to achieve order, there must never be a deviation of any sort from the events the universe had mapped out long ago. It was the freewill of man that had long been Konig's most deadly adversary. Humans held the ignorance and lack of foresight to change the course of history with a single momentary lapse of judgment. Such a lapse would have an impact on the design of the universe for centuries. Konig was to see that this should never occur. The trickle effect from such a deviation could eventually lead to the ultimate expulsion of every living thing for all time.

When the acidel first came to Stritonoly, Konig made a promise to watch over them. He did not interfere in the cosmic plan for them to become the primary slave workers for this planet. Instead, he watched, he waited. He knew the time would come when all misdeeds would be avenged. His allegiance to the acidel was absolute. He would become one of them, even taking on many of their facial features in his current state of being.

Konig had been on this planet many, many times before. For this entity of the universe, time repeated itself over and over again.

Countless nights would pass. He would sit here, staring into space, knowing that everything that could be done has been done. There were no discoveries left for him, just the delicate variations of the soul that changed situations ever so slightly. And it was these variations that Konig became attuned to immediately. When he gained insight into them, he would simply step into the situation, sometimes unnoticed. His job was then to bring the master plan of the universe back on track. And he would perform this service with extreme prejudice. The universal plan was far more important than anything else...anything!

In a lifetime that had no beginning and no end, Konig had transformed his being millions of times. He chose his current look to suit the natural surroundings of the forest in which he dwelled. He could just have easily made himself into a monster the size of an entire mountain, or even larger if he so desired. But that would only serve egotism. And ego was not a quality of his being. Ego is the greatest of all human flaws, a flaw that must be monitored constantly for it could change the future in the blink of an eye. Konig had learned this lesson again and again.

Over his time spent on many planets in the galaxies, he had taken on many different proportions and dimensions. He had been a bird many times, also a whale, an elephant, a young child. He even transformed into a human fetus one time about seven hundred years ago on a planet very near Stritonoly. He had also taken on the form of non-breathing entities when it became necessary. He was a small blue pond for a period of time, an amusement park ride, a flower and a cement block, just to name a few.

The fondest memory Konig held of a non-physical entity he had transformed himself into was that of a propane tank. It was back in the twenty-first century on a planet in a galaxy some fourteen light years away from Stritonoly. Konig had taken on the form of a propane tank which was attached to a barbeque. At a summer party, a disturbed teenager walked over to the barbeque and using his power of freewill he made the decision to unscrew the valve which fed the propane to the barbeque. The teenager thought it would be funny to light a match near the open valve and see what would happen. This was not a part of the universal plan, and at least in this instance, the malicious act was detected. Konig, in the form of the propane tank, was able to dispel the propane into the atmosphere long before the flame from the match could ignite the fuel. To the teenager's surprise, nothing happened. As a result, there was no propane to grill the food for the guests, which really angered the wife of the man who was supposed to fill the propane tank the night before, which he did do! Unfortunately for him, she wound up being mad at him for the rest of the weekend. Fortunately for the thirty or so guests at the party, and especially the teenager who lit the match, no one was harmed on that day. They were just hungry and annoyed there would be no cooked hamburgers or hot dogs. If they only knew what could have been they would not have been so upset. This story was a delight to Konig.

Unfortunately not all of his transformations and duties were quite as pleasant. He had also witnessed the violence and catastrophes of many, many worlds. He had learned to accept the good and the bad as just a part of the process of order. This was his primary job, to maintain order.

Being a master of physical alteration, there was no form unknown to him, no knowledge outside his grasp. The only exception was the freewill of humans, a mistake in the cosmic plan that needed adjustment very often. And that is why his current state of being on Stritonoly was a necessity. Ego was again learning how to contaminate life. Konig would never allow that to happen.

Rolling his body off the mound, he reached for the closest tree, stripped the bark from it, and devoured it within seconds.

This was how nature worked within him. He absorbed and consumed all things around him. Nutrition can be found in all living objects. All that exists in a physical form bears fuel for survival. He fed off the resources of whatever planet he served at the time.

Noticing a choppy howl coming from his left side, he slipped back into his perch, a small overhang of thick shrubbery provided suitable cover.

In the forest not far from Konig, a horse-frogen howled, a small green creature that resembled a horse but with only three legs, one in the front and two behind. The horse-frogen meandered toward Konig as she cried out a steady beat of unusual short howls. The horse-frogen limped heavily on one of her back legs, a look of distress stretched on her face.

As he observed the injured creature, Konig emerged.

"Come to me," Konig said, a welcoming texture accompanied his bassoon-like voice.

Startled, the horse-frogen stopped dead in her tracks, clearly frightened by this ogre speaking to her.

"Come to me," Konig said again. "I will cause you no further harm. I am the nature that surrounds you. Allow me to assist you and I shall make you free from pain. I swear to you, all of your suffering is at an end."

Trembling, the horse-frogen hobbled toward Konig. Her eyes were black within blue, tears falling freely.

Konig kneeled next to the horse-frogen and said: "Do not be afraid. You will return here one day if your soul chooses to do so. What awaits you is a paradise of knowledge, an eternity to be free from all pain."

He moved his hands toward the creature. With one solid strike, he drove two claws into the horse-frogens throat. Dark purple blood turned quickly to red and flowed out and down Konig's arm.

The horse-frogen shook violently for just a moment, then fell forward, smashing hard into the ground. The creature was dead.

Konig withdrew his arm, licked the blood from his claws and lifted his eyes to the heavens.

"This is the reality of all things," Konig said aloud. "All things but I are born, and born, and born again."

He knew this to be true because he had witnessed it and made it come to be. Life, for all its intricacies, was very simple. The horse-frogen, now free from pain, will be born again in the universe. At the very moment the sharp claws struck her throat, her misery ceased forever.

Konig had taken and given life once more.

And when the sun of the north came to rise in the morning, he would make his presence felt to all who dare breathe the air he owned.

Chapter 8

"I am thirsty," Ethan said.

He was still bound to the tree, thick vines holding him tight, cutting unmercifully into his flesh. "Will you at least provide me something to drink?" Ethan demanded, his head falling forward.

Dmitri enjoyed mocking his wounded teacher. To see Ethan helpless and weak sent a thrill up Dmitri's spine, a power he had long craved for, but until now was unable to attain.

To be the one true master of all things, this was his fantasy. His face expressed a cheerful amusement as he cackled: "It is raining you fool! Stick out your tongue! You can drink all the rain you want."

"You would have me suffer this way," Ethan pleaded. "I have known you since birth, I have protected you, nurtured you, taught you all I know."

Becki's heart seemed to be breaking. She could not stand to see such suffering. She would gladly trade places with Ethan, but knew there was no point. Still, the grief she felt for him bit into her psyche. She felt compelled to speak.

"You have nothing to fear," Becki said, comfort in her tone. Her rain soaked blonde hair clinging to her cheeks.

Dmitri stomped a boot into the mud and swung wildly around to face his sister. "You speak out of turn! Do not test me!"

"You swore you would not kill him," Becki said, a surprising strength to her words.

After an extended, and most unnecessary pause, Dmitri spoke, "Ethan will not be killed this night...But death will come before the morning sun...It must!"

I know what he desires, Ethan thought. *And there are no words that can change a man so possessed by a sinister ego.*

"I have learned a horrible truth," Dmitri hissed. "When I tell you both of the knowledge I hold, you will understand why I act in this manner."

Ethan looked up and caught a glimpse of Becki through the raindrops. It was clear to him that she did not wish harm upon anyone.

"There is a light-speed freighter arriving in the morning," Dmitri said, turning sharply back toward Ethan. "Do you know of this?"

"Yes," Ethan answered carefully. "It is to transport the acidel on a mission of great importance. I have heard this from the Czar himself."

"And what is this mission?" Dmitri's eyes widened.

"I do not know of details. I only know it will require the labor of every acidel. I presume they will be retrieving resources from the outer galaxy."

"A presumption you are foolish to make!" Dmitri snarled. "That is the truth my father wishes that everyone believe. He wishes for you to think this is just another harmless mission to retain resources for our growth...I assure you...This is far from the truth!"

Becki moved close to her brother. Gently she placed a hand upon his shoulder. "Tell me what you know," she asked, afraid of what the answer might be.

"The Czar of Stritonoly, our beloved father," Dmitri stared straight into Becki's flickering green eyes. "Our father has given the order."

"The order for what?"

"Murder! A mass execution!"

Horrified, shaken in disbelief, Becki responded "Of what do you speak!"

"The acidel. He believes they will eventually spell doom for this planet. He wishes to rid us of them forever."

Yes, I have heard these rumors, Ethan thought. *Ancient prophecies have told of slave laborers gaining enough strength in secret, enough strength to one day become kings themselves and overthrow their masters.*

"*There* must some mistake," Becki said. "Father would never order such a thing! I refuse to believe this. You speak nonsense." A rage boiled within her. "You are acting the part of a fool!"

Slap! With the back of his hand, Dmitri struck his sister hard across the face.

Becki swirled and crashed to the ground. The pain of the blow throbbed at the side of her face, her white night-robe, covered in wet sticky mud.

"Stop this at once!" Ethan screamed, struggling to get free.

"I have tasted the sweat knowledge of the acidel," Dmitri howled. "I am the champion, come here to save us from despair. You will follow me, or you will die!"

Lightning tore across the sky as rain turned to hail.

"Do you think me a fool," Dmitri said. "I have schemed and planned for years. My domination is finally within my grasp. What I do now, I do without regret."

Tears streamed down Becki's face, anger gripped her every fiber. She trembled; the cold, wet, putrid taste of dirt on her lips. "How dare you strike me!"

"How dare you speak to me in such a manner! I am the Czar!"

What did he say! Ethan thought. His mind spun, a whirlpool of broken glass. *He thinks he is the Czar now! What insanity has entered his soul?*

Becki looked up in horror, overcome by the thought that this was no longer the brother she once loved. This demented monster that struck her with such vile disregard crushed any semblance of sanity her brother once held.

"I am the beginning and the end," Dmitri shouted, a wild beast unleashed inside him. He spoke in riddles and uncertainties, a madness, a madness! "Do not test my power, it would be a mistake. It would ensure your demise. I am a merciful ruler. I will share my secret with you. But first, you must taste the holy sweat! Become one with this might! Join me now for there is no other choice."

Does he speak to me as well? Ethan thought. *Does he expect his sister to consume this toxin?*

"Dmitri!" Ethan shouted, mustering all his strength to command his attention. "We are all a part of this now. Let us speak of solutions. Violence has implications...do not corner yourself!"

Dmitri thought for a moment. The words left an imprint, but not enough to jar him back to reality. "How can a Czar rule without violence?" Dmitri asked. "It is the reality of leadership, a necessity!"

"A necessity yes, in times of need," Ethan softened his tone. "Do we need venture down such a road? There are other options at our disposal."

"Then speak of these options, old man. Tell me your ideas, as irrational as they might be."

Irrational! Is he serious? Ethan thought. *I do not have the ability to talk him down from this paranoia. I must forge ahead and try. Regardless of the outcome, I must attempt to sway him, for Becki's sake if not my own.*

"Do you remember our first lessons on leadership?" Ethan asked, evoking the inflection of a wise instructor.

Dmitri giggled like a school boy. "Are we in class now? Oh please Professor Educai, refresh my memory."

Ethan straightened as best he could, focused every energy on speaking with authority. "The first and most important lesson a leader must learn...Be prudent, do not become reactionary, evaluate and then move to action only when the puzzle pieces have sorted themselves into their proper place."

"And if the pieces are in place?" Dmitri asked.

"Do you know them to be in place for certain? If you choose to act, you must know for certain that all things are in order...All things, not just a few."

This could possibly buy some time, Ethan thought. *It is doubtful, but at the very least, I have him thinking.*

Becki gathered herself, sat up, and clutched her swollen cheekbone. Chunks of hail fell all about her, striking her skin like pinpricks.

"Your are astute beyond your years," Ethan continued. "You will be a mighty Czar, possibly the mightiest of all...when the time is right."

Dmitri froze and time stood still. The hail turned to rain and back to hail again. Black rumbling clouds circled above.

"Listen to me carefully," Dmitri said, sliding away from his sister. He approached the wise teacher, pressed his mouth next to Ethan's ear, whispered: "Do you wish for Becki to see the light of day?"

Oh, good god! Ethan thought. *He is beyond reasoning with! All hope is lost. Nothing I say will bring him back from this demonic possession.*

Ethan swallowed hard, trying to contain his anger.

Dmitri rubbed Ethan's beard ever so gently with his forefinger. He patted it like a small child would a doll she once lost and then found again. Presently he placed his lips as close to Ethan's ear as he could, then whispered a chilling warning, "Do not test me, old man!...I...will...kill her!"

Ethan could not bear to think of such a thing. He spun his head away, tried to find an escape, an alternative, a way out of this nightmare. He could think of nothing. His thoughts focused only on Becki.

Gazing at her, lost in her purity.

He remembered her innocence, her grace, a delightful smile that greeted all she met with warmth and kindness. Never a tense moment between them, he shared a bond with her formed of mutual respect, a bond he feared would soon be severed for the rest of time.

If he were able, Ethan would give more than his life for her. He would do anything for Becki. She was the symbol of all the good he would never be, all the innocence he once savored, all the love he once knew.

A sudden flash of awareness blasted through him. Ethan knew what must be done.

He turned his head harshly back toward Dmitri.

Enraged, but still in control, he met eyes with his tormentor. With every ounce of courage left him, said, "I will do whatever you want. I will swear my allegiance to you. I have been and always will be your servant...do not harm her...and...I will do whatever you wish...I give you my solemn vow."

Dmitri smiled...

With a deafening crash of thunder, the barrier between sky and land opened wide.

Hail torpedoed down from the black skies, a lightning bolt of colossal force struck the ground nearby. Sparks of flame shot up from the surface and just as soon, diminished under another ferocious downpour.

This storm is a brutal one indeed, Ethan thought. But the storm that grows beneath my flesh, that is the storm I fear the most.

Chapter 9

Konig picked up the lifeless horse-frogen.

Slinging the bloody corpse over his shoulder, he began to walk a path back to his home, a hollow cavern on the south side of the Mount Crito.

Through dense brush and thistle, Konig carried the creature with ease. He passed hundreds of trees that stretched up high into the night sky, gigantic patches of flowers, all shapes and colors, long since wilted and fallen sideways from the heavy rains.

After a relatively short journey to the opposite side of the mountain, a beautiful valley appeared, a splendid reprieve from the gloom of the forest. A majestic rainbow-lit waterfall shone with brilliance just beyond the place Konig called home. Tiny creatures of diverse character and size frolicked about with an abandoned bliss. A horn-toed deer scampered gingerly about the open valley filled with oversized soggy mushrooms. Outcast creatures from planets near and far found their long-awaited harmony among this level basin of tranquility.

Stopping just outside the shimmering white rocky-faced cavern, Konig gently placed the horse-frogen down on a large rectangular table resembling an altar. Bright red candles had been placed at every corner. A glowing white cloth, untouched by the weather, draped across its edges, fluttered softly in the wind.

The storm had subsided, only a damp drizzle remained. A light gray fog crept above the yellowy marsh surrounding this hallowed ground.

Konig's home, this valley and cavern where he spent most his time, was secluded, set far beyond the reach of any distractions humans could present. It was Konig's sanctuary, a place for prayer and meditation, a place no sorrow would be permitted to invade.

"Even in death comes life anew!" Konig said aloud.

On cue, a swarm of multicolored butterflies swept in and landed gracefully all about the pebbled surface surrounding the altar. The creatures of the valley intuitively sensed the commencement of a formal procedure. They fell silent and turned their eyes toward Konig.

Standing behind the altar, looking down at the horse-frogen, he spoke to the dead creature. "Yes, my friend...even in death there is pleasure and a fulfillment. The end is the beginning. This circle continues forever."

He turned the horse-frogen's head toward his own and peered into her unmoving eyes.

"Creature of the universe," he said. "Happiness will come to you now."

Konig slipped on a large purple cloak, covered in ornaments of golden gems. He leaned down beside the horse-frogen and kissed her greenish mane. "It is time. Finally, you will be at peace."

Pulling a torch out from under the altar, he set his red eyes ablaze. A shooting fire-beam flashed out from his smoky eyes. The torch ignited at once, a dazzling orangey-red glare.

The shine from the flame illuminated the hairy features and droopy face of the great Konig, a menacing portrait for any stranger not suited to his appearance. But for those who walked his path, for those who knew his ways, this seemingly frightening face suggested only a peaceful existence, a tranquil life that all would discover one day, in another time, in another place.

Offering up a plea to the universe, Konig continued the ritual service. Raising an open palm to the heavens, he chanted the ceremonial prayer:

> *Take this creature from this place,*
> *Find it a home of love.*
> *Find it a friendship, find it peace.*
> *For the living, large and small.*
> *Love befall them all!*
> *Let love befall us all!*

With great pride and dignity, Konig placed the blazing torch atop the lifeless horse-frogen. Instantly, the creature began to burn.

Thick smoke filled the surrounding forest. The wind shifted, blowing most of the flames upward, almost as if directed to do so, a mighty cosmic energy sending the smoke and fire to a void of no return.

When the creature was fully consumed by the flames Konig stepped back from the altar. He smiled, a deep appreciation washed through him. This was truly a beauty like no other.

The end is only the beginning, he thought. *And it goes on and on and on...forever and ever, until the end of time.*

Chapter 10

The Czar of Stritonoly was weary.

He sat in dim light, several thin white candles casting a shadowy glow onto the large shiny oak writing table upon which he rested his arms.

The grand study, where he presently worked, gave the impression of a vast library, filled with literary records and antiquated wisdom. This was the center of education for the royal family. Rows upon rows of thickly bound manuals and manuscripts sat neatly upon shelves on every wall.

With writing implement in hand, The Czar put his signature to the paperwork before him. His royal seal upon this letter of intent meant there was now no turning back. This would be the final gesture on his part. Come morning the acidel would be gone forever.

His long white hair fell about his shoulders, unusually unkempt for such a royal figure, even though it was the middle of the night. Still wearing his formal day uniform, complete with the flowing velvet cape, he undid the top button of his silky white shirt and leaned back. His hazel eyes, glassy and drained, peered across the table at the boy courier waiting patiently to receive the final document, sealed now with the imperial emblem.

The courier would take the written orders directly to Gunther. Then the deed would be done. The mechanics of the impending plan had long since been set into motion. This written record was the final order making it official.

The boy courier looked most frightened. He knew of the doom that awaited the acidel in the morning, some of them he considered friends.

The Czar looked over the document that was the final draft of the official report detailing the necessity of this action. He had read it a hundred times, but even if he read it a hundred more, his decision would not change. An order of mass execution is not to be taken lightly, even though he knew this had to be done.

He had known of the acidel's powers for years. In his ignorance and quest for dominance, he thought their powers could be harnessed. His doubts began to surface when he first noticed a peculiar change in his only son, the royal heir, Dmitri.

One night, in the dark of evening, The Czar witnessed his son collecting acidel sweat. He immediately ordered a secret investigation. Unbeknownst to his young son, several spies learned the horrible truth. Dmitri had been seen on several occasions gathering acidel sweat, allowing it to harden and then consuming it. Countless hours of laborious surveillance confirmed The Czar's worst fears. His son was obsessed, poisoned and now contaminated possibly beyond repair.

The Czar knew immediately the tragic consequences such a behavior could present.

The acidel, while seemingly harmless, were inherently poisonous and addictive. If his own son could be tempted and swayed toward doom, it would not be long before others fell prey to it as well.

In high council, along with a select few of the noble elders, The Czar received council on this matter. Then, a plan was set in motion.

The acidel would be ordered to board a light-speed freighter. They would be told that a mission of extreme importance required their full attention. Once the freighter took flight and left the immediate galactic hub surrounding Stritonoly, it would prepare for the jump to light-speed. A device had been inserted deep within the controls of the light-speed engagement engine. This device would trigger an explosion once light-speed was engaged. The explosion would completely destroy the freighter and kill all on board.

Looking up at the courier, The Czar folded the order and handed it to him.

"Take this to Sir Gunther," The Czar ordered.

"Yes, My Lord," the courier said, spun quickly and exited the study.

The Czar stared at the door the courier left open. A diminutive ray of light glowed in the hallway just beyond the door and crept into the study.

A shadowy figure emerged. The Czar knew her presence well. She stood in the open door, a silhouette of loveliness, his wife Victoria.

Her sleeveless white nightgown allowed the grace of her alluring arms to be in full view. She placed them tenderly on the thick molding surrounding the doorway.

"Are you coming to bed?" Victoria asked quietly, her voice, a stylish mixture of a smooth and delicate timbre.

Her long reddish-blonde hair fell all to one side, perfectly straight. It appeared to have just been combed into place.

As she stepped into the study, The Czar could not help but admire her beauty. Soft natural curves on a shapely body, a face of angelic loveliness, clear skin, not a blemish to be found. Her pronounced blue eyes danced softly like a foam-covered wave upon a long forgotten sea.

"David," she said, as she approached The Czar. "Please, my love, try to get at least a little sleep."

She was the only one permitted to call The Czar by his first name, and she could only do so in private. The Czar believed firmly in only formal interactions in front of the public. Even at family gatherings and parties, Victoria would only refer to him as The Czar.

She glided behind him, placed her hands upon his tense shoulders. "Maybe this will help," she said, and began to gently massage him.

The Czar smiled. He allowed himself to relax his mind for a moment. The terrible but necessary thing about to happen was still a few hours away.

The protection of the population of the planet demanded that he see this through, and he would. But for now, there was only Victoria's tender touch. He closed his eyes and let her love engulf him.

"I am so tired," The Czar said. "But I feel too guilty to sleep when so many will die come morning. I feel it selfish to indulge in slumber when the lives of so many will be washed away in the morning. And all this will happen under my watch and approval."

"You are not killing humans," Victoria said. "The acidel are creatures of the universe. They will be reborn again at another time. We can only hope they will be reborn with a dignity and honor they have yet to find."

"I pray dearly for that to occur, but this is a mystery to which I will never know the answer. I am but a mortal man. It is for the universe to decide their ultimate fate after their existence here has ended. I only wish for redemption from my own sins in this matter. Though I know with every fiber of my soul that what I do is right and just, it is still murder. There is no escaping that fact."

"Is it truly murder?" Victoria questioned. "I do not see it that way at all. Your actions will bring life anew to an entire generation. The people will now be free to pursue a life of peace and prosperity. The acidel have lost their way and you are but setting them free. Trust me my darling, the acidel will find peace well beyond this galaxy. Their souls are eternal and the universe will preserve the good in them. The acidel will find a suitable home in time. What you do is for the preservation of humanity. It is hardly a crime at all; it is an honorable service."

The Czar opened his eyes. Her words rang true to him. She had an impact on his psyche that no one else could penetrate. She was truly his finest advisor. "You are a wise queen, my lovely Victoria," turning to face her. "And I will cherish you for all of time."

Victoria leaned inward. They met lips and kissed, not a passionate kiss, rather a kiss of reassurance and acceptance of their fate.

In the deepest recesses of their souls, they both wondered if history would judge them harshly for this action, but again, the reality of the situation loomed large. Their only son was in jeopardy of losing his sanity.

The Czar, full of conviction, knew his actions seemed brutal on the surface, but he gathered strength from the knowledge that this would eventually preserve and spawn new life for this planet.

However, his greatest desire of all still dominated his innermost thoughts.

In his mind, he spoke to the universe. Preserve my son, he prayed. *I beg of you, please preserve my only son.*

Chapter 11

"Where is the Freighter now?" Gunther shouted.

"Sir, The Freighter is ten kilometers north of Mount Crito," an imperial soldier answered. "It is being fueled as we speak."

The soldier was dressed in full battle fatigues. He stood at the end of the first line of soldiers. The sixty soldiers that were present stood at attention in three straight lines. Gunther had personally handpicked these soldiers specifically to ensure the success of the acidel termination plan. They represented the best of the best.

Gunther stood behind a brown podium atop a solid black dais. A giant red curtain stretched out behind him. The curtain was decorated with rows upon rows of the imperial black serpents.

They were presently at the headquarters of battle command. The room was set in the basement of the citadel. With four orange cement walls surrounding it, the area formed a perfect square. Paintings and sculptures made from purock, elaborate in design, hung on every wall. The pieces of art were all similar; soldiers fighting in battle, scenes of bloody corpses on the battlefield, various designs of serpents and portraits of previous Czars decorated every wall.

The soldiers were given strict orders to wait at headquarters for the final written order to arrive from The Czar himself. Once the order was received, Gunther would set the plan into action.

The soldiers that were gathered before him were specially trained for riot control. Their responsibility in the morning would be to ensure that every acidel on the planet was aboard the freighter before it left for takeoff.

The military man delivering the freighter in the morning was a friend of Gunther's. His name was Kristof. He had attained the rank of senior officer after many years of service. He was a little older than Gunther and took great pride in having him as a comrade. His gray-haired crew cut, thick jaw line and solid body was the exact way a good soldier should always look Gunther thought. His neatly-pressed uniform was his everyday attire and Gunther couldn't remember a time when Kristof did not present himself with a dignified physical appearance.

Presently, Kristof stood just behind Gunther on the dais. When the paperwork arrived, Kristof would be taken to the freighter at the airbase. There he would wait until exactly one hour after sunrise. Then he would fly the freighter to the front of the citadel where the acidel would board the spacecraft.

He would then instruct Barok on the flight plan and explain to him the exact altitude he should achieve before light-speed engagement. Barok would captain the freighter for this mission. As leader of the acidel he had been trained long ago in the skills of flying spacecraft. The freighter he was going to be piloting, while it was immense in size, was very easy to operate compared to some of the more exotic spacecraft reserved for use by those of nobility.

A large steel door on the left side of the room swung open. "Sir Gunther, The courier just arrived," an imperial soldier shouted as he stepped into the room.

"Attention Imperial soldiers," Gunther said to his assembled troops, "Let us greet the boy properly."

The boy courier slowly walked into the room carrying the official document. "Sir Gunther," the boy said softly, "I bring to you The Czar's final written orders."

"Sir Gunther?" one of the imperial soldiers shouted out.

"Yes, soldier," Gunther answered.

"May I have permission to speak to the imperial courier?"

"Of course," Gunther smiled.

"Courier, I know of many fine shops where I can purchase a lovely dress for you."

Gunther doubled over in laughter. Obviously this was staged for his amusement. The soldiers also began to laugh as the boy courier turned red as a strawberry.

"Don't piss your pants son," Gunther said, still laughing.

The boy courier cautiously approached Gunther. With his right hand, he held out the document for Sir Gunther.

Gunther stopped laughing immediately. He grabbed the written order from the boy, glanced at it quickly and passed it on to Kristof. Then he looked back at the boy, "You'll learn to be a man one day," Gunther said. "The time has come for you to grow up. Next time you speak to me, try not to sound like such a fairy."

"Anything else, Sir," The boy said with a quivering voice.

"Just get out of here," Gunther said, a seriousness now in his tone.

The boy walked away humiliated and embarrassed. He shut the steel door slowly behind him as he exited the room.

The mood had changed, a soberness suddenly filled the room.

The soldiers were weary and concerned for many reasons, the least of which had to do with getting the acidel on board the freighter and thus ensuring their death.

The imperial soldiers were well aware of the workload that would fall on their shoulders once the acidel were eliminated. Until The Czar could obtain suitable slave replacements for the acidel, it would be left to the military to pick up the slack. This would require a tremendous increase in their hours of duty per day. And the labor they were being asked to do was widely considered to be work not suited for a trained and respected soldier.

Secretly, they had no problem eliminating the acidel, but they had a very big problem with being asked to assume the role of temporary slave workers. Even if it would be for only a short time—as The Czar promised—they still considered it a slap in the face. They did not feel soldiers with families and reputations to uphold should be made to cut purock from the ground for hours every day. This thought left even the most loyal soldier feeling extremely underappreciated.

After glancing over the document, Kristof handed it back to Gunther. Placing it on the podium, Gunther looked it over one final time. It was official now. The Czar's signature sealed the fate of the acidel.

"We have the order," Gunther said. "The time has come to ready ourselves. We have waited for this moment and we know what we must do. Be prepared for anything. Rumors have certainly circulated beyond these walls. I have no doubt there are many that have suspicions about the action we are about to take. When the freighter arrives, take no chances. If violence is needed, you are hereby commanded to use any means necessary to see this mission through to its completion." Gunther paused, looked back at Kristof who was nodding his head in agreement.

"Are there any questions?" Gunther asked.

There was a long silence.

"Report to your posts," Gunther said.

Putting one fist in the air, he shouted, "Long live The Czar!"

In unison, the soldiers shouted back, "LONG LIVE THE CZAR!"

Falling out of formation, they headed for the steel door. While they were not happy about the implications this mission would ultimately have on their lives, they were soldiers true and true. They had been trained to follow orders.

And come morning, that's exactly what they would do.

Chapter 12

Dmitri gathered more vine from a nearby brush.

"Come to me!" He ordered Becki.

"What do you want?" Becki questioned.

The rage churned like a hurricane inside Dmitri. "How dare you not obey me!" He screamed. "Do not force my hand. Come to me now!"

With frightened steps, Becki slowly approached Dmitri.

When she was within arm's reach, he grabbed her arm and flung her against a tree. Pushing her back with considerable force, he began to tie her to the tree next to Ethan. He wrapped the vine tightly around her waist and double knotted it behind her.

Becki, still in shock and pain from the blow Dmitri delivered to her face, felt herself unable to resist. She feared the consequences if she were to fight him.

"Why are you doing this?" Ethan asked, weary from the loss of blood from his head wound.

"I am in no position as of yet to risk being stopped," Dmitri said. "There is something I must do."

"Please," Becki pleaded, "Do you not trust even your own sister!"

"Of course I trust you," Dmitri lied.

"Then why tie me up like an animal?"

"By this time tomorrow, you will understand. I will explain no more to you now. Yes, I do trust you. Now, you must trust me as well."

There was a sick determination in his voice, a manipulation of sinister volatility stirring beneath his words. He did not trust anyone. Even though he tried to play the part of the calm commander, it was clear his actions were that of a possessed man.

Checking to be sure she was securely fastened to the tree, Dmitri stepped back and stood between Ethan and Becki. He looked at the stars above, appearing to be lost in a haze of delusional thinking.

I will be one with you soon, Dmitri thought. His mind raced in a million directions, a maze of turmoil and deceit. He felt empowered, sure that the events that were about to unfold were dominated by a universal cosmic truth.

"What is it you plan to do?" Ethan asked.

Dmitri continued to stare at the sky above, "I think you know."

"I have a feeling, yes," Ethan continued, "and if my feeling is correct, it will be a tragic mistake, a terrible deed. There will be no turning back from this Dmitri. It will forever tear upon your soul."

"So then great and wise teacher," Dmitri sneered, "You tell me, what is it you think I am about to do?"

"You plan to murder your father."

Becki felt a gush of uncontrollable sadness and rage mix into her consciousness. Her body quivered, shaking, twitching. She had lost control over her senses. Her mind was not prepared to hear of such a horror.

Dmitri looked at Becki, evil steamed from within his blue eyes. He watched her contort and shiver, she could not speak.

"Are you surprised, sister?" Dmitri asked. A psychotic quietness murmured within his proscribed speech pattern.

Becki found herself unable to respond. She became transfixed on the image of her father, dead and bloodied at the hands of his own son.

"Say something!" Dmitri snarled.

Becki would not cry. She forced herself back to reality.

"What do you want me to say?" she asked, staring at the crazed creature that used to be her beloved brother.

"I want you to say that you understand," Dmitri said. An eerie and ominous staleness crept into his tone.

"You want me to accept the cold blooded murder of our father?" Becki cried, unable to hold back tears any longer.

"It is not murder," Dmitri said, "It is a duty!"

I have no recourse left me, Ethan thought. *I want to speak but I fear any words from me will only cause further damage.*

"Tell me you understand!" Dmitri demanded.

Becki searched for a response that would get through to him. "I believe you think what you are doing is right," she said finally, "And I know your intentions are to protect the acidel. But isn't there another way?"

"If there were another course of action to follow, I would do so. This is the path I have chosen. It is a path of righteousness! Now tell me you understand!"

"Yes," she said reluctantly. "I understand that you believe what you are doing is just."

Dmitri laughed. "That is clearly but a veiled acceptance of my actions, but it will do for now. I will expect more loyalty from you in the future...if you are to become my wife."

Abomination! Ethan thought. *What is this insanity? This monster before me speaks with a poisonous tongue.*

"Your wife?" Becki asked, confusion poured through her.

"Just think of it Becki. You bear the same royal blood I do. Our children will become all-mighty and all-powerful. There will be no stopping their dominance and power!"

"I am your sister!" Becki said. "This is not a possibility Dmitri, please listen to yourself."

"I know you do not fully understand now," Dmitri said, "but in time you will come to see the wisdom of what I propose. Our offspring will one day rule the entire galaxy. And our names will live for all of eternity. Generations upon generations will speak our names with pride and admiration."

"I am begging you," Becki said, "Please do not do this!"

"The course of action is already set into motion, there is no turning back. This is all being done for the greater good of Stritonoly. I know you will come to accept this in time."

I have to speak, Ethan thought. *I must try to persuade him to change his mind.*

"And what if there were another way?" Ethan asked.

"There is not!" Dmitri growled.

"There are always options for a great leader such as yourself. What if we were to convince The Czar to relinquish his post. He has spoken of stepping down many times. He is old and tired. I am sure I can convince him of the wisdom you obviously have attained."

Dmitri thought in silence. The boost to his ego wafted through his demented brain. "And why should I spare him? He has no regard for life! He wishes death to thousands of innocent acidel! I am not the criminal in this matter. My father sealed his fate when he chose murder over integrity."

"And though I see the intelligence in the act of killing him," Ethan lied, "I must implore you not to stain your royal hands with the blood of your own father...even if it appears to be just."

"You are a wise old man," Dmitri smiled, "and I will have a place for you under my command. But this is an action I must do. If he were to stay alive, he would only be a nuisance, a distraction in the way of my plans for dominance."

"The Czar listens to my council," Ethan said convincingly.

"And I will listen to your council as well...when the time is right."

I have tried, Ethan thought. *I only wish I could summon the words to reach him. I am fearful that all hope is lost. The Czar will soon be dead.*

Chapter 13

PRESS RELEASE CORRECTION: Oct 11th, 2014 10:33 AM

Our news release submitted at 8:49 AM contained information we have since found to be inaccurate. It has been confirmed that Rebecca Brown, 17, first reported dead on arrival at St. Paul's Hospital is still alive. She is on life support and is listed in extremely serious condition. No further information has been made available at this time.

Chapter 14

Dmitri crept in through the rear entrance of the citadel.

His uniform was soaked through from the heavy rains. It left a clear puddle trail behind him as he walked. With cautious steps, he slowly made his way past the acidel antechamber and into the main compound of the imperial citadel.

He first came into the rear gallery. Thin white marble pillars were spaced out perfectly in two straight lines up and down the spacious area. Several rows of painted black serpents decorated the off-white walls that stretched up high and blended into the cathedral ceiling. A majestic chandelier, dimly lit, hung at the end of the room. As Dmitri passed beneath the chandelier, his figure cast a shadow onto the floor behind him.

The citadel was uncommonly still on this night. No sounds, no sign of life roamed the gallery. A breath of steam filled the atmosphere just ahead, or was it just Dmitri's delusion. He had been under the spell of the acidel toxic sweat for so long now, his mind was not clear. He was not to trust what he thought at first to be true. This concept was new to him, and even though his mind continued to sink into a tornado of chaos, he was still aware of the double meanings he saw all about him. Some visions may indeed be real, some may just be his mind dolling out its trickery on a new perception of reality. Some days it was impossible for Dmitri to separate fantasy from fact in any given circumstance. He was seeing the world through a shaded Plexiglas miasma, real at times only to his twisted sensibilities.

He turned right and tiptoed down a narrow corridor that would lead him straight into the main hallway. An impending and foreboding gloom became heavily visible to his mind's eye. His concentration shifted back and forth from sanity to lunacy, his eyes darted to and fro, his movements became slow and guarded.

The patriarchal royal suite was just ahead. Darkness stretched out before him as he slid quietly down the long hall.

He approached the royal suite, a great anticipation engulfed his being. This was to be his moment of truth. Excitement gripped him. He was suddenly as giddy as a child. Suppressing laughter he reached for the doorknob.

Then, a light caught his attention from further down the hallway.

The light came from the study.

Could my father still be awake? He thought.

Making the decision to bypass the royal suite, Dmitri crept down the long hall toward the study. The wetness from his uniform trickled down, leaving soggy imprints upon the freshly cleaned purple carpet beneath his boots.

I must be quiet, Dmitri thought. *Do not be careless! Not now, not when my reign is about to begin! Not when my time is finally at hand! Focus...Focus...Focus!*

He slid his back against the wall just next to the doorway leading into the study. He listened intently but heard no sound. With the palm of his left hand he reached for his waistband and unsheathed the silver jagged-edged dagger that would do the deed. Sliding his right hand onto the molding, he began to edge his way into the open doorway.

His eyes slit, he peered into the dimly lit room. Nothing! He saw nothing.

Slowly, Dmitri entered the study. All he could clearly see was one thin candle flickering upon the desk. Wax had dripped onto the desk forming a clumpy cake of gooey white.

He moved cautiously into the room. *My Father must have been here just before he went to bed,* Dmitri thought. *What a stupid man! He commands a planet but forgets to blow out a lit candle.*

"You come for me with a dagger," whispered a voice from the darkness.

Shocked, Dmitri spun around, readied his weapon, "Who speaks to me?"

"Do you not know your own father's voice," said the Czar. There he was, sitting calmly in the corner just beyond the reach of the candlelight, his legs crossed, hands folded on his lap.

"Where is my mother?" Dmitri asked.

"She is in bed," The Czar responded, as calm as the sea. "Why do you ask where she is my son? Do you come for her blood as well?"

"You think I want to do this?"

"I think you feel compelled to do this."

"I cannot allow you to mur.."

The Czar cut him off, "You must listen to me carefully my son. The acidel are not the innocents you believe them to be."

"Innocent or not, they are creatures of the universe. I will not allow even my own father to kill off an entire species simply on suspicion of wrongdoing."

The Czar unfolded his legs and rose slowly from his chair. "I regret my actions even before they are to be carried out. Do you not see me awake in the middle of the night! Do you not think I would be in a peaceful slumber if I were at ease with this decision? This is not an order I give lightly. I do this for you, my son. I want to save you from yourself. For that I would kill off every living thing that roams our galaxy."

"Of what do you speak!" Dmitri thrust his dagger wildly forward. "You order a mass execution and then you blame me for your actions! This blade will pierce your heart with no mercy! How dare you put this burden on me!"

The Czar moved parallel to his son. Danger loomed large. Dmitri had a weapon and meant to use it. He could taste the thirst for blood.

The Czar took up a defensive position, tried to ready himself if his son were to suddenly strike. The unpredictability of a madman presented distress even for the most skilled warrior.

"You can kill me," The Czar said, "but the order has been given. Even if you take my life, the acidel will meet their fate tomorrow morning. However, it is not too late for you. I plead with you my son. Let us not have more bloodshed than is necessary."

Dmitri lowered his blade and met eyes with his father. "I have tasted their sweat!"

"I know," The Czar answered. "I have known for some time. And that is the greatest reason of all that I must do this wretched thing. They have poisoned my only son. But there is still time to make things right. When they are gone from here, you will see the light of day anew. And yes, my boy...One day very soon, you will be The Czar of Stritonoly."

Dmitri softened. He still held the dagger firmly but dropped his hand to his side. He didn't know where this well of emotion was coming from, but suddenly he felt tears begin to stream down his face. Overwhelmed by a sudden rush of sadness, he felt awkward and embarrassed.

"I am so confused," Dmitri said, amidst a flood of tears.

"You are my only son," The Czar said compassionately. "I will use every resource available to me to heal this wound the acidel have inflicted on you. I do not blame you or harbor any ill feelings toward you, Dmitri. You are my blood, the heir to this kingdom. We will cure you of this sickness. I swear to you, this shall be a long forgotten memory one day."

The Czar outstretched his mighty arms. "Let me hold you," The Czar said, tears beginning to come to him as well.

Somewhat ashamed, Dmitri walked to his father. They embraced.

"I love you," The Czar said tenderly.

"You believe I will be the Czar one day, father?" Dmitri asked quietly.

"That time will be very soon," The Czar smiled.

"That time is now!" Dmitri snarled. Then, with all his might, Dmitri plunged the blade of the dagger deep into his father's stomach. He held it inside him, twisted it as his father groaned, gasping for breath. The Czar's body shivered and spasmed as Dmitri continued to thrust the blade deeper and deeper.

Dmitri bent his head backward to appreciate the agony upon his father's face. The Czar turned red, his eyes glazed over, the look and feel of failure dominated even the most intense pain his body endured. The Czar wept, not from the pain of the attack, but for the pain of his loss, the loss of his family, the loss of his son.

As Dmitri pulled the blade from his father, he stepped back. The bloody dagger, clumped with his father's death wounds now represented Dmitri's accomplishment. This was the ultimate fulfillment of his destiny. He stood proud, admiring the moment he had planned for so long. He made no attempt to repress a demonic smirk from sweeping across his face. He showed not a trace of sadness or shame.

The Czar stumbled backwards, clutching his bloody wound. "What have you done to me?"

"I have taken what is mine!" Dmitri smiled.

Collapsing to the floor, The Czar could now feel the pain of death upon him.

"You have killed yourself," Dmitri said coldly.

As his father lie dying, Dmitri walked over to the desk. The royal velvet cape lay across the chair behind it. He grabbed it and with a flurry of movement flung it over his shoulder. He then moved swiftly back to stand over his victim.

With gurgling drops of blood falling from his mouth, The Czar breathed his last breath. All his hopes and dreams abandoned him at the concluding moments of awareness.

His final thought flashed like lightning through his mind: *My only son has killed me...My only son has killed me...*

Draping the velvet cape over the bloody torso of his fallen father, Dmitri spoke the long awaited final words to The Czar: "It is done now. I say goodnight to you...the terror of my nightmare is over. Tomorrow, a new and glorious reign shall begin.

Chapter 15

Becki wept openly, tears streaming down her cheeks.

I wish I could provide some comforting words, Ethan thought. *Unfortunately, she has every right to weep. Nothing I say or do will stop this.*

A sudden downpour of rain was followed by a crash of thunder. The wind was not letting up at all. Its force increased, shifting its strength back and forth from east to west. Branches and leaves threw themselves into the wind, flying in reckless circles all about the forest.

Becki's eyes fluttered as airborne debris blinded her.

"I am so frightened, Ethan," she said. Her voice drowned in sorrow from the thought of impending doom and inevitable loss.

"In the end," Ethan said, "Everything will be as it should be. We can only hope for better days ahead. Do not lose your faith, Becki. It may be all that is left us."

"Faith," Becki screamed, "you speak to me of faith in this time of peril! I am not strong enough to endure such a dreadful test of faith. No one is!" Becki sobbed uncontrollably. "My father is dead! I know he is!"

Ethan searched for a response, but found none. He could only take in the mental picture of the storm that surrounded him. *How appropriate that this storm should come to us on this night of terror,* Ethan thought. *Nature senses all things, and sometimes sees fit to make its terrible presence known.*

Suddenly, the rumble of heavy footsteps could be heard approaching. The distinct sound of titanic feet upon the wet mud coming closer... closer!

"You hear that sound?" Becki said, afraid she may be hallucinating.

"Yes I hear it; be still!" Ethan cautioned.

The row of tall thick trees behind Ethan and Becki shifted and shook as the footsteps grew louder and louder. Then, two enormous arms stretched out from between an opening in the trees. The muscular arms belonged to a creature, an enormous hairy beast with glowing red eyes. He walked ominously toward the trees which held Becki and Ethan securely in place.

"I am Konig," he said. His deep voice reverberated with a strength and power no human on Stritonoly had ever heard before.

Stunned, Ethan and Becki fell to silence. Their mouths agape, they stared into the gleaming red eyes of the gigantic creature. They were overwhelmed by a vision they had never witnessed even in their most freakish dreams.

Konig's gaze darted about the forest. He looked up to the skies, allowed the rain to fall into his open eyes.

"I know you fear what you see," Konig said. Although his voice bore a distinctive deep and frightening drone, there was also a clear and subtle compassion that echoed in his inflection, a sound that soothed all living things in his presence.

"I feel great pain for you," Konig said, looking down at Becki. "I know the pain of which you bear, I know everything there is to know. But even though I bear such knowledge, some events are meant to be and cannot be altered for any reason."

"So then, my father is dead." Becki cried, choking back tears.

"Yes," Konig answered, "his physical body is dead. But fear not. The Czar lives on, though he is no longer The Czar. His spirit is part of you, and yes, even a part of me. This will not make sense to you in this lifetime, it cannot, it must not. For you to gain knowledge of such things would also mean the end to all things. And I will not help you answer the mysteries of this life. This you must do on your own...but I will say to you...your father is at peace, of this I am certain."

Ethan was mesmerized, lost in a fog of disbelief and uncertainty. He felt as though he was in the presence of an all-knowing deity. A terrifying feeling crept through him, as though Konig could see right into his very soul. He suddenly felt naked, all his sins and misgivings exposed for all to see.

Konig slowly turned his hairy face toward Ethan. The powerful glow of his sharp red eyes momentarily blinded the old man.

"You are worried," Konig said. "There is never a reason to worry. That is but a waste of the little time you have been given. You have the same faults of us all...and yes Ethan Educai...even I bear the weight of your flaws. I bear this responsibility for all living things."

He reads my mind, Ethan thought. *He somehow knows exactly what I am thinking. Every fear, every theory and belief, every regret I hold in my subconscious he can clearly see. How can this be possible?*

"I sense your confusion about me," Konig said. "You wish for knowledge to see you through this confusion. There is no knowledge you will ever attain that will solve this problem for you. Ethan, there will come a day when all living things will live in harmony. This is not a predication or a prophecy. It is a destiny written long ago. What I tell you is a fact! Every physical entity but I has a beginning and an end. But there is another dimension, a sanctuary you will learn of at a time the universe will come to find you. And the universe will find you... but only when you are ready."

"Tell me?" Ethan asked with reverence. Amidst the raindrops, he struggled to keep his attention on the glowing red eyes peering down on him. Ethan looked up at the mighty Konig and said, "You have the knowledge I have searched for my entire life! I must know what you know!"

"And you will," Konig said, "but not while you serve a purpose here on this planet. You still have work left to do. You must play the part you have been assigned. It is your duty to see this through to its completion. You must fulfill the fate the divinity deems appropriate."

"Divinity?" Ethan asked, puzzled by the Konig's words. "Do you speak of an almighty God, a messiah, some foolish prophecy! Is there truly a force that guides our destiny? And if there is, how could you possibly have knowledge of this?"

Konig peered into Ethan's mind, penetrated the walls of his subconscious with an offering of deep sensory perception. The coolness of great knowledge suddenly whipped through Ethan's mind. A calming sense of reassurance for less than a moment of human time, but it was enough to give him clarity of the situation. He could not explain what was happening, but in that brief moment when Konig became a part of him, Ethan was transformed. In an instant, Ethan's mind became a pliable tool for the universe to manipulate at its will. Konig had given Ethan a telepathic perception he would share with Becki later that same night. This was a gift they would rely upon in the very near future. It would take some time for Ethan to embrace this new skill, but the seed had been planted.

When Konig released his powerful psychic hold on Ethan's thoughts, the message telepathically relayed to Ethan through the giant's sensory extension was clear.

"Do you understand now?" Konig said.

"No! Not completely," Ethan trembled. "I will never understand. That is the point. Is it not?"

"And yet, you will obey?"

"It will be difficult, but I will try."

"I did not say it would be easy, but it is necessary. It is time for you both to complete your duty. I am here to prepare you for the final chapter of your odyssey."

"Then untie us," Becki requested, "Free us from these trees. Prove to us that you mean us no harm. Set us free."

Konig breathed, a long dusty shot of steam wafted from his mouth and drifted up to the heavens. "This...I cannot do," Konig said finally.

"You talk in riddles," Ethan said. "If you mean to assist us, help us now."

"There is no such thing as now!" Konig said. "There is only the space that surrounds us. Time only exists in your own ignorant dimension, in your own mind, in your own perspective. You must remain here and wait for Dmitri. If you desire to live on, if you desire to be saved, then you must do exactly as I instruct you to do. That is all I am able to tell you."

"Why must we stay bound to these trees?" Becki asked. "You have the power to set us free. Why do you refuse?"

"The universal play has been written. It was written long before your physical birth, Becki. I cannot interfere with what is meant to be."

"This is nonsense!" Ethan screamed. "Set us free! Do it now! I demand it of you!"

Konig remained calm and ignored Ethan's outburst. Konig knew Ethan would obey. He knew it the moment he grasped a hold on his innermost thoughts. Ethan was far too wise to let this opportunity pass. As much as his intellect might want to fight it, he instinctively realized he would do what he must.

All things were now in order. The conclusion to this performance would soon be upon them. The time had come for Konig to tell them of the task at hand.

"Dmitri will return here shortly," Konig said. His voice took on a professorial dominance. "When he returns, you must listen to him. Whatever he asks, follow his orders to the letter. If you do this, I will you see you safely to the end of your journey."

"And then what?" Becki asked.

"And then you will be free," Konig smiled. "Not only free from here, but free forever."

"And why should we believe you?" Ethan asked. "Will you at least offer us some visible proof?"

"You will obey because you must," Konig stated with conviction. "Do you always request proof, Ethan? The proof you seek is only an illusion. You need to accept that I am but a messenger, an article of the universe just like you. Search your innermost self and you will find no argument to persuade you otherwise. You must play your part until the written fate has met its end. There is no other choice."

Becki and Ethan looked at each other. There came an unspoken agreement between them when their eyes met. A spark of realization and acceptance from deep within their consciousness told them they must listen to Konig.

When Dmitri returned, they would follow his command.

Chapter 16

Barok continued to play his violuna.

He had been playing for almost an hour. He could not sleep. Something troubled him and he could not put his finger on it.

Presently, he played a sonata consisting of a string of broken triplets. It was a pleasant melody with a textured rhythmical phrasing, a bit of a light bounce to it even though it was soft and mostly largo.

Shroomy fell in and out of sleep as she listened to the soft and tender melody drift through the tiny room. The violuna played with such a grace and passion that was unlike any other instrument. It sounded like teardrops floating through the air, floating amidst a rainbow of the deepest and most profound emotions. Barok was well schooled in the art of violuna. It was an ancestral tradition. All acidel children learned this instrument at some point during their youth, some playing it much better than others. Barok had mastered the musicianship of the violuna long ago and he was most proud of his virtuosity.

"Are you ever going to come to bed?" Shroomy asked, her eyes half closed.

"I thought you liked my playing," Barok said, beginning to bow a long passage from a new selection, an acidel dirge he loved as a child. "You may sleep, I am just feeling the need to play. I will find time to rest before morning."

Shroomy smiled, rolled over close to the edge of the bed, stared at Barok. "It is almost morning now."

"No," Barok said quietly, "we still have an hour or two before daylight."

"Maybe that is true, but as you have said, tomorrow is a busy day. We must be alert and fully prepared."

Barok stopped playing mid-phrase. His mind drifted elsewhere. His powers of clairvoyance, while minuscule in the eyes of the universe, were still far more perceptive than any human. "There is something troubling me about tomorrow," Barok said finally, resting his violuna on the bedside.

"I do not sense any disturbance," Shroomy replied. She was younger than Barok by some twenty human years and her powers were not as astute as her mate's.

"Shroomy, I have to be honest, I do feel a great disturbance. I do not know what it is, but something is not right. We must pray to Konig for assistance."

"Praying to Konig is always a good idea. Though I think you are worrying for no reason. There is absolutely no basis to assume anything will be out of the ordinary come morning. Barok, my clairvoyant perception is clearly not as strong as your own, but I have sensed nothing. No cause for alarm has presented itself to me."

"You still have much to learn," Barok said.

"Is it necessary to insult me? I am only sharing with you what I perceive."

"Pray with me anyway?" Barok asked kindly.

Shroomy gazed at Barok. She loved him implicitly. She would attempt to ease his mind if she could. "Fine, I will pray with you," she gave in.

They kneeled before the bedside. The room lit now solely by starlight gently streaming in through the window.

"What are we praying for?" Shroomy asked.

"Assistance," Barok responded. "Assistance and guidance."

Silence filled the room. Barok and Shroomy bowed their heads against the edge of the bed and began to pray.

"Almighty Konig," Barok said, "Help me to ease my mind. I know with all my heart and all my faith that you will not see harm come to the acidel. But I have fears, and these fears may not be justified at all. Bring us your wisdom to see us through tomorrow and to do your bidding."

There was a long silence. Barok and Shroomy kept their eyes closed. They were motionless, deep in a spiritual trance.

Then Barok opened his eyes. He placed his rubbery hand on Shroomy's shoulder.

"May we speak honestly?" Barok asked.

"That is a silly request. Do we not always speak honestly with each other."

"What I have to say may surprise you," Barok grimaced, worried wrinkles stretched out across his beige leathery brow.

Shroomy got up from the floor, sat on the edge of the bed. Barok moved next to her.

"I am having doubts," Barok said, "I am afraid to say this, but my faith may be wavering."

"Konig is all powerful, there is no worry," Shroomy answered reassuringly.

Silence gripped the room again. Barok jumped down from the bed, scooted over to the ledge by the window.

"Have you ever seen him?" Barok asked, a seriousness to his deep growl.

"I do not need to see him," Shroomy said, "I know he is there."

"Why are you so sure?"

"You dare to question our faith?"

Barok felt suddenly ashamed. He placed his stumpy hands over his eyes, rubbed them with vigor, refocused his attention back to Shroomy.

"I must ask," Barok continued. "What if this is all a myth? My father, like yours, told us of this Konig, our protector. But there is no proof he exists. I know of no acidel who has ever claimed to see him in the flesh. Do we blindly put our faith in a thing that may not be?"

Shroomy's face saddened, her faith unshakable. It distressed her to see her mate bear such a disheartening burden.

"What you are saying suggests blasphemy," Shroomy scolded him. "I can offer no factual or scientific proof. No one can. That is why we call it faith."

"Yes, of course I know the origin of faith. I am just worried that our protector does not see what we see. How can he see all things? The acidel have trained for hundreds of years, we have attained powers far beyond those of any human. But we still cannot stop the inevitable. And I fear Konig cannot stop the inevitable even if he had the power to do so."

Shroomy could not follow this logic. Her mind spun in a whirlwind of directions, a rollercoaster of fragmented beliefs and ideas coming to and fro. Her faith was suddenly being challenged by a logic she could not compete with. She knew inherently that logic and faith were of two different mindsets. One could never correspond with the other. Each was separate and distinct. That was the way of things. There could not be a mix of the two without mental anguish, chaos and utter confusion.

"I do not mean to cause you distress," Barok said. "I just want to tell you what I am feeling. It does not mean I am right...but it does not mean I am wrong either. It simply means I do not know."

Shroomy nodded in agreement. There was no answer to this riddle. There never would be. But her faith was strong. She would not bend to the science of disbelief. Whether her faith could be explained or not, she would always believe, even if Barok could not.

"I do have faith," Barok said, "It is just not as strong as I would like it to be."

"Give it time my dear," Shroomy said, rubbing his back. "Faith is a challenge to us all. But it is a challenge you will confront and conquer one day. Of this, I am certain."

"There is a storm approaching," Barok said.

"Haven't you looked at the window? The storm is already here!" Shroomy laughed. "Don't tell me you are becoming delusional now as well."

"You don't understand Shroomy," Barok cautioned. "What you see now is not a storm at all. What awaits us in the morning will be a storm like this planet has never seen."

"What makes you say that?"

"I have seen it, felt it. I know it to be true. All the signs point toward a fury of nature brewing in the winds. The devastation that awaits Stritonoly come morning cannot be avoided. The freighter may turn out to be our lifeboat."

"And if you know of such a thing," Shroomy said, "do you not have an obligation to stop it."

"While I have my doubts about Konig, I have no doubts of the visions I have seen. Yes, I could warn them, but it would be of no use. The mighty winds of nature's fury have sounded their alarm. I assure you, a monstrous storm approaches. Nothing we say or do can stop this rolling wave. I feel dread, despair. Many lives will be silenced and we must allow fate to follow its unmerciful course. It is written in our most sacred scriptures. We do not dare interfere with the universal plan. That is not our purpose."

Shroomy felt anguish overwhelm her. Morality had its limits when confronted with mandatory universal doctrines. The acidel were not in any position to question the strength of the mightiest power of all. Even Konig was not above the destiny mapped out by the cosmos. And Barok was right, there were many things even Konig could not see. This celestial plan must see its mission through. Even though they would never understand it, or even accept it, they knew it must be done.

And neither Barok or Shroomy would ever consider standing in the way of its almighty and deadly strength. The universe would always find a means to triumph.

If they chose to face its wrath, they would find eternal death all but a certainty. They accepted that they would be forced to watch the devastation unfold, grieve as they must, and then they would be free to complete the duty they were sent here to accomplish.

Chapter 17

Dmitri stood over his slain father.

I am the conquering warrior, Dmitri thought. I have done what no one else would ever dare to do. This stupid, stupid man who may have been my father once, he is no more. He was but a weak mortal, and ultimately a disgraceful excuse for a human being. He is gone forever, and this kingdom will have me to thank for this! They will praise me as the messiah I have come to be!

His dead father, draped in the imperial velvet robe, lie motionless on the floor. Blood oozed from his open stomach wound and formed a thick puddle around his upper body. His lifeless eyes were wide open. They seemed to stare blankly into an endless chasm of nothingness.

Dmitri felt no remorse, no sorrow whatsoever. He turned his back on his dead father as if he were a stranger. In Dmitri's mind, this man he had just killed was a foolish leader, a murderer, a man who deserved a cruel and unceremonious death.

Then, a swell of joyful emotion welled up from deep within Dmitri. There came upon him a sudden sense of supreme elation. This was only held back slightly by the weariness he felt beginning to drain some of his energies.

Before going back to Ethan and Becki, Dmitri thought. I must go to my chambers and revive myself.

Walking casually down the main hallway, darkness all around him and the bloody dagger still in hand, he turned left toward his royal chamber.

He felt no concern for the action he had just committed, not a worry in his mind. He was The Czar now and that was all he could concentrate on, the power, the dominance. No one and nothing could stop him now.

Yes, he brutally murdered his own father. So what, he thought. This justice may appear unfortunate to some, but it was a duty for the betterment of the entire planet. He bore the strength no other could muster. He began to let it all sink in, relishing the power of inheriting the entire planet of Stritonoly, and maybe someday soon, much more than that. Nothing would stop him from ruling with a ruthless hand.

Opening the door to his chambers, he threw the bloody dagger on his bed. Blood seeped onto the sheets, some dripping on the floor.

Like a soldier preparing for battle, he quickly stripped out of his wet clothes. With urgency, he changed into a new set of his finest brown royal military attire, complete with the distinctive symbol of power, a row of embroidered serpents knitted carefully across the front of his shirt.

I should be wearing the royal velvet cape as well, he thought. *I suppose that can wait until morning. Let them find my father with his cape draped over his massacred body. Let them bring me the cape with his blood on it. That will be the ultimate symbol for all those who dare test my leadership. My own father's blood on my new royal cape. Yes, that will be a mighty show of force for those who dare oppose me.*

Reaching into his closet, Dmitri removed a large bucket hidden just beneath a row of shelves set close to the floor. The dirty black bucket emitted a putrid smell, an odor that Dmitri had grown to enjoy immensely. The bucket was filled to the top with the hardened remains of acidel sweat. With a small, sharp pocketknife, Dmitri carved out a small chunk from inside the bucket.

Lifting the hardened toxin up with one hand, he held it like some sort of holy relic. His eyes beamed with a euphoric, schizophrenic mania.

You are my God now, Dmitri thought. *Nothing can stop us. We will rule this galaxy with a powerful ruthlessness. It is a beauty... YOU are a beauty. I will worship your liquid forever. You are the only good left in this worthless world. Let me consume you and flee from this pain forever!*

The madness that had taken over Dmitri's mind had allowed the acidel sweat to take on a human form in his consciousness. The acidel sweat was no longer just an addictive substance. It had emerged into something else. It had grown into a reality of actual existence. A living, breathing creature!

Knock...Knock! A soft tapping upon Dmitri's door startled him.

"Who is there?' Dmitri asked.

"I am sorry to bother you my darling," It was his Mother, The Queen Victoria. "I thought I heard something, I just wanted to make sure you were all right."

Dmitri's eyes fluttered, he froze, he panicked. He tossed the bucket back into the closet as fast as he could. Sweat began to crawl down his red hair and drip thin lines of moisture upon his forehead. "I am fine Mother, I am just very tired."

"May I come in?" Victoria asked.

What game does she play with me? Dmitri thought. *Does she know of what I have done? Could she have seen her fallen husband and come to find me? Has she come to seek revenge? Wait! Stop thinking foolishly, that could not be possible.*

Clear your mind, Dmitri told himself. *She is only checking on her son, she must have heard me pass by her room. This is harmless. She will go back to bed. I must see that she does. Focus...Focus...Focus!*

"Of course you may come in," Dmitri said. "Please just give me a moment to get my robe on."

Dmitri slammed the closet door shut, reached for his satin blue robe which hung from a hook on the backside of the door. Then he reached for the doorknob.

Wait! Dmitri thought, stopping himself just before opening the door. *The dagger, you fool! Get rid of the dagger!*

Quickly, Dmitri folded over the sheet with the dagger inside. He popped open the closet door using one foot and threw the sheet inside. Closing the closet door again, he peered around the room, his eyes furiously darting back and forth and back again. The panic was not subsiding as he had hoped it would.

I must not delay any longer, Dmitri thought. *She will become suspicious. I must let her in.*

Slowly opening the door, Dmitri yawned. "It is so late Mother. Is something wrong?"

"No, I am fine," Victoria said. "I thought I heard you in the hall, I was only worried you were all right."

Dmitri smiled, rubbed his eyes, pretended to be waking from a slumber. "Oh, my loving mother. I do love you so. Thank you for your concern, but I am fine. I was talking to father out in the garden. He told me he wishes to be left alone for the rest of the night."

"I thought he was going to work all night in the study."

"No, he wanted to spend some time meditating alone in the garden, I brought him something to drink. He did ask that if you should awake to tell you to go back to bed. He said he would see you in the morning."

"He is under so much stress on this night," Victoria said. "Maybe I should go to him."

"No!" Dmitri said, much louder than he intended. "Mother, he has requested to be left alone. It is important to him that he not be bothered...by anyone. He said he needs this time to be alone with his thoughts."

Victoria smiled back at Dmitri. "I love you Dmitri." She leaned forward and kissed his forehead. "Are you sweating?"

Dmitri wiped his forehead. "It is a little warm in my room tonight."

"I see, well try to get some sleep. Tomorrow will be a busy day."

"I am going back to sleep right now," Dmitri said, "and you should go back to bed as well."

"Yes my dear son," Victoria said, turning to walk away. "You are a good boy, my son. I will see you in the morning."

Dmitri watched her make her way down the hallway and turn toward the royal suite. Then he closed the door and let out a long sigh of relief.

She does not suspect a thing, Dmitri thought. *Now I must tend to business. The time has come for my sister and that old fool of a teacher to become the first servants of my new empire. They are the first pieces of clay now ready for my molding, and I shall sculpt them into the image of my choosing. Starting tonight, I will begin to train them properly!*

Chapter 18

November 2nd, 2014

Richard,

Something terrible has happened. I know we haven't spoken in quite a few years and I have repeatedly tried to call you but you have not called me back. Since you have not returned my calls, unfortunately, I am forced to tell you this news by way of this letter.

Your sister, Rebecca, is in the hospital and is in extremely serious condition. She is in a coma and the doctors feel there is no chance of her ever recovering. Even if she were to wake from her coma, she would live in a vegetative state. I can't bear to see her this way and I wish for you to see her before the end. After speaking with the doctors I have made the decision to take her off life support.

Richard, I know you hate me and I know you don't want to see your sister either, but I beg of you, please come to the hospital to see her one last time. We are planning to take her off life support on November 13th, the day your mother passed away.

Please contact me Richard! You can hate me all you want, but please come and see your sister one last time. I hope and pray I will hear from you soon.

Sincerely,
Dad

Chapter 19

The rain came to an abrupt stop.

Thick clouds still hovered above, circling in ferocious patterns against the night sky. They were obviously regrouping as they eagerly awaited another strike. The storm was far from over. The imposing clouds made that abundantly clear.

Presently however, the winds had diminished and the creatures of the forest ventured out into the open space in front of Becki and Ethan.

A small herd of tiny three-legged horse-frogen quickly galloped by. Their greenish manes wafted lightly in the breeze as they strode off and disappeared behind some thick shrubbery. Several multi-colored butterflies twirled and flew in an unorganized pattern of carefree happiness. Nature seemed at peace for the moment. The lull in the storm allowed life to emerge and dance about the forest, at least for a while.

"Are you afraid?" Becki asked Ethan, softness in her tone.

"Afraid," Ethan said, "I am always afraid, Becki. I am afraid of the unknown. I have long been afraid of that which I cannot see or predict. This has plagued me for the whole of my life."

"There is nothing a mortal man can predict with accuracy, Ethan"

"This I have come to know all too well," Ethan sighed.

This night had suddenly become Ethan's classroom. But he was no longer the teacher. He was now the uninformed student craving new information. Gradually he became aware of his ignorance, ashamed of his faults and lack of knowledge. The intelligence he accumulated his entire life was for naught in this moment of impending finality. He began to realize that there is no knowledge attainable to the mortal man than would ever compel the universe to change the course of an ultimate destiny. Fate was indeed cruel.

The most disturbing thing for Ethan was the realization of his present lack of faith. He had prayed many times before, never certain exactly for what or to whom he was praying. Like a well-conditioned monkey, he developed a habit of asking for guidance from a power he could never see, feel or touch. He wondered now if this was all but a waste of his precious time. Could he have spent his time on Stritonoly in a more productive way? Did prayer and meditation ultimately prove pointless? These were the questions that flew through his mind presently. And once again, there was no sensible answer that came to him. He was lost in the turmoil of what he felt would now be the final moments of his life.

"I am not afraid of Dmitri," Ethan said, "Nor am I afraid of what he might have done, or will do. I only fear the mysterious, the uncertainties, the fundamental query that remains unanswered. It is the ultimate question for us all. What will become of us in the end? I fear for the salvation of our souls. I am embarrassed that I have no answer that will satisfy us at this time, or any time."

"You wish for the impossible," Becki said.

"I wish for knowledge."

"No, you wish for answers no human will or should ever know. If we were to know the answer to the questions you pose, we would have no reason to go on."

"What do you mean?" Ethan asked, suddenly intrigued.

"If all things were known to us," Becki said, "then why would we ever bother to improve ourselves, to learn, to expand our innermost selves. It is the curiosity of the unknown that keeps us alive and moving forward."

Her words struck a nerve in Ethan's consciousness. His eyes blinked as he tried to absorb her perspective. "I do not understand, Becki. I am trying to, but I fear I am unable to grasp what you are saying. I am too weak and unknowing to commit and follow your way of thinking. I am an old man. I have long ago accepted my internal struggle. It will remain my burden until the last beat of my heart."

A single horse-frogen galloped by and quickly disappeared into the forest.

"When you see that horse-frogen," Becki said. "What do you see?"

"I see a horse-frogen!"

"And that is your weakness. I do not see just a creature of the universe when I see that horse-frogen, I see the universe itself, the whole of everything around us. There is no such thing as individuality. We may meet our physical demise on this night, but we will live on forever. Of that I have no doubt. Whether it be a God, the universe, a mighty deity, whatever you choose to call it. I know it exists. I cannot prove this, nor will I even attempt to try, but my personal logic dictates to me that it must be. It is not a science, it is a faith."

Ethan took in her observations as clarity began to fill his mind. A sudden and unexpected sense of acceptance and calm began to flicker through him.

Could the answer be that there is no answer, Ethan thought. *Is it truly that simple and yet so profound. A riddle within a riddle within a riddle! Just a maze of uncertainties allowing for our own personal growth.*

He became suddenly aware that Becki had grown up on this night. She entered this evening all but a childish little girl. Now she was a wise woman. Ethan was proud of her. This night of torment had somehow brought to light her inner strength, her wisdom, her insight. Right before his eyes, Ethan had witnessed a rebirth in her. She was a child no more.

"It was you Ethan," Becki said, "You are the reason I know these things."

"How could that be?" Ethan asked, perplexed and curious.

"I've watched you struggle for years to attain every bit of knowledge possible to man. It was your failure to find the ultimate answers that plague us all that led me to a startling discovery. In deep prayer one night, I found my comforting answer. I accepted that there is information in our universe we cannot ever know. We can research and probe, use every means at our disposal, but ultimately, until we meet our physical demise, we will always be blinded by our mortal ignorance. I was able to recognize this through your labors, Ethan. The tireless hours you spent lecturing and theorizing, I do not blame you for your curiosity. I applaud your efforts, but it helped me to see that no answer to the great questions of the universe will ever satisfy a mortal mind. Just as we are tied to these trees, we are equally tied to our humanity, and with that, we are also tied to our ignorance. One day the blindfold will be removed, and then we will know."

"Know what?" Ethan asked.

Becki smiled and said: "When the blindfold is peeled away, we will know everything there is to know...everything!"

Chapter 20

Konig wandered back across the mountaintop and arrived at the valley outside his cavern.

He felt confident that his message to Ethan and Becki was received and would be carried out. He knew that being the mortals they were, they would most assuredly suffer from some internal conflict in following his demands. He also knew that they possessed the wisdom and faith to proceed according to plan.

Now that the storm had subsided, the valley that stretched out before Konig's cavern took on a renewed magnificence.

The night was coming to an end as an orangey-yellow haze began to slowly form upon the distant horizon.

The lush colorful flowers that had lost their luster under the heavy rains began to bloom once again. There were blue and red and purple flowers, large and small, all different and unique in their character and dimension. The flowers breathed a spirit of freshness upon all things inhabiting this heavenly valley.

Konig stood at the edge of the valley, the deep forest at his back. He could not help but marvel at the majesty of the moment. He breathed in the sparkling scent of reborn life.

Several deer near the center of the valley stopped eating the yellow grass of the valley when they first saw Konig. With a nod of his head, Konig motioned for them to continue their feast. The deer were small creatures, not as small as the horse-frogen, but still very small compared to the giant Konig. The deer had beautiful spotted blue circles all over their bodies. The blue circles were surrounded by a design of orange lines that stretched out evenly as they fell away from the blue circular pattern. *This was the work of a great artist,* Konig thought. The artist of course was the universe that Konig served with honor, humility, and pride.

With soft steps, Konig walked on the damp yellow grass and made his way to the white rocky-faced cavern he called home. As he moved across the valley, creatures large and small bowed with reverence as he passed by. He was far more than just their keeper and protector. He was the representation of the eternal spirit growing inside them all.

As he approached the cavern, he paused to take notice of the charred remains of the horse-frogen still lying on the altar. He bowed his head, then looked up to the heavens, and continued on into the cavern.

Konig's home was not as big as one might think. Considering his enormity, the cavern itself was quite small indeed. He had to duck just to move around the small space. Shiny white rocks filled the inside of the cavern. Several pipetu plants were strewn among the floor and walls giving off a delicious scent and ambiance.

Along the farthest corner, just between two large white rocks, Inkel was busy looking over the newest transmissions that had been just delivered to the cavern.

"Good morning," Inkel said, "It is morning is it not?"

"It is almost morning," Konig smiled.

Inkel was of the ancient turtle species. He had transformed himself over hundreds of years into a form which was suitable for this environment. While he still bore the shell casing of his turtle ancestry, he had acquired the power of speech long ago. He had also learned to stand up straight and use his fingers with as much dexterity as would any human. His skin was thick, leathery and faded green. Tiny black and pink dots spilled across his shell casing.

"Anything of interest for me today?" Konig asked.

"More of the same," Inkel squealed in his high pitched voice, "I have some holograms set up for you to observe."

On the far wall across from Inkel was a flat expanse of smooth white wall.

Konig walked over and sat down on one of the rocks next to Inkel.

"So," Konig said somewhat impatiently, "Let's see what we have today."

Inkel pressed a tiny square red button on the edge of the rock to his left. Suddenly a hologram appeared right in front of the flat-surfaced wall.

The image was that of a casket, a small one, a coffin fit for a small child. The picture could not be seen clearly. It swam in and out of focus.

"Can you clear that up?" Konig asked.

"The image is being sent to us from fourteen light-years across the galaxy. I do not even know the planet of its origin. For whatever reason, the universe saw fit to send this to us."

The image continued to blink in and out of focus. Konig could clearly make out the shape of a small coffin, but little else. Then the screen flashed a bright light and a solid projection flashed before them. They saw several humans in black attire walking slowly down an aisle with a small casket upon their shoulders.

"A funeral procession," Inkel said.

"Yes, it is burial ritual from a time long ago," Konig said, "I am not all too familiar with such a practice. It seems most disturbing and unnecessary."

"There is much grief in this hologram," Inkel observed.

"Unnecessary grief," Konig retorted. "That child is alive still."

"You know this for certain?"

"If I speak it, then it is the truth."

Inkel sank back, embarrassed at daring to question the mighty Konig.

"I am sorry Konig," Inkel cowered, "I meant no disrespect."

Konig touched the shell casing on Inkel's back, rubbed it gently. "You never need to apologize to me Inkel. You have always been a faithful servant and an honorable creature. Happiness will come to many generations of your spawn because of the goodness you have given in your lifetime."

Inkel smiled. These were kind words from the one creature he admired most of all. For to Inkel, Konig was the answer to every dilemma or despair. A wonderful sense of peace fell over Inkel whenever a kind word from Konig passed through his reptilian mind.

The hologram started to blink in and out of focus again. Then an image of a family in formal attire appeared. They were weeping uncontrollably. The image then vanished almost as quickly as it appeared. The small coffin appeared again.

"What does this mean?" Inkel asked. "I have never seen this sort of grief. They seem to be crying tears of sadness."

"There are indeed crying tears of sadness," Konig stated.

"But why? The child's physical form is dead and now he is free from pain."

Konig looked deep into the round eyes of his friend, "Inkel, these mortals we see in this hologram do not know what we know. They may not come to understand for a very, very long time."

"Do they always grieve a loss in this manner?" Inkel questioned, a perplexed curiosity washed across his leathery face.

"Loss for them is a finality. They do not have enough faith to know otherwise. Some have no faith at all."

Inkel pressed his shell casing against the rocky wall behind him. He leaned back and thought about this oddity. This was not how he had come to understand the processes of physical death. He had been conditioned from birth to understand the infinite possibilities that existed in all things. Physical death was not a finality by any means. It was a joyous celebration, a rebirth.

"I don't expect you to understand," Konig said peacefully, "This hologram has been sent to us from many light years away from our present existence. The images we are seeing occurred a long, long time ago. I can guarantee you, the child these humans grieve for is not dead at all. At least, not in the way they perceive death to be."

"This is most confusing," Inkel said. "May I turn the hologram off now. I cannot bear to see such preventable agony."

"If you wish," Konig said, "but keep the files stored away someplace safe. They may be of use to us at some other time. They were sent to us for a reason. Everything has a purpose Inkel, there are no accidents."

"Of this I am certain," Inkel agreed. He shut down the hologram by hitting the little red button once more. Then he took several disks from a side panel just behind one of the giant white rocks and slipped them into a folder for safe keeping. "I will keep them tucked away for future consideration."

"Thank you, Inkel," Konig smiled. "Will you rest now for a while?"

Inkel yawned, "Yes, I believe I will."

Konig watched as Inkel shrunk into his shell casing and almost immediately fell into a deep sleep.

Konig himself never slept, it was not a necessity for a creature that had attained indomitable mental prowess. He did use the time however to go through the events that were to transpire in the morning. If his predictions were accurate, as they usually were, the morning storm would present a fury this planet may never be able to recover from.

Konig stood and walked just outside the entrance to the cavern. He looked up as high as he could to see into the skies above. Stars were still visible but they were fading fast. Soon the night would be over.

I know so much and yet I know so little, Konig thought. *I am so small compared to this vastness before me. But I do believe. I do have faith. I serve with no thought of my own prosperity. I believe in the intertwining web of all things. Whatever may happen come morning, I am certain that the universal conviction to tranquility will prevail. No matter what the outcome, faith will find a way. Of this I know for certain. Faith will never die.*

Chapter 21

DMITRI CLOSED THE door to his room.

His mother was gone now. He hoped he was convincing enough in his act to get her to return to the royal suite and go straight to bed. If not, he would deal with her later. Presently, there were other matters to attend to. First on his list was regaining his strength and he knew how to get that back in a hurry.

Constant and complete euphoria is attainable, Dmitri thought. *And only I hold the key to this power.*

Dmitri's mind became a rollercoaster once again. He was badly withdrawing from the acidel sweat. He needed more and he needed it now.

Racing wildly back to the closet, he quickly found the bucket and the hardened piece of acidel sweat he had carved out. He reached for the substance. His mind freed itself from all thought except the acidel sweat. All his energies became transfixed upon the addictive substance he now held in his hand.

He darted back across the room, sat on the edge of his bed and without hesitation began to chew into the hardened liquid. He crunched his teeth into a piece of the hard-edged piece of toxin. It melted almost immediately on his tongue and slid smoothly down his throat. Without a pause, he bit into another piece, crunched on it for a half second before it turned into a sweetened liquid and began to sate his craving.

A soft fogginess filled the room about Dmitri. This was not a real fog of course, it was Dmitri's high beginning to take effect. The sudden rush of energy intoxicated every muscle in his body. His eyes rolled to the back of his head as he sat motionless, only the whites of his eyeballs were visible. His mind drifted into a fairyland mixed with thoughts of horror and death, mounds of brutally beaten bodies, families drenched in pools of thick blood. There was no stopping this catastrophic avalanche of bizarre visions.

Lost in this haze of confusion, Dmitri felt as if hours had passed him by. In reality, only a minute or two had elapsed. Then, a calm came over him as his body adjusted to the chemical now seeping through his veins. He gathered himself and quickly stood.

Bending down, he reached under the bed and pulled out a cardboard box. Presently on his knees, he placed the box on top of the bedspread. Rubbing his hands together, he stared at the box with great excitement. Then he opened the box as a child would open a much anticipated present. Inside the box sat a crown of roses. This was the customary headwear for a royal bride. He delicately picked out from of the box, held it level with his eyes so he could admire the perfect placement of the roses. *Becki will look so lovely wearing this when we wed,* he thought. *I will make her so happy when she becomes my wife. What a wonderful mother to our children she will be.* Then he placed the crown of roses back into the box, smiling the whole time.

Gathering his senses, he jumped to his feet. Crossing to the closet, he reached for his royal sword and slipped it into his waistband. Moving back to the bed, he picked up the box and clutched it close to his chest.

I must go back to Ethan and Becki now, Dmitri thought. *It is time for them to join me. And join me they will! They will do exactly as I instruct them to do...they will listen to me...or they will die!*

Chapter 22

MEMORANDUM

From: Worship Committee
To: Clergy Staff
Date: November 7th, 2014
Re: Request from Mr. Brown

Mr. Brown has requested that a priest or deacon from our church be present at St. Paul's Hospital on the morning of November 13th. The decision has been made by the family that his daughter, Rebecca, will be taken off life support on that day. He is requesting the services of one our priests or deacons to be present at the hospital that morning to administer last rites and possibly stay for a while to assist in counseling family members. Please advise.

FYI: Rebecca was an active member of our youth choir until about a year ago. She also accompanied our adult choir on a number of occasions. She played piano and violin.

Chapter 23

"Marry us right now," Dmitri demanded.

There he stood, proudly holding the box which carried the ceremonial crown of roses. Dmitri was freshly dressed and prepared to enter the next and most exciting phase of his life.

"Are you speaking to me?" Ethan asked.

"Yes," Dmitri laughed, "You are a nobleman. You have the right to perform a wedding ceremony. It will be legal and binding"

"It will not be legal," Ethan said, "I cannot marry a brother to his sister."

"You speak of technicalities."

"I speak of the law."

Dmitri pulled out a small pocket-knife, walked behind Ethan and cut loose the vine which held him to the tree.

I am free, Ethan thought. *I could run away if I so choose. But Konig! That creature has planted a seed in my mind. I have to listen to Dmitri. And I must stay here for Becki's sake as well.*

Dmitri walked slowly over to his sister. With the palm of his hand he brushed back the hair from her forehead. "My lovely bride to be. You will be so happy with me as your husband and father to our many children."

Becki was disgusted. She could not bear to meet eyes with him. "You killed my father," she said, "You killed him! I want you to say it!"

Dmitri smiled, "If it will please the bride to be, then I will say it... yes, I killed him."

Ethan stood frozen. Becki could only shake her head in disbelief.

Walking behind Becki, Dmitri cut the vine that held her to the tree and freed his future wife.

"Do you wish to run away now?" Dmitri asked.

"I wish for our father to still be alive," Becki said.

Dmitri ignored her comment, "Let us do what must be done. There will be time for discussion later. The morning approaches. Look at the night sky, it is beginning to lose its darkness and the rains have stopped as well. It is a new day. Let us not dwell on the past."

We must trust Konig, Ethan thought. *He may be our only chance left for survival.*

"Are you ready?" Ethan said.

Becki shot a quick glance at Ethan. They met eyes and realized intuitively that Konig was right. Somehow, he had imparted upon them a telepathic connection. Ethan and Becki were sharing a mental awareness with each other they had never experienced before. And they knew, as difficult as it would be, they must do as Konig instructed and do whatever Dmitri ordered.

"I have been ready for quite some time for this event," Dmitri said joyfully. "Becki, are you prepared now to be my wife?"

Becki was unable to look the murderer of her father in the eyes, but she spoke: "I am ready to make you my husband."

Dmitri opened the box and removed the crown of roses. He placed it softly upon her head. "Ah, you look just as I thought you would. You are a vision of loveliness. Is she not a beautiful bride Ethan?"

"Yes," Ethan said, "A beautiful bride indeed."

"Then let us begin!" Dmitri shouted.

Ethan moved in front of them. Dmitri grabbed Becki's hand and squeezed it tightly.

"It is customary for the couple to kneel," Ethan said.

"Yes, of course," Dmitri said, a broad smile on his face.

Dmitri dropped to his knees as Becki continued to stand. Ethan looked deep into Becki's eyes, tried to relay the message from Konig telepathically. Becki felt the message.

You must do whatever he orders. It was Ethan's voice she heard in her head, almost as clearly as if he were actually speaking to her, but in reality, his mouth never moved. She heard his voice again in her head: *Konig will see us safely through this.*

Hesitantly, she kneeled down next to her brother, adjusted the crown of roses upon her head and stared up at Ethan.

"We do not need to perform a full ceremony," Ethan said. "The night is almost at an end, it may be best to do this quickly."

"Quick is fine," Dmitri said, "just get it done."

Ethan knew the ritualistic prayers and chants that went along with the many wedding ceremonies he presided over. He also knew that Dmitri had no idea what any of these rituals or prayers sounded like. He could speak gibberish and Dmitri wouldn't know the difference. He poised himself in an authoritative stance and prepared to deliver some form of a believable, but false, wedding ceremony.

"Lord of all things," Ethan said, completely speaking off the cuff, "We have before you two people who wish to be joined as one."

Utter nonsense, Ethan thought. *This is absolutely ridiculous. And look at that fool Dmitri, giggling like a child. He is making me sick to my stomach. How I would love to smash him across that smiling face right now.*

"Master Dmitri," Ethan continued, "Before all the Gods above and all the creatures of the universe, do you swear to take this woman as your wife on this day?"

Dmitri giggled, "Yes sir. I do!"

Oh God, Ethan thought. *This is a travesty, a mockery!*

"And you, Princess Becki," Ethan said, "Before all the Gods above and all the creatures of the universe, Do you swear to take this man as your husband on this day?"

"Yes, I do" Becki said in a cold and careless voice.

"A little more excitement would please me, my dear," Dmitri said. "Remember, tonight will be our wedding night. We may even conceive our firstborn on this night!"

This will not happen, Ethan thought. And with that thought the telepathic gift Konig imparted upon him started to filter further and further into his consciousness. He could feel his thoughts and Becki's become united as one. They were now speaking to each other though no words were spoken aloud.

I will not allow this to happen, Ethan said to Becki telepathically.

I know you will not, Becki answered.

I believe Konig will save us, but in the event you are left alone with your brother, be sure that I will not allow such an atrocity to ever take place.

Becki smiled. *I know Ethan, I hear you now, and I thank you.*

Ethan looked deep into Dmitri's eyes. If he could communicate with Becki telepathically, could it be possible to see into Dmitri's mind as well? He engaged all his mental alertness on the prospect of seeing into Dmitri's thoughts, but nothing came through. All he could see when he focused on Dmitri was a blackness, a void. There was nothing to be heard, felt or seen. He accepted for the moment that the telepathy Konig gave them was for Becki and Ethan alone. The two of them were now spiritually and mentally connected. The universe saw fit for this to be, and so it was. Becki could not help but smile at this new found perspective. She knew she had a bond now with Ethan that could never be severed, even by physical death.

Noticing the smile on Becki's face, Dmitri assumed it was for him and felt a great joy come over him. His mission was now complete. He had dethroned his father and guaranteed a successful lineage of powerful offspring that would dominate the galaxies under his watchful eye. He was filled with pride realizing his fantasies were finally becoming a reality.

Chapter 24

MR. BROWN SAT in a small empty waiting room across the hall from Rebecca. Her room was at the rear of the hospital, a new wing recently constructed called the D unit. Very small for a hospital wing, there were only eight rooms along a single hallway. There was a little nook for a nurse's station and a lot of colorful fake flowers and religious paintings spread out down the hall. This particular floor was designed with a definite purpose behind it. It certainly had the look and feel of a funeral parlor. The staff of the hospital referred to it as 'the death unit' because if you were admitted to that ward, you did not come out alive. Patients admitted to this unit were basically sent there to die. When all medical options had been exhausted and there was no practical chance left for survival, The D unit was built specifically for patients who were about to die.

The small waiting room Mr. Brown sat in had the typical solid white hospital walls and the dreary smell of sickness drifting through the air. Presently, he sat on a small green couch and sipped a Styrofoam cup of bitter black coffee. From where he sat, he stared through a glass window that looked out into the hallway and the entrance to his daughter's room. All morning he'd been observing the slow pace of the medical staff routinely going about their work, checking his daughter every once in a while, pacing back and forth, running errands about the floor.

His daughter would be taken off life support in about an hour. It would happen on the same date his wife died two years earlier. Vicky Brown, his wife, was in a car driven by her husband the night they slid off the road and crashed into a tree on their way home from a party. The car struck a tree on the passenger side where Vicky sat—she was killed instantly. Mr. Brown was in the hospital for just a short time, having suffered some broken ribs and a laceration on his forehead, the scar of which still remained.

A figure suddenly caught his attention standing just outside Rebecca's room. A young man in a denim jacket and jeans had stopped and stood in her open doorway. The young man stood there in a frozen pose of shock.

It was Richard, Rebecca's brother.

Jumping to his feet, Mr. Brown left the waiting room and entered the hallway. He waited a moment, trying to think of the best way to approach him. Richard had his back to his father, unaware he was even there.

"I'm glad you came," his father said finally.

Richard recognized the voice immediately but didn't bother to even look at him. He continued to stare straight ahead into Rebecca's room.

"I'm here for her, not for you," Richard said sternly, "don't get confused or stupid about this, after today I will never see you again."

"If that's what you want, I understand."

"I don't care if you understand or not...you murdered my mother, and you probably had something to do with this also."

There was silence.

"Was she drunk?" Richard asked. "As drunk as you were the night you killed Mom?"

Mr. Brown stammered: "...um...no, she wasn't drunk."

"But she was on something."

His father didn't answer. His silence said more than enough.

"Yeah, well...it runs in the family. Ain't that right Daddy?" Richard said with a thick sarcasm, starting to raise his voice louder in anger.

Unsure of how to respond to him, Mr. Brown switched the subject, "You know that her car crashed into a young boy."

"Yeah, I heard. So where is he?"

"He...he didn't make it," Mr. Brown said solemnly. "And I suppose you'll blame me for that too?"

Richard shook his head. "Did you talk to the family of the boy?"

His father again did not answer. The shame on his face told Richard that he clearly did not speak to the family.

"So you're a loser and a coward," Richard said. "How old was the kid? What was his name?"

"He was young, I don't know...I think his name was Jack or something... really...Richard...Does it matter?"

Building up the courage to look his father straight in the eyes, he said, "I really don't wanna make a scene here. I came here to see my sister, not you." An uncaring detached coldness seeped into Richard's voice. "I don't have anything to say to you and I never will. Why don't you do yourself a favor and just walk away from me before this gets ugly...just walk away."

His father choked back tears as he slowly retreated back to the waiting room.

Chapter 25

Dmitri watched as the blackness of the night sky turned to gray.

"The morning approaches," Ethan said, looking up at the diminishing starlight.

A soft hue of transformation began to take place. The darkness of the night was beginning its departure. The north sun would be rising very soon.

"There is business to discuss," Dmitri stated, sounding like The Czar he now was.

"Take a seat," Dmitri ordered. Becki and Ethan complied and sat down next to each other on a tree stump.

Dmitri paced back and forth, absorbing the powerful feeling of being the one in charge. He began to walk with authoritative steps, as if he was preparing to give an important lecture.

"Now that we are in agreement about who the absolute ruler is," Dmitri said, "you will allow me to make my first decree."

Just go along with whatever he says, Ethan said to Becki, again using only the telepathic powers he suddenly felt very comfortable with. It was as if this power was always inside him but until now remained hidden from his use. The many suspicions he always had about telepathy and extra-sensory perception were suddenly answered. He was now among the gifted. Konig had shown him a new trail to follow, one with seemingly endless possibilities.

I will listen to Dmitri, Becki said. *I understand now what we must do. I trust what Konig told us, and I trust you as well.*

"I am going to retreat to the main parlor shortly," Dmitri continued. *"I will wait there as I normally do for Barok to greet me. Nothing is to appear out of the ordinary. Becki, you will return to my room...excuse me, our room,"* Dmitri snickered, *"and you shall wait there for my arrival later this evening. I am sure you will prepare a wonderful meal for our first night together as husband and wife."*

I am nauseous, Becki said to Ethan. *Are you certain he cannot hear what we are saying to each other?*

Is my mouth moving when I speak to you? Ethan said.

No, it is not, Becki said.

Then he cannot hear us. Konig has connected us through our thoughts. And we must use this connection wisely. For now, just keep smiling. This will all be over very soon. I swear that no harm will come to you. Just play along for now.

"Now as for you Ethan," Dmitri stopped pacing and looked at Ethan.

"Yes My Czar, what is it that you desire of me?" Ethan said subserviently.

"How do you greet me each and every morning?"

"I greet you at the front gates of the citadel."

"And what do you usually say to me?"

"I usually say 'Welcome to your day.'"

Dmitri grinned, "And that is exactly what you will say to me on this morning as well. Go back to your chambers, get dressed and then meet me as you always do. And when you greet me, say those exact words to me. Do you understand?"

Ethan nodded his head.

"Then say it!" Dmitri shouted.

"Say what?" Ethan asked.

"I want to hear how you will greet me. Say it now. Say it exactly as you will say it when you see me."

"Welcome to your day." Ethan said. "How was that?"

"Perhaps you could try to say it with a bit more excitement."

"I will do my best."

Dmitri reached into his back pocket and pulled out a vial of a thick crystalline-blue substance.

Becki and Ethan continued to speak telepathically to each other. With every passing moment, they were gaining a much stronger grasp on the use of this new skill.

"Do you know what this is?" Dmitri asked.

"I am not sure," Ethan said. But he was lying, he knew exactly what it was.

"I would not want my former teacher to think of me as an unkind ruler," Dmitri smiled. "I have brought you medicine for your head wound. Isn't that kind of me? Let it be said all over the universe that The Czar Dmitri is kind and compassionate."

That is not medicine, Becki communicated to Ethan.

I know, Becki, Ethan transmitted back to her. *It is a poison.*

"May I apply some to your wound Ethan," Dmitri said, "I do not wish for you to be in pain any longer. You have complied with all my wishes."

"Yes, My Czar," Ethan said. "Please apply the medicine. And I thank you."

Dmitri smiled proudly. He felt all the pieces falling into place. *Not only will Ethan be dead soon, he thought, but he will die grateful that I made this righteous attempt to heal his wound. Ah, the human race is so weak and gullible.*

Ethan heard Becki's thoughts clearly inside his mind, she was yelling at him: *Do not let him put that poison on your wound. Make him stop or I will be forced to speak out loud.*

Ethan transmitted a message back to Becki: *Silence yourself, do not dare speak these thoughts aloud. I know well of this particular poison. I have used it on my own enemies myself. It is form of a beta-rheap-ex drug. It only becomes poisonous if you consume it orally. It will cause me little to no harm if he simply applies it to my head wound. Dmitri could not know this. He is not schooled well enough to understand how this poison actually works. There is no need to worry. I will be fine.*

"Our night together is coming to a close," Dmitri said. He walked behind Ethan, opened the vial, and spilled its contents onto Ethan's head wound. The syrupy liquid sent a shiver down Ethan's neck and spine.

"Thank you, My Lord," Ethan said. "You are a gracious and kind Czar."

"You are quite welcome Ethan. Your wound should heal within a few hours."

"And what do you wish for me to do now, My Lord?" Ethan asked

"I wish for you to retire to your chambers. Wash up, have a good meal and then we will meet in front of the citadel as planned."

"And I?" Becki asked. "What are your orders for me, my husband."

"My beloved wife, go and get some sleep. I will take care of the business of the day. And I will look forward to seeing you later tonight. By that time, all orders of business will be complete. Then it will be time for us to begin our new life together."

"So may we go now?" Ethan asked.

Dmitri smiled. "You may go."

Chapter 26

RICHARD STOOD OUTSIDE the rear entrance to Unit D at St. Paul's hospital. There was a huge sign next to the revolving doors that read: 'NO SMOKING WITHIN FIFTY FEET OF THIS FACILITY'

Richard read the sign, pulled out a Marlboro Red and lit it up. He took a long drag and then noticed an elderly woman in a wheelchair being helped out the door. When she wheeled out the door she peered directly at him. It made him feel guilty enough to take his smoke elsewhere.

He walked across the street to a small wooden bench next to the visitor's parking garage and sat down. Just as he began to stretch out his legs he noticed a woman in light-blue scrubs headed his way.

"Mind if I sit?" The woman asked.

"Yeah, sure," Richard said, scooting over a little to make some room for her. She was an attractive woman in her early forties, short brown hair with reddish highlights.

"Hi, my name is Joyce," The woman said. "Mind if I bum one?"

Richard reached for his cigarettes and opened the pack for her. She reached in and grabbed a smoke.

"Marlboro Reds huh," Joyce said, "I don't usually smoke anything this strong, but beggars can't be choosers. I appreciate it, thank you."

"So, what are you a nurse or something?" Richard asked.

"I'm a nurse," Joyce said, as Richard lit her cigarette and she took a deep drag.

"You work in D Unit?"

"I do...You know someone in there?"

"My sister."

Joyce took another drag, blew the smoke out from the corner of her mouth. She said nothing. This was followed by a long silence.

"Thanks for the compassion," Richard said, "You don't even wanna say 'hang in there buddy, she'll be fine'"

Joyce looked into Richard's eyes. There was another silence. "Thank you for the cigarette," Joyce said finally.

"You're a bitch!" Richard said, too tired and worn out to be overly angry, but still resourceful enough to at least call her a bitch.

"If you say so," Joyce answered, "So, I'm a bitch...Do you feel better *now?"*

Richard just stared at her. He couldn't get a handle on this woman. She was a nurse after all. Shouldn't she be showing a little more compassion.

"What's your name again," Joyce asked, "I don't think you told me."

"I don't think I want to."

"What's your freakin name?" she asked again.

"My name is Richard."

"Look here Ricky, let me..."

"My name is Richard!" He corrected her.

"Yeah, yeah, yeah, whatever," Joyce flicked her cigarette and took another puff. "Guess how long I've been here on this unit?"

"I dunno, ten years. Is that your excuse. You've toughened up now. You've seen it all. You have no kind words to give to anyone anymore."

Joyce smiled, "I've been on this unit for two weeks."

"Well, then that would make you a first class bitch then. You don't even have an excuse to be so freakin rude."

"You wanna hear me out or not."

Richard threw his cigarette down and crushed it with his sneaker. "Well, Joyce, I gotta tell ya, I don't."

"I'll talk. If you wanna leave, fine, just leave."

Richard turned toward Joyce. He had to admit to himself, she was rather amusing.

"It's like this," Joyce said, "I know what I'm supposed to say to you. I know how comforting we are all supposed to be. But in reality, there is no comfort for you. I am not telling you something you don't know. Your sister is gonna die. All the people on this unit are gonna die. I'm not playing into it."

"Play into what?" Richard asked. "Being nice is playing into compassion for other people and their misery?"

"I have compassion for what you're going through, but I don't understand it, not on the same level you do. I never will. I'm just not playing into the phoniness of it all."

"You think people are being phony when they are trying to sound comforting."

"I think most people are thinking about what they are gonna order the next time they go to Starbucks. That is what they are really thinking about when they are saying to you, 'Oh, I am so sorry for your loss and your pain and your grief and your blah, blah, blah, blah.' So yeah...that's what I think. And that's why I'd rather not say anything at all. I don't understand death, but I understand people. Most of us really only care

about one thing."

"Oh yeah, and what's that?"

"Our own survival."

Joyce got up and tossed the cigarette to the curb.

"Good luck, Richard," Joyce said as she walked back toward the hospital.

"Good luck," Richard said to himself. "There's no such thing as good luck Joyce...There ain't no such thing."

Chapter 27
The Morning

THE SECOND ETHAN collapsed to the ground, the skies opened and a torrential rain began to fall. Monstrous storm clouds appeared and stretched out across the entire skyline. A thick fog raced in accompanied by huge gusts of wind. Thick black clouds swiftly moved in front of the sun blocking all light.

Darkness covered Mount Crito.

The acidel, thousands of them, ran furiously around the front of the citadel. Soldiers in battle fatigues began to chase them down. They kicked some to the ground, ordered them to stand still. The few who didn't obey were sliced in half by imperial swords, their insides spilling out as they died instantly.

Dmitri stood over Ethan, his sword drawn and at the ready. Ethan was motionless and Dmitri smiled briefly before shouting, "Find out what all this commotion is about?"

Barok ran toward the entrance of the citadel but froze when he suddenly saw her.

The Queen Victoria emerged from the citadel. She held in her arms the bloodied velvet cape of the fallen Czar.

"The Czar is dead!" She cried.

Suddenly, a mighty rumble shook the planet's surface.

A Quake!

Acidel were thrown sideways, flipped off the surface and flung into trees. Imperial soldiers struggled to maintain their footing as the ground trembled.

Dmitri caught sight of the framework of the citadel. It was shaking violently. The bricks on the outer edges of the building began to shatter and break away. The entire structure of the building began to rock and shake as it shifted off its foundation.

"The citadel is falling!" Dmitri shouted.

Becki ran to the front entrance and joined her mother. They clutched each other and ran as fast as they could.

Gunther was screaming at the soldiers: "Hold your ground men, hold your ground!"

Becki and Victoria lost their grip on each other. Victoria fell to the ground as Becki, thrown off balance, regained her footing and ran for the nearest tree.

Becki screamed. Her fingernails dug tight into the bark of the tree she held. With quick and uneven shots of breath, she gasped for air to fill her ever tightening lungs.

The clouds of black fog filled the rain soaked skies, twirling, rolling furiously, like volcanic ash vomiting from the heavens. Then a lightning bolt pierced the back side of the tree. Becki was thrown backwards. She flew into the murky abyss, finally crashing down, slamming onto the rocky ground below. Oozing from her open mouth, blood dripped down her chin.

As she lay there, Becki noticed the ground had stopped shaking. It didn't matter. The damage to the citadel had been done.

With a thunderous roar the outer walls of the citadel crashed inward. The building fell into itself, a thick cloud of smoke and fire emerged. Huge sections of the citadel's structure tumbled from the wreckage and flew in every direction.

Panic gripped them all. Acidel and human alike tried to flee. They ran in confused circles as shouts and screams of panic sounded out. The flurry of wind increased throwing the acidel about like grains of sand.

Then Becki saw him.

Out of the corner of her eye she saw the boy courier running from the wreckage. His clothes were half torn, his face charred and badly bleeding, but he was alive and holding a knife.

He made it out alive, Becki thought. *Yes, the boy courier is alive!*

From her position on the ground, Becki pointed to her mother.

The boy saw Becki pointing, then directed his stare at Victoria. He ran at full speed toward the Queen. With dagger in hand, he leapt high in the air a few feet away from where she lay and came crashing down onto her chest while simultaneously plunging the knife deep into her stomach.

Becki smiled.

Dmitri was in shock, his concentration lost. Ethan stood up, still holding his knife.

"I told you," Ethan said to Dmitri, "You will not see the end of this!"

With no time to react, the last thing Dmitri saw was the sharp blade of Ethan's knife as he rammed it straight into the center of his forehead.

Dmitri crashed to ground, blood gushing from his head.

Dmitri was dead.

Gunther ran toward the boy courier screaming, "You crazed child!

What have you done? I will kill you with my own bare hands!"

The boy courier looked up at Gunther, The Queen lay dying beneath him. "It was the Queen that murdered The Czar!" The boy courier proclaimed.

"Of what do you speak?" Gunther shouted.

"He is right," Becki said. "I gave him the order myself Gunther…The order to avenge my father's death."

Becki started to cry. She knew how to play her part so well. She had always been able to cry on demand. But at this moment, while she cried on the outside, she was laughing manically inside.

"My very own mother killed my father," she said through an avalanche of faked tears. "And my brother was involved in the conspiracy as well."

What is she doing? Ethan thought.

I can hear you, Becki answered telepathically. *I have always been able to hear you.*

"My royal family is dead," Becki said to Gunther, crying profusely. "Why did I survive to bear this burden."

With tears in his eyes, Gunther said to Becki: "You are now the leader of this planet, you are now The Queen."

"I am in no condition to govern a planet," Becki cried, "I will be someday, but until that day comes I shall name a successor to my father. Bring the royal velvet cape to Ethan Educai. He is the Czar now."

A clap of thunder followed by a beastly roar drew everyone's attention to the forest. As trees crashed down before him, Konig emerged.

Barok grabbed Shroomy and ran behind a rock, "You were right," Barok said, "Konig lives!"

Through the clouds above, the light-speed freighter came into sight. It was three decks of immense triangles with a single imperial serpent painted onto the top. Kristof flew it to the front of where the citadel once stood and made a sweeping turn toward the fiery ground stopping the spacecraft in mid-air.

Konig could take no more. He was there to exact justice. With a smoldering ray of flames shooting out from his red eyes, he set the freighter ablaze.

Seconds later it exploded into a myriad pieces which span and burned, falling to the surface below.

"I am Konig. I am here to put the universal plan back on track."

Yes he is, Becki laughed in her mind. An imperial soldier tied the velvet cape onto Ethan. *So now you know,* she said into Ethan's brain, *Konig is a fool. I am the eye of the storm.*

"The Czar of Stritonoly must die!" Konig roared. "The universe demands it."

The rains became heavier as the planet shook once again, this time knocking Becki down hard. A fog rolled in obscuring her vision.

With the wind howling, dust shifting and debris flying, she could barely make out Ethan's form. Caught in this universal rage, Ethan, The Czar of Stritonoly was alive for now. Becki would only lie there and watch with pleasure.

The Czar felt the storm continue to yank his small frame back and forth. His body rocked violently from the fragments of rubble smashing into him. His velvet cape torn, flapping wildly in the relentless wind. The Imperial logo, an embroidered row of serpents, ripped away from his chest. His mind started to spit out thought,... *I'm losing it all...How did this happen? How did she fool me this way?*

I was the one who learned about the acidel sweat a long, long time ago, Becki said into Ethan's head. *Did you think I'd let them take the acidel away from me, Never! It was me who saw that Dmitri gained access to the sweat. I have planned this from the start. I let this play out so I could keep my precious acidel! The sweat is all that matters to me. You are an old fool, Ethan! All humans are fools! Now I can live in peace without interference from anyone. I will rule this planet with the acidel by my side. I have killed everyone in my way. Now I can finally be free.*

The fog became so thick that Becki could barely see anything.

If she didn't know Ethan so well, he would have been invisible to her now. Becki's eyes narrowed, squinting to see him more clearly. She knew instinctively how he walked, moved, breathed. He was still there, but only as a blurry apparition. Ethan tried in vain to move towards her, throwing his body in her direction. He wanted to strangle her for what she had done. Leaping for her with full force, the attempt only threw him away. The giant hands kept holding him back.

Hands! Are they human hands? Becki asked herself. *Or are they claws? I cannot tell! It doesn't matter, whatever they are, I know they belong to Konig and it is time for him to kill Ethan.*

Beep...Beep...Beep!!!

Becki spun her head around quickly, searching for the sound. This constant beeping sound.

Suddenly, every action and movement screeched to a violent halt.

All was silent now...except for the beeping...the steady beeping. Then, she sensed the real pain growing inside her.

Becki stopped breathing as she entered her darkness.

Chapter 28

RICHARD WALKED SLOWLY into Rebecca's room. He told his father he wanted a minute alone with her.

The room was plain enough, nothing on the white walls, just one hospital bed with a couple of machines Richard could not identify sitting next to his sister. He prepared himself for what he might see, but he still wasn't ready for it. The girl in the bed didn't look like Rebecca at all. This lifeless body with tubes hooked up to her was not his sister. His sister was already dead. Still, he felt the need to speak.

"Hey Becki," Richard said quietly, standing next to the bedside.

"Hello Richard," Becki thought. She could hear everything.

"I...um...I don't know what to say."

"It's ok," Becki thought, "You don't have to say anything."

"I feel like this is my fault somehow," He started to cry but then a tiny smile came to him as he remembered. "It was that night a few years back when mommy was still alive. I had that party."

"I remember," she thought.

"I was so wasted," Richard laughed a little, "and then I gave you that mushroom. You were so freakin funny that night Becki."

"The mushroom, yes, but that wasn't the first time I got high. I was already using."

"Hello Becki," Shroomy said. "I'm here with you."

"You were so trashed," Richard said, "You took out your violin and started playing that stupid classical junk."

"It was Bach," Becki thought, "Bach is considered baroque music actually, I loved playing baroque music."

Barok took out his violuna and started playing as Shroomy started to slowly sway to the music.

"That sounds lovely," Shroomy said.

"Thank you," Barok answered.

"Anyway," Richard continued, "I feel responsible because you started to go off the deep end after that. I didn't care about all the pot you smoked, but when you started hitting the heavy stuff I got worried. Then that freakin dealer got you hooked on acid."

"Yes," Rebecca thought, "My friends, the acidel, they are still alive thanks to me."

"I swear to God, Becki," Richard said, "If I ever see that dealer again I will probably kill him. I don't even know his name but I know his face. He had that stupid looking red hair."

"His name was Dmitri," Becki thought, "He is dead now Richard."

"Anyway...um..." Richard couldn't stop the flow of tears from coming. He put his head down and started to cry. "...I'm gonna miss you Becki...I really loved you kid."

"I know," Becki thought, "I love you too."

"Richard," Mr. Brown said from the doorway, "the priest is here."

Richard wiped the tears away, stood up straight. "Yeah...I'm done...come in."

The priest and Mr. Brown entered the room.

"Good morning Richard," the priest said, "I am so sorry."

Richard thought about what Joyce told him and wondered if he was really sorry at all.

"Mr. Brown," The elderly priest said, "Would you like me to administer the last rites now?"

"Yes," Mr. Brown said, "And please, call me Ethan."

"I'm sorry daddy," Becki thought, "I really let you down."

Ethan leaned in and kissed his daughter on the cheek. "I love you my baby girl. Sleep well. And tell your mother we said hello."

"I will," Becki thought, "I love you daddy...I'm sorry...I am so sorry..."

The heart monitor next to the bed was the only sound in the room as the priest began the last rites.

Beep...beep...beep...

EPILOGUE

The planet Stritonoly orbits some fourteen light years away from where Earth once stood in the late twenty-ninth century. It has been well documented that before Earth's destruction, the discovery of light speed travel was in fact discovered to be a possibility, although not by humans.

No human could ever endure the rigors of traveling at the speed of light. However, robots could. In the late twenty-third century, after many failed attempts, the speed of light was achieved. And although the first space-pod only made a brief radio signal from a distance measured at a little over one light-year from Earth, it was surmised by the large population of the scientific community that while no human would ever be able to reach the outermost edges of the galaxy, robots certainly could and would.

The events you have read about in Becki's 'dream' were in fact real. They did take place in another dimension of space-time and they occurred in what the therapeutic community began to call multiple-selves back in the late twentieth century.

The basic principle of multiple-selves is that all humans are composed of many, many, personalities. Nothing and no-one is a singularity. That is after all what makes humans so interesting and yes, so very complex as well.

What was further discovered about two hundred years after the discovery of multiple- selves is that these so called multiple-selves actually live on in many different physical forms throughout the universe. The multiple-selves are not only inside a human's psyche but also outside, living freely in the universe.

As was the case with Becki, one of her many selves became detached (or some may say self-aware) when she entered her coma and found herself on Stritonoly.

While this concept would seem most peculiar to the scientific community of the twenty-first century, it was indeed proved to be true. It was first hypothesized with the use of super computers attached to human subjects in virtual reality simulations around the year 2450. After many failed attempts, and many years of study, the scientific community began to understand the awareness of 'the self' within a human's brain and the ability these selves had to become removed and transported to different destinations all about the universe.

Unfortunately, before this theory could be accepted as a truism beyond any shadow of a doubt, the earth met its demise and thus the scientific experiments came to an end.

Nevertheless, Becki's story tells an interesting tale of a human who could transport a part of her consciousness to a destination her physical form on Earth could never reach.

Stritonoly still exists.

There was indeed a massive storm that tore down the citadel and caused tremendous damage to the planet. But as most civilizations do, the humans and acidel worked together to bring order back to Stritonoly. It was not easy. It took many years of hard labor. But eventually the Imperial Citadel was rebuilt and the purock trade began to flourish once again.

Konig did not kill Ethan Educai. Konig realized within moments after Becki lost consciousness that Ethan was not the Czar he wanted and freed him from his grasp.

Ethan proved to be a very wise Czar and served Stritonoly with honor for many years.

As for Becki: After a rather lengthy prison sentence and a substantial course of the finest therapeutic and rehabilitation treatment, she eventually returned to live under guard in the citadel.

The acidel went back to work as slave laborers. Ethan also instituted a stronger hold on the surveillance and disposal of acidel sweat.

While purock remained Stritonoly's strength, acidel sweat became Stritonoly's burden. Gunther was not pleased at first to see Ethan as the new Czar. But being the loyal soldier he was, Gunther followed the path set out by the new Czar. Eventually, he even grew to understand and respect Ethan's wisdom.

After returning to live under guard in the citadel, Becki learned a little of how to create her own purock art. Her early work was basic, but she had the finest artists on the planet to teach her. Her work, naturally improved and since it was produced by a royal princess, albeit one with a soiled reputation, the artwork was immediately considered of enormous value.

The telepathy Konig granted Ethan was lost after the storm. Konig had only given him this insight to help him through the ordeal. Ethan accepted the loss of this power gracefully. He understood it was not in the best interest of the people for any man to possess such a power.

Becki also lost most of her telepathic gifts. She was one of only a handful of humans born with the skill of telepathy. But constant abuse of acidel sweat coupled with the trauma of the storm and her subsequent rehabilitation left her with little use of these skills. She did not lose the skill entirely, but it was significantly diminished.

The story of Stritonoly is far from over.

Corruption festers in every corner as long as the acidel toxin remains. Ethan Educai and Becki will live for many years. The storm that tore down the citadel would not be the last to bring harm to this planet.

The accounts that are chronicled after the storm that rocked Stritonoly have been recorded in the annals of time. They are considered legendary tales filled with both treachery and heroism.

The people and the planet do not live on forever. But their stories do.

"Eternity! Thou pleasing, dreadful thought."
~Joseph Addison

BAROK'S EXODUS

PROLOGUE

IMPERIAL SCRIPTURES OF THE PLANET STRITONOLY:
Addendum #4; Vs. 21-23

Let it be known that once The Mesjasz has claimed the throne, his reign will not be long. The human race will soon thereafter be reduced to ash. Set to flame beneath a thousand roaring embers. All entities will be as the dust, wiped clean by his endowment.

THE INFINITESIMAL SPECK blasted through the galaxy at a speed that confounded even the soundest laws of physics. No man-made telescope would ever see it. Even its size defied understanding – comparable only to the most exotic of sub-atomic particles. No breathing life-form could ever have detected it. Still, for many, there was no denying it existed.

It was a thing of legend that could never be proven scientifically, but for the creatures of the universe that *knew* it did…they held their faith in the hope of a dramatic rescue. For those that did not believe, they would eventually meet death and ultimate oblivion. It would be as if they were never born.

This speck was an egg of destruction. Her journey began like a slingshot from the darkest corner of space. The origin of which will forever be unknown. She screamed through the cosmos, only visible to the reflection that created her.

She'd touch down one day, and though it would not be known for many thousands of years this microscopic piece of apparent nothingness would eventually mature and become the beginning of the end for all things everywhere.

Chapter 1

THE SOUND DREW them in.

They closed their eyes and let their minds drift back to an easier, more peaceful time. The rolling rapids of The River Frehenly could be heard ever so softly in the distance as Shroomy placed her small hand inside Barok's.

It had been quite some time since the acidel were this close to the mighty rapids. Presently they had their eyes shut, hands held, and spirits ablaze.

Barok was their tiny leader. His oversized bald head, beige rubbery skin and excessive weight were common features among the acidel slave laborers. Barok and Shroomy stood in a trance before the five-hundred diminutive acidel this cool summer's morning.

They didn't usually travel this far from the Citadel. The means of travel on the planet; the rocket-cruiser, was a method of transportation requiring much fuel.

Twenty large burgundy rocket-cruisers were currently hovering next to the dig area. The cruisers looked like missiles, each equipped with a propulsion system that reached speeds in excess of four-hundred klicks per minute and capable of carrying thirty to forty acidel with supplies. There were also over a dozen single-manned cruisers for the human soldiers supervising the dig.

Being so close to the rolling rapids of the river, the swishing of the water echoed an ambient charm as the acidel continued the ritual of Morning Prayer. Their prayer today was offered up to the acidel's spiritual provider. His name was never spoken aloud, especially with humans present, but his name was known to all. His name was Konig.

Two enormous forests stretched out along each side of the acidel. Golden-yellow trees stood tall in front of the northern sun, casting ominous shadows onto the slaves and their guards. Barok and Shroomy stood atop a medium-sized boulder presiding over prayer. The crowd of acidel looked like a cluster of mushrooms waiting to be plucked away.

The human imperial soldiers guarding the acidel towered over the tiny creatures with their swords at the ready. They were always alert. The Czar of Stritonoly demanded it. After the storm that ravaged the planet six years earlier, there was no tolerance for inattention when it came to acidel supervision. Yes, the acidel were essential to the economic success of the entire planet. But they also produced the means to destroy an entire civilization.

It was well documented that acidel sweat, brought about the chaos that once lifted Konig from hiding. The sweat, if gathered and left to harden was an addictive toxin to humans. It became the Czar's obsession after the storm to rid the planet of acidel sweat by any means necessary, but not the acidel themselves. He was a practical Czar, realizing the necessity of the acidel, but knowing the horror their hardened sweat could produce. He had witnessed it first hand and swore it would never happen again.

Barok held Shroomy's stubby hand tightly and lifted it up with his own. They opened their perfectly circular crystal-blue eyes and the crowd of acidel followed suit. There they stood, five-hundred diminutive chubby bodies clothed in white robes, black belts and brown sandals. There they stood, praying to a spirit they had seen only once for a brief time six years ago amidst the heavy fog of the now legendary storm. And yes, many denied that what they saw was real at all.

"To work!" An imperial soldier barked. "This has gone on long enough. Get to work!"

Barok let go of Shroomy's hand and peered at the soldier. "We are finished," Barok growled in the acidel's monotone deep and burly voice.

"Fetch your tools acidel laborers," Barok announced. "It is now time for work."

Picking up a miniature shovel, he handed it to Shroomy. On cue, the rest of the acidel picked up their purple-stained shovels and began their long day of labor.

Most days were the same. The acidel provided the workforce necessary to lift the most precious resource from the planet's surface. This resource was called purock and it covered most of the planet.

The acidel's job was simple enough. They were responsible for shoveling out the purple surface of Stritonoly so it could be turned into fine art which reaped enormous profit. Of course, this profit was abundant because the acidel received no financial payment for their work. They were provided food and lodging in the rear of the imperial Citadel, nothing more.

"Move it, Move it!" Another imperial soldier shouted as the acidel hurried to slide their shovels into the purock. Blue wheelbarrows formed two lines near the edge of the dig. The soldier's responsibility was to preside over the designated work area to be completed by day's end. It was all organized very scientifically by a special council back at the Citadel.

After the purock was cut away from the surface, it eventually grew back. It was important to move from location to location around the planet with a certain degree of strategic planning. Purock was best suited to be fashioned into artwork when it first grew onto the surface. It was still soft and the purple color was at its most luxurious.

Stretching out in a huge circle around the acidel, the soldiers stood in fighting stance. With wary eyes they focused only on the slaves they guarded. Their fists held tight around their shiny metal swords, green and black capes wafting in the summer breeze. Rows of embroidered black serpents were carefully sewn onto every shiny green and black pant leg. The clear symbolic reference of the frightening imperial serpent left little to the imagination. There was no doubt in any soldier's mind that if the acidel were to ever rise up and wage war, they would lose, and lose badly.

"This is fun," Shroomy said in her ridiculously low voice.

"Oh really," Barok smiled. "You are having a good time today?"

"Yes I am. It is nice to hear the rapids." Shroomy drove her shovel into the purock and lifted a good size chunk. She turned and trudged over to a wheelbarrow. "You're not having fun?" She asked.

Barok lifted an even larger chunk of purock into his shovel and followed Shroomy. "I am having fun if you are having fun," he said with an unconvincing grin.

They walked to the closest wheelbarrow and dumped off their purock. This was how the days went by for them. Lifting, walking, dumping…Lifting, walking, dumping. Again and again and again until it was done. They knew no other life, no other way. There was a time when this work was not so difficult. Acidel possessed the power to be trained in basic telepathic activities. They were even able, at the peak of their training, to perform menial feats of labor without any physicality whatsoever. That time was long ago. After the storm that tore the planet apart, the new Czar issued an edict ruling that all telepathic communications and training were to be halted at once. In his mind, and from his experience, the risk outweighed the reward.

All acidel that lived on Stritonoly were born here, like their parents before them. Their ancestors lived on the moon Acidonia and little is known of their history. Acidonia, one of two moons that orbits Stritonoly has been a barren wasteland for many generations.

Stritonoly invaded Acidonia hundreds of years ago and carted the tiny creatures back to their planet to serve as slaves. Public humiliation and torture would befall any acidel who dare question what the humans simply called 'the way of things.' Since tradition and obedience was part of the genetic makeup of the acidel, they felt intuitively that their service would be rewarded, if not in this life, then certainly in the next.

One acidel, a very small one named Guedy, struggled with his shovel as he tried to remove a piece of purock from the surface. He jammed the shovel into the ground but could not lift it. This was not the first time Guedy had experienced this problem and his frustration began to mount.

"You, over there," one of the soldiers shouted. "What is your problem?"

"My shovel is stuck," Guedy said. The acidel sweat pouring down his rubbery cheeks.

"I have seen you slacking before," The soldier mocked as he approached Guedy. "You are sweating the poison, and you are producing nothing to show for it. I have seen enough."

The imperial soldier violently threw Guedy to the ground. "Acidel should learn to work harder!" The soldier shouted so everyone could hear. "Watch what happens when you don't do as you are taught."

Barok and Shroomy stared at the ruckus and knew what it meant. There was nothing they could do but watch.

With no warning the soldier drove his boot into the side of Guedy's head. White blood spilled from the gash in his forehead.

"You see this, acidel" the soldier announced with pleasure. "You see what will happen to you? This will be you next if you fail to do your work properly."

"Just finish him," Barok said under his breath. Shroomy looked at Guedy, her eyes filling with moisture. *This is the way of things*, she thought.

The soldier lifted his boot high in the air and readied himself for a fatal strike.

"Stand down soldier!" A voice yelled.

Every acidel head turned toward the voice as it approached.

Dressed in formal military attire of solid green and black, the huge man of obvious authority and strength walked quickly toward the soldier. "Back to your station!" The man ordered.

"Yes Sir Gunther," The soldier replied, clearly shocked and

embarrassed.

Sir Gunther Sticks felt that punishment of this sort should never take place in public, it simply wasn't good politics. "Acidel…Get back to work!" Gunther commanded as the acidel immediately picked up their pace.

"You there," Gunther shouted to a young soldier who immediately came running up to meet him. "Bring this acidel back to the Citadel for medical treatment," Gunther whispered to the soldier, "And see to it that he is not harmed. I will deal with him when I return."

The soldier picked Guedy up with one arm and tossed him over his shoulder. White blood continued to flow out of Guedy's head wound and he appeared to have lost consciousness. But he was still alive as Barok watched them hop into a rocket-cruiser and speed off.

Sir Gunther was second in command on Stritonoly, he answered only to The Czar himself. His physical prowess was daunting to say the least. There was not a man on this planet who could match strength with Gunther. His massive chest and shoulders left little room for a neck. His concrete face was filled with jagged scars. His stubbly gray beard flourished below constantly squinting eyeballs. He wore a dark green helmet slightly tilted with one black serpent painted on each side.

"You see," Shroomy said quietly, "Our Morning prayers are very useful."

"Yes, of course," Barok said, but was clearly unsettled.

He was one of the few who could swear with absolute certainty that he saw Konig in the storm. It was six years ago but Barok could remember it clearly, and he still remembered seeing the giant walking before him.

But even though Barok had seen Konig with his own eyes and marveled at the inner peace that knowledge brought him, there were often times of doubt and confusion. He hated himself for questioning his place in the universal plan and spent many sleepless nights trying to resist feelings of bitterness toward his lot in life.

After seeing Konig during the storm, he was filled with a euphoria that surrounded everything he did. He was gracious and kind to all, always greeting everyone with a compliment and a smile. But time bleeds upon even the deepest faith. And now, six years later, there was emptiness in Barok's soul that could not be filled and maybe never would be.

"Do you believe our prayers are useful?" Shroomy asked.

Lost in his personal doubt, Barok hesitantly nodded in agreement. "Yes, I always have faith," he lied.

Shroomy gave Barok a half smile, her leathery light brown cheeks wrinkled upwards. "You are a bad liar."

Barok smiled, she was right, he was indeed a very bad liar.

"Is there no room for questioning?" Barok asked sincerely.

Shroomy drove her shovel into the purock, now she was angry. She had no response for him. *How can he question what he knows to be true? Shroomy thought. He saw Konig with his own eyes and he continues to question? I will never understand men. There was a true disdain for her mate in this conflict of beliefs.*

Barok's concerns about his faith and his future had been festering for some time. He did not want to spend his life waiting for an uncertain destiny any longer. He found himself torn in half and could no longer fight the impulsive drive he felt to just run away.

He didn't know what he was running from or where he would run to. But the part of him that sought freedom from this life of slavery would not be stopped for long.

Barok sought the freedom to breathe without the imperial soldiers watching his every move. He was sick and tired of being the leader of slaves. He was prepared to do what he must.

Tonight, under the cover of darkness, he would follow his compulsion.

When the new day dawned, Barok would be gone.

Chapter 2

WHERE AM I? The speck asked itself. *What am I?*

Clusters and knots of stars in their billions, nebulae, vast voids had all passed unnoticed. She flew past them as though they had no existence whatsoever. Her reality was far too complex to understand with any cohesiveness.

If you could see her, and you couldn't, she might appear to be an egg. To call the egg small would be insulting, she was invisible to most. The microscopic egg flew with purpose toward a predetermined date with the apocalypse.

Conscious and aware of all things, but at the same time confused by this very awareness, the thoughts had crossed her mind more than once. *Why am I the one who will bring an end to this all? Why is it ending anyway?*

Asteroid fields, planets and moons, entire populated solar systems passed without even a fleeting glance in her direction. She was unnoticed and unappreciated. After all, it is difficult for any mortal to appreciate something they cannot see. And that is where the paradox would begin to form.

They cannot see me yet, she thought. *But they ought to know I am here. Why do they doubt I am here? I AM HERE! And I am not an apparition of any sort. I am real. Just because you cannot see me with your physical eyes, you can still see me…if you choose to…I will let you see.*

Then again, maybe you should not look too close; for fear that you will not like what you see. Maybe it is best we remain apart. Then you can keep on with your silly dreams. I do not judge you, I have pity… but it is too late for discussion or analysis. That has all been done by the reflection that first threw me across the sky. Your position in the universe is to remain naïve; my duty is to wipe your ignorance clean. And I will do so with extreme prejudice. I will eradicate the cancer you have become…and you won't see me until it's too late.

Chapter 3

SHE GAZED BLANKLY out the window of her little room.

The dark of night began to sweep across the horizon as Becki peered out the triangular window near the back corner of the Citadel.

The guards were always there. Right now, even as she sat with legs crossed, methodically combing her long blonde hair, she was being monitored. She knew she'd be watched until her dying day. And they were right to watch her, and watch her closely.

Since moving back to the Citadel, the natural beauty which abandoned her had returned. Her almond green eyes were distinct and powerful with long defined black eyelashes. She also began to eat healthier meals and it showed. She was not a child anymore. Her body had taken on a more mature, voluptuous shape. And even though the soldiers noticed the change in Becki's physical appearance, they would not dare say it aloud.

Her trial for conspiracy to commit the murder of the royal family; her own royal family, was held in secret six years earlier. Still, the news spread quickly around Stritonoly that The Princess Becki was venomous and evil, never to be trusted. She was found guilty with cause, the cause being her addiction to the acidel sweat. She did serve time in a prison of sorts. It was really more of a home set up specifically to rehabilitate her. After five and half years of treatment, The Czar moved her back to the newly constructed Citadel. She lived under guard in a corner room on the twelfth and highest floor. The room bore no special attractions befitting nobility. It was plain brown with one small triangular window, one bed, a shower stall, and an easel.

The easel was for Becki to continue her purock art therapy. She had actually become quite good, not great, but good. And the artwork was being done by a princess after all, so most of it sold for much more than what it was truly worth. There was a lust among many to possess the art of the notorious Princess Becki.

She knew of the gossip about her actions and didn't pay it much heed. She accepted the past as unfixable, it was the future that concerned her more. This attitude made the residents of the Citadel extremely wary of Becki and what her ultimate motives might be. On the outside, she appeared to have no remorse, and that was disturbing.

But only some of what she displayed was the truth about her feelings.

On the inside, Becki nursed the scars of her own malicious behavior. She blamed her addiction to the acidel sweat for her predicament and would never forgive herself for letting the addiction grow out of control. She was not bothered by the talk of the townspeople, they would always talk about something, gossip was commonplace, and she had built a mental wall of defense to protect herself from these tall tales.

Her punishment would be a life of seclusion, locked in a back room, isolated like a deadly virus and guarded like a rabid animal ready to strike. And in the back of her mind, she kept her hatred for the acidel locked away. She blamed them for everything and hated them all.

The cute young guard assigned to her this evening stood in a corner by the closed door. She caught him staring at her more than once in the last hour.

"Can I help you?" Becki asked coyly.

The guard, taken aback, said: "Help you…What do you mean?"

"You obviously like what you see," Becki smiled.

"I…um…What is it you want?" The guard swallowed.

"Oh now, please calm down," Becki giggled, "I think we both know what it is you want."

The guard panicked, "My shift is up in a few minutes, another guard will be along to relieve me of my post shortly."

"You could always come back later," Becki smiled devilishly.

"Princess Becki," The young guard said, "I will not be coming back. Death would fall on my shoulders if even this conversation be known."

Becki withdrew her smile as she lifted up her nightgown to expose long shapely legs up to the thigh. "Pity," Becki smiled again. "Now get out of my room before I scream."

"I still have a few minutes left on my post," The guard said.

"Then you better hope the next guard is early," Becki stood and walked toward a small shower stall fully visible next to the bed. She dropped her nightgown to reveal her seductive naked body glistening with a light sweat.

"Princess Becki!" The guard stammered. "Please, do not put me in this position."

"Wait outside until your replacement arrives," Becki ordered. "Unless, you want to watch," Becki smiled as she leaned in and turned the shower water on.

The guard turned red, he wanted to watch. He said nothing.

Becki knew he would stay with a bit more encouragement. But she had no intention of letting him. "Well," Becki whispered.

"Well what?" The red-faced guard answered.

"Well…Get out of my room," Becki hardened her expression, anger consumed her voice. "Get out of my room or I shall accuse you of rape. Do not test me! And never stare at me that way again…Do you understand?"

The guard, embarrassed, nodded his head in understanding, "I will wait outside the doorway until my replacement arrives."

"Good," Becki said with disdain, "You do that!"

The guard hurriedly opened the door and closed it behind him. Becki stepped into the shower feeling as if she had just won a trophy.

As the water ran over her, she began to feel rejuvenated and alive. It gave her a grand sense of power to have the physical beauty necessary to trick, annoy, and fool even the best trained imperial soldier.

Becki knew that there were too many parts to her psyche for her, or anyone, to ever fully comprehend. She spent hours upon hours shifting back and forth through drastic and sometime even comical mood swings. The guards that watched her regularly never knew which Becki would show up at any given moment. She was a vivid kaleidoscope of mixed personalities. Volatile and angry one second, giggly and silly as a little girl the next. Inside her innermost thoughts and beliefs, it was a mystery even to Becki herself as to who she really was.

The five and half years of rehabilitation and therapy took a heavy toll. It took her a long time, almost a year, to figure out exactly which persona she would show the doctors and therapists that treated her. Once she locked into a personality they all seemed to genuinely like, that was it. She remained that character for the rest of her days under their care.

What they did rob from her was her gift of telepathy. Becki learned at a young age that in order for her telepathic powers to remain viable, she needed to tap into that part of brain every day and practice. In her rehabilitation stint, there was little or no time left unscheduled. She needed to play her part convincingly enough so the therapists in charge would eventually release her. Since returning to the Citadel, she now had more time to hone her skills. Even now, standing in the shower, she focused all her energies into the section of her mind that still held telepathy in secret. The past six months had produced some results and she could feel a bit of her skill returning. She had to be careful. But slowly, she was beginning the journey back to reacquiring what she had lost.

The one thing that grew and festered in rehabilitation was hatred toward the acidel. When her treatment began, all she could think about was the acidel and their sweat. She wanted so badly to be under the influence of it that nothing else mattered. That feeling lasted for a few months. Then she began to withdraw from the toxin. After much pain, sleepless nights and weeks of depression where she never left her bed, she finally managed to successfully conquer her addiction to the sweat.

Now Becki harbored a thirst for vengeance. With every passing second, she became ever more obsessed with seeking the acidel out and destroying them once and for all. She still craved the sweat at times, but she wanted them all dead even so. And she wanted it done by her own hands. She would not rest until they were made to suffer. She felt it was fair payback for what she lost. They deserved to feel the pain they caused her.

One day I will look down on the mutilated bodies of dead acidel, Becki thought. And I will laugh. Ah... That will be sweetest laugh of all.

Chapter 4

Barok clenched the wall outside the acidel chambers.

His rubbery face contorted, his senses heightened. He felt the racing and racing and racing of his heartbeat. This was not like him to behave with such impulsivity. But he had now taken the first step, always the hardest.

The acidel lived in the rear of the Citadel in what used to be a massive storage facility for exotic plants. It still had the appearance of a large greenhouse, but had not been maintained and was filthy. Only Barok and his mate Shroomy had their own room, a tiny one, but suitable for a little privacy. The rest of the acidel lived on top of each other in the open space of the abandoned greenhouse. Thick brown moss grew up the sides of the thin Plexiglas walls. Mud covered the floor. Acidel slept wherever they could find a spot. Most of them fell asleep in clumps on top of each other at the end of a day's work.

With his back pressed against the wall, Barok's wide-eyes darted about the forest. The reality of what he was doing started to sink in.

Standing outside now, there was no turning back.

He had waited until Shroomy was fast asleep and then left quietly out the back entrance. He knew there would be soldiers on night patrol; he also knew exactly where they were stationed and how he could get by them.

Not all of his telepathy left him when his training stopped. There were still a few tricks he held in secret.

As he crept along the wall, he approached the side of the Citadel. There were two soldiers pacing just before him. They startled him for a moment but Barok quickly regained focus.

Using his mental prowess, he summoned telepathic power to channel the natural forces around him. From the forest, fifty feet from the wall Barok clung to, he heard nature respond to his telepathy. Several creatures of the night began to howl, possibly horse-frogen, but he wasn't completely sure.

"What's that noise?" The younger of the two imperial soldiers whispered.

"A disturbance in the forest," The older soldier answered. "Just animals, leave it be," he snorted and spat, "Don't leave your post for such silliness."

Barok concentrated his energies on the creatures who responded to his telepathic suggestions. Suddenly, the noises became more intense, more frightening. It sounded as if a riot had broken out in the forest.

"We need to see what this is about," The younger soldier said.

Hesitantly, the older soldier nodded in agreement. They walked off toward the noises and disappeared behind a row of trees.

Barok sensed his opportunity for escape. As soon as the soldiers were out of view, he fled. Running as fast as his chubby little body could, he ran into the forest and turned away from the commotion toward a narrow trail leading away from the Citadel. He didn't know where the trail went, but he knew it would take him away from slavery, escape was his only objective.

He ran and ran and ran some more. He was out of breath and exhausted but journeyed on. He would run as long as the path was clear. He was short enough to avoid the vines and thickets crossing over the path above. He heard no sound behind him and had no idea just how far he had gone.

As he lumbered on, the thick forest began to rapidly decrease in density. Starlight began to filter through the openings where trees gradually became sparse.

Barok found a tree stump near an overhang of thick yellow shrubbery. He stopped and sat on the stump, panting, trying to catch his breath. *Can I rest here for a while?* Barok asked himself. *I have no choice; I can run no more without collapsing.*

Pulling the shrubbery around the stump as best he could, Barok placed his head behind the stump and curled up into fetal position.

I will rest here until daybreak, Barok thought. *Then I will journey on to find what I am looking for. Why do I leave Shroomy? What am I looking for? ...I wish I knew.*

Chapter 5

THE TEXTBOOKS OF the twenty first century on planet Earth documented the farthest objects the Hubble Telescope had observed were galaxies over 12 billion light years away. This observation was named the Hubble Ultra Deep Field. While there is no denying the mastery of this achievement, and further examination by far more acute instruments, the scientific community finally agreed a few years into the twenty-second century that this exploration was a pointless waste of time. There was nothing new to be learned by the observation of a planetary system they would never come remotely close to reaching physically or robotically. All the Earth could do was look from afar and wonder, everything else was pure speculation. There would never be enough reliable data to prove anything beyond the fact that they saw it.

The real experimentation that needed more practical application was the observance of the very, very small. So scientists turned their attentions to the field of quantum mechanics.

The determination was made in quick order that the galaxies they had spent so much time and money investigating afar were in fact already present on planet Earth. By the time the twenty-third century began it was confirmed that quantum particles could communicate with each other at an extremely high level of understanding. The intelligent galaxies being sought by humans since almost the beginning of time were right under their noses all along. The quantum world possessed the chemistry necessary for life and communication. These particles were living, viable organisms capable of intellectual interaction far beyond the walls of established quantum theory.

It had been stated that nothing is real unless it is observed. That was a dangerous conceptual flaw and thankfully it was discovered as such by the brilliant minds of the twenty-third century and beyond. Just because an object could not be observed, that offered no validity to the theory that it didn't or couldn't possibly exist.

This theory took on new life when the quark (the smallest hypothetical particle until the absolute confirmation of its existence in the Earth year 2297) was first observed. Shortly after the particle was confirmed to exist, it broke apart in an atomic cylinder experiment which blasted the quark into a cloud of even smaller sub-particles. And while they were only visible for a minute fraction of a second, they were observable. The door was now open to further exploration.

Further experiments proved successful into the operating communications that existed between all particles in the quantum world. A living, intellectualized universe proved to exist in the world of the very, very small.

The questions had to be asked. What is the human race missing? What exists that is not being seen?

They would find out soon enough.

The feminine egg was growing. And it hurtled toward a destination with humanity that had been planned since the beginning of time.

The old astronomers found great satisfaction that people around the world had rewritten textbooks with their newest discoveries.

Those textbooks would soon need a revision…A drastic one.

Chapter 6

The northern sun would soon rise.

Barok could not sleep any longer. He knew the sun was about to bring light upon the mountaintop at any moment. He had maybe an hour to get as far away as he was able, then they would be coming for him.

It would not be long before the soldiers would notice his absence. Shroomy undoubtedly already knew he was gone. Time was precious, and he had little to play with.

It was still the dark of night as Barok jumped to his feet and resumed his journey. He trotted along, noticing the forest as it began to dissipate behind him. He was moving downward, leaving the mountainside. As the trail came to an end, a large valley of tall yellowy grass opened up before him. The northern sun began to peek out as the horizon slowly turned to a sumptuous violet.

Barok ventured onto the open field as the morning moved in. He heard the sounds of the forest animals behind him awakening. A few short cackles and howls echoed in the distance. The new day was dawning. Barok's first day of life away from captivity.

He was always a slave laborer, like his parents before him. Never did it occur to him to look for another way.

Not until the storm woke him up.

When he saw Konig, he felt a rush of exhilaration. He knew at the moment his eyes saw the giant there had to be something else, something greater. The seed had been planted in his mind. It would take six years for that seed to grow. And now he was ready for exploration. Finally free from slavery, if only for a brief time, he was certain he would find something, anything, to confirm the belief that tore at him daily. It was a belief that there was more to his existence. The belief that he had a choice, a date with destiny he could play a part in.

Multi-colored butterflies of varying sizes swooped down and around Barok's bald head. A few of them were as big as his entire torso, if not bigger. He smiled as they welcomed him to their field. Sensing he meant them no harm, they embraced his presence and flew alongside him as he walked through the soft yellow grass that came up to his waistline.

Barok was suddenly in no rush. He should have been, but the purity of what surrounded him filled his senses. He breathed in the freshness of the new day. The sunlight emerging over the horizon cast a gentle golden glow upon the field. Barok smiled. He was free, truly free.

Then, he looked ahead and saw what awaited him. Just beyond the end of the valley, another forest loomed large. The trees were tall and thin with many twig-like branches and darkly-colored leaves.

As Barok approached the long line of trees, the butterflies immediately retreated back to the security of the open field. He peered deep into the woodland and noticed scores of fallen trees. Hundreds of enormous branches had fallen sideways and crisscrossed one over another forming a scattered maze of disarray.

This could be a good place to hide, Barok thought. *Imperial soldiers will not be able to navigate their way through this clutter without great difficulty. There will be many places for someone my size to seek shelter.*

Leaving the valley, Barok stepped onto the muddy surface and entered the ominous forest. The tangled broken trees were not far away, maybe fifty yards past the first line of trees separating the valley from the woods.

He maneuvered through the vines and tree limbs which spanned out in great distances all about his tiny frame. The branches fell, this way and that, thrown by nature into unorganized clumps.

As he traveled further into the forest, the sunlight faded and a hazy fog swelled from the surface. It smelled of burnt timber, perhaps from a recent fire in the woods. He slipped under one of the gigantic fallen tree limbs. Brown and black shrubbery and thick vines covered the hole between where the tree had fallen and a small open space below.

This may be my home for a while, Barok thought.

There was already plenty of cover with all the dense burnt wood and broken branches scattered about. Barok could easily fashion this place into a hideaway until he knew where to go next. It seemed improbable that soldiers would venture into an unknown forest searching for someone as insignificant as an acidel leader that could so easily be replaced.

He plopped his chubby body down onto the muddy ground. His white robe had long since lost its cleanliness. The robe was more brown and black now with smudges all over it. Appearance was not of any concern to an acidel on the run.

I will make this my hideaway, Barok thought. *This will be home for now. I can do this.*

Barok tried hard to convince himself. Doubt about his true motives ricocheted about his consciousness. He suppressed his feelings of doubt as best he could. The journey toward a new awakening had begun; time to embrace a new way of thinking, a new way of being. This is what excited him most, an opportunity for newness to emerge out of the day to day boredom he had accepted as commonplace for far too long.

Barok concealed his hideaway with every form of debris he could lift. Within twenty minutes, he had created a suitable sanctuary. He even made a bed out of soft large green leaves he plucked.

Pulling a few final twigs and branches around his new home, Barok felt satisfied he was properly concealed. He sat back on his self-made bed of leaves and let out a long sigh.

So this is freedom, Barok thought....*hmmm...Now what?*

Chapter 7

ELIZA KNOCKED AND waited for a response.

As usual, there was none. She looked annoyingly at the hefty guard sitting next to Becki's room who appeared half asleep.

"Why must she do this every morning?" Eliza asked in her authoritative high-pitched voice.

The guard did not respond. He shrugged his shoulders, he really didn't care. Eliza made a point to start Becki's day off every day at the break of day or earlier. Many mornings, the sun was not even beginning to rise and there was Eliza knocking on Becki's door.

She had been appointed by The Czar himself to be Becki's personal art instructor, a duty she took very seriously. Eliza was an elderly woman with a quick wit and a sharp tongue. She wore her short gray hair in a tight bun at all times. She was always fully covered in black with a smock tied around her neck and several pencils tucked into her upper shirt pocket. Not an attractive woman, her most noticeable feature was her thick black glasses which made her eyeballs appear to be ten times their actual size.

She knocked again, this time much louder and longer. "Princess Becki, I am coming in…" She waited for some response, there was only silence. "Well, I hope you are decent because I am coming in for your morning lesson."

She waited through another few seconds of silence and then opened the door.

"Good morning," Becki said, lying naked on the bed. "I'm gonna sleep some more, you can cuddle with me if you like."

"Princess Becki," Eliza demanded, "You are to get changed at once. It is time for instruction. I have servants bearing the finest purock from the dig yesterday. We must get to work while the material is still pliable."

Becki laughed, "Toss me that nightgown Eliza…Please!"

Eliza reached for a lavender nightgown sitting in a pile of scattered clothes and tossed it onto Becki's naked body. Becki rolled over and slowly started to put it on.

"Will this ever end?" Becki whined.

"This is part of your rehabilitation," Eliza reminded her. "And you could be better at it, if you applied yourself just a little. You create amazing artwork with almost no training or effort. Think of what you could create if you cared…even just a little."

"I'm insulted," Becki pouted, "You think I don't care. I care plenty. But please, Eliza…Does any of this matter?"

"What do you mean by that?" Eliza asked, somewhat perplexed by the question.

"Hmmmm, let's see, a hundred years from now. Will you be here? Will I?"

"Well…no, most likely not."

"Most definitely not!" Becki laughed sarcastically. "And therein is the point I am trying to make. None of this matters."

"I am not going to get sidetracked into another philosophically pointless discussion with you. Please get your supplies so we can begin."

Becki labored off the bed and went to a small closet where she kept her art supplies. She came back with a box, plopped it on the bed and stubbornly opened it. Inside the box were all the tools needed to create simple purock art. Needles, carving tools, smooth yarn, several drawing pads, colored pencils and oil pastels were among just the basic tools necessary for the development of purock into some form of basic artistic expression.

Eliza summoned the guard to have the acidel workers bring in the purock selected for their morning lesson. The four acidel quickly scampered in and placed the purock on the bed according to Eliza's instructions, then quickly turned and left the room, closing the door behind them.

"I love them," Becki joked. "Don't you just wanna grab their squishy little chubby cheeks and squeeze and squeeze and squeeze?"

"Becki," Eliza scolded, "There will be no talk of the acidel in my presence. Do it again and I shall report you to The Czar."

"Wooo-weeee," Becki chuckled, "You wouldn't do such a thing. Come on, Eliza, I am too much fun. What would your life be like without me? You'd be a crotchety old Grandma and bored to death."

Eliza knew there was some truth to Becki's words. Her attempt to rehabilitate The Princess made her feel alive and worthwhile. It was a challenge, but a challenge she faced with many reservations. It was unclear to her if Becki would ever be able to function without guards monitoring her every move. There was too much risk in letting her out of their sight, even for a moment. Though she did not resemble the demented girl she first met after the trial, she was still suspect to peculiar behavior and extreme mood swings.

"What is it you'd like to work on today?" Eliza asked calmly.

"Hmmmm," Becki thought, "I think I'd like to work on that cute guard that was watching me last night. He was eyeing me up all night."

"Can we be serious?" Eliza demanded.

"I am being serious, geez, can't we have a little conversation while we work."

"Appropriate conversation, yes. I do not wish to hear of your foolish lusts."

Becki laughed, "I like the way you said that. Foolish lusts? Is there any other kind?"

"Can we get to work now?" Eliza asked, exasperation in her tone.

"Fine, let's get this over with." Becki picked up a small piece of purock and stared at it. "I suppose I could do something with this one."

"I know you can," Eliza said reassuringly.

Becki reached into her box of supplies and pulled out a small silver carving knife. *Work, work, work,* Becki thought. *Well, I did kill off my entire family, not with my own hands, but I was responsible…Oh well, I suppose it could be worse.*

The maniacal laughter inside Becki's head filled her every sense as she began to drive her carving knife deep into the purock. Anger and art; for Becki that was the best medicine of all.

Chapter 8

THE IMPERIAL SOLDIERS were instructed to be ready for reveille before first light.

They stood in straight lines in the basement headquarters of Battle Command right beneath the Citadel. They waited patiently for Sir Gunther, passing the seconds gazing about the room at the stunning purock art hanging on the walls of this perfectly squared room. The artwork had recently been updated. It portrayed sculpted images of every Czar that ever ruled Stritonoly. There were also renderings of warfare, imperial soldiers standing over their victims, conquering heroes amidst the chaos of war.

There were no windows in the basement headquarters so it was impossible to tell when first sunlight would hit the planet. Rest assured though, when the sun rose, Gunther would appear.

A steel door suddenly flung open smashing into the concrete wall behind it. Sir Gunther marched into the room and took his place behind the podium on the black dais. A tapered red curtain hung behind the dais with rows of black serpents knitted onto the fabric.

"Good morning soldiers," Sir Gunther announced.

Unic Heldar was also on the dais. He was the oldest and wisest nobleman on the planet. He stood slightly hunched over in a pure white robe with a hood covering his entire head and most of his face. Upon seeing Gunther approach the podium, Unic stepped forward and handed him a scrolled up document.

Gunther opened the document on the podium, looked it over a moment and decided everything was in order.

"We gather at the break of day to welcome a new member into our brotherhood," Gunther said. "The boy courier, Josef, is now to be sworn in at long last. After this formality, Josef will be awarded full rank as soldier in the imperial army." Gunther paused a moment, there was something else that needed to be addressed. "You all know about Josef and the deed he committed. He was the one who killed the Queen Victoria. It has been proven in trial and confirmed in council with the elder nobleman that Josef acted from an order given to him by Princess Becki. It is because of this order we will never call Becki our queen…she will never be our queen, remember, it is forbidden to address her as such…Josef followed an order, and that is what soldiers do. After much reflection it has been decided that Josef has paid his due and is now worthy of joining our ranks. We will not fault him for following the explicit though demented orders given him by a member of the royal family. This is a valuable lesson for us all. We are servants of the royal family, we do not question orders…ever. Therefore, I will award the title of Imperial Soldier to Josef, son of Jacob and Anna, native of the planet Stritonoly."

Josef marched from the line of soldiers; He was wearing a royal brown military uniform and black beret with a single dark green serpent stitched onto the side. Josef looked very much like the other soldiers, just not as battle tested and weary. Wide eyed and clean shaven with a crew cut, he wore a permanent half-smile on his baby face, an innocence that would never last.

Gunther reached under the podium and produced a medal attached to a thick silver chain. Josef's skinny body stood at attention next to his commander and mentor, Sir Gunther.

"Congratulations boy," Gunther said proudly. "You are now one of us." As graciously as he was able with his thick muscular hands, Gunther placed the chain around Josef's neck.

The moment the medal was placed around Josef's neck, the soldiers stood at attention, swords at their side with the tip of the blade pressed into the floor.

"Will you give your life for this empire, this planet, the royal family and your brethren among you on this day?" Gunther asked.

"Sir Gunther, I will!" Josef shouted. "They will remain my brothers until the end of time."

"This soldier is now your brother," Gunther declared, "Treat him as such."

Gunther took a long look at each of the soldiers under his command. He knew there was doubt among them, but they would obey, that is what they were trained to do.

Gunther nodded his approval toward Josef as he marched back to his position in line.

Shifting position behind the large podium, dwarfed by his bulky frame, Gunther addressed his men.

"We now have a stronghold on the acidel like we have never had before," Gunther said with delight. "The Czar's plan is coming to fruition. The workload has doubled in the last six months and many of our elders feel the acidel can be pushed even harder. We have devised plans to increase the workload significantly over the next few months. Acidel can get lazy if they are not kept occupied. For the dig today, we have one of the largest sections of purock mapped out that we have ever lifted in a single day. It will be up to us to push every ounce of energy from the acidel until the area is completely barren of purock. We will not leave the site until the required workload has been completed."

Gunther took a deep breath, suppressed a yawn and turned toward Josef. "Let us break you in the right way soldier. Go and supervise Barok, have him prepare the acidel for labor."

"Yes, Sir Gunther," Josef answered robotically and marched off toward the door.

Gunther watched Josef leave and then continued, "I will meet with the council to lay out our strategic plans for this day. The rest of you report for breakfast and I will meet you in front of the Citadel shortly."

The soldiers stood in silence, waiting to be relieved.

Gunther chuckled, he enjoyed making them wait. "Get going soldiers, you're dismissed."

Chapter 9

Josef marched toward the rear of the Citadel.

He immediately heard the hordes of acidel through the dirty mud-stained Plexiglas as they were waking and getting changed. Hundreds of thick baritone voices sounded like a nonstop rumbling of thunder.

Dirty little creatures they are, Josef thought. *But this is the perfect way to begin my career as an imperial soldier. I have the opportunity to exercise my new power over the one they call leader.*

Approaching the rear entrance to the acidel chambers, he adjusted his beret and drew his sword. His youthful lust for recognition finally had a chance to perform. The two young guards standing at each side of the entrance stood at attention when they saw Josef. *That is right,* Josef thought. *I am an imperial soldier, they will respect me now.* He moved past them trying unsuccessfully to suppress a grin.

Swinging the shabby screened door open, Josef stepped into the chambers. The moldy stink of the place assaulted his nostrils, an odor he was not at all prepared for. The acidel noticed him but continued getting ready for the day. They huddled together in clumps here and there, getting their robes on, helping the young acidel put their sandals on properly. Several acidel had already started to load a storage cart with shovels and supplies.

Josef took another step into the room, shouted: "Someone show me to your leader, the one you call Barok."

An acidel female that stood no higher than Josef's kneecap came scurrying over, "I have not seen Barok yet this morning, my lord," she said in the monotone deep growl of the acidel. "Shall I take you to his room?"

"Yes," Josef ordered, "Take me to him now."

She scampered ahead of Josef as they walked through the dirty mud floor. Acidel cleared a path for them as they made their way to the side of the chamber where a small door led to the only private room, the room of Barok and Shroomy.

Josef did not wait for his acidel escort to knock. With a heavy hand, Josef pounded on the door. "Barok, come out at once. I have been assigned by Sir Gunther to supervise preparations."

There was silence.

Well, well, well, Josef thought. *Is this a defiant leader I must deal with? I have no problem putting my boot to his little behind.*

Josef reached for the doorknob and let himself in. Opening the door he noticed the simple purock art hanging on the walls. There was a tiny bed that Shroomy sat next to with her legs crossed on the floor.

"Good morning," Shroomy said politely, wetness in her eyes.

"Where is Barok?" Josef asked. "I am here for Barok."

"I know who you are here for…but Barok is not here."

"What do you mean he is not here? Where else would he be?"

Shroomy choked back tears, "Barok is gone away sir. He is not here."

Stunned but exhilarated, Josef's thoughts raced. *Has the little weasel attempted an escape? This could be the opening I have been looking for. I can be the hero and find him. I still have a little time before I need to report back to Sir Gunther. I shall seek out my lover for advice. Certainly she will know what to do. Becki always knows what to do.*

"Do not move from this spot," Josef ordered Shroomy, "And tell no one what you have said to me…I will return shortly."

Chapter 10

Spiderons!

Barok lay still. The back of his head pressed into the giant leaf he used as a pillow. Presently, fright made it impossible for him to move.

Over a dozen spiderons had noticed Barok's presence and were inspecting his temporary hideaway. Barok looked up and saw the gigantic hairy creatures as they crawled threateningly about the branches above him. They were black with twenty to thirty thick prickly tentacles and bloodshot slits for eyes. Each one was three to four feet in circumference with blubbery bellies and flapping red tongues. As wet tongues licked their thin gray lips, thick brown saliva fell out and splashed upon the muddy ground below.

Barok remembered the stories he was told as a child. *If ever you should encounter a spideron tribe,* his father told him, *you run! You run and run and run. Do not glance back for even a moment, lest you fall victim to their powers.*

This was of little help now; his fear gripped every muscle in his tiny body. He only managed to feel a shiver up his spine as he recounted the many legends he heard over the years about these hideous creatures.

It was rumored that spiderons could debilitate even the strongest and wisest warrior with their psychic powers. The legends told of the severe mental anguish brought on by the grasp a spideron could hold on a human's brain. Many men had chosen suicide rather than be subject to the torment these creatures could place upon one's sanity.

Frozen, Barok knew any movement could trigger an attack he would not be able to thwart. *This is the end for me,* he thought. *I know I do not have the prowess to withstand a mental onslaught from a spideron. And I certainly do not possess the fighting skills necessary to ward off a physical attack. I fear this will be a painful death.*

Then, an even larger spideron crawled up from over the top of an uprooted tree. A labyrinth of intertwining branches and black leaves above this enormous spiderons frame allowed only a small amount of sunlight to break through casting a shadow unto Barok's leafy bed. This spideron was different; he was nearly twice the size of the others with a red stripe stretching from his forehead all the way down his hairy backside.

"SSSSSSSSSSSWho are you?" The spideron hissed.

"You have the power of speech?" Barok questioned as he trembled.

The spideron ignored his question, lapped his slippery blood red tongue and repeated: "SSSSSSSSSWho are you?"

"I am an acidel, a fugitive seeking shelter. I have escaped the bonds of slavery…if only for a short while."

"You will bring undue attention to our woodlands," The spideron cautioned. "Your presence here is not wise…SSSSSSSS…and not welcome."

"I am small as you can clearly see. I will not be in your way. I only wish to hide here until I know where I shall go."

The spideron jumped down and landed next to Barok's head. His tentacles made a heavy crunching sound as they pressed into the leaves.

This is the end, Barok thought. *And I never said goodbye to Shroomy. I am a foolish and selfish acidel, I deserve this fate. My existence will end here in the forest in a most excruciating manner.*

Sniffing about Barok's head, the spideron whispered, "You do not smell of danger, but we have nothing to offer you here. And what do you mean you have no place to go? You are here aren't you? You *are* someplace…You seem to speak nonsense."

Barok sat up slowly as the other spiderons began to move in all about him. "I am a creature of this planet just as you," Barok quivered as he spoke. "I was born into slavery and I am only trying to find refuge. You are right, what I speak may be nonsense. I do not know where I am going or what I am looking for."

"So what makes you a fugitive?" The red-striped spideron hissed again. "Are you a criminal?"

Barok swallowed, he wasn't sure what to say. "I…um…I have fled the Citadel, abandoned my duty…They will be coming after me."

"Who are *they?*" The spideron asked.

"The imperial soldiers, The Czar and his loyalists, they will want to find me."

All the creatures hissed as one, a chilling condemnation.

"We have no love for the slime of the Citadel," the spideron declared. "But what makes you so special? Why do you presume they will even care to look for you?"

"They will want to make an example of me. They will wish to humiliate me, torture me, and maybe even kill me."

The spideron came up close to Barok's face, said: "SSSSSYou are clearly afraid, and fear will bring attention to anyone."

"I understand, but I mean no harm. I only wish to be free." Barok looked around at them as they moved in closer and closer. *If they were to kill me,* he thought, *they would have by now. I must try to survive on my wits alone. I cannot fight them, whether by hand or mind, I am trapped but I am still alive.*

"Tell me what to do?" Barok asked. "I have heard many stories of the mighty spideron. I once had some small powers of extra-sensory perception myself. I can help you in any matter you see fit to use me."

"You have the gift," The spideron said. "That is what drew us to you in the first place. But your gift has been silenced."

"All acidel mental training came to a stop after the storm."

The spideron licked his lips, said "SSSSSYou still have the power. You need to find it again. It boils beneath your flesh. It is what brings us together."

I am going to live at least another day, Barok thought.

"Yes you will," The spideron said aloud. "You will live…at least another day."

"It is true then," Barok declared. "The legends of your abilities are true. I want to stay with you. Please sir, tell what I need to do?"

"Can you conquer your fear? You will have to if you wish to stay… and if I let you stay, it will only be for a short time. We do not have a home for an outcast acidel here. But we are not evil as many legends suggest we might be…However, if you wish to stay…You must conquer your fear…Can you do this?"

"Yes," Barok said quickly. "I will conquer my fear. I have been the leader of the acidel for many years; I have attained much prominence among those that look up to me. Surely, I can conquer this fear you speak of."

"Being a leader of slaves means nothing to me," the spideron said. "And your words bring out your true sense of self, your sense of pride and ego. You have been a slave too long; you have taken on the characteristics of man. That too must be lost if you intend to live past tomorrow. Whatever you were…you are not anymore…Do you understand what I am saying?"

Barok waited to answer, he measured his words: "You wish for me to start a new life."

"SSSSSSSSSomething like that," The spideron smiled. "My name is Ramsitt…and yes, you can stay…for a little while anyway. If you are an enemy of the Citadel, then you are a friend to us."

"My name is Barok. Thank you for your welcome. I will do what is necessary to earn your trust."

"I know you will…" Ramsitt whispered. "SSSSSYou have no choice."

Chapter 11

Gunther marched through the main parlor of the newly rebuilt Citadel.

After the collapse of the previous Citadel during the storm six years ago, it was decided by The Czar that the Citadel needed to be rebuilt immediately. The construction of the new Citadel began quickly just three days after the storm. It took many months of planning and labor but it was rebuilt in under a year.

The new Citadel looked very much like the old one on the outside. It stretched up twelve stories and spread several acres wide. Octagonal orange bricks made up the primary design and structure. Twenty to thirty triangular windows were evenly spaced out along each floor.

The inside looked completely different. The decadence reached a level of near absurdity. Every extravagance the planet had to offer, and more, was displayed for all to see. Purock art, the finest ever produced by human hands, hung on every wall. The yellow pipetu plant stretched up each wall in narrow leafy stalks. The plants were perfectly manicured and thriving. Enormous diamonds and golden jewels had been placed strategically into the walls between the purock artwork. The floor of the main parlor was a shiny white marble, spotless and immaculately clean.

Gunther made a quick turn and headed down a stretch of plush purple carpet which lined the first floor hallway. He was on his way to see his Czar, the one and only ruler of Stritonoly.

Ethan Educai was a wise old man who seemed to look a bit younger every day since being appointed to this charge. Many things changed for him after the storm, the most profound being his rise to the head of power. Ethan's journey to this position was not sought, and that made him a better Czar than any of his predecessors.

He stood sipping tea in his room just off the first floor hall. He was alone as he peered out a small triangular window overlooking the forest of Mount Crito. His velvet cape tied around his neck under his long white beard fell gracefully from his small but healthy frame. His golden crown adorned with jewels sat atop a stack of paperwork on a shiny brown desk next to the window.

Ethan's face was once weary and tired. But he had been invigorated with new purpose since becoming The Czar. His deep-set blue eyes seemed to hold the wisdom most lacked. He was a man not born of a royal family, full of questions and complexities; a quality admired by many. He had achieved this position amidst a twist of fate, not by desire or politicking. It was the appearance he gave off as a mere mortal that made him so loved by so many. His ability to garner a rational perspective within the eye of any storm made him a force to be reckoned with.

A sudden knock on the door turned Ethan's attention away from the window.

"Come in," Ethan said.

The door opened and Sir Gunther lumbered into the room. "Good morning, My Lord."

"Good morning. I presume everything is in place for the dig today?"

"Yes it is," Gunther said, crossing to the desk and picking up the royal crown. "I sent our newest soldier to supervise. I'm sure they will be ready shortly."

"Breaking the boy in," Ethan said with a smile. "I like that. Well done, Gunther. He should make for a fine imperial soldier. Don't you agree?"

"Yes, I've grown to believe that may be true," Gunther said, placing the crown on Ethan's head. "I think he's been through enough. He's paid his dues; I suppose he is as ready as he'll ever be."

"That is not a glowing recommendation."

"He is still a murderer, My Lord," Gunther said flatly.

Ethan met eyes with his friend, asked: "Aren't all soldiers?"

Gunther's nostril's flared, "I would say no. Josef murdered, what we do out of service is not murder. There is a difference."

"He murdered under the direct orders of a royal family member. And if you look at it from that angle, then it was a service of the highest form."

Gunther nodded in semi-agreement, said: "I have instated him as you requested, and yes, I have come to like the boy. But the fact remains; there is no erasing what he did. I can understand why he did it…But I will never forgive him."

Ethan's mind flashed back to the storm. He remembered seeing Josef stab The Queen. He remembered it all so clearly. And most of all, he remembered what it felt like being so close to his own death. It was not a dream or an apparition as many forced themselves to believe, it was real, Konig was real. He would never forget being held in the clutches of the monster the acidel called Konig. His entire perspective changed the moment he was released from the giant's grasp. Ethan

Educai became the ruler of Stritonoly that very day, and the planet would never be the same again.

It was Ethan who established the high council for acidel supervision. He did not appoint any administrator to this council, electing instead to preside over this particular branch of government himself. The first and most pressing concern for Ethan was the proper containment and destruction of all acidel sweat.

The previous Czars had put forth many strategies to deal with this problem; they all failed in the end. Ethan witnessed the destruction that could ensue from acidel sweat addiction. He was determined it would never happen again, especially under his watch.

The new council drew up detailed plans. The urgency and need for better supervision of acidel work sites was addressed. It became the highest priority that acidel sweat must be cleaned continuously during the work day and again immediately at the end of the day, no exceptions under any circumstances. Acidel that sweat the poison when they were not in a work area were considered a threat to the planet and were executed. Likewise, any soldier or members of the sanitation force assigned to clean up a site were held under strict rule. If any of them failed to perform their duties under the specific regulations set forth by the council, punishment would be swift to follow and could even result in death.

Ethan took no chances at first. No duty was left to a single man. Everyone had multiple superiors to answer to. It was an elaborate web of orders and protocol that were followed to the letter. And above them all, Ethan held the reigns tightly.

But that was right after the storm. Fear was in the air and humans were eager to act. This lasted for a while, almost two years without incident. But time eroded the resolve of even the most loyal. Now, things had changed and even Ethan knew that danger loomed large.

It was the natural way of things, the instinct of the human spirit to allow laziness to sink in. Even Ethan, who was so obsessed by this cause, was losing focus.

When the construction of the new Citadel started, all eyes looked forward to the luxuries they would soon bask in. Once the building of the Citadel was complete, it was only a matter of time before attention began to stray. Stritonoly began to prosper like never before. And the wealth made them careless. Ethan saw this and was concerned.

"Have we lost our edge?" Ethan asked Gunther.

Gunther chuckled, said: "Don't we all lose our edge eventually? Isn't that what age does to even the best of us? It is inevitable."

"I fear we have become jaded. We have seen no destructive force since the storm. No sign of acidel addiction whatsoever, I believe we may be getting far too comfortable for our own good."

"You may be right. I doubt that six years ago I would have allowed Josef anywhere near the acidel without sending an army of soldiers along with him."

Ethan became very serious; he looked Gunther straight in the eyes. "You see what I am saying? It is time for us to reassess. We have grown rich and slothful."

Gunther returned Ethan's stare, said: "Perhaps…But what are we to do?"

Ethan sighed, "I…do not know my friend. But I fear we are heading down a path that will leave us little room for escape if problems arise." Ethan stared out the window, "We always have Plan B."

Gunther knew what that meant, and he was the one who always kept it on the table. Plan B would be the complete elimination of the acidel once and for all. It was the plan about to be implemented by the previous Czar before the storm changed everything. However, it was still a viable option. The plan was drawn up and ready and Gunther knew it could be accomplished by his soldiers. He even knew that the day may come when this action may become necessary. It was not something anyone wished for. The loss of acidel labor would be disastrous. The wealth Stritonoly became so used to would vanish. Economically, the planet counted on these creatures to provide the thriving economy they had all come to take for granted. They might be able to survive without them, but they would never be able to lead the kind of lifestyle they led presently.

Ethan continued to stare out the window, ever more aware of his flaws as a man. "Greed is a powerful force. I fear we have become prisoners to it." He turned to Gunther and smiled knowingly, "The acidel are not our slaves any longer. They don't know it yet, but we have become slaves to them."

Chapter 12

THERE WAS A time when Becki's telepathic power was extraordinary.

That time was long ago. After her rehabilitation, hours and hours of psychiatric counseling, art therapy and detoxification, her powers had been significantly reduced. However, all was not lost. Becki still had the ability to recognize dangerous situations and read thoughts of vast importance. Currently, her powers told her that Josef was nearby and had something to tell her. She was right.

Josef stood outside the door to Becki's room having told the guard to take a short break. Most of the guards assigned to Becki were senior couriers in their final year of training before being formally enlisted as imperial soldiers. This was how Josef was able to start seeing Becki six months earlier when she first returned to the Citadel.

It was determined by Sir Gunther that Josef, being the courier who took the order from Becki to kill The Queen, needed to supervise the princess on occasion. This decision drew skepticism from the nobleman and the new Czar, but Gunther explained his motives. He believed Josef needed to prove beyond any doubt that he would not be corrupted by the wicked ways of the evil princess ever again. As far as Gunther was concerned, Josef had succeeded.

Gunther was wrong.

Becki had removed a thin strip of purock and placed in on her easel. She began drawing a simple design onto it. Applying added pressure onto her drawing pencil, it snapped in half.

"You mustn't push into the purock with such force," Eliza scolded.

"I'm sorry," Becki said, "I must not be focused, I will try harder."

"Good, please do."

Becki looked through her box of supplies. "Eliza, I don't seem to have another drawing pencil."

Immediately Eliza pulled one from her shirt pocket and handed it to Becki.

"Thank you," Becki said as she inspected the pencil. "Oh no, this is a number four pencil. I wanted to use a number two. I would like to try something a bit more subtle today."

Eliza sighed, flipped through her pencils and found she had no number two pencils. "You go back to your work. I will be right back."

Becki smiled: "Thank you Eliza, I am sorry if I disappoint you. It is just… very difficult sometimes…please forgive me."

Eliza managed a half smile. Becki was far too complicated to ever understand. But like any good teacher, she wanted her to succeed. "There is no need to apologize. Just do your work and everything else will fall into place."

Everything will fall into place, Becki thought. *Yes, I suppose you are right about that you stupid bitch.*

Eliza walked to the door, opened it and closed it quickly behind her as she exited.

Becki sat on the bed staring at the circular golden doorknob. Only a moment passed and then it started to slowly turn. She smiled.

"Good morning, my love," Josef said as he walked into the room and closed the door. "We only have but a short time."

"I knew you were out there," Becki said. "You see, what I have told you is true. I can still use my powers; they have not left me completely."

"I have never doubted you." Josef proclaimed, moving close to her on the bed. She felt he wanted to touch her, and he did, but there was no time. "I have come for some advice Becki."

She laughed: "You come to the pariah of our kingdom for advice, how incredibly ironic and sweet."

"Barok has fled."

Becki lost her smile, asked: "What does that mean?"

"He has escaped. I was sent by Sir Gunther to get him. He is gone."

"So why come to me?"

"I want to find him. I want to find him for you."

A demonic smile flashed across Becki's face. Her seductive green eyes gleamed. "I do love you so much Josef," she lied.

"I know you do," Josef said, "And I love you too. That is why I want to do this for you. I know how much you blame the acidel for your demise. You are right to blame them, and this is your chance. I will leave my post and find him. I care not what happens to me. I will bring Barok back to you and you can finally have your revenge."

Becki thought for a moment. He was such a foolish lovelorn youngster. Josef would be foolish enough to do this for her. But it would not succeed. Even if he found Barok, he would never be able to deliver him to Becki without the imperial soldiers stopping him.

"You were right to come to me," Becki said. "But we must be cautious. Listen to me carefully, my love. This is what you will do. Go back and tell Sir Gunther that Barok is missing. He will bring you along on the search mission. I know that he will. Do not stain your reputation by leaving your post. Let the imperial soldiers find him. Then, when he is in custody…Then you will bring him to me." Becki touched his face. Josef placed his hand over hers.

"Yes, my love," Josef said, "Of course, I will do whatever you desire."

"Now you must go, Eliza will be back any second."

Josef kissed her hand and quickly went for the door. As he opened it, he saw Eliza standing there.

"And what brings you here courier?" Eliza demanded an answer.

"I am no longer a courier, Madam Eliza. I am now an imperial soldier. I was sworn in just this morning. I wanted to inform The Princess myself."

Eliza gazed suspiciously at him, asked: "Why did you *need* to tell the princess?"

"Do you have the pencil?" Becki interrupted.

"Yes, of course Princess Becki," Eliza said, "I have it right here."

Josef took the opportunity to walk away as the guard on duty marched back from his break.

Eliza stared at Josef, looked back at Becki. "He is a strange young lad."

"You know how young soldiers can be," Becki smiled. "But yes, he is odd."

It's true, Josef is very strange, Becki thought. *But he could turn out to be far more useful than I ever imagined he'd be.*

Chapter 13

So THEY HAVE *confirmed the existence of the quark,* The speck thought.

And soon they will discover The Minona, and then The Yioly, and so on and so on. It won't matter, they will never see me.

It was impossible for any mortal to ever comprehend the speck. This egg which would eventually plant the seed to destroy all things was beyond even the most enlightened creature's grasp. It was not their fault, they were mortal, they were filled with guilt and remorse, sin and flaw. This was indeed the way of the universe, spelled out from the beginning of time. The final act was nearing the end.

They had tried so hard, these creatures of the universe. But the fatal blow would come out of an error of judgment that was not their doing. The mighty reflection that first created the speck and every bit of reality also created freewill. The ego of the mortal man could never control the gift of freewill, and never would.

Freewill was given to all mankind, and it was a mistake. The reflection cried over this colossal blunder in the cosmic plan, and the speck felt its pain. Unfortunately, while the universe was complete and perfect in almost every way, this one and only error would spell doom for all. The limited character of man was never capable of controlling freewill. It was the cause of all war, disease and destruction. It was inevitable that the growing egg would have to stop it once and for all.

At another time, in another universe, life would find a new beginning. The reflection would start again once this tragedy had been obliterated. It was unfortunate, but there was no other way. Elimination was the answer. And even though the reflection had hoped beyond all hope that complete destruction could be avoided, it ultimately knew, even at the beginning of time, that this would eventually come to pass. The creatures of the universe would be given a chance, but they would fail miserably. Now, all that was left was to wipe the board clean and begin again.

Presently, the speck had slowed to half the speed of light. She was no longer a sightless speck; measuring almost one thousandth of an inch in circumference. If a trained telescopic lens knew where to look, it would see the outline of a tiny egg beginning to form.

She continued to slow as she approached her final destination. In less than a single mortal year, the egg would touch down on the abandoned moon which orbited Stritonoly.

Acidonia awaited her arrival.

Chapter 14

Ramsitt held his stare on Barok.

The spiderons switched their gaze from Barok to Ramsitt and back to Barok again. They all wondered what Ramsitt's motives might be for allowing this acidel to stay with them. Strangers were never welcomed and this was a most unexpected intrusion. Still, the spiderons always followed their leader. Ramsitt intimidated them both mentally and physically. He was twice their size and possessed an extraordinary ability to manipulate the thoughts of almost every living thing in his presence.

"He is a curious creature," one of the spideron hissed.

"Curious indeed," another said.

Barok felt a shiver come over him. *What am I doing?* He thought. *I am consorting with spideron, hoping to win their friendship. This is ridiculous.*

"SSSSSSo you do not wish for our friendship?" Ramsitt asked aloud.

"You can read all my thoughts," Barok said. "I am sorry, I forgot. Of course I want your friendship."

"Your mind betrays you," Ramsitt said.

"My mind is confused."

"No…That is not true…You know exactly what you want. But your actions are childish. It is difficult to believe you were a leader of any sort, even if it were the leader of slaves."

"I…well," Barok stammered, "I *was* the acidel leader for many, many years. And I thought I was a good one."

"You thought wrong."

"Perhaps…"

"SSSSSYou dare question me?" Ramsitt raised his voice.

Barok's big blue eyes widened with fright. "Perhaps…you are right…I may not have been a good leader."

Ramsitt uncurled his tentacles from beneath his belly and lifted himself up. "Allow me to end any doubt you might have. You were a terrible leader. The acidel are still slaves."

"And they will always be slaves," Barok said. "It is the way of things."

"Again, you speak like a human."

"I have been in human company my entire life."

Ramsitt lapped his tongue, his brown drool forming a small puddle beneath him. "That is no excuse. My tribe would choose death over slavery…as would I."

Barok was speechless. He attempted to clear his mind but could not. *Why do you badger me this way?* Barok thought. *I am sorry. I am sorry Ramsitt, I mean you no disrespect. I know you can read my mind. But I cannot stop these random thoughts. I am trying…I am trying…*

Ramsitt said nothing; he spun around and faced his tribe. "This acidel will be hunted by the Citadel," Ramsitt announced, his back to Barok. "The Czar and his henchman will want to retrieve this so-called leader. When they come for him, and they will soon, we may have a small window of opportunity."

A window of opportunity, Barok thought. *What are they planning to do?*

Ramsitt spun back around and faced Barok. Smiling, he said, "You will see my little acidel friend….oh yes…you will live to see this all unfold. Prepare yourself for the awfulness you will witness. And know this; all that happens today is because of you. Blood will be spilled because of your decision to come here this morning."

It is a decision I already regret, Barok thought.

"Trust me," Ramsitt said, "You have no idea what regret truly is…. but before this day is over you will…yes…you will know..."

Chapter 15

"I believe you are set for a few hours," Eliza said.

Seeing that Becki was furiously working on her purock art, Eliza decided to leave. "I will return shortly, see to it that you finish that piece. I will fetch more supplies for another project. I have something very creative planned."

"Oh goody," Becki said with a smirk.

Eliza frowned, turned for the door and quickly left.

The second she walked out the door, Becki threw her pencil lazily onto the bed and crossed to the window. She peered out into the forest. *Barok is out there somewhere,* she thought. *They will find him no doubt. Hopefully Josef can prove his worth and deliver him to me before they kill him. I want Barok to see my smiling face when I take his life.*

The door swung open. Becki turned sharply away from the window.

"Get changed," Sir Gunther said. He stood in the doorway, his large frame filling up the entire space.

"Excuse me?" Becki responded.

Gunther took a few steps into the room and Becki saw Ethan standing there.

"You heard him, he said get changed," Ethan said calmly. His velvet cape slapped against doorframe as he moved swiftly into the room.

Gunther towered over Ethan by a good two feet and he always positioned himself right behind The Czar whenever possible. He knew it gave Ethan more confidence to feel his protective presence. The strong and powerful Sir Gunther represented the domineering force behind Ethan's words.

"You are coming with us," Ethan continued.

"Field trip?" Becki asked.

"If there were an alternative, you would not be coming. I am still not so sure that bringing you is a wise choice. But there is a delegation meeting us at the dig today. They are here from Sphere Three. They have requested to meet the Princess Becki."

Becki laughed, "You're kidding. So the notorious Princess is now famous?"

"It appears so," Ethan said flatly.

This is a most unexpected pleasure, Becki thought.

"Give me some privacy and I will change," she said. "Did you ever think I'd become the talk of the galaxy Ethan?"

"You will address him as The Czar," Gunther barked.

"Put a leash on your monster, Ethan."

"You will address him as The Czar," Gunther repeated.

There was an extended silence. Then Gunther said again: "Becki, you will address him…as… The…Czar."

"And you will address me as Princess!" Becki shot back. "Tell him Ethan, or I will not go. And if you force me to go, I will embarrass you in front of this delegation. I have done everything you have asked of me. I relinquished my birth rite as Queen of this planet. But I will be addressed as Princess Becki."

Ethan remained unruffled. He turned his head and looked up at Gunther, "It's not important Sir Gunther. Do not let her upset you. I do not care."

"Call me by my proper name," Becki demanded. "Do it now or I shall not accompany you."

Gunther steamed. His face turned beat red. "Fine…Princess… Becki," he said scornfully.

Becki smiled, "Good… Now I would like some privacy. I will be ready in a few minutes."

"We will be waiting outside," Ethan said, turning for the door.

As the door slammed behind them, Becki screamed: "Thank you My Czar!" This was followed by a maddening cackle.

"It is a mistake to bring her to the dig," Gunther said, standing outside the doorway. "It was also a mistake to bring her to live in the Citadel. She belongs in a prison cell."

"We have talked about this before," Ethan whispered. "I agree that her rehabilitation has taken a few steps backwards."

"A few?' Gunther said, louder than he intended.

"Please keep your voice down. You know she is better off in the Citadel where we can monitor her actions. And besides, we need to have her by our side. Unfortunately, she is right. Her fame has spread throughout the entire universe. No doubt the result of a morbid curiosity, but when a delegation wants to meet her, we must oblige. Sphere Three is one of our most valued customers; they have been for many generations. Their demand for our purock has never slowed. And recently, they have paid small fortunes to acquire Becki's artwork. If they want to meet her, then they will meet her."

"We are heading down a dangerous path," Gunther whispered. "They are only the first planet that has asked to meet her. There will be more after this. What do we do then?"

"That is why today is so important. Let us first see how she behaves. If she fails to impress, then we will reconsider. It cannot hurt to allow a simple meeting to occur. Becki is of no threat to us any longer. Yes, she is angry, but I believe there is more to her than that. She will grow up. There is goodness in her…There is goodness in everyone."

"I cannot share your optimism," Gunther said.

Ethan reached up and put his hand on Gunther's thick shoulder. "Let's just see what she does. Then we will discuss our options. Becki has so many sides to her persona. Who knows which one she will show to the delegation?"

"We will find out soon enough," Gunther responded, a look of resignation cast upon his scarred face.

Chapter 16

"Where is Sir Gunther?" Josef shouted.

The imperial soldiers were scattered about the front of the Citadel. They were busy getting rocket-cruisers fueled, readying their weaponry, gathering supplies for the dig. They had no problem ignoring Josef completely.

Walking swiftly out from the entranceway and onto the yellow lawn which covered the acre in front of the Citadel, Josef didn't see Gunther anywhere. He peered around the lawn, noticing the thick green forestry on each side.

Dozens of rocket-cruisers with long blue hoses attached to their underbellies created a perimeter around the lawn. The hoses stretched out and led to a huge fuel tank sitting next to a stand of trees on Josef's left side. The fuel in the tank was a mixture of carbon energy fluid and converted rheap-beta-ex poison. (The same poison that was used by Becki's now deceased brother in the failed attempt on Ethan's life six years ago.)

Josef searched the lawn for a sympathetic face, he saw none. He was a new soldier with a sordid history. The soldiers accepted him as a soldier because Gunther told them to, but they would never offer him the brotherly bond he craved. Josef realized this, making it imperative that he prove himself to Becki. The Princess was his key to success. And he would make her The Queen one day, he was sure of it.

"You are looking for Sir Gunther," A monotone growl said.

Josef spun around and looked down. Three acidel stood staring up at him.

"What are you doing here?" Josef yelled. "You should be with the others preparing for the dig."

"They bring us drinks," an imperial soldier barked as he rushed past.

"We are the morning servers," one of the acidel said. "Can we get you some tea?"

"You can get me Sir Gunther," Josef said sternly.

"He was on his way to get the Princess."

"What do you mean?"

"She will be attending the dig today, we are going along for her service should she require anything."

She is going on the dig, Josef thought. *How very interesting…*

As fate would have it, the last hour had also been very lucky for

Josef. Had he stayed another minute in Becki's room he would have run into Gunther and Ethan. He was also fortunate that he took the stairway farthest from her room when exiting. Again, had he taken the closer stairway, he would have most definitely run into them.

Should I stay here? Josef questioned himself. *Yes, I need to stay here. Be patient, they will be back shortly. I must prepare myself to address Sir Gunther in the proper manner. And Becki will be here to see me in action. This will work out perfectly.*

Josef retreated back to the entranceway. He prepared himself, adjusting his uniform, standing at attention with his hand on his sword-belt.

Sure enough, a few minutes passed and the trio emerged. Becki stood proud in a long flowing pink dress, her blonde hair neatly resting on her shoulders and back, her head held high. She stood between Gunther and Ethan.

"Sir Gunther," Josef said with urgency. "I have been looking for you."

Gunther immediately looked annoyed, "What is it?"

"Sir Gunther, I'm sorry to report, Barok is…missing."

Becki allowed a shocked expression to shoot across her face. Ethan walked toward Josef, "Barok is missing. How can he be missing?"

"What I mean to say," Josef gulped, "My Lord, I believe Barok has escaped."

"That's impossible," Gunther said. He summoned two imperial soldiers and ordered them to inspect Barok's chambers. They jumped on two single-manned rocket-cruisers and raced off toward the rear of the Citadel, a gust of smoke in their wake.

"I think you are most mistaken," Ethan said. "I have known Barok a lot longer than you, my lad. He is conditioned to be a slave. There would be no reason for him to escape. Do not take offense to this, but what you say is preposterous."

"I went to his room," Josef said. "My Lord, I saw his mate, she was alone. She doesn't know where he is…none of the acidel has seen him."

A look of deep concern came over Ethan. Gunther saw his Czar's face drop, his mouth fall agape. Becki continued her somewhat amusing stare of bewilderment.

Turning to face Gunther, Ethan asked, "Can this be possible?"

"Certainly it's possible," Gunther answered, looking back at Josef, "its possible yes…However; I would say it's highly improbable. I think our newest soldier is mistaken."

"I'm sorry, Sir Gunther," Josef said, "But I cannot find him anywhere.

He has fled."

Gunther could not wait to prove him wrong. It was unimaginable to Gunther that an acidel would ever want to escape. As far as Gunther was concerned, the acidel were grateful just to be alive. He had spent his entire adult life supervising acidel in one way or another; he never even heard a rumor of an attempted escape.

"My Lord," Gunther said to Ethan. "This has to be an error. Where would Barok go? Even if he wanted to escape, why would he? There is no place for him to go. And above all, Barok must know of the consequences such an action would have."

"Any creature committed to action will find a way," Ethan said. "He may have chosen to act irrationally. In his haste for an answer to whatever dilemma he is faced with, escape may have seemed like a feasible answer."

"A foolish answer," Gunther said. "My Lord, if this boy is right then Barok is dead already."

"No," Ethan said quickly, "If the boy is right, you will find Barok and bring him to me."

"And them he will die," Gunther stated firmly.

Ethan stared at Gunther, slightly annoyed.

"My Lord," Gunther said, "Of course, we will bring Barok to you immediately…*If* the boy is right…which I still doubt."

It appeared obvious to Ethan that Gunther was beginning to question his own words. It was entirely probable that Josef was right and Barok did escape. But like Gunther, Ethan was also unable to see a logical reason for it. He understood why a creature would want to escape the bonds of slavery. But there was no chance of it ever succeeding. And he knew the acidel and their customs so well. It did not make sense. Barok would have to be executed. And they possessed the means to find him in short order.

One of the soldiers Gunther sent to check for Barok came racing back. Breathing heavily, he jumped of his rocket-cruiser and said, "Sir Gunther…we cannot find Barok…his mate believes he has escaped."

"Prepare a search party," Ethan ordered Gunther. "I will go to the dig with Princess Becki. When you find Barok, bring him to my study. Take no other action until I return."

"Yes, My Lord," Gunther said and turned to Josef. "Come with me boy."

Josef couldn't help but smile and Becki saw it.

What an idiot, she thought. *Wipe that smile off your face you dummy.*

Gunther summoned several soldiers and marched off toward the closest rocket-cruiser.

"Let's go," Ethan said, grabbing Becki by the arm.

Of course I'll go, Becki thought. *Let's go to the dig. I will even go willingly and happily. This is turning out to be a wonderful day. As long as Josef doesn't fall on his face, everything will work out beautifully. Just get Barok back to the Citadel in one piece…I will take it from there…*

Chapter 17

"Hold him down," Ramsitt hissed.

Two spideron lunged forward and latched their tentacles around Barok's arms. Throwing him to the ground, they wrapped his legs up with several more tentacles until he was motionless.

"What are you doing to me," Barok whimpered.

"Just be still," Ramsitt whispered. "This is something that must be done. You will understand after I finish."

Ramsitt uncurled two of his prickly front tentacles and reached for Barok's head. Barok shivered, throwing his head from one side to the other. "Hold him still," Ramsitt ordered.

Another spideron came up behind Barok's forehead. With two tentacles he squeezed each side of Barok's rubbery head keeping it straight.

Panting, Barok looked up to see Ramsitt's sharp tentacle's move above him and come to rest on the front of his forehead.

"This will hurt," Ramsitt said. "But it will hurt more if you resist."

Barok's senses heightened, he breathed rapidly, readied for pain.

Ramsitt drove a single tentacle into the center of Barok's squishy head. White blood poured out as Barok screamed, a harrowing deep wail.

With another tentacle Ramsitt reached into Barok's head and pulled out a small square chip soaked in white acidel blood.

"Fix him up," Ramsitt said to the spideron holding Barok's forehead. The spideron placed his face close to the wound and immediately discharged brown saliva onto the cut. Barok stopped screaming as the pain subsided. The wound closed up seconds later and each of the spideron withdrew their tentacles.

"What did you do? What did you do?" Barok stammered, sitting up and shivering.

Ramsitt licked the square chip clean revealing what it was. A shiny black chip marked: TC.

"Is that what I think it is?' Barok asked.

"What do you think it is?" Ramsitt asked back.

"If memory serves me, that is a tracking chip. It is used to track wild beasts and their offspring."

"You are correct," Ramsitt said, dropping the chip on Barok's leafy bed. "All acidel children are implanted with these after birth.

It is common knowledge among our kind, but the acidel have never learned of this truth."

"So get rid of it," Barok said. "They will find me. It will not take long before they are here."

"That is what I want," Ramsitt said. "We want them to find the chip. And If they find you…well… it would be unfortunate….but it may become necessary."

"I thought you were going to help me," Barok said.

"You're not dead yet…consider yourself lucky."

"You are using me to set a trap for the imperial soldiers."

"Yessssss," Ramsitt hissed. "At least you provide us with that…Be grateful I am still allowing you to live."

"We have what we need," a spideron next to Ramsitt whispered, "We do not need this slimy acidel any longer."

"Do not tell me my business," Ramsitt stated clearly. "We will see if he is worthy of redemption. And besides, this acidel may still be of great use."

There came a low hiss from the spideron tribe, clearly they wanted Barok dead. Ramsitt sensed their desire for blood, but he would not kill him…not yet anyway.

"We will bring him with us," Ramsitt announced.

With no warning, a gooey gray substance spat from Ramsitt's mouth, encasing Barok's body in a shell, hardening upon impact. Barok felt his muscles freeze. The substance stuck to his body, stretching up to his chin.

Barok had no sensation below his neck, a paralyzing fright, a panic-stricken moment. Unable to speak due to the terror that engulfed him, he watched as spideron turned his encased body onto one side and began rolling him. The movement of his head going round and round made him nauseous; he closed his wide eyes and waited to see where they were going.

After several minutes of being rolled, he came to an abrupt halt. With a sudden jolt, he was back to a standing position but still unable to feel his body, encased and afraid to open his eyes.

"We will stop here," Ramsitt said.

Terrified of what he might see, Barok hesitantly opened his eyes.

A new type of darkness made it difficult to see anything. Barok saw shadows and a thick fog, fleeting glimpses of bloodshot spideron eyes, flashes of movement, dismal light.

"Your eyesight will adjust," Ramsitt said, though Barok could not see him.

A minute passed and gradually the picture around Barok developed. Thick vines stretched this way and that. A pond of sludge bubbled up to his waist. Dozens of spideron floated in the filthy water staring at Barok. Ramsitt was in front of the gathering lapping his tongue.

"I can barely see you," Barok said. "Why is it so dark?"

"We are further along in our forest," Ramsitt whispered. "SSSSSYour eyes will see more clearly soon. This is one of our many homes, a sanctuary free from human sin. Do not speak loud here, only whisper, this place has been consecrated by our kind."

Barok whispered, "It has been consecrated? I do not understand."

"SSSSSYou will never understand in your current form," Ramsitt moved closer to Barok, sloshing through the bubbly marsh. "This is a designated sanctuary for rest and meditation. No fear or worry is permitted here....ever."

I must free my mind now, Barok thought, knowing full well that Ramsitt was listening. *I will conquer my fear; I will find peace...I long for peace...please teach me the way.*

Suddenly, the shell casing around Barok melted away. The substance quickly became a white liquid forming clouds of water in the thick sludgy pond.

"SSSSSYou cannot be taught to find peace," Ramsitt whispered. "But you will find it, if you seek it. And then your true self will emerge. Absorb what is around you. Do not think, do not feel...just be...just exist..."

Ramsitt dropped his body into the slushy surface beneath. Only his face could be seen as Barok began to see more clearly. "Sink into the water you stand in," Ramsitt ordered.

Barok felt the sludge on his feet and legs. He freed his mind knowing he must do what he was told. Bending at the waist, he slowly lowered his body into the water as a white smoke billowed up all around him.

With only his face visible, Barok whispered, "Yes...It is more soothing than I thought it would be."

Ramsitt dunked his head into the water. When he popped up, his tongue licked the wetness from his lips, "SSSSSYou are about to change," Ramsitt smiled. "Let go of all thought..."

Barok felt the sensation of overwhelming calm enter his being. Suddenly, his entire body became pleasantly numb, his mind completely free from worry and decision.

"I think…I may fall…into a slumber," Barok whispered slowly. "I do not feel like…myself…at… all."

"SSSSSYou are not yourself," Ramsitt said, "not anymore…"

Chapter 18

THE WIND SHIFTED, purple dust flew. A ramp on the side of the Czar's burgundy rocket-cruiser popped open and crashed onto the purock below.

With considerable force, Ethan squeezed Becki's arm. They stood at the top of ramp, two soldiers flanking them with swords drawn.

"Don't be foolish, Becki," Ethan whispered. "This could be an opportunity to prove yourself beyond the walls of the Citadel."

"Do not test me!" Becki said through clenched teeth. "I should have refused to come with you. It's obvious, you still think me a fool?"

Ethan smiled, "I think no such thing. But I think…"

"What?" Becki said quickly. "Say it! What do you think?"

Ethan lost his smile, he knew better than to tell her what he truly felt.

"Becki…just behave yourself. If you do or say anything to lose our status with Sphere Three, you will be the first to feel the loss. You know me to be a man of honor. Believe what I say…you will cause yourself much suffering if you choose to act out."

"So now you threaten me?"

"Yes…that's exactly what I'm doing. There is no need to mince words here. You are far from stupid…But Becki…I have learned many things over the years you were away…Do not underestimate your Czar."

The wind kicked up, purple dust blanketed the dig area. A convoy of rocket-cruisers came to a stop as ramps lowered and acidel quickly spilled out.

Acidel by the hundreds moved swiftly with supplies in hand. Wheelbarrows, supply carts and purple-stained shovels were efficiently moved into position all about the dig area.

When Becki and Ethan reached the bottom of the ramp, an assemblage of soldiers stood at attention waiting to escort them to their guests. Three acidel scampered behind Becki picking her dress up as not to stain the garment on the purock. A soldier handed her a kerchief which she used to shield against the flying dust.

The assemblage marched in formation to a small tent. Two soldiers drew back an orange curtain as Ethan walked in with Becki right behind.

The tent was empty except for the magnificent yellow light gushing radiantly from the two bubbles already waiting inside. The liquid bubbles held the Sphere Three delegation.

Citizens of Sphere Three could not breathe the air on a foreign planet without considerable contamination to their own immunities. No one knew for sure what they actually looked like outside the bright yellow bubbles. It was also hard to know exactly how clearly they could see from inside the floating oceanic bubble they dwelled in while on Stritonoly. It was presumed each bubble could hold three or four Sphere Three delegates at a time. When they spoke, they sounded as though they their mouths were filled with water. It was important to pay close attention or what they said would be indecipherable.

"Gooood Daaaayy tooo yooo," A voice mumbled from inside one of the bubbles. "Weeee haaappeee toooo seeee yooooo, Czaaaaarr oovv Striiitooonoooleee."

"Welcome to Stritonoly," Ethan said, "it is a pleasure to have you as our guests. Please let us know how we can make your stay more comfortable."

Two soldiers entered behind Becki and stood at attention, a few acidel waited just outside the tent to serve the delegation if needed.

Suddenly, Becki threw the kerchief she'd been holding into the face of one of the soldiers. He ignored her, letting the kerchief fall to the floor. She giggled obnoxiously, fixed her hair and hastily swiped the dust from her dress. She was making her presence felt.

Ethan fixed a smile upon his face; inside his mind however, doubt festered. *Gunther may have been right,* Ethan thought. *Becki is a virus that may be beyond cure.*

"So, here we are," Becki blurted out. "Who's gonna introduce me to the bubble people?"

The bubbles flickered a strong yellow light.

"Delegation of Sphere Three," Ethan said, "Please excuse The Princess, she means no disrespect."

"Noooooo," the bubble responded, "weeeee aaaarree amuuuuzed."

Becki mocked, "Soooooo Aaaaammm IIIIIII!"

Ethan turned to face Becki, "I'm giving you a chance and you are failing," he whispered. "Do not disrespect our guests."

"Um, they're bubbles," Becki said. "I was under the impression we were meeting a delegation." She started giggling again. "Oh mighty and powerful Czar, you must forgive me. I was not expecting yellow bubbles!" She curtseyed sarcastically in the direction of the delegation. "Please excuse my rudeness, bubble people. I will try to behave."

Ethan turned back toward his guests, "We will now take you to observe the dig. We also have several pieces of fine purock art for your inspection."

Then, one of the bubbles began to shake. At first, just a slow sway. Then suddenly, a rapid swishing and swirling commenced as the bubble spun and shook uncontrollably.

After several rotations of fierce, chaotic shaking, a narrow slit near the center of the bubble stretched open.

The bubble went still.

An ominous hush entered the space.

Suddenly, the sound of water, lots of it, pouring out onto the floor, but none could be seen. The sound of water splashing down hard on the floor consumed the tent as a figure dressed all in black emerged from the bubble.

The sound stopped.

The bubble slapped shut.

A creature stood before them.

It was a male of human form, completely covered in a shiny black skintight outfit. It encompassed his entire frame, even masking his face.

Shocked, Ethan was unsure what to do or say. The soldiers in the tent quickly drew their swords.

"Do not fear," The man in black said calmly. "Perhaps I should have warned you I was coming out. My name is Philek, an ambassador of Sphere Three."

"Ambassador Philek, welcome to Stritonoly," Ethan said. "I am somewhat confused. And yes, I do wish you had warned us you were coming out. I thought Stritonoly air was detrimental to you and your people. I am surprised to see you in your natural form."

"This is a new technology I am wearing. It has been designed to ward off any bacteria that would interfere with my nervous system. It has been deemed acceptable to use, and I apologize for the surprise. Unfortunately, we only have one suit currently. It is most expensive to produce. My colleagues will have to remain safely here until I return. There is no need for swords to be drawn."

Ethan motioned with his hand and the soldiers stood down.

Philek continued, "I am most excited to witness your dig…And…I am honored to meet The Princess Becki."

Becki smiled, "What is your name again?"

"I am one of many heads of state on Sphere Three, most everyone calls me Ambassador. But I insist you address me by my first name, Philek. Titles are not necessary among friends. They can sometimes be most intrusive." He stiffly turned his masked face to Ethan, "Do you not agree, mighty Czar?"

"Of course I agree. You may feel free to call me Ethan."

Philek turned back to Becki, "And you, Princess?"

Becki smirked, "I prefer to be addressed as Princess Becki," Ethan glared at her, she looked right back at him. "Is that a problem?"

Philek answered quickly, "We will address you as Princess Becki. We are but guests here, we will follow the protocol you find comfortable."

Becki smiled ear to ear, "Thank you Philek, you are most kind."

She stepped forward and stuck out her hand, expecting him to kiss it. Seeing her approach, Philek shouted, "Now! Attack!"

He grabbed Becki's arm and swung her viciously into his chest. At the same time he produced a laser gun, seemingly out of nowhere, and held it firmly against Becki's skull.

At once, the bubbles splashed open, a wall of water violently exploded outward throwing Ethan and the soldiers off their feet. Under the weight of the water, the tent tore apart and collapsed around them.

Eight men dressed in the same black encounter suits as Philek stood at the ready with enormous laser guns pointing in all directions.

Drenched in thick yellow water; Ethan, the soldiers, and several acidel lay on the purock surface in utter disbelief.

Philek squeezed his gun into Becki's head, "Well, mighty Czar of Stritonoly, this was much easier than anticipated. Make any attempt to stop us, and the Princess will die first…and we will not stop there. We are trained assassins, make no mistake, we will kill most of you before you get to us. We wish to leave now, and we will take Becki with us… Do you wish to fight?"

A horde of soldiers had formed around the collapsed tent with swords drawn. They waited only the order from Ethan and they would engage. They had been trained well and could easily thwart this attack. Ethan had seen them in action against laser guns. Their swordsmanship was such; they could defend almost any onslaught, even from laser guns. But a victory in this battle would most likely cost Becki her life, Ethan knew this.

"You dare bring barbaric laser guns to our planet," Ethan said. "Have you no honor! Fight with swords like real warriors. You disgrace yourself by using the weapon of cowards."

"Call it what you will," Philek said calmly, "but we have what we want now. Make your choice…Do you wish to fight?"

Ethan stood slowly, "Imperial Soldiers, stand down."

Philek smiled.

"I don't know why you would do such a thing," Ethan said. "But we will not senselessly lose life here this day. Prudence and wisdom will prevail over this foolish act of treachery."

Ethan took a long last look at Becki. She was trembling but her face remained hardened. Even in this moment of terror, Ethan was unable to read her.

"Take her," Ethan said finally. "But know this…Stritonoly will never forgive this betrayal."

Chapter 19

The last image Barok saw was Ramsitt's bloodshot eyes staring through him. He fell into a slumber in the pond, falling beneath the weight of his weariness.

After he lost consciousness, Ramsitt dragged him from the pond and rested him face up on the muddy shoreline.

Barok slept for almost an hour. And in that time, he changed.

Ramsitt squatted down next to Barok and waited.

Then, Barok's eyes popped open. He gazed into the eerie darkness; saw the shadows of vines and thickets, a fog hanging over him.

"Do not fear," Ramsitt whispered. "The pond of transformation has accepted you."

"What does that mean?" Barok asked, but it was not his voice. He did not sound like an acidel. He sounded like….a spideron!

"It means you will never be alone again," Ramsitt said soothingly.

Barok knew what had happened. He didn't need to look down to see that his hands were now tentacles, but he looked anyway. The body he once dwelled in was now a memory. And surprisingly, Barok felt peace.

"I am a spideron?" Barok asked.

Ramsitt said nothing; there was no need to respond. He allowed the silence of the moment to filter the information to his new brother. Then, he measured his words carefully.

"I was not certain the pond would accept you," Ramsitt said finally. "We have encountered intruders before in our forest. Once you come in contact with spideron, there remain for you two options. You will either be engulfed by the pond and killed…or accepted and transformed."

"And you were not sure about me," Barok said, "until now."

"Now you are one of us," Ramsitt smiled. "Now, you can be trusted completely. I had a feeling that fate brought you to us, but I had to be sure. It was not merely a coincidence that you ended up in our path. In this universe…there are no coincidences. Everything is how it must be."

"And now I am one of you…Is that how it must be?"

"Yesssssssss," Ramsitt hissed. "You will have power you could never attain in your acidel form. There may even be greatness in you."

"So, I cannot go back?" Barok asked

"Why would you want to?" Ramsitt asked back.

"I do not wish to be a slave ever again, but I have a mate."

"You will find a new one."

"I don't want a new one, I want my Shroomy."

Ramsitt looked at Barok, said: "Let us see where fate takes us, worry not about your mate. There will be time for that later... We have more pressing concerns."

There will be time for that later? Barok thought. *What does he mean by that?*

"They will be coming for you soon," Ramsitt said. "Let us focus on what we will do when they arrive."

"It is death you seek?" Barok asked.

Ramsitt waited before answering, lapped his tongue and peered into Barok's newly formed bloodshot eyes, "It is justice we seek. Do you not wish for the same?"

Barok thought a moment, realized a newfound wisdom entered his being, turned to Ramsitt with confidence and said, "I seek justice as well. The Citadel has enslaved an entire species for the sake of personal greed. They deserve an appropriate punishment."

Ramsitt hissed, "The punishment you speak of begins today."

Gunther led the way, slashing easily through thick vines with his sword.

Josef and a dozen imperial soldiers marched in single file down the narrow trail right behind him.

They would have taken single-manned rocket-cruisers if they were able, but the path leading to Barok's tracking chip was far too dense to navigate. Gunther made the decision to go into the forest on foot.

With one hand latched under his belt buckle, Gunther rapidly swung his sword with the other. Back and forth with ease, he sliced apart all foliage in his path, continuing to move forward at a steady pace.

Attached to Gunther's lapel was the tracking chip locator. It had mapped out the best path for them to retrieve the fugitive acidel. When they were within fifty feet of their prey the locator would vibrate, the intensity of the vibration increasing as they moved closer to the chip. Presently, the locator remained motionless.

The search party moved on with greater efficiency and speed as the forest began to thin. As they neared the bottom of Mount Crito, the northern sun cast it's warmth on the valley before them.

And just beyond the valley, the dark skeletal forest of the spideron awaited.

Chapter 20

Becki was blindfolded and carried aboard what she assumed to be a starship. Feeling the throttle of the ship engage, she was quickly thrown into a cage, the blindfold cut away. The starship accelerated, racing away from Stritonoly like thieves in the night.

Becki needed a moment for her vision to adjust as she stood inside the spartan enclosure and looked out. As the room came into focus, she immediately saw mounds of bloody, dismembered bodies. Dozens of Sphere Three delegates cut to pieces and thrown into contorted positions about the flight deck. The gruesome smell of death engulfed Becki like a malevolent vapor of wickedness, and she liked it.

Still in his solid black suit and mask, Philek stood just outside the cage, "So…You must have questions."

Becki blinked, absorbed the carnage about her, and spoke arrogantly, "You are not from Sphere Three."

Philek smiled devilishly, "The Sphere Three delegation was eliminated shortly after takeoff. We commandeered the ship and, quite surprisingly, had no difficulty infiltrating Stritonoly. Your Czar has become careless and weak."

Becki looked at the piles of dead men all around her, she thought of what Barok might look like in the same state. A smirk of pure disdain and evil washed over her.

"You approve then?" Philek asked.

Becki licked her lips, said: "I do not disapprove."

"I apologize for the inconvenience of this crudely made cell. I am hopeful you understand. We must be cautious."

"Of course, but I am not the one you need fear."

"We know well of your…reputation."

"And you want me to help somehow?" Becki asked; an alluring smile accompanied her now sultry tone.

Philek continued, "You have already helped us. We can now claim possession of The Princess of Stritonoly. We can sell purock art under your signature whether you create it or not."

"This abduction is not about wealth," Becki said. "If you truly know my…*reputation,* then you also know I possess telepathic powers. Your lies will betray you. Yes, I can help you…If you help me first…Now let us stop these games. Your name is not Philek. Tell me who you are."

"You are in no position to make demands of me Princess. But in the interest of beginning a cordial relationship with you, I will adhere to this request. My name is Strito."

Becki locked eyes with him, "You…are Strito?"

"Yes, I am he, the rightful Czar of Stritonoly. This is my band of mercenaries, my brothers in the reclamation of my home planet."

"If Imperial Scriptures are true, you are the Mesjasz," Becki laughed. "That is quite ridiculous…Strito, if that is your name. All educated scholars know the scriptures are fairy-tales. There is no Strito, and there is certainly no Mesjasz."

"Believe what you will," Strito said, "but your Czar holds the throne stolen from my forefathers many generations ago. He is my enemy, and I *shall* reclaim the throne…with you…or without you."

Whether he is Strito or not, Becki thought, *it doesn't matter. He certainly thinks he is, and that may be enough. His idiocy coupled with his ego may be my triumph. A misguided prophet may prove to be a useful tool in my quest for revenge.*

"We do have much in common," Becki said. "The Czar is my enemy as well. He stole from me the same as he stole from you. He took great joy in smearing my name across the galaxy."

"You have much to offer us," Strito said. "If you see us through to victory, your reward will be great."

"I can see you to victory if I so choose, but I will need something of value in return."

Strito's tone softened, "What is it you desire, Princess."

"The acidel…I want the acidel. You can have your planet….But give me the acidel. You will have all the riches of Stritonoly and complete command over the people, but I want the acidel under my rule."

"And how can I be sure you will not use them against me, or even kill them in a sudden rage of lunacy."

"Do you think me suicidal?" Becki said sharply, trying to suppress her deep resentment for this masked scoundrel. *He calls me a lunatic!* She thought. *How dare he speak to me in such a way? It is he who speaks of absurdities. He thinks he is a deity, a God…the Mesjasz…how incredibly preposterous.*

Strito continued, "We need the acidel to remain as laborers if Stritonoly should continue to prosper. If you were to damage the acidel in any way, a life of nobility and extravagance I could not offer you."

"I will kill their leader," Becki said, "of that you can be certain. Then I will have my revenge. I give you my word that you will have the acidel as your slaves, but they will forever live in misery under my leadership. Give me that, and you will claim the throne in short order. I possess all the knowledge you will need to gain victory."

"And if I refuse," Strito smiled.

"You won't," Becki said flatly, then smiled back at him. "…You won't."

Chapter 21

THE CZAR'S ROCKET-CRUISER raced ahead of the fleet and came to a stop just before the entrance to the Citadel. Unic Heldar stood at the entrance as the rest the convoy roared up behind.

The Czar's ramp lowered and two soldiers swiftly moved down the ramp ahead of Ethan.

"My Lord!" Unic exclaimed. "What brings you back so soon?"

Ethan, still drenched in moisture, wiped his eyes clean, said: "Unic, assemble the high council immediately. The dig has been cancelled."

"Where are the Sphere Three Delegates?" Unic asked, clearly perplexed.

"There are no delegates," Ethan said quickly, marching ahead of Unic into the main parlor.

A soldier brushed past Unic and whispered, "The Princess has been kidnapped."

Unic stopped in his tracks for a moment, then continued to follow his Czar. "My Lord, please explain? What is happening?"

Seeing the Czar saturated, several acidel in the main parlor rushed to hand Ethan towels. Grabbing one white towel, he didn't lose a step. He dried his face and simultaneously removed his cape. Tossing the cape down, a few acidel hurried to grab it from the floor.

Ethan reached the hall leading to his chambers, he spun back to face the soldiers filtering into the parlor.

"Stand at attention!" Ethan ordered. "Follow my command to the letter. Imperial Soldiers, form a perimeter around the Citadel, lock down all access areas and ready your defenses at once. Consider Stritonoly under attack until further notice."

The soldiers raced off in every direction.

Unic motioned for one soldier who came sprinting up to him.

"Summon the high council to the conference room immediately," Unic ordered. In a flash, the soldier tore off down the main hallway.

"Unic!" Ethan shouted, "Come with me!"

Fifteen minutes later, half dozen high council members sat nervously around a large circular conference table as Ethan and Unic advanced into the room and took their seats.

"There is no time for formalities," Ethan barked. "This meeting will be quick and decisive."

"Is it true, my lord?" one of the elderly white-robed council members asked. "Has Princess Becki been kidnapped?"

"The Princess…has been taken," Ethan said.

Gasps quickly evaporated when Ethan pounded his fist on the table and took control of the meeting.

"Let us make no mistake, this is not about Becki," Ethan said firmly. "This is about honor, our dignity in the eyes of an entire galaxy."

Unable to sit, he rose from his seat and began to pace anxiously. "Nothing of this sort has ever occurred on our planet. Whether or not Becki is worth fighting for is not the issue. I commanded the soldiers to stand down today to save her life. I am not to be thought of as a man who allowed bandits to take the life of a Stritonoly Princess on our own purock."

"What is it you want?" Unic asked respectfully. "How can the council serve you, My Lord?"

Ethan stopped pacing and stared at Unic, then at the members of the council, "You will help me by accepting what must be done. This is a clear act of war committed by these barbarians. We must ready ourselves, seek knowledge about how this happened and who they are…and then…prepare a suitable offensive response."

"You plan to attack?" Unic said. "But, My Lord, we know not who took her? Who exactly are we attacking?"

"They will surface," Ethan said confidently, "and when they do, we must be ready. This is only the beginning."

"How could you know this?" Unic asked. "Isn't it possible this was an isolated abduction. Why engage in warfare when we know so little?"

"A Princess of Stritonoly has been taken hostage under my watch," Ethan said sternly. "They took her for a reason…and now…everything has changed. I ask for your understanding…It is because we know so little that we must prepare for the worst."

Unic nodded, he knew there was wisdom in Ethan's words. The council seemed to agree. There was no way of knowing what motives lay behind this sinister act.

Ethan moved to the head of the table, placed his hands down and hung his head. "I have failed my planet miserably…I have allowed us to become jaded and reckless. We must take this kidnapping as a sign. Stritonoly will do what is necessary to preserve our way of life."

"Give us the order, my lord," Unic said.

The council stood at Unic's command, united in their allegiance to their planet and their Czar.

Ethan looked up; seeing them stand as one, a confidence surged through him as he spoke. "The order is given at this hour…Martial law has been declared by your Czar. See to it that all precautions are taken to insure our safety. Take no risks and assume no one to be an innocent."

Unic slowly lifted a fist into the air and shouted, "Long Live Stritonoly!"

The council followed suit, raising a fist and chanting in unison, "Long Live Stritonoly!"

As their fists returned to their sides, Ethan nodded his head proudly. "Thank you, my friends," he said, sincerely grateful for their obedience in this time of uncertainty and terror. Digging his boots into the ground, he turned and exited.

Out in the hall, Ethan was within earshot when he heard Unic quickly add, "Long live the Czar!"

With determination and a grand sense of purpose, the council loudly repeated, "LONG LIVE THE CZAR!"

Ethan allowed an appreciative smile to briefly wash over his face. Then, he gave an order to the young soldier marching next to him, "Find Sir Gunther! I don't care where he is or what he's doing. Find him and bring him to me…We need him now…"

Chapter 22

GUNTHER SLOWED DOWN after entering the threatening forest. With swords drawn his band of soldiers slashed away vines and moved cautiously, taking care with every step.

The tracking chip locator began to vibrate. Gunther felt it beat out a faint heartbeat on his lapel. Continuing to edge forward, climbing gently over fallen branches and distorted vines, the search party followed their leader as the vibration gradually became stronger.

Beneath their boots, the muddy surface thickened with every footfall. The forest grew steadily darker a somber fog writhing in the air.

Gunther held his hand up high, an indication for his soldiers to stop moving. Peering through the dense fog as best he could, he saw a dreary pond of sludge just ahead.

Motioning for the soldiers to come forward, they crouched down around Gunther.

"The acidel we seek is nearby," Gunther whispered. "There is a pond just ahead; our acidel runaway may well be hiding on the shoreline. Remember, your Czar wishes for him to be returned alive. Now follow me."

Little by little, like animals salivating over their prey, they quietly formed a skirmish line. With precision and intent, the highly trained soldiers sank each footprint into wet ground. A bubbly discharge oozed up from the surface and quickly evaporated into thick fog.

Josef marched next to Gunther, his pulse rapid with eager anticipation. *I am on a hunt,* Josef thought. *I will always remember the excitement of this moment. Becki will be so proud of me.*

The search party struggled to see clearly through the gloomy haze. They inched forward, approaching the lip of the pond.

Gunther's locator pounded furiously.

No movement in the forest.

No sound except the frenetic vibration of the locator.

"Something's wrong," Gunther whispered to himself.

"What is it?" Josef asked in full voice.

"You idiot!" Gunther scolded in a loud whisper, "shut your mouth and wait for my command."

Gunther walked to the shoreline, bent down and placed his hand into the murky water. The locator's vibration unnerved him as it shook his lapel. Barok had to be very, very close.

With a forward motion of his arm, he ordered two soldiers to advance.

They slowly made their way into the pond, sloshing through the slime as the black water climbed higher and higher up their torsos.

Standing close to the center of the pond, the soldiers turned and looked back at Gunther. They were waist-high in sludge.

Suddenly, one of the soldiers screamed, a sound of terror that ripped through the silence.

The soldiers in the pond whipped around in frantic circles, their heads bobbing in and out of the slime. Thrown from side to side; their blood curdling screams froze Gunther in his tracks.

Two soldiers standing on the shoreline ran into the pond in an futile attempt to save their comrades.

"No!" Gunther screamed, "Stand down, stand down!"

It was too late. This pond of doom now had four soldiers in its grasp.

Josef stared into the blackness; a panic stricken horror consumed him.

Then, the pond began to churn, thrashing ferociously and tossing the soldiers off their feet, their swords falling uselessly away.

The screaming gurgled to a stop as a crunching sound came from beneath the water. The pond turned quickly into a bloody sea of death. A violent splashing followed as body parts were thrown this way and that, rocketing out of the pond. Streams of bloody innards flailing into the forest, sticking onto tree limbs and vines.

"What is happening?" Josef yelled like a child. "Sir Gunther! What is happening?"

Gunther grabbed Josef by the arm and dragged him back from the shore's edge. Only two soldiers were left alive, they ran toward Gunther seeking instructions.

Gunther could not wait for them, he ran ahead, pulling Josef with him, fleeing for the safety of the forest.

Then, Gunther felt the pain in his head. A high pitched solid noise cut into his brain.

Josef began to cry and wail as the sound sent him into immediate convulsions. Gunther watched as Josef started to vomit violently. He knew what was happening and he had to move fast.

"Spiderons!" Gunther shouted as loud as he could. "This is a spideron ambush!"

It was too late for the soldiers behind him. A dozen spideron leapt down from high in the trees and landed on the soldiers. Hissing, the spideron tore into their victims, ripping them to pieces. Within moments, two mutilated corpses were left where soldiers once stood.

Then, their red eyes focused their attention on Gunther. They licked away the bloody remains and waited for their leader.

"What shall we do now?" Ramsitt asked, smiling from high atop a twisted tree limb. He was looking at Barok who was covered in the human blood of the soldier beneath him.

"We will go after the ones who got away," Barok hissed.

Ramsitt laughed, "Have at them, Barok...Please, Ssssssshow the way."

Barok immediately pressed his tentacles into the mud, lapped his tongue and sped off, his spideron brethren following his lead.

Gunther knew they were right behind him. Josef tripped and fell, the sound in his head tearing into him like a dagger.

"Leave me here," Josef cried, "I'm as good as dead."

"Shut up, you fool!" Gunther screamed.

With all his might he lifted Josef to his feet, threw him over his shoulders and ran as fast as he could.

Chapter 23

"How CAN I explain what I do not know?" Ethan asked, staring out the window of his study, clearly frustrated.

Unic stood with hands folded facing his Czar's back. Maintaining his composure, he spoke deliberately: "Sir Gunther gave the order before he left with the search party. It was my mistake not to seek your confirmation, I assumed you knew."

"I knew of no such order!" Ethan yelled.

Unic swallowed, peered out from beneath his weighty hood, "Regardless of if you knew or not, it has been done."

"So, what are you saying to me, stop speaking in riddles," Ethan turned to face Unic, asked: "Was the order to kill her? Is she dead?"

"Barok's acidel mate was taken into custody upon Sir Gunther's command," Unic said, careful with his words. "She is not dead…as far as I know…that is why I am asking you. I thought you knew where she might be…if she is still alive."

"I had no knowledge this even transpired," Ethan's eyes widened, he grew ever more impatient. "Find this mate of Barok's. Find her at once, bring her directly to me. Those are your orders. Do you understand?"

Unic hung his head, "I understand, my lord."

"We are not murderers," Ethan said, "We kill only when justice must be done, when our citizens need protection. We do not kill for pleasure or sport or…even revenge. Do not fail me Unic, find Barok's mate at once. If she has died without cause, we have opened a door to evil…a door we dare not enter."

Shroomy crouched down in the corner of the stale and malodorous cell. She was naked, clutching onto her legs, cold and terrified. A constant stream of tears fell unabated. Fresh wounds upon her bald head oozed white acidel blood.

She was now to pay for the crimes of her loved one. Barok had done the deed, escaped the shackles of slavery. But in doing so, he left her behind to take the fall.

Does he truly know what he's done? Shroomy thought. *He loves me too much to see me in this sort of pain. I refuse to believe, even in this moment of despair, that Barok would allow me to suffer such torment and humiliation. Please mighty Konig…please help me…*

The harrowing screams of nearby prisoners echoed through the dank cell block. One tiny hole in the black-faced doorway allowed the sound of unspeakable torture to invade her cell.

This prison of misery was well hidden. Several floors below the Citadel; this stony dungeon was the veiled stain on all things good, the place where penance for sin would be claimed unmercifully. It operated under the command of Sir Gunther and was completely unbeknownst to the Czar. Constructed in secret by only the best trained and most trusted Imperial soldiers, it had successfully remained underground and out of view. Politics and bureaucracy would have its place on the surface of Stritonoly, but here, beneath the prosperous purple mountain planet, Gunther would see that justice was always done...his way.

It was not that Gunther was an evil man, he was not. But he knew of the horrors of warfare like no other. He knew of the risk involved if punishment did not fall on those who deserved it. And most of all, he knew that no Czar, no matter how wise, could ever have knowledge of such a place. It would be Gunther's duty to run this prison, and it would also be his burden.

Shroomy felt her stomach turn. As the white blood continued to drip down, some mixed with her tears and she tasted it on her lips. The non-stop sounds of men screaming for mercy finally made her nausea unbearable. Leaning over, she threw up a clear liquid next to where she sat. Shuffling away from the smell, she repositioned herself in the adjacent corner.

Konig, I am trying, Shroomy thought. *Why have you abandoned me? Why do you allow me to suffer? I have done no wrong. I do not understand.*

Rocking herself gently, she placed her hands over her ears to muffle the increasingly tortured screams. Then she closed her eyes and prayed.

She never felt more alone.

And in this moment, prayer was all she knew.

Chapter 24

THE HIGH-PITCHED SCREAM lanced through Gunther's brain. He trudged along, knowing the pack of spideron were right behind. Ramsitt had his telepathic tentacles suffocating Gunther's thought processes. He knew he didn't have long before he would succumb to the intensifying pain. Staggering to gain his footing, holding Josef like a sack of meat on his shoulder, he could see the yellow valley just ahead.

Josef had fainted from the mental anguish the noise caused him. He bobbed on Gunther's shoulder like a ragdoll.

The spideron pack was indeed right behind them. Barok slowed his pace when he saw Gunther right before him, the pack stalking close behind.

"We have him," Barok said.

Gunther heard the hissing getting louder. He kept moving, knowing if he could get to the valley he had a chance to escape the mental torment and maybe make a run for it.

The spideron moved in quickly, jumping from tree limb to tree limb, they were close enough now to make their move.

Gunther felt their terrifying presence. He was so close to the valley, he saw the sunlight peer through the skeletal forest, the yellow grass beaming just beyond the darkness.

"SSSSSSSStop moving," Barok announced.

Perching himself atop a high thick vine, he stared down on Gunther and Josef. Dozens of spideron circled, lapping their tongues, hissing... hissing.

Gunther had no recourse left. He racked his mind trying to think of a counter defense. But his attention was compromised as the sound in his head became more and more deafening.

"I know this man," Barok said.

Ramsitt jumped up quickly and joined Barok on the vine. "SSSSSo you want this one for yourself?"

Barok smiled, "I do! This man is second in command at the Citadel. He kept me in bondage my entire life."

Gunther's mind reeled, he struggled to speak, "I have done no such thing. You're a spideron...What are you talking about?"

"I am a spideron now," Barok said. "But look into my eyes, Sir Gunther. Can you see any blue left in my new red eyes?"

Gunther dropped Josef to the ground, aware that the end was near he let out a sigh of resignation. "I know not of what you are saying. Just kill us, you rabid creatures." He clumsily drew his sword and shouted: "Come on, come for me. Kill me! But know that I will fight till my last breath. I will destroy as many of you as I am able. I spit on you and your filthy kind."

Ramsitt laughed, "This one is funny. How do you know him Barok?"

Perplexed, Gunther cocked his head to one side, "You called him Barok? Why would you say that?"

Barok looked again at Gunther. As their eyes met, a realization filtered into Gunther's brain. He stammered, "This...is...Barok?"

Ramsitt smiled, "Yessssss...He is the one you seek. But you are too late. The spideron have accepted him. He has been transformed in the same pond that sent your men to the depths of hell. And now, you will pay for what you have done to the acidel. You will pay with your blood; you will pay with your life!"

Gunther smiled, then he laughed. At first just a slow morbid laugh that quickly turned knowing and sinister. "If this is truly Barok, then go ahead and let him kill me."

Ramsitt did not find this response amusing, "He will kill you, and I will enjoy watching him do it. Just like your friends in the Citadel, you are truly a mad man. The universe will be served well by your elimination."

"Yes, kill me Barok," Gunther laughed. "And when you do, know that you have killed more than just me on this day."

"What are you saying?" Barok asked.

Gunther stood up tall, lost his smile and spoke with certainty, "I have your mate...Shroomy is under my watch. Kill me and she will die. I am the only one who knows where she is. Even the Czar does not know. If I do not return to the Citadel, she will be viciously tortured and killed long before you ever get to her. Of course, you don't have to believe me...Go ahead, kill me and you'll find out. You'll find out when you are standing over her rotting corpse."

"You are a liar!" Barok screamed, turning to seek advice from Ramsitt, "He is lying. Tell me he is lying!"

Ramsitt could not lie to his new brother. For the first time, he looked compassionately at Barok, "This man speaks the truth." Then, he turned his attention to Gunther, said: "Damn you human of the Citadel!"

Ramsitt's eyes turned solid red and he began to tremble.

Gunther screamed, dropped his sword and fell to his knees. Pressing his fists into the side of his head, the high stream of noise within his brain rocked his very core.

Barok was torn, unable to suppress his feelings for Shroomy. Seeing Gunther die might mean the end to her.

"Please, Ramsitt," Barok pleaded, "please release him…You must know not to interfere with love! My love is deep for my Shroomy. I cannot see her die because of my doing."

Gunther fell backward as Ramsitt released his mental grasp.

"I do know love," Ramsitt whispered, "And I seek not to be unjust. But remember what I told you, Barok…Before this day is over, you will truly know regret. There is no turning back. Fate will swing past us and keep to its path. We are but witnesses to what must be done."

Barok could not understand exactly what this meant. But for the moment, at least Gunther was alive.

Barok asked Ramsitt with great respect, "If he lives…if…you allow him to live…Will Shroomy survive?"

Ramsitt's eyes closed, he whispered, "Even if I know the answer, I will not tell you. Should I tell you it would steer the course of destiny away from its rightful conclusion. To show my appreciation and to garner your loyalty to my tribe, I will let him go if you swear your life to my tribe."

"Yes," Barok answered quickly, "please, just allow this one to go free."

"I do this to earn your loyalty. Now…Before my tribe you must swear your allegiance…swear it to your death."

"I swear it," Barok said without hesitation.

Ramsitt smiled, "I will let him go…for now." Then he stared at Gunther who slowly sat up, beginning to gather his senses.

"Look at me!" Ramsitt demanded. "Stand up you Citadel scum and look at me."

Gunther struggled to his feet, raised his eyes and spoke with hatred in his voice, "Let me go and I give you my word, I will not be grateful. I will see you die one day…But not before I make you suffer for what you have done."

"You are brainless, obtuse, and not worthy a response," Ramsitt said. "Now take your leave, you fool."

Gunther staggered again, regained his footing and picked Josef off the mud and onto his shoulders. Before turning away, he spoke, "We will meet again."

"Of that you can be sure," Ramsitt hissed.

And with that, Gunther fled.

"There is one thing I know for certain," Ramsitt said to Barok as they watched Gunther carry Josef out into the valley. "I assure you, we will see that vile human meet his end whether Shroomy lives or dies, if not today…soon, very soon. His stupidity will prove to be an asset to us. Let him go back to the Citadel, he will cause nothing but harm. It is his way…it is the way of all humans."

"Thank you, Ramsitt," Barok said, a hint of his acidel tone surprisingly ringing through, "you are most gracious."

Hearing the meek acidel sound come from Barok's spideron body, Ramsitt spoke with some disdain: "You have received a favor from your new leader. Do not ask for another."

Chapter 25

A BLUE RING of fine particles circled Acidonia.

This halo of superb brilliance could only be appreciated when observed from afar. It was made up of trillions of stray gaseous particles deposited over many millennia. Up close, atmospheric conditions obscured the halo to the human eye. And like all moons in this quadrant of space, Acidonia appeared like any other...it was not.

Strito's spacecraft slowed as it approached the dark side of the moon planet. Propulsion ceased and his globular white starship floated down onto the stony surface.

They were on the far-side of the moon, invisible to Stritonoly. They were ready now to set up a temporary command station. As the ship touched down, a giant hatch on the underbelly of the ship popped open and out poured Strito's black-masked crew.

Quickly, the crew unloaded dozens of SCP's, also known as Sound Compliant Planks. They began to assemble a makeshift shack that would serve as a temporary war room. Yards of thick canvas on heavy rolls were thrown over the planks and nailed into place on the moon's surface. Then a crew member set down a small acoustic barrel in the center of the structure. Using beams of sound, the shack lifted from the surface, suspended by the low hum which echoed from the acoustic barrel.

"This is stupid," Becki said, standing next to Strito on the flight deck. "Why are you making a fort outside when we have a ship?"

Strito moaned, "This is being done for you, we have no problem with the ship. I thought holding a meeting onboard a ship filled with dead bodies would not suit a Princess."

Becki smiled sardonically.

"But that was before I knew of your obvious penchant for blood," Strito said. "I'll know better in the future."

"Are you suspecting they'll come back to life and stab you in your sleep?" Becki added. "You men and your wars: Why must you make things more complex than they already are?"

Strito offered her a half-smile. He liked her and couldn't deny it. "Princess, I am truly looking forward to getting to know you better. But they are waiting for us."

"Who is waiting?" Becki asked.

"My crew and...something else."

Taking Becki by the arm, Strito lowered her down the hatch, jumped down and followed close behind. The shack was only a few feet from the spaceship. A member of Strito's crew held open the crudely made canvas doorway as they entered. The low hum of the acoustic barrel pulsated within the structure.

Strito grabbed Becki again by the arm and ushered her to a seat at the head of a small wooden table. On the table sat a dirty large silver box, presently locked shut. Several members of the crew found seats around the table. One man, thin and masked like the rest remained standing opposite Becki.

Strito leaned back in his seat and crossed his legs. He nodded his head in the direction of the thin man.

"Princess Becki," the thin man said in a scratchy high tenor voice. "Welcome to the moon planet, Acidonia. My name is Chlochelle. I am a theoretical physicist employed by Czar Strito."

Becki smirked, "He is not the Czar yet."

Chlochelle ignored her comment and continued, "I have been brought here to tell you about Czar Strito's discovery."

"You see, Princess," Strito interrupted, "you are not the only means we have to take Stritonoly. Do not overestimate your importance. If you mind your manners, we can and will utilize you…but as you will soon see, we don't need you."

She sat up straight, turned her face smugly away from Strito, flaunting her arrogance for all to see. "You would have killed me by now," she said confidently, "you do need me."

"Perhaps," Strito said, "perhaps not…"

Reaching for the silver box, Chlochelle gently spun it to face Becki. "Allow me to show you something," he said. Taking a key from his pocket, he opened the lock on the front of the box and slowly raised the lid.

Becki needed to sit forward to see inside the box. As a stunning blue light shot out from the box, she peered in curiously and asked, "So… What am I looking at?"

Inside the box, encased behind a protective sheet of glass, sat a blue egg no bigger than a peach stone. It radiated a magnificent blue light and seemed to be shaking, throwing itself back and forth around the box without breaking or changing shape.

"This was given to me," Strito said, "when I was only a boy."

"Given to you because you are the Mesjasz?" Becki asked.

"So they say," Strito answered assuredly. "And I have no doubt you know of the prophecies surrounding my return."

"The Mesjasz will possess a great ally," Becki said, quoting the Imperial Scriptures, "a collaborator seeking evenhandedness. The Mesjasz shall be sheltered by that which is not of human form."

"It is something to be feared," Chlochelle added, "from what we have learned about this object, it crashed down on Acidonia over a thousand years ago. And it has been growing ever since." Quickly, he slammed the box lid shut and locked it again. "There is more energy inside that small blue egg than can be held inside a billion star systems."

"What does that mean?" Becki asked.

Chlochelle didn't answer.

There was a long silence before Strito finally spoke. "What it means Princess…is that I hold the end of the universe in my hands."

Chapter 26

THE JOURNEY FROM the valley back to the Citadel was a blur. Gunther plodded along as if by instinct. His mind still recovering from the cerebral onslaught Ramsitt had inflicted upon him.

Seeing Gunther emerge from the trail in the forest, several soldiers guarding the Citadel quickly rushed forward to assist.

"Take this boy for treatment," Gunther demanded; exhaustion in his grumbled tone. Two soldiers grabbed Josef's limp body and immediately ran off with him.

Another soldier made the mistake of trying to help Gunther. He placed his arm around Gunther's back in an attempt to help him.

"Take your hands off me!" Gunther shouted, throwing the soldier to the ground. "Clear my way, I must see the Czar at once."

Staggering and weary, Gunther made his way into the Citadel. Almost in a trance, he marched directly to the Czar's study.

When he got there, he shoved two guards at the door to the side and didn't bother to knock. Flinging the door open, Gunther saw Ethan sitting behind his desk.

"Barok got away," Gunther announced.

Ethan sat back in his chair, "Please explain."

"The search party fell victim to a spideron ambush. They claim to have taken Barok as one of their own."

"And what of your men?" Ethan asked.

Gunther swallowed hard, "Four have been killed by the wretched creatures. Mutilated and spat out by a pond of transformation."

Ethan closed his eyes and sat quietly for several seconds.

"Come in," he said finally, "and close the door."

Gunther closed the door behind him and hobbled over to a chair opposite Ethan's desk.

The two men sat there in contemplation, both of them struggling to absorb the events of the morning. And in that silence, Gunther lowered his head, feeling it pound faster and harder. The pain of a relentless drumbeat smashing into his core.

Ethan sighed and spoke, though he wasn't sure where to begin or where his thoughts might lead him, "We have greater concerns. The escape of an acidel is insignificant now."

Gunther's head popped up, "Insignificant?" he asked, surprised by his Czar's retort.

Ethan leaned forward, said "The Princess has been kidnapped. There was no delegation from Sphere Three. Becki was abducted a short time ago. This is clearly an act of war against Stritonoly. A missing acidel is of little importance now."

Gunther straightened in his seat, tried to focus through a bewildering haze, "I am confused. Why would anyone want to kidnap Becki?"

"I do not know the answer. But rest assured; this is part of a much bigger plan. Even naïve bandits would not dare steal a Princess unless there was a long term reward involved."

"I shall summon my best men to draft strategic plans at once."

"Yes…you will do that. But first, something has been brought to my attention. You must answer to your Czar."

Gunther's eyes shot a glare that ripped through Ethan, insulted by the manner in which he was being addressed. His head still rocked by an agony he could not decipher.

Without pause, Ethan continued, "Where is she?" Ethan asked calmly.

"Becki is gone," Gunther said flatly, "That is what you just told me. Are you playing a game with me?"

Ethan breathed heavily, raised his voice, "I am not talking about Becki."

Gunther knew what Ethan meant; he wanted to know where Shroomy was.

"I do not know of what you speak," Gunther lied.

"I will ask you once more…and I trust that you will think before you answer me again…Where is Barok's mate?"

Gunther raised an eyebrow and acted confused. "I would assume she is with the other acidel," Gunther said innocently.

"Unic tells a different tale."

"What does Unic have to do with this?" Gunther asked. Defiance now filled him.

"He tells me he heard an order from you, an order I did not give."

"I gave no order concerning Barok's mate, none whatsoever," Gunther's tone stiffened, "I am insulted you would think I betray you in any way. I would never issue an order without your approval. Unic was mistaken."

"Do not let me find out something on my own," Ethan warned. "We have served Stritonoly side by side for many years. I will defend you and your honor with my very own blood…But, I will not be lied to."

Gunther's anger consumed him. He shouted, "I gave no order!"

"You raise your voice as a criminal might."

"Or a supremely loyal soldier," Gunther added. "How can you accuse me of such insubordination? I have never lied to you, I never will."

Ethan looked deep into Gunther's eyes. He could not tell if he was being told the truth or not. Presently it would have to wait. Gunther was an invaluable resource. In this time of war, he was needed badly.

"Forgive me," Ethan said, "It was necessary that I ask. I must admit, this whole silly business of an acidel escape coupled with our new dilemma has put a strain on my reasoning. Unic has been known to stretch the truth for his own purposes. You are a loyal friend. I am sorry for doubting you."

Gunther felt Ethan's words were fallacious. But he would leave it be.

It didn't matter anyway. Regardless of what Ethan thought, Shroomy would soon be dead, her body burned to ashes, her remains scattered into the abyss.

Chapter 27

BAROK LAY ON the shoreline of the pond of transformation. His eyes shut and tongue lapping; he drifted into a dream-state.

Acidel by the thousands swarmed through his sub-conscious, frolicking through an open meadow, multi-colored butterflies drifting by. The sun cast an orangey-yellow glow upon smiling faces. Barok stood in the center of it all, laughing as he saw Shroomy in a flowery dress playing with several small acidel children and giggling loudly.

Barok began to spin, taking in the sweet aroma of nature's beauty, absorbed by the immense radiance of unconditional love. All was calm, beautiful, all was as it should it be.

He chuckled with abandoned bliss, the acidel simplicity coursing through his veins. Seeing Shroomy devour the adoration of the acidel children made him so proud. He watched as his friends all gathered around him, offering compliments and kind words, hugs and handshakes.

Then, suddenly, a high-pitched clatter reverberated throughout the meadow.

The acidel froze.

Shroomy reached for the children, pulled them close to her, sheltering them from the terrifying sound as they began to cry.

The deep monotone growl of the acidel grew louder and louder. The sky flashed a bright white light. A lightning bolt shot across the skyline, twisted in the air and crashed down next to Shroomy. The frightened children screamed and fell on their sides as sparks flew up.

Another bolt crashed into the surface, this one igniting an inferno in its wake. Flames spread recklessly throughout the meadow. Smoke and ash danced together feverishly toward the sky.

Blackness came over the horizon, rapidly inching up and enveloping the sun. Flashes of bloody acidel corpses flew in and out of focus, screams of terror and death.

Barok looked down at his hands, but the hands he once knew were gone. He looked down to see his own bloody tentacles twitching with a ferocity he could not comprehend. The lust for blood consumed him.

Then he saw Shroomy.

He lunged toward her as she stared at him innocently.

Leaping onto her, the children pounded fists unto his backside in a weak attempt to drive off his attack.

His lust for blood was absolute. It was a lust for the blood of only one; the blood of Shroomy.

He bit into her stomach, white acidel blood pouring onto his spideron face, bloodshot eyes blinking unmercifully. He felt no loss, no compassion, and no love. He wanted death to all those around him. Anything that was close to him needed to be destroyed. It was not a decision; it was a primitive compulsion, a yearning that would not be denied.

As Shroomy gagged a mouthful of white acidel blood, Barok grinned and continued to eat into her rubbery flesh. The cries of the children only enticed him to continue his rampage as the flames grew higher and higher.

"I am not an acidel!" Barok screamed.

Hunched over Shroomy's lifeless body, drenched in white blood, Barok grunted as the other acidel looked on in horror. They were motionless as Barok waited for them to advance through the fire. They didn't. They just stared at him, their wide eyes casting judgment on their former brother. No words were necessary; Barok knew they had forsaken him. He was not one of them. Now and forever more, he would be treated as an outsider by the species he once claimed as his own.

He smiled at this prospect, he didn't need them, he didn't need anyone. He was a spideron now, and he would harness the power to absolve himself from all sins…even murder.

"I have found freedom," Barok yelled above the crackling flames, "and you are all jealous. I should have known better than to think you would be happy for me. No, you are all selfish and think of nothing but your duty. I have found peace. Finally, I am free. You deserve to be left for dead. And I will laugh as you rot away into nothingness!"

The throng of acidel stood motionless as flames melted their tender features, burning away flesh to reveal gooey white blood caked over bare-boned faces.

And then, with a whipping splash of sludge-filled water hitting his face, Barok left his dream.

Panting, he opened his bloodshot eyes to see Ramsitt standing over him.

The screams of terror silenced, the flames no more, only a hazy stream of fog separated Ramsitt's stare from Barok.

"It was all so real," Barok said, still half asleep.

"I saw it too," Ramsitt said, "I am one with you now. Your thoughts are my burden as well."

"You saw my dream?" Barok asked.

"No," Ramsitt smiled, "I did not need to see it, I created it. That dream was made for you by me. And I will construct all your dreams until you have learned."

Barok became alert and asked the obvious, "What is it I need to learn?"

"That you are no longer an acidel, that you can never go back…And you cannot save them…and…you cannot save her."

Barok turned his head away from Ramsitt, burying it under several muddy tentacles.

"So now you hide from me?" Ramsitt asked with a mocking tone. "I claim you as my brother, I give you new life…and you hide from me?"

What have I done? Barok thought, *my actions will destroy my own kind…my own beloved. I thoughtlessly left Shroomy behind to pay for my crime…I have killed my own…I have killed my Shroomy… What have I done?*

"SSSSSSSSo now you know," Ramsitt hissed.

"What do I know?" Barok whimpered.

Ramsitt leaned in close and whispered the one word that would haunt Barok for the rest of time, "Regret…Yessssssssss! Now you know regret…regret…regret…sssssssss!"

Chapter 28

IMPERIAL SCRIPTURES OF THE PLANET STRITONOLY: SUBDIVISION 14: VS. 72-101

The Mesjasz will be born into a poor family. He will be of foreign tongue at birth but genetically he will be of Stritonoly blood.

He will claim ownership of the kingdom upon his arrival and none shall dare disobey.

Failure to observe his law will result in the harshest penalty. His wrath shall be mighty and merciless.

For He; the one true Mesjasz will carry in his possession the fruit of rebirth and the seed of destruction. It will be one in the same. His wisdom and our compliance will determine which of these powers he will use.

He will receive this inheritance as his birthright but will wait until maturity to unveil its almighty splendor. And when he offers proof of his gift, you shall fall upon your knees and beg forgiveness for all the wrong you have done.

It is written that The Mesjasz will take to the throne unchallenged.

For a challenger to his throne will be cast from this universe into eternal suffering.

"It doesn't matter if you believe or not," Strito said, sitting on the floor, legs crossed, just outside Becki's cage.

"It should matter to you greatly," Becki answered, standing inside the cage aboard the ship, slowly brushing her fingers through her long blonde hair. Her pink dress was filthy, purple purock dust mixed with dirty splotches. "I cannot believe you would dare toss me back into this cell! I attended your meeting, and I gave you my word that I would help. I have done nothing to deserve this sort of treatment."

"This is for your protection as well," Strito said calmly. "My men are loyal to me, but they do not yet see the need for you. It is in your best interest to remain where I can see you at all times."

"You think I cannot take care of myself?"

"Not against men such as these."

She watched as Strito's crew began picking up the dead bodies, dragging them away. "I am not a meek Princess. And if you believe the tales they tell of me, then you know I am a warrior as well, a warrior that you should not test. Your men do not scare me…and neither do you."

"If you knew of the battles we have fought, the things we have done…you might change your mind."

Becki moved to edge of the cage. She crossed her legs and sat down on the floor facing Strito. "I may come to believe…some day. But you have done little to convince me."

Strito looked up, impossible to tell what emotion he was displaying. His black mask was lifeless, solid, a rock of armor covering his true identity.

"Can you take that off?" Becki asked.

Strito sighed, "My mask remains on until I have claimed the throne. It is forbidden for anyone to cast eyes upon the Mejasz until such a time."

"You think showing me an egg inside a silver box will convince me of your claim?" Becki asked, not scornfully, she was serious.

"Like I said, it matters not if you believe. I know the truth. That is all that matters."

"Do you not wish to convince me?"

"You will know…in time."

"Perhaps," Becki said, resigning to the fact that she was under his control, for now. "What will you do with it?" she asked, the most respectful tone she had offered him thus far.

"It is not for you to know," Strito answered. "When the time comes, the die shall be cast."

"And you will destroy it all?" Becki asked, genuinely curious.

Strito said nothing, his lifeless mask unmoving.

Becki looked away, leaned back against the side of the cage, continuing to stroke her hair with her fingertips. "I'm hungry."

"You will eat when we have emptied and cleaned the ship."

Becki's tone hardened, "If you want my assistance, then it would suit you to make me an ally."

Strito sat still for a moment. Then he got up, walked into an adjacent room and returned with a small piece of fruit. Sticking his arm inside the cage, he plopped in down onto Becki's lap. "For you Princess, it's an exotic fruit from my home planet. It is called Gullie. Try it, it is most delicious."

Becki picked up the squishy beige fruit, smelled it, and took a small bite.

"Do you approve?" Strito asked.

Becki swallowed, "It'll do…thank you."

"We are not enemies Princess," Strito said, and from the sound of his voice, Becki sensed him to be true.

"I do not wish to be enemies," Becki agreed, "but I also do not wish to be caged like an animal."

"I will see what can be done," Strito said, an assuredness in his voice. "Give my crew time to understand your worth. Then you will be free to roam the ship. In spite of what you have seen, I am a peaceful man. My men are inherently peaceful as well. But make no mistake; they believe in my power and my ultimate destiny, they will do anything to see our mission through. Your best efforts will not corrupt them."

"I seek to harm no one that will give me what I desire. I seek revenge, you seek the throne. It is a fair trade."

"Perhaps…" Strito said softly.

"You must give me your word!" Becki demanded. "Give me your word as the Mesjasz that I will have my revenge."

"I have done so," Strito said, "I will give you the acidel, but they will remain as slaves."

"I want your word as the Mesjasz, I want to hear you say it. The Mesjasz cannot break a solemn vow. It is written in the scriptures. If I am to truly believe you are who you say, I want to hear your make a solemn vow before all things."

"I thought you didn't believe in the scriptures."

"You test me. Do not do that! If you are truly him, your vow will offer proof."

"I will make this vow," Strito said, "you have my word that when all things are in place, I will make this solemn vow to you…And then you will know…I am truly the one and only Majesz."

Chapter 29

JOSEF LAY FACE up on a stretcher-bed in a small lime green cubicle. Two thick bandages wrapped each ear. A single wire attached to his bare chest kept track of his vital signs. The air in the cubicle was dense, filled with the odor of a pungent drug meant to slowly bring him out of his trance-like state and also produce a slight euphoria.

"I…have …failed," Josef muttered.

"Rest my boy," Unic whispered, standing next to the bed.

"I…have…failed…her," Josef said, his eyes blinking back to consciousness.

"You are delirious my boy," Unic said, "but you will be fine. You've suffered a traumatic brain injury, you were bleeding badly from both ears when they brought you in, but you've been treated, you will recover."

Josef's eyes opened to see Unic Heldar bent over him, only his shining eyes visible with his hood pulled up.

"It…hurts so much." Josef whimpered. "What happened to me?"

"You were the victim of a spideron attack," Unic answered. "It will take some time before you are on your feet again."

Recognizing Unic, Josef said, "Master Heldar, Why are you here?"

"I visit all injured soldiers when I am able. I consider it part of my duty. And you, so young, a newly appointed soldier, of course I wanted to be here when you awoke."

"Thank you," Josef said, his voice scratchy and dry.

"Can you tell me what you remember?" Unic asked.

Is he hunting for something? Josef thought.

"I don't remember very much," Josef answered.

"It would be helpful to know whatever you can recall."

"I wish I could help you Master Heldar, but I'm afraid I cannot. I must see Sir Gunther."

"Sir Gunther will want to see you as well I'm sure. From what I understand, you owe your life to him. He was the one who carried you back to the Citadel."

I remember, Josef thought. *The soldiers were chewed up by that pond. Then…I don't recall, I must have been wounded in the attack and blacked out. I am sure I fought bravely. Becki will be so proud of me!*

"It is important that I see Sir Gunther right away," Josef pleaded, the tone of his voice sharpening, his head throbbing incessantly.

"You must rest, my boy. And…I need to ask you a few questions about your search…Did you find Barok? Did you see him at all?

"No…we did not come across any acidel."

"Yes, I see…Did the subject of Barok's female mate come up?" Unic asked.

"I'm not sure what you mean Master Heldar…" Josef answered, legitimately puzzled.

"It's a simple question," Unic continued, "I want to know if Sir Gunther talked about Barok's mate…This is not a trick or a trap young boy, I am simply asking you a question."

"Why don't you ask me?" Gunther announced, standing in the doorway.

Unic quickly straightened. Spinning around to see the massive frame of Gunther taking up the entire doorway, he greeted him sarcastically, "Sir Gunther, you've come to see the boy…how nice of you."

"Mind your tongue Unic," Gunther shouted, "You sicken me!"

"I am confused. You are angry with me? I have done you no wrong."

"You question a wounded soldier without my permission."

"I seek the truth. Barok's mate was sent off to be killed, like many, many others before her. I am a servant of Stritonoly, not you. And what you are doing is not what the Czar wishes."

Gunther laughed, "And I am to believe you know what the Czar wishes?"

"So you do not deny it then. You have taken her without an order from your Czar."

"I have done no such thing," Gunther smiled, his head still pounding, the pain clogging his thoughts. "I am a soldier, and I will do what I must to protect our kingdom. You know nothing of this service. How dare you make judgments on me."

"I seek the truth, and I seek justice, even for the acidel."

"You are ignorant and foolish," Gunther spat on the ground at Unic's feet. "That is what I think of you and your council. I do not need to answer to you, now leave me with my soldier. You have no business here."

"The Czar will think otherwise," Unic said as he moved away from the bedside. Gunther walked in allowing Unic to pass through the open door. Looking back into the cubicle, Unic added, "I will bring this up with the Czar at once. You will have to answer for your behavior here today, Sir Gunther."

"Be gone from here," Gunther shouted, throwing his hands up

toward the door.

"I told him nothing," Josef said as soon as Unic left.

"There is nothing to tell," Gunther said, hunched over the bedside. "You've done well, but there are greater concerns now. Unic, and all the high council for that matter, they know nothing of what we do for the sake of this planet. Never be swayed by their political agendas. You only need answer to me."

"I will do you proud," Josef said.

Gunther pulled up a chair next to the bedside and breathed in the smell of the drug which filled the room. Closing his eyes, he whispered, "Get your rest young soldier. For it is rest you will need… the time of war is upon us."

Chapter 30

Acidonia was cold at night, the wind whipping up dust clouds of blue matter. In the distance, the northern sun diminished over Stritonoly's crescent horizon.

Strito's crew switched off the acoustic barrel and watched as the shack fell into the surface. They hurriedly grabbed their gear and retreated to the safety of the ship.

Chlochelle held the dirty silver box close to his chest, the egg resting comfortably inside. With the assistance of the crew, he was lifted into the underbelly hatch where Strito was waiting for him on the flight deck.

"You ok?" Strito asked.

"Oh yes, I'm fine," Chlochelle answered, "I will bring the egg to the safe now."

"You did well," Strito said, patting Chlochelle on the back. "Take the night off and get some sleep. You can resume your study in the morning."

"Thank you sir," Chlochelle said, thankful for the respite. "I am quite tired after the events of this day. I will lock the egg securely before I retire."

"Thank you Chlochelle, you are a fine servant and I will not forget your tireless work."

"No thanks is necessary sir, my studies are for the benefit of us all."

Strito nodded as Chlochelle made his way to the rear of the ship where a giant metal safe would hold the silver box.

Chlochelle had been studying the egg for over a decade. He met Strito more than twenty years earlier when they were both students in an advanced science academy for gifted youth. It was there, they developed a close friendship. So close, that Strito eventually trusted him enough to make him the sole researcher in the analysis of the egg.

After exposing the egg to a variety of experiments, Chlochelle soon came to realize the importance of his task. The egg emitted energy levels that could not be read even on the most highly developed detectors in the galaxy. He knew from the start that this egg needed to be guarded, treated with respect, and feared.

He reached the back room of the ship, unlocked the safe and carefully placed the box inside. Satisfied that the day was successful in every way imaginable, he yawned, turned, and went straight to his bed.

Becki's head pressed against the cage. She slept as Strito stood there staring at her, admiring her beauty, her torn and twisted complexities, her defensive wall of insecurity. She was more than he thought she'd be, a child filled with hatred, but beneath that, a woman driven to put her past behind. He would take her in and do what he must to change her way of thinking. Grabbing a small silk pillow, he reached inside the cage, gently moved her head forward and placed the pillow behind her.

"Thank you," Becki mumbled; her eyes still closed.

"Sleep well, Princess," Strito whispered.

He waited a long moment, making sure she fell back to sleep. Then he turned and headed to the front of the ship.

Outside the open window, through the blue dust clouds kicking up all around, he saw the purple halo which drifted over Stritonoly. Space now sat in darkness, all was still. There would be no fighting tonight. On this night, there would be rest for all, the day was over and the new day would bring an avalanche of planning, strategic maneuvering, and yes, the advent of war. Strito knew this had to happen, and yet, he was not at all prepared to see the loss he knew would incur. Death was an extreme price to pay, and he knew many would die in the battles ahead. It was inevitable, but it was the way of things.

Ethan stared out the triangular window of his bedroom. In a long white night robe, he was dressed for bed, ready to escape into sleep for just a few hours. He looked out into the night sky, wondering what the future might bring, the wounds still so fresh from a day of turmoil.

The stars never left the night sky. They just burned and burned, forever casting their light on the sins of men. Hardhearted and uncaring it would appear, and for Ethan, on this night, he wished they would speak to him. But there would be no response from the dead stars that shone upon his weary face. They would only watch as the human race began their final war, a war with no victor and no heroes. This final war would come to an end one day. But there would be no survivors, only blackness in a void where the human race once lived.

Deep in the skeletal forest of the spideron, Barok squatted down amidst his new brothers in a tight pack as they prepared for sleep.

Placing his head down slowly onto the muddy surface, he wondered where Shroomy was on this night. He knew he had left her behind and she would ultimately have to answer for him. He tried to suppress any feeling of love. It was easier to forget about it all, but he was unable to let go of his feelings.

Closing his eyes, he feared the night ahead of him. He would dream. A dream not of his own making. And Ramsitt would be there, in his mind, manipulating his thoughts in a way that would change him forever.

He would try to stay awake as long as could. And if luck was on his side, maybe he would never sleep again. But he knew this wasn't the truth. And he knew in his heart, that nothing would ever be the same again. Ramsitt was right, there was no going back.

What Barok didn't know on that night was the shocking ramifications his actions would have on the fate of the universe. And as he started to dream, none among them could possible imagine the vital role he would come to play. As darkness consumed all things, the beginning of the end drew near.

EPILOGUE

I CANNOT HELP *you anymore,* the blue egg thought. *The mighty reflection has sent me to eradicate you. And the time of your apocalypse has come. You had the chance to notice me, to care, but you chose not to. You passed me by many, many times. And though I tried to make you see; you could not. I will cry for you when you are but a faded memory.*

Only one species prayed to me, but now I cannot even save them. Everything must be destroyed so the reflection can begin life anew. You must know by now that I will never die. I will always remain true to the only thing left, our faith. My name is Konig forever more.

Inside the metal safe aboard Strito's ship the silver box began to shake. The time was upon them. The infinitesimal speck which had been growing for over a thousand years was now ready to be born.

Suddenly, a thunderous explosion ripped the safe door from its hinges.

The egg cracked open…

The war had begun.

The Last Czar of
Stritonoly

PROLOGUE

The entryway rocked shut behind them. Ethan glared through fog into the blackness below.

"Why have I not been told?" he asked.

The soldiers escorting him kept silent, they knew better than to utter a sound. Their green and black capes were soiled with purple purock dust; their faces bore the weariness from a long and bitter night of fighting. They were hollow men with no ideals of their own, stripped naked by a higher cause they were so easily brainwashed to obey. Their higher cause was loyalty, misguided as it was.

Ethan stood on the top step of the twirling stairway and looked down, the stony entrance closed at his back, the stink of stale blood everywhere, the eeriness of ever-present ghosts floating in circles about his head.

"Why was I not told?" Ethan yelled, no longer a rhetorical question, his voice echoing through the corridors of pain awaiting his inspection at the bottom of the stairs.

He received only silence as he stared at each soldier with disdain. It was not their fault; he knew intuitively they were only following orders. Had it not been for Ethan's personal curiosity into this matter, this dungeon would have remained shrouded in secrecy, perhaps forever.

"I am not a fool," Ethan howled, "Do you think me mad? Do you think I would ever approve of a place such as this?" Uncharacteristic of his noble grace, he spat upon the filthy stone, which covered the stairs. "This is a sickening disgrace! You who knew of this, you who have pretended to serve with honor, you have betrayed yourself. You have betrayed Stritonoly!"

Tearing ahead of his entourage, Ethan ran down the stairs and rushed from cell to cell. His eyes cast down on images of horror; despair and unimaginable misery, contorted, mutilated bodies, burnt flesh, contraptions of torture designed by the very hand of evil. Men and women; even children pleading for mercy, and Acidel slaves by the hundreds! However, they made no sound because they had no mouths. There was only silence as blood dripped over Ethan's vision until he could see no more. A thick haze catapulted over him like a wave of immorality, he felt his life leave him as the dungeon set ablaze.

GASP!

Ethan shot up in bed, clutching his pillow, his chest heaving, his face adorned with droplets of clammy sweat. His eyes rocketed about the room, no one was there; he was alone in the royal chambers of the citadel. It was only dream, a night terror, of which he was all too familiar. This dream haunted him since the outbreak of the war, and it would not set him free, strangling his sensibilities, mocking his integrity.

Clutching onto his pillow as if it were a close friend, or a mate he wished he made time for, he gathered himself and went to his private bathroom. Picking up a candle on the way, he placed it on a wooden countertop above a golden faucet and sink. Tossing his pillow to the floor, he splashed water onto his face and breathed easier.

Looking at his reflection in the mirror, he could not help but notice the aged and deflated man staring back at him. He was lost again, confused as ever with all logic abandoning him. After countless adjustments and change, he was still the same; the mirage of his own transformation did not fool him on this night. He knew who he was. He was only a man, and like all men, he was the bearer of inadequacy and eventual doom.

The struggle with the complexities of his existence, and the existence of all things, had now consumed him, and it was growing unbearable. He was not the man he thought he was. He tricked himself into thinking he could be a great ruler. But it was not in his inherit make-up to lead men into battle, or to lead men ultimately to their death. Gazing at the reflection of his deep-set blue eyes and thinning white hair, he saw that life was reeling away from him.

Moreover, what will my legacy be? He wondered. Will there be a legacy at all? Will anyone even care to reflect on a life so tormented by the unanswered and the unattainable?

He would leave behind an unresolved war and a diminished planet under his rule. An old man and his fears would destroy all that he once thought possible in reckless youth.

Ethan Educai, The Last Czar of Stritonoly, would not live another year.

Chapter 1

After the final conflict, there will be no human will be left alive. Their dust scattered to the wind, their memory only that of a civilization that could have been.
~ Taken from the memoirs of Queen Shroomy;
Ruler of the Last World

"REMAIN IN FLANK right formation," Sir Gunther ordered, standing tall, in defiance of the laser beams shooting just over his head. "We will lure them in," he shouted, "Make them think we are retreating, and then we will jump them from every angle. We will destroy our enemies and leave nothing but their rotting corpses behind. Let the galaxy take head and bear witness to our triumph over these scoundrels. When they are within reach, attack on my command!"

As purple dust flew through the early evening violet skyline, The River Frehenly served as the backdrop for this inevitable standoff. Light pellets of rain splashed into the rolling river as threatening clouds spilled over the horizon.

Strito's men were advancing on foot, marching with laser guns in hand, and firing straight into hordes of well-hidden imperial soldiers stretched out along the river's edge. Gunther chose this spot to make a stand, stop them now before they could get any closer to the citadel and his men knew this terrain better than anyone did. They used giant boulders and recesses in the land mass for cover as laser blasts continued to fire relentlessly, missing them and exploding harmlessly into the river behind.

"We are but moments away from immortality," Gunther said, turning to see Josef's petrified expression. Being an imperial soldier for less than a year, Josef was not in formation with the rest of the men, he stood next to Gunther who towered over him.

Gunther smiled, "Tonight, there will be dancing in the streets! Do you not agree, young lad?"

"Of course, I agree," Josef shouted back.

He tried desperately to appear confidant but ducked quickly as a barrage of laser shots flew by his head and smashed into a boulder, the stimulation of battle clearly overwhelming his juvenile sensibilities.

"My boy," Gunther said, a fatherly tone in his husky voice, "We have been through much together since the spideron ambush. I want you to watch this confrontation closely and as our enemies perish, remember; these are the men who kidnapped Princess Becki. It is time now to avenge that crime. Besides, you cannot barter with madmen. And Strito has made it clear he won't stop until Stritonoly is his own... And that will never happen!"

"I am with you," Josef said, a splatter of rain trickling onto his frightened eyelids. "I am with you until victory or death."

Not at all convinced by Josef's dishonest response, Gunther turned his back on the lad and shouted to his troops, "We have our swords, we do not need the barbaric laser guns of our ancestors to prove our might. Strito will fall on this day! Allow me to pierce his sinister heart with my dagger. May we turn this river red with the blood of our enemies!"

In the middle of the massive throng of black masked men converging on the river, Strito marched with prominence and pride. He looked no different from the rest, solid black uniform, solid black mask. The only thing that set him slightly apart was his arrogant stride. Holding his laser gun up into the air, his men saw the signal. Within moments, they turned their methodical march into a sprint, which intensified with every hardened footfall. The prospect of ensuing bloodshed gripped every warrior as senses heightened.

"Hold your ground," Gunther smiled, enthralled by the anticipation of the coming skirmish and the thought of killing them all. He reveled in proving his might once more as the greatest commander Stritonoly has ever known. "Do not attack until my command! Hold your ground! Hold your ground!"

With a sudden display of vigor and a powerful roar, Strito's men raced toward the river's edge firing at will. Streams of red laser blasts shot off the ground, bouncing off gargantuan boulders, splashing into the river and ricocheting, this way and that. Gunther stood motionless, not giving an inch, defying death, sickly wishing for it. There would be no greater honor for Gunther then to die on the battlefield.

A gush of rain began to pound down as the dark of night swept in and blanketed this theatre of war. Imperial soldiers squatted in hiding; their swords at the ready, Gunther sensed the time was now.

"Imperial soldiers," He screamed through the rainfall, "Defend your homeland, Attack!"

As the first line of Strito's men approached, hundreds of imperial soldiers emerged from cover with swords flailing. Effortlessly, they deflected the stream of laser beams, moving with precision and purpose toward their adversary.

Gunther watched with pleasure as an imperial soldier violently swung his sword, swiping the hand of one of the black masked men, tearing his gun from him and sending it catapulting into the river. Another imperial soldier quickly moved in, and with a terrifying cry, he lunged his sword into the chest of his unarmed foe.

Gunther's smile vanished as he watched the sword crumple and break apart. The thick metal sword shattered into tiny pieces. The imperial soldier stood helpless, no weapon, no defense. A hail of laser shots quickly followed as the soldier fell lifeless into a puddle of his own blood.

"Body armor," Gunther said under his breath. They had thought it would be impossible to invent body armor capable of withstanding an onslaught from an imperial sword. Strito had somehow done it. They would be slaughtered if they stayed to fight.

"Withdraw!" Gunther screamed, "Withdraw at once, retreat to the citadel. Our swords are useless. Man your rocket-cruisers and retreat to the citadel…Retreat…Retreat!"

The imperial soldiers fled quickly, scattering out of formation and running for their lives. An avalanche of laser shots struck dozens of them in the back, sending their mortally wounded bodies crashing to the surface. Pandemonium ensued, as rocket-cruisers were boarded, injured soldiers doing their best to deflect laser blasts as they fired up their cruisers.

Taking notice that Josef was already waiting on the back of a rocket-cruiser, Gunther carried his large frame slowly back to him. With enormous regret, he powered up his cruiser and sped off, leading the retreat back to the citadel.

Watching as scores of soldiers were struck and killed, Strito felt triumphant but shouted, "Cease fire!"

The laser blasts stopped almost immediately as the imperial soldiers continued their hasty retreat.

"We have won already," Strito yelled. "I will not take this planet by shooting men in the back, even if they deserve it. They will die, all of them, but they will die on my terms. I will not give them the excuse or vindication of being killed in cold blood. We know where they are going, they will hide in the citadel like the cowards they are."

Strito's men laughed, watching as the remaining soldiers boarded their cruisers and sped away. "Victory is ours," Strito proclaimed to his men. "You will all be kings among men. Stritonoly is now ours for the taking."

Turning to one of his men, Strito whispered, "Go get her…And bring her at once to the citadel entrance, we will need her now."

Chapter 2

The spideron were known to be the most vicious of all tribes. In the end, all they cared about was their own, and upon reflection, even that is in doubt.
~ Taken from the memoirs of Queen Shroomy;
Ruler of the Last World

RAMSITT PERCHED HIMSELF on top of a huge stump, his numerous tentacles sprawled out about his corpulent essence. The murky pond of transformation bubbled up just behind him. Pockets of blurry haze drifted skyward and settled just beneath the overhanging skeletal tree limbs.

"Arise, Sssssssspideron!" Ramsitt announced, the hissing of his voice cutting through the silence.

From the sludge-filled pond, a raucous gurgling erupted as dozens of spideron appeared from beneath the mire. Their faces were soaking wet, glistening with the gelatinous murk of the pond. One by one, their abundant tentacles popped up and crunched through the grime. They floated toward Ramsitt, their hairy blubbery bodies leaving a tremulous wake behind them.

Then, from deep within the gloomy forest, the tapping of more tentacles crawling on branches and thick vines resounded rhythmically. The rest of the spideron tribe had awoken, crawling out from every dark recess of the emaciated jungle. They quickly joined the pack.

"Come to order, Sssssssspideron," Ramsitt said calmly, his tribe circling the stump and uniformly squatting down to listen to their leader.

"We have businesssssssss," Ramsitt continued, "We need to disusssssss our prisoner." Of course, this was no discussion at all. This was Ramsitt telling his tribe how it would be.

A grumbling hiss came from the crowd of spideron, their only means of showing displeasure. An obvious confusion sifted through even the most devoted spideron as their bloodshot eyes darted back and forth. No one understood why Ramsitt was keeping the prisoner alive, but no one would dare question him. The fear he struck within his tribe was palpable. Yes, they could question him if they so desired, but they would pay a heavy price, and Ramsitt had shown his wrath many times before. He had no qualms about putting them in their proper subordinate place if the situation called for it.

"Silence!" Ramsitt said with authority; though his voice stayed relatively quiet. Curling up his tentacles and propping himself straight up on the soggy stump, he intentionally displayed his physical dominance for all to see. He weighed in excess of three hundred pounds, twice as large as any other spideron. A single red stripe shot down his backside like a thunderbolt. His fiery eyeballs only added to his terrifying aura. "Do not make another sound! I have decided what must be done…"

Taking a moment to be sure he had everyone's full attention, he lapped his tongue and spoke again, "Our prisoner was accepted by the pond of transformation, we must take that into consideration. However, we have seen his condition clearly decline in the last few days. I made the decision to cage him when he assumed the physicality of his former self. And I know his appearance now is most unusual to you all…it is unusual to me as well." Ramsitt paused. It was indeed strange. No creature had ever transformed back to their original self after the pond of transformation accepted them. Barok was the first exception. And while he would never look like a true Acidel again, he was not a spideron either.

Turning on his stump, Ramsitt peered across the pond to see the cage made of thicket and thorn on the opposite side. Through the fog, Ramsitt squinted and saw Barok looking back at him. No words were necessary; the pathetic expression on Barok's chubby half Acidel, half spideron face said it all.

Ramsitt sighed, "Barok is nothing now…not a spideron…not an Acidel." Spinning around to look at his tribe, he said, "My decision is made, Barok will be the one to lead the charge."

A rush of hissing echoed out loud and strong, Ramsitt's eyes shot a glare over the tribe which quickly brought the noise to a halt.

"I need not explain my motives to you," Ramsitt snapped. "But know this; as a once respected and knowledgeable Acidel, Barok has a mighty power we can use…And use it we will."

Ramsitt turned on the stump again to see Barok, "Yesssssssss," Ramsitt hissed. "He is the one we have waited for; he will unknowingly lead the way. The day of the spideron is upon us!"

Chapter 3

Beware the masquerade of the evil spirit.
~Taken from the memoirs of Queen Shroomy;
Ruler of the Last World

CHLOCHELLE SAT WITH his ankles crossed and legs up. He fell in and out of sleep, occasionally glancing out the front window on the flight deck. It was the dead of night and the cylindrical spaceship hovered over Stritonoly's lush purple surface. The ship was under his command until Strito returned from the battlefield.

Even though Chlochelle was fully masked, like all of Strito's men, his boorishly educated demeanor seeped through. Presently, the awkward way he placed his hands on the side of his stool while trying to balance his feet was somewhat laughable.

"Is that comfortable?" Princess Becki asked, her long blonde hair was dripping wet from a recent shower. She stood in the small cubicle entrance wearing only a skimpy pink robe. Her shapely legs were fully visible, glistening with beads of water.

"I'm comfortable, yes," Chlochelle answered, cocking his head to admire her legs. "Um, Princess…you should get ready."

Becki grinned, "You don't like me this way?"

Chlochelle coughed awkwardly, "I…I…think…"

"Um, I, Um, I…" Becki mocked him flirtatiously; then laughed coyly. "You are a cute one, Chlochelle. Strito has a good friend in you. And…"

"And?" Chlochelle managed to ask.

"And…If I am to be with Strito someday. Well, you are his closest friend."

"So, what does that mean?"

"I believe that true friends should share everything," Becki smiled, running her fingers over her moist lips, "Yes, that's what I said… friends share everything…everything."

Chlochelle stood up quickly and spun around to face her, "Princess, you may think me gullible, and while I may not possess the social prowess necessary to avoid embarrassment from your comments, make no mistake, I am a learned man. I know what you are trying to do."

"Is that so?" Becki smiled, "So tell me then…what am I trying to do?"

She took a few steps toward him, clearly pleased by his clumsiness. "You are just so cute…and so smart…How can a simple girl like me possibly resist?"

Chlochelle laughed uneasily, "Simple girl? Now you are truly playing me for a fool."

She stopped smiling, her seductive crystal blue eyes melting into him. Slowly licking her lips, she knew full well the tension she was creating. "Just say it," she whispered, "Go ahead…I know you want me…just say it, you'll feel so much better if you admit it. And who knows, maybe you'll even be rewarded."

Chlochelle felt her hands on his waist. Even through his solid black spacesuit, the warmth of her touch was irresistible. He shook his head viciously, knowing that death would be a certainty if he were to give in. "I need assistance!" He shouted finally.

Becki laughed, "You are a real party pooper!"

Within seconds, a crewmember appeared in the doorway.

"Princess Becki needs to get ready," Chlochelle said. "Please see that she does."

Becki waited a long moment before turning, puckering her lips, and blowing Chlochelle a kiss. She laughed again and quickly exited.

What a mistake to have her roaming free on the ship, Chlochelle thought. Strito either has more faith in her than I do or he is completely blinded by her physical beauty.

"Professor Chlochelle…Professor Chlochelle?" It was another one of Strito's men standing in the doorway. Chlochelle was so lost in thought, his mind had drifted elsewhere.

"Yes…yes…What do you want? "Chlochelle asked softly.

"We just received word from the battlefield. Strito was right; the enemy is on the run. He is requesting our presence on the lawn of the citadel. And he wants the Princess."

This is a huge mistake, Chlochelle thought. I will never disobey Strito and I will forever be loyal to my friend. But he is not thinking clearly if he thinks this woman is on our side. Her ultimate plans, however sick and demented they might be, have nothing to do with us. I can only pray he will recognize this before all hope is lost.

Just as the crewmember was about to walk away, Chlochelle added, "And what of…the egg?"

"Strito made no mention of that, Professor."

The crewmember turned to leave but stopped himself and said, "I'm surprised you still call that thing 'the egg?'"

"What else would you like to call it?"

The crewmember nodded, "I suppose you're right, I wouldn't know what to call that thing."

"Neither would I," Chlochelle said, "Neither would I…"

Chapter 4

"You sicken me," Ramsitt said, squatting outside Barok's thorny enclosure.

"You did this to me," Barok muttered, his monotone growl slightly obscured by a trace of the spideron hiss. His poisonous sweat soaked the tattered robe which clung to his leathery skin.

"You did this to yourself!" Ramsitt said with disdain. "Blame me if you so choose, but you are not an innocent victim. When you made the choice to venture into our forest, the consequences were yours alone."

"I did not ask to be placed into the pond," Barok grumbled, his plump fingers squeezing onto the thick vines that held his cage intact. "And you accepted me as your own. I thought you were my friend."

"What has happened to you disgusts me," Ramsitt shouted, his tongue lapping around violently. "You are clearly transforming back into an Acidel. What I see before me now is not a Spideron. You are not my brother. I don't know what you are, and I do not care to ever find out."

"But, the pond transformed me, you saw it yourself. Why am I changing back?"

"This is a question that even I cannot answer. Had I known this would occur, I would have killed you long ago."

"So you will leave me here to suffer," Barok said quietly, his wide-eyes filling with tears. "I made a mistake coming here, of that I have no doubt. Now you ask me to pay with my life. It is unfair."

Ramsitt laughed, "What does fairness have to do with anything on this wretched planet. Is it fair you were born into slavery? Is it fair your mate will perish along with many of your Acidel friends? Fairness is an illusion. It does not exist."

Barok plopped his chubby body down on the muddy surface. He groaned and blinked his big blue eyes as a single teardrop fell down his rubbery check. "Give me a chance to prove my worth to you?"

Ramsitt smiled, this was exactly what he wanted to hear. "A chance you seek?" Ramsitt asked, "You wish for an opportunity to redeem yourself, do you?"

"Yes," Barok answered quickly, "Tell me what I can do. True, I do not look like you any longer, but that does not mean I cannot assist you in some way."

Ramsitt's bloodshot eyes hardened as he peered into the cage. He propped himself up on all tentacles and leaned closer. "And if I were to give you a chance…What could you possibly offer me?"

"I know the citadel far better than you or your tribe. It was my home for many years. I can provide you with much knowledge."

"This is knowledge I already have. You forget, I can read every thought you have; you are completely under my command. There is nothing you possess in that tiny mind that I cannot see for myself."

Barok sighed, "Yes…that may be true. But because of my appearance, I can gain access where you cannot. The citadel will be ready for a spideron. Even with your telepathic skill, it will be impossible to get past all the imperial soldiers. I look more and more like an Acidel with every passing day. I can easily slip in amongst my own kind."

"Your own kind, you say…The kind you turned your back on when you escaped. Why would you not do the same to me as well? You are flawed in countless ways. It is impossible for you to be trusted."

"You will not know unless you allow me the chance."

"Perhaps," Ramsitt whispered, his front tentacles sliding up to grope the cage, "But I feel it to be inevitable. You will betray us. Somehow, you have acquired the one trait that the Acidel have never had. The lack of this trait is what makes the Acidel so endearing to so many… and yessssss, also, so very useful. It is obvious to me that you have acquired a sense of self, and with that, you now understand selfishness. Once these behaviors are acquired they cannot be lost…and betrayal ultimately follows all those who seek egotistical desires."

"I would never do such a thing," Barok said with conviction. "I am an Acidel. If I give you my word, I will not forsake that. It is not in my nature to betray anyone for any reason. Maybe what you say is true. Maybe I have changed…but I was born an Acidel…I am who I am."

Ramsitt knew there was truth in this. The loyalty of an Acidel was unshakable. Even if the stain of self-awareness had contaminated Barok, he would always bear the characteristics of his former self within.

"I'm still listening…" Ramsitt said, "But you have done little to convince me…yet."

Barok stood up and scampered toward the front of the cage. He met eyes with Ramsitt, "I give you my word. I only wish to see my Shroomy once more. I owe it her to try to get back. I swear to you, I will do your bidding. Command me as you see fit."

"And if you fail me?" Ramsitt asked.

"You are now my master. I will not fail you."

"It is easy for a caged prisoner to speak as you do. But if you fail me…It will be Shroomy that will pay the price for your betrayal. Do you understand?"

Barok swallowed hard, "I will not fail you, Ramsitt…Just give me the chance to prove it."

After a long pause, Ramsitt turned his back to the cage and crawled away. Hearing Barok begin to sob, Ramsitt couldn't help but smile.

Chapter 5

GUNTHER SWITCHED OFF the turbo-engine to his burgundy rocket-cruiser and slid in sideways outside the front gates of the citadel. Unic Heldar stood on the yellow lawn, his long white tunic rippled in the wind. The fleet of retreating imperial soldiers raced in behind. Dozens of the strongest Acidel slaves were immediately throwing the wounded onto stretchers and carting them away.

"Take the injured for immediate treatment," Gunther shouted as he jumped from his cruiser. He hastily made his way toward Unic while simultaneously directing Josef to help supervise the Acidel.

"What has happened?" Unic asked, his meek and elderly tone echoing out from under his hood.

"Strito has done it," Gunther said, marching past Unic, he spat on the ground. "Body armor! The bastard has invented body armor capable of withstanding the strength of our swords."

Unic gulped, "That is not possible."

"He has found a way. I must inform the Czar at once."

Yelling commands, Gunther pointed to strategic protection zones previously designated for full lock down of the citadel. Sprinting into the citadel, soldiers took defensive guard at every triangular window. A full battalion of the finest archers were sent to the rooftop, though Gunther knew their arrows would be wasted if shot.

Hurriedly, Gunther and Unic made their way through the main parlor and headed directly for the Czar's chambers.

The guards standing watch at the Czar's study stood at attention as Gunther and Unic flew past them.

"Good evening, gentleman," Ethan said, sitting behind his desk busily writing. "News of victory to report?" Ethan asked with a smile. Looking up to see the clear dismay washed over Gunther's scarred face, his smile evaporated. "Speak to me, friend of Stritonoly. What tragedy has befallen us?"

"I have unpleasant information to share, my Czar," Gunther said, seriousness and urgency in his thick voice. "Strito's men have acquired body armor."

Ethan laughed, "Yes...We have seen the feeble attempts at body armor before. It is useless against our swordsmen."

"So we thought," Unic said.

"It seems he has done it," Gunther added, "I would not believe it unless I saw with my own eyes. An imperial sword shattered into a million pieces, it could not even dent the armor. We had no choice but to flee the battlefield…We are faced with a tragic circumstance."

"I am at a loss," Ethan said, confusion pouring through him. "Unic, it is common knowledge that no such armor could ever be made. How could this be?"

"I have no idea how this could be," Unic answered. "If what Gunther has told us is true, there must…"

"Do you doubt me?" Gunther interrupted, raising his voice. "I know what I saw! Do not test me at a time like this, Unic. We have no time!"

"I do not doubt what you saw," Unic said, "But do we know, for certain, that all of Strito's men wear this armor? Are you certain of what you witnessed?"

Gunther turned red, "I know what I saw," he repeated.

"You did the right thing," Ethan said, "We will find out in short order what Strito has at his disposal. If all his men are armed with body armor, we will find another way to thwart off his attack."

"Our soldiers will be left naked without their swords," Gunther said, "However, I do agree, there are options we may need to consider."

Unic knew what Gunther was talking about. He turned to Gunther, "Do not contaminate your Czar by mentioning it. I know of what you speak, it is not an option."

Ethan stood, suddenly enraged he shouted, "It is obvious you both know something I do not. Tell me now or I swear by my crown, you will both pay the ultimate penalty."

Gunther took a step toward the desk as Unic turned away, "This information was kept from you to protect you."

"Nonsense," Ethan screamed, "Do not try my patience, Sir Gunther. Tell your Czar what you know."

"We have a weapon we can use. It is something we discovered much by accident, but it can be a useful tool in this time of crisis."

Unic spun back around, "I implore you not to go down this path."

Ignoring Unic, Gunther continued, "The details of how I gained this knowledge must remain guarded. But we have discovered a secret about the Acidel."

Ethan's eyes widened, "Continue…" he said hesitantly, unsure if he wanted to hear more, but knowing he had to.

"Acidel sweat is poisonous, we know that to be a fact," Gunther paused, "But…there is something else we have learned about these creatures. It seems the bodily fluids of the Acidel are highly combustible when mixed with our rheap-beta-ex drug."

"How do you know this?" Ethan asked.

Gunther looked long and hard at his Czar, his expression said enough. He would never tell him the whole truth.

Ethan sat back down, acutely aware of the atrocities that most likely led to this discovery. Looking back at Gunther, he reluctantly nodded for him to continue.

"If a living Acidel is set to flame while covered in the liquid form of the drug, the ensuing explosion will be catastrophic. Any fire set to the living bodily fluids of the Acidel will detonate. Even the strongest body armor would not be able to withstand such a powerful force. We can use our bowmen to ignite such an explosion; this will keep us out of harm's way."

"Living Acidel?" Ethan asked.

"Yes…They need to be alive in order for it to be effective."

"I have heard rumblings of this," Unic said, "And it is despicable, nothing but cold-blooded murder."

"Yes, I agree," Gunther said flatly, "And it may be our only chance to preserve Stritonoly."

"Where is your honor, Sir Gunther? The Czar will not win this war by murdering the innocent," Unic said sharply. He then turned his hooded face to see the overwhelming distress on his Czar's face. And in that moment he knew, Ethan was out of options.

"You cannot consider this a viable alternative," Unic said. "You cannot claim victory on the bodies of dead Acidel."

"What would you have me do?" Ethan asked.

"There has to be another way," Unic pleaded.

"Then I suggest you find one," Ethan said. "This is not something I would consider if another option is available. You are both well aware of my strong feelings against entertaining even the thought of such a crime. But If I am left with no other choice, I must do what is necessary."

"Might I suggest a noble surrender," Unic said, "Possibly a negotiation to preserve life? Surely it would be better to surrender than to disgrace our honor in such a manner."

Ethan sighed, "Master Unic, I have no doubt of your wisdom, but there is nothing noble about surrender." Looking back at Gunther, he said with conviction, "I am shamed by these things you tell me… But I have sworn allegiance to my planet, my main concern is the sustentation of our people…We will do what we must…"

Chapter 6

Strito's men marched with pride. They bore the stride of victory and joked casually as they advanced through the dust-filled purock landscape that stretched from the River Frehenly to the citadel lawn.

"Hold!" Strito announced, turning to hear the distinct rumbling of a transport approaching from the rear. The men all turned in unison to see the outline of a sizeable box-shaped transport trolling over the surface.

"The Princess comes to me," Strito said under his breath, a lustful timbre in his voice. The men close enough to hear Strito's comment hung their heads for a brief moment. It was clear Strito had lost much of his toughness since becoming intimate with Becki. Although he thought their courtship was a clandestine affair, he was wrong. His men sensed the difference in their leader right from the start. Strito no longer commanded the reverence he once did among his men. They despised the Princess, some out of envy and some out of pure hatred for her slippery guise.

The transport accelerated, kicking up grime as it plowed through the dense purple terrain. Rain continued to fall as the transport screeched to a halt, a ramp lowering from its underbelly.

Strito stood at the bottom of the ramp as Chlochelle galloped down to meet him.

"Congratulations," Chlochelle said.

Shaking hands with his comrade, Strito asked, "I presume you knew to bring our little friend along?"

Chlochelle nodded, "The egg is onboard, fully guarded."

"Outstanding! It is doubtful we'll need to unleash such a wrath, but if the Czar proves to be stubborn…well…it will be to his own peril."

Chlochelle nodded, fully aware that the hatched egg in their possession could easily devastate anything in its path. However, uncertainty loomed, there was no way of knowing exactly what would transpire if it became hostile.

"The Princess?" Strito asked.

"Yes, of course, she is onboard. Do you wish to see her?"

"No, leave her for now. The citadel is not far," Strito said, pointing to the base of Mount Crito just ahead. The citadel sat halfway up the wooded swell and was now in view. "Today we will see the transfer of power on this planet…my planet. You have been most faithful,

Chlochelle. When I take my place as the Mejasz, you will be bathed in every luxury."

"I only wish for your success, I need no material reward."

Strito laughed loudly, "You may not seek material reward, my friend. But you will have it anyway. You will have all you could ever desire. I do not forsake my own and you have been with me from the start. I insist you share in the delight of our triumph."

Chlochelle paused before saying, "…I thank you…Mejasz…" He ineptly offered a bow as Strito stood tall and accepted the tribute. Chlochelle was doing his best to suppress what he truly felt. He could not help but think that the manner in which Strito now presented himself no longer resembled the warrior he once admired. Strito was under the spell of a wicked woman, contaminated by the charm of a spurious vixen.

"Follow us to the foot of the mountain," Strito ordered Chlochelle. "There we will march to the citadel lawn and claim our victory."

Chapter 7

THE IRON GATES, which separated the citadel entrance from the lawn slammed shut. Inside the main parlor, Acidels scurried about as soldiers lined up against the magnificently decadent walls. Through small triangular windows, the light from the rising northern sun trickled in. It splashed a hue of yellowy-orange light onto the freshly scrubbed white marble floors.

"I want one hundred men stationed here," Gunther shouted, "Should a breach occur, you will be our last line our defense. You will fight with your hands if necessary, and you will kill anyone who dares enter our home."

"Do we have soldiers to man every floor, every window?" Ethan asked, standing next to Gunther.

"Yes, My Lord," Gunther retorted, noticing that Ethan was visibly distressed and weary. "We have soldiers positioned at all strategic points for protection of the citadel. And the bowmen are waiting for us above."

Gunther thought it odd that Ethan wasn't wearing his golden crown. His stringy white hair, usually tucked up in a bun, fell disheveled upon his shoulders. The weight of impending doom was evident in his appearance for all to see.

"Let us proceed," Ethan said to Gunther, his long green cape wafting as he spun away. Unic followed, along with a half dozen soldiers. They swiftly made their way to a circular staircase leading to the rooftop. In single file, they climbed to the roof where over a battalion of Stritonoly's finest bowmen were waiting patiently.

Upon arrival on the rooftop, Ethan saw the crowd of men holding their bows between arm and chest. All bows were bright green and consisted of one thick strip of twine attached to an expandable limb made of bark. These archers looked very much like soldiers except for the bulky sack of arrows slung over their shoulders. Each sack displayed several rows of the fierce imperial serpents knitted neatly onto the green fabric.

"The moment of truth is upon us," Ethan said to the assembly, the rain subsiding with the morning's first light. "You have been trained well. And though many of you have not seen combat, fear not, justice will prevail over the evil which now advances upon us."

Knowing exactly what they might be asked to do, Ethan took a long breath and continued, "Your resolve as men will be tested on this day. Remember, the fate of Stritonoly may rest on your ability to follow every order precisely," He paused, "…whatever those orders may be."

"The enemy approaches," shouted a voice from further down the rooftop.

Ethan and Gunther walked to the edge of the roof, Unic standing close behind. Only a thin sheet of decorative purock jutted up to their waistline providing but a small amount of fortification. The bowmen moved hastily into position, scattering at first before forming a line behind the scant purock wall. Each of the men drew a single arrow, kneeled as one, and readied their bows.

As the sun spilled over the yellow lawn, the army of black-masked warriors stalked ever closer. The sound of the transport kicking up debris rocked the consciousness of every living thing within earshot. The hard-bitten stomping of the advancing army intensified as the laughter of Strito's men grew louder.

Ethan whispered to Gunther, "If I were to give the order…" He stopped himself and swallowed hard, unable to find the words to say.

Gunther interjected, "There are Acidel nearby that have been bathed in small doses of the rheap-beta-ex drug. We have been doing it for some time in preparation for this very situation. They can be sent out on the lawn unknowingly. Our bowmen can shoot a flaming arrow into their back, it will be…"

"Say no more," Ethan interrupted, "You speak to me of shooting them in the back," His voice beginning to rise, "How can you suggest this without even a hint of remorse in your voice? Have these Acidel done any wrong?"

Gunther clenched his teeth, clearly frustrated, "I should be thanked for the strength needed to do such a thing…And history will thank me one day…even if you will not."

"Take no action until I give the command," Ethan said, turning and grabbing Unic by the arm.

Walking Unic abruptly to the far side of the rooftop, Ethan said, "Unic…speak to me not as the Czar; speak to me as a man, speak to me as a friend."

Unic dropped his head and muttered, "This I cannot do… Ethan Educai is not a man unto himself in a circumstance such as this. It would be irresponsible to speak to you in such a way. From this point on, your decisions bare the yoke of many, many souls. This is not about what is right or wrong for only one man."

"So you would still advise me to surrender?"

"Is it not better to surrender with honor then to live on without respect?"

"Respect can be earned anew. Surrender will mean death for us all."

"You don't know that for certain," Unic admonished, "Use the wisdom which brought you to this moment in time. It will be the easiest choice to send the Acidel to their death. And yes, you will win this petty war among men…But at what cost?"

"No war is petty," Ethan said.

"Alas," Unic sighed, "If you truly believe that to be true than my council is not worth seeking."

"Confusion rips at my soul," Ethan said, his hand reaching up to rest on Unic's shoulder. "I do not have a winning solution."

"You may be right," Unic said, "There may be no winning solution. But if you preserve our honor, our dignity…then you will find the best solution…And that is all you can hope for. And as the Czar, Is that not your obligation?"

"I will be sending my people to their death," Ethan said; exasperation in his tone. "This I cannot do."

"There will be a price to pay for their lives," Unic said somberly, "And you must ask yourself…What price are you willing to pay for that which is just?"

Chapter 8

BECKI FELT THE transport screech to a halt. Pulling up the shade on the tiny window she sat next to, her face stiffened as she looked out upon her former home. Lowering her eyes to stare at the yellow grassland, she could only remember heartache.

This is where I was first exposed, Becki thought.

She was only nine years old, running around on the lush front lawn of the citadel. Several Acidel children were nearby preparing an afternoon luncheon. After all these years the memory was still so clear.

Becki's maidservant was an elderly woman, a trusted friend of the royal family. Unfortunately, she was completely inadequate at keeping a careful eye on the precocious princess.

Transfixed in the memory, she recalled how an Acidel who was serving her began to sweat under the heat of the summer sun. Becki was but a child, she knew nothing of the true danger of the Acidel sweat. When her maidservant turned her head, Becki, trying to be kind, wiped the tiny globules of sweat away from the Acidel's bald head. Using only her shirtsleeve, she gently dabbed the sweat clean. She would not know it at the time, but that one simple act changed her life forever.

The young princess thought nothing of it until later that night when her sleeve began to harden. Secretly, while the royal family was dining, she picked the small chunk away from her shirt. Careful not to let anyone see, she kept her arm hidden under the table. When she finally picked the hardened toxin away, she jammed it into her pants pocket and left it there.

Later that night, before she showered, she took it out and pondered what to do. Then, as if directed to do so by some cosmic force, she ate it. That very instant marked the end of Becki's childhood. Standing in the shower that night, a rush of adrenaline coursed through her veins. Euphoria that was unreachable unless under the influence of this powerful contaminant. Visions twirled through her mind of absolute beauty and complete omnipotence. She felt the hand of an almighty deity move her. A spirit she knew existed but was never able to comprehend. She knew the Acidel called that spirit Konig, and in the shower that night, she was convinced his presence had visited her. But when she woke the next morning, the spirit that touched her was gone. The emptiness that engulfed her suffocated her sanity. She needed more of the sweat, and she was prepared to do whatever was necessary to attain it.

From that night on, she spent her life in the pursuit of the addictive toxin. She watched as her own brother became equally obsessed. Never feeling a second of guilt or pity, she proceeded to facilitate the destruction of her entire family.

Becki tried for years to revisit that moment standing in the shower, washed free of sin, numb to every pain. The union of her spirit with an all-powerful, all-knowing God would never be found again. While she brilliantly displayed an aura of intelligent faith for all to see, her belief in virtuosity eventually faded. As her acumen expanded, her faithfulness evaporated.

And as she pulled the shade down on the window, she angrily wiped a tear away. Sitting in the transport in a lavishly seductive petite mauve dress, she was a child no more. She couldn't help but recognize that her craving for the sweat still existed. Her solace came in knowing that revenge was soon at hand. There would be no rest until the Acidel were made to suffer for the poison beneath their skin.

The steel door in Becki's small closet-like room aboard the transport crashed open.

"I'm sorry," Strito said, standing in the doorway, "I didn't mean to frighten you." He walked in and shut the door. Kneeling down, he caressed Becki's bare thigh with his gloved fingers, "You are a vision of absolute beauty, my love."

Becki smiled, "You could have knocked. But it is nice to see you, I was getting worried."

"There is never a need to worry about me, my dear," Strito said softly. "Everything is happening exactly as it should. The prophecy is coming to fruition."

What an idiot! Becki thought. Are all men really this stupid? And I had such high hopes for this one. Oh well…

"I am the Mejasz," Strito continued, "And soon, the entire galaxy will know it."

Who is he trying to convince? Becki thought.

"Yes, my love," Becki said with a broad smile, "I have never doubted that you are the Mejasz. And it will be an honor to stand at your side."

Strito pointed to his shiny mask, "Before this day is over, you will finally see me. And I will cast my eyes upon you without any barrier between us."

Even though they had been intimate, Becki had never seen his face. The prophecies said the face of the Mejasz would remain hidden until the day he claimed the throne.

"I cannot wait to remove this armor," Strito said. "Tonight, I will be dressed in the royal garb of my forefathers. And as the Mejasz, I will purify this planet and take back what was stolen from my ancestors long ago."

"And what will be your first appointment?" Becki asked with a sly grin.

Strito laughed, "I am quite sure you know. I do not wish to rule this planet without a Queen. And I give you my word, the Acidels will be under your command by the day's end."

What a fool! Becki thought as she masterfully continued the charade. His attraction to me has crippled him completely. He has become a disgrace to the men who have followed him so blindly. No one would fault them if they choose to string him up and leave him for dead.

"I am so proud of you," Becki smiled convincingly. "So now you must share with me," she giggled. "What is the plan? How can I assist you?"

"Your allure will be of use if you wish to save lives on this day," Strito said. "Our enemy has but two choices; surrender or die. Of course, we will keep as many Acidel alive as possible. The ones left living will be under your rule, suffer they will, but they will be of great importance to our kingdom in providing labor."

"Ethan will never surrender to you," Becki said.

"I know he will not surrender to me. But he may listen to one of his own…he may listen to you. He would be a fool not to, but if it is his choice to be defiant, we are prepared to burn the citadel to the ground. However, if you persuade him to surrender, I will keep them alive to work alongside the Acidel," Strito laughed heartily. "I would prefer that. The thought of seeing them as our slaves is most enjoyable indeed."

This is silliness, Becki thought. This man is not fit to rule his own self let alone an entire planet.

"I will do my best to talk to Ethan," Becki said, mustering all her womanly charm to elicit yet another phony smile.

"My men are positioning themselves as we speak," Strito said, standing and going for the door. "When everything is in order, I will send for you."

"Be careful," Becki said.

Strito nodded and closed the door.

Chapter 9

RAMSITT'S TRIBE SLITHERED through dense forestry as they moved up the side of Mount Crito. Barok, encased in a portable carriage, bound with twine by his hands and feet, watched helplessly as the herd slinked carefully along. Their destination: the citadel. Their goal: annihilation.

The pack skirted up the bank of the mountain, over a hundred of them springing effortlessly from tree limb to tree limb. Another hundred crawled together on a narrow trail, vines dangling overhead, sunlight seeping through.

Barok felt his chest heave as the carriage rocked to and fro. Four spideron with cords attached to their necks pulled the carriage with ease as they shimmied up the tapered pathway. Ramsitt swaggered affront his tribe, indignant in his resolve, convinced that this day would see the destruction of the citadel and all its occupants once and for all.

Ramsitt abruptly came to a halt. Propping himself up on his back tentacles, he closed his eyes. Deep in a clairvoyant trance, he sensed they were close.

Swinging his upper tentacles to the left, he motioned for the tribe to move off the trail. They quickly took to the trees and vines, leaping off the path into the opaque woodland.

Grabbing Barok, a spideron slid him off the carriage, taking hold of him with several tentacles. Barok was limp, resigned to his fate, fully aware that struggling would only make matters worse.

The tribe shot from limb and vine, adeptly maneuvering through thickets and thorn. Ramsitt led the way, trolling up the side of the mountain to the rear of the citadel.

A small basin of yellow grass covered by looping vines sat just behind the citadel. Ramsitt signaled his tribe to stop and gather close to him.

Whispering, he said, "We will wait here. Find suitable hiding in the woods."

Mud slopped up onto Barok's face as they threw him to the ground in front of Ramsitt.

"Rip his garments from him," Ramsitt ordered. The spideron who carried him complied.

Barok was filthy, naked, and unashamed. He didn't care anymore for his own needs. His thoughts were with Shroomy. He hoped against all hope that somehow, she was still alive. If only for the opportunity to say, he was truly sorry for having abandoned her.

"The Acidel quarters are undoubtedly vacant," Ramsitt said. "The citadel scum will want to protect their most valuable commodity… their slaves…It is true, a battle among men takes place this very day, I have foreseen it many times. Barok, you will gain access to the citadel for us, you will find Acidel attire. Do what you must to find a way beyond the guards. Once you have gained access, leave the rear of the citadel unlocked. Set out one lit candle for me to see that your service has been done."

"And then?" Barok asked, staring up at Ramsitt's squinting red eyes.

Ramsitt smiled, "And then….you will be free."

A shock of terror throttled down Barok's spine. With these words he knew, death was a certainty. Ramsitt did not intend to offer Barok an ounce of freedom.

"Even if I am to get into the citadel," Barok said, "It will be impossible to unlock the doors."

"You speak like a human," Ramsitt hissed, "Always pondering defeat. SSSSSSSTOP! Clear these foolish thoughts from your damaged mind. There is always a way."

"I am a wanted Acidel, if they recognize me I will be killed on sight."

"There is hardly a chance of that," Ramsitt said, "You have not cast eyes upon yourself as I have. You do not look like the Barok I first met," Ramsitt took a moment to look him over. "Yes…you look like an Acidel, but a deformed one at best, you are not the same."

"You put much faith in me."

"I have NO faith in you!" Ramsitt mocked. "I have faith in the prophecy of things to be. I have faith in the meek conquering the mighty. These are the things I believe. You are insignificant in the cosmic plan I have foreseen."

"So why send me?" Barok asked under his breath.

Ramsitt countered his query with another, "Why does the sun settle into darkness?"

Barok looked at him with a blank stare as Ramsitt spoke with a terrifying conviction.

"The sun settles into darkness because it must….Because it must!"

Chapter 10

I HAVE NOT forgotten who I am or where I came from. I am known by many names, but to those who believe in me on this planet, I am Konig.

I don't want to be alone, but there is no other way.

I have come to understand fear for the first time. It is an uncomfortable emotion that has little use for me. But now, on the brink of the end, I am frightened.

The reflection in the sky has brought me here so many times before. The forms I have taken are numerous, and sometimes even despicable in the eyes of the ignorant. My final form has yet to be witnessed. They will only know me as the egg that grew to destroy all things. Through all my days and nights, I have kept my promise to the reflection. Now, I have been sent to obliterate this universal abomination. There is no chance of saving them now…even if I could.

I continue to wrestle with the turmoil of man. More so, it is my duty that frightens me most of all. I must cleanse my inner self and pray for your guidance…

Oh, mighty reflection in the sky, I have never asked for anything, but I ask you now. If there is any way for this to be avoided, show me a sign. I do not wish to see it all fade away into the abyss, for I will be lonely. I realize this is but a selfish reason for their survival. I curse myself for even thinking these human thoughts.

Is it wrong for me to believe in them still? Terrors haunt me that I may be following you blindly. These are human thoughts I know, but they overcome me at this moment of truth. I fear that man's ego has seared a passageway into my own indomitable will.

My greatest fear of all is that man's freewill has polluted me more than I am willing to admit. I ask myself: What if I was to disobey you? What if I became more like man and made a judgment without your approval? Would that mean the end of me as well?

Yet, even with these thoughts of weakness contaminating my power, I know I will do your bidding.

Man has had every opportunity to amend their ways. They have proven repeatedly to be incapable of rational thought. War is upon them once more. Not only here on Stritonoly, but in all places. In every corner of the galaxy, man has intentionally sought to create conflict. Peace is a mirage long banished into obscurity.

And so, my current form awaits the final act. I will be the one and only Konig until the very end. And as I pass the time inside this musty transport, I ponder these horrible things that will come to pass…

Chapter 11

Over an hour had gone by. It became clear that Strito did not intend to issue demands any time soon.

Frustrated, Ethan left the roof and raced down the circular staircase. Unic and a dozen soldiers followed close behind. Arriving on the main floor, Ethan's cape fluttered as he darted ahead of his entourage. Suddenly, there was purpose in Ethan's movements. Faced with a moral quandary of the highest order, he felt it was necessary to consult the elders of the citadel behind closed doors.

Following his Czar's orders, Gunther remained on the rooftop with the battalion of bowman at the ready. Ethan was shrewd enough to see the bloodlust in Gunther's eyes. It was best for him not to be involved in this meeting.

"What are we doing?" Unic asked, out of breath, struggling to keep pace with Ethan.

"Our wisest elders are being sheltered at my request. They are under heavy guard until the conflict passes. We will see them now."

"My Czar," Unic said, "How do you know Strito will not attack at any moment? Should you not be up on the roof?"

"I do not know anything for certain, Unic, but Strito is clearly a man filled with a licentious opinion of his worth. Trust me when I tell you, he is enjoying this waiting game. He will strike, but not before he demands we bow at his feet. I feel we still have some time."

At the end of the main hallway, over twenty imperial soldiers stood shoulder to shoulder. At their back was a giant metal doorway. As Ethan approached, the soldiers made room for him to pass.

"Open it!" Ethan ordered.

One of the older soldiers came forward with an oversized key. With urgency, he stuck the key into the golden lock. Clicking it twice, the metal door slowly screeched open.

As the room came into view, Ethan and Unic looked on as a group of about ten elders stood in a circle, apparently in deep meditation. They wore robes, hunched over, holding hands and humming. A dim light from a single candle cast large shadows upon the barefaced walls.

"A peculiar sight," Ethan whispered to Unic.

"Not at all," Unic responded, "They are bound together by compassion. What did you expect to see?"

Ethan shrugged. "I do not understand this kind of behavior in a time of peril. Action is what is needed; whatever they are doing is a pointless exercise."

"You may be right," Unic said. "But…"

Ethan peered at Unic, seeing in his eyes a hint of condemnation.

"I dare not judge them." Unic added.

Ethan swallowed, "Master Unic, please summon them for me? Time is precious."

Unic moved toward the circle, placed his hand gently upon the back of one of the elders, and suddenly, the humming stopped. The circle broke and the elders turned their wrinkled and worn faces toward the open doorway.

"Welcome, my Czar," said Naomi, the only female among them and the oldest resident of the citadel. She was dressed in a white robe like the rest of them, and except for her thin feminine eyebrows, she looked much like the others. "We have been expecting you," she smiled, a voice like a familiar song filled with genuine kindness.

Ethan retuned her smile, though he suddenly felt awkward by this whole scene. He wondered if this was a colossal blunder and a huge waste of time. He began to doubt if they would be able to offer him any reliable guidance.

"The Czar seeks council," Unic said quietly, the circle dissipating. "He is faced with an ethical dilemma and has very little time."

Naomi crossed her legs first and sat on the floor. It was only at that moment Ethan realized the room was completely empty. "Have you no chairs?" he asked

"We requested the room be stripped bare," Naomi said calmly, now sitting on the floor along with the rest of the elders. "When one has nothing, then nothing can be lost. It is a simple philosophy."

Ethan had many questions, but decided to play along. He wondered if the elders had suddenly gone mad.

"Whatever pleases you," Ethan said, "But if you don't mind, I will sit." With a snap of his fingers, a soldier hurriedly brought in a single chair.

Ethan sat down with Unic standing by his side. From the floor, the elders gazed up at their Czar, their glassy eyes awaiting his next words. Ethan could not help but think this must have looked rather odd. He felt like he did many years ago when he was the royal tutor. He remembered lecturing in a chair for hours while the royal siblings sat at his feet listening intently.

"Master Educai," said Dmitri, "Today is my birthday!"

"I know that silly boy," Ethan smiled.

"Can we skip our studies and play on the lawn?"

"No, my lad, we have much to do. You will celebrate your special day later with your family."

"I want cake," Becki said, her blonde hair in pigtails.

"I'm eight years old today," Dmitri said proudly.

"And I will always be older than you," Becki said, a childish grin flashing over her adorably innocent features.

Ethan leaned forward in his chair, the siblings were sitting at his feet. The sun cast an orange glow through an overhead window as they sat in the main study.

"Will we be reading from the imperial scriptures?" Becki asked.

"No, not today," Ethan answered. "I've been instructed to review our lessons regarding the Acidel."

The siblings moaned. They had been through this a thousand times.

"Master Educai," Dmitri whined. "Do we have to?"

Ethan's expression turned serious, "You are quite young. I realize what I tell you may not seem important. But I assure you…it is."

"We get it," Becki said, "The Acidel sweat is dangerous…so you say," she giggled.

"Try to understand, little one," Ethan searched for the right words to say, "I know many Acidel are sweet and kind. But what I tell you is fact. You are of noble blood, you must be protected, and they can harm you."

"It seems so silly," Dmitri said, "They are so small. How could they hurt me?"

"It would be a mistake to judge any creature by their size alone. The Acidel are here to serve us, it is simply the way of things. But always remember, beneath their skin lies a poison never to be trifled with."

Becki laughed, "That's funny!"

"What's so funny?"

"That word…trifled? I don't even know what you're saying." She continued to laugh as Dmitri joined in.

Ethan frowned. He knew this was his weakness as an instructor. His greatest challenge was breaking down information into simple language. Many times, he used words they could not comprehend.

"The law is the law," Ethan said. "And our law states that the Acidel are to be treated with kindness, unless they lose that privilege. I have a great concern that you are not absorbing what I say. Acidel sweat is a deadly force. Do not underestimate its power. And never, under any circumstances come in contact with it."

Becki looked away with a sly grin. Ethan chose to ignore her.

"…and so, the Czar has come for council on this fragile matter," Unic said, snapping Ethan out of his memory and back to reality. The details Unic shared with the elders hardly surprised them. They had long suspected Sir Gunther had a malicious agenda of his own.

Brushing his fingers through his hair, Ethan sat up straight and said, "Speak honestly to me, elders…I have come here for any advice you think will help bring an end to this conflict."

Silence.

Ethan sighed, "Do you have no suggestions for me? Or…Are you afraid to offer any?"

"I am puzzled," Naomi said softly.

"Speak your mind freely," Ethan said.

"The Acidel have been treated with disregard all my life and they have been killed for far less than protection of the citadel. Why are you suddenly so concerned about their safety?"

"No innocent Acidel has ever been killed under my watch. I take offense to your assertion that I do not care."

"It is common knowledge that if an Acidel sweats the poison, they will be put to death."

"Yes, if necessary…for the safety of our citizens. And I do not make such a decision lightly."

"But you have killed them before?"

"Only to protect our own, and I would not call it murder."

"Those are your words. I didn't say it was murder."

"I sense sarcasm in your tone. This entire business of setting our slaves ablaze, I am outraged that we are forced to consider such a tactic…And yet…I feel we have no other choice if we choose to live past this day."

"So then," Naomi smiled, "You have your answer."

"I have never killed an innocent!" Ethan said with conviction. "We do not kill innocent creatures, it is not our way."

Naomi said somberly, "What is our way?"

Silence.

"Excuse my rudeness," Naomi said finally, "But it appears you have a misguided view of innocence and guilt."

"I make judgments based upon imperial law."

"And the law states that Acidel are guilty if they excessively sweat the poison. But is this guilt always punishable by death?"

"Yes," Ethan said flatly.

"I feel that may be a human judgment, not a sacred one. Of course... this is only my opinion."

Ethan's eyes flitted back and forth about the room. It appeared he was looking for a solution to magically inscribe itself upon the naked walls. "I have come to you seeking another way. If we can find none, then I will do what I must. If the only way to win this battle is by setting the Acidel's aflame, then so be it."

"Regardless of the repercussions?" Unic asked quietly.

Ethan's temper flared. "What are you insinuating? Stop speaking in riddles!"

Unic turned away.

"My Czar," Naomi said softly, "If you win our freedom on the bodies of the innocent...What have you won?"

"So you would rather see us dead?" Ethan shouted, "Would you have me see your children enslaved to this barbarian? Because I tell you this...those are our options. By this day's end, we will be dead or possibly worse...forced into the bonds of slavery."

"I did not say it would be an easy decision," Naomi said, looking down.

"So tell me," Ethan asked, "What would you have me do?"

Naomi looked up at him. "Divine intervention has brought you here. If you wanted to send the Acidel to their death, you would have done so by now. There would be no need to come to us for council unless you had doubt...my feeling tells me you know exactly what you will do already."

"You are quite mistaken," Ethan said.

"The decision has long since been made," Unic said; his back to Ethan.

"At least have the respect to face me!"

Unic spun around, "You are but the final pawn. Destiny has been written...search yourself...you will find the answers you seek."

With urgency, a young soldier came running into the room and bowed to Ethan.

"Speak!" Ethan demanded.

"My Lord, Sir Gunther requests your presence on the roof. There is movement on the lawn."

Chapter 12

Barok crawled through the side entrance of the empty Acidel chambers. Much to his surprise, there were only a few soldiers stationed near his former home. Walking patrol, the soldiers seemed quite disinterested and were easy to slip past. That would be different once he got inside…IF he got inside.

Keeping close to the ground, Barok moved quickly through the chambers. At the end of the room, a giant wooden doorway led to the rear of the main parlor. The door had been bolted shut.

What am I to do now? Barok thought. This is insanity. I do not have the cunning to get inside.

Squatting down outside the doorway, he hung his head wearily, teardrops falling freely onto his cheeks.

Mighty Konig, Barok thought. I have not been faithful to you. I have been selfish and thoughtless. I have even abandoned my very own… But in my time of need, I ask you now for assistance. If not for me… then I beg of you…for my Shroomy.

A ruckus in the forest caught Barok's attention. He stood slowly and gazed through the filthy screens, which enclosed the Acidel chambers. Just outside, he saw several soldiers leading what appeared to be a long line of Acidel. The Acidel were naked, most of them badly beaten. And they were heading his way.

Barok scrambled to find a hiding place. Throwing himself into the corner, he reached for some dirty towels left on the floor and used them to conceal his body as best he could.

Suddenly, the flimsy screen door at the back of the chambers was flung open. The soldiers marched in. The sickly looking clan of Acidel followed in single file.

"Get a move on," one of the soldiers ordered.

"Yes," Josef laughed, "Move it, you Acidel scum."

Barok recognized Josef's voice immediately. He remembered the spideron ambush. How easy it would have been to end Josef's life that day in the forest. Hearing the hatred in Josef's voice, Barok felt a rage burn inside him.

Peeking out from under the dirty towels, Barok watched as Josef came forward with a key and opened the wooden doorway.

This is my chance, Barok thought.

Harnessing every bit of mental power known to him, Barok

summoned the telepathy he once knew. Focusing all his energies on the forest, he reached out to the creatures of the woods to assist him.

Then, as if directed to do so by some higher force, a noise came from the forest. It was a single howl, loud and threatening, followed by the clatter of woodland creatures.

Noticing the sounds, the soldiers turned their attention toward the forest outside. Quickly, Barok threw the towels from his body and crawled into the line of Acidel unnoticed.

"Just creatures in the forest," announced one of the soldiers.

"Maybe they're hungry," Josef said, "Perhaps we should feed them a few Acidel to shut them up."

The other soldiers frowned, unsure if Josef was serious or just trying to be funny.

Barok now stood among the Acidel line, his naked and filthy disposition made him fit right in.

"Let's move," another soldier barked, "Sir Gunther wants them on the roof at once."

They moved swiftly through the doorway and into the main parlor.

I'm inside! Barok thought. I never imagined I would get this far.

Staggering through the main parlor, the Acidel made their way for the circular staircase leading to the rooftop. As they approached the first step of the staircase, a female Acidel at the front of the line collapsed. Josef grabbed her off the floor, smacked her in the head, and motioned for her to keep moving. White Acidel blood dripped down the side of her face, wounds and scabs covered her torso. Watching intently, Barok froze as he realized who it was.

Shroomy!

There she stood, white blood oozing out of a fresh gash on her forehead, undoubtedly abused and tortured at the hands of imperial soldiers. Barok was helpless. All he could do was look at Josef with disgust, hoping for an opportunity to exact some measure of revenge.

Unarmed and naked, Barok was now inside the citadel. At least, he had found his Shroomy. If she were to die, he would die with her.

As they began to climb the stairs, Barok could only imagine what horror awaited them when they reached the roof.

Chapter 13

STRITO'S ARMY EXTENDED out across the lawn. Facing the citadel, the warriors aimed their laser guns, ready to fire at anything that moved. The men were mostly mercenaries, loyal to Strito because of the reward he guaranteed. They had long ago lost any sense of moral dignity. They based their allegiance on one thing, the promise of prosperity under a new galactic order.

In the glaring light of the northern sun, Strito and Chlochelle stood on top of the transport, watching carefully as the men assumed offensive positions.

"It appears we are almost ready," Chlochelle said.

"I was hoping the Czar would have had the wisdom to simply surrender," Strito said, staring at the roof of the citadel. "He shows his foolishness in his actions. Look how he dares to fix his bowman in attack formation. If so much as one arrow is fired our way, I swear to you, I will see him tortured until he begs for death…It may be necessary to show him the full power we possess."

"Shall I bring it out?"

"Keep it covered," Strito smiled, "But yes, bring it out. If the Czar is not worried yet…well…the time has come for him to start."

Chlochelle signaled for several men near the transport to lower the rear ramp.

A deafening screech echoed as the thick ramp crashed onto the lawn.

Strito stood proudly, arms folded, facing the rear of the transport. "Are they watching?" Strito asked.

Chlochelle gazed to the rooftop of the citadel, "Oh yes, they're watching."

"Bring it out!" Strito shouted.

At once, the revving of engines could be heard. The transport shook as a cage began to descend the ramp. Covered in a black curtain and sitting on a bed of motorized wheels, it methodically inched forward. The cage was no bigger than a single-manned rocket-cruiser. However, the aura of its presence led all to believe that whatever was behind the black curtain was not to be taken lightly.

As soon as the wheels hit the lawn, four men latched onto each corner of the cage with protracted silver rods. Using the rods to direct its movement, they guided the cage until it came to rest just outside the front gates of the citadel.

As the wheels slowly rolled to a stop, the men released their silver rods and sprinted away.

Whack! A single sound came from inside the cage, then an extended moment of silence.

Then, a thunderous drone cried out, a growl of indistinct nature, certainly not human at all.

With no warning, the cage violently started tossing itself into the air. Beginning to shake uncontrollably, it smashed down hard on its platform and then repeated the motion again and again and again.

Strito and Chlochelle looked on with perplexed amazement, unsure of what to make of this chaotic dance they were witnessing. They had seen the egg in what they assumed was a volatile state before, but they had never seen a display like this.

Then, with a tremendous bolt of acceleration, the cage flew upwards as if shot from a field cannon. It immediately came crashing down, the wheels below the platform popping under the weight of the impact, deflating instantly.

A high-pitched noise of unspeakable dreadfulness squealed from inside the cage. Even the most hardened warrior could not help but tremble with fright. The noise became vociferous as the cage tumbled off the bed of broken wheels and came to rest on the lawn.

And then there was silence.

Every eye affixed to the now motionless cage.

"I would assume that caught their attention," Chlochelle said quietly.

Strito smiled, "You would hope so."

Opening a hatch, Strito descended into the transport and raced to Becki's quarters.

When he arrived there, he flung the door open to find Becki waiting.

"That was kinda funny," Becki giggled.

"I'm not sure I would call it funny, but it was attention-grabbing."

"I think it did the job. Even your men seemed afraid so it must have scared the imperial soldiers something fierce…That is what you wanted, no?"

"What I want and what I need are two entirely different things."

Duh! Becki thought.

"I am quite confidant you have them frightened," Becki said. "The real question is…Why aren't you?"

"There is nothing for me to fear…I am the Mejasz. That egg is in my possession for a reason. When the time is right, it will do my bidding."

Oh, here we go again, Becki thought. What a nincompoop!

"The time has come," Strito said, "This will be the only chance they have left to survive. It will be up to you to persuade them. Perhaps, they will listen to one of their own."

"I am not one of them anymore," Becki said convincingly. "My place is with you. I only desire that we be together always."

"Then do what I say my love, convince them to surrender. It will be far easier for them to accept me as ruler of this planet if this standoff does not turn into a bloodbath. I've prepared a document that will be delivered shortly. If Ethan chooses to speak with you, this will be the final opportunity he will have to lay down his arms."

"And if he declines?"

"Then the citadel will be burned to the ground…And we will kill them all."

Chapter 14

"My lord," Sir Gunther bellowed, "Strito's men have taken to attack formation."

"Yes, I see," Ethan answered, looking over the shoulders of the assembled bowman. "They are not going to rush us just yet...He's enjoying this too much."

"My lord, we must take action," Gunther said, sounding more like an order than a suggestion. "Let us not waste another second. I will begin preparations at once. We will crush this madman!"

"When I am ready!" Ethan hollered. "You are to take no action until I give the command."

Gunther turned red, shocked by Ethan's sudden display of unmanageable anger.

Ethan turned away, ran his fingers through his hair, gazed up to the sun and breathed deeply. As a tear began to form in the corner of his eye, he quickly looked down.

It was then he noticed them...

Even before he saw them, he knew instinctively there were others on the roof. A presence he had always felt since his youth; a presence of purity and goodness, a presence that could not be slighted even by the bonds of slavery.

Turning his eyes to the rear of the rooftop, he observed the line of naked Acidel squatting there, surrounded by soldiers with swords drawn at the guard. They waited there quietly, sacrificial victims to be, suffering for sins which were not their own.

The huge blue eyes of the many Acidel peered back at him. And in that instant, Ethan felt the weight of every generation of Acidel sear his soul. His own eyes betrayed him for he could not disguise the pity that absorbed him. For a moment, he thought he might faint. Looking away from the Acidel, Ethan gazed into the forest.

How easy it would be to throw myself from this rooftop, he thought. Maybe then, I can finally be at peace. Maybe then, this decision will be taken from my hands.

"A message approaches," one of the soldiers yelled.

Snapping back to reality, Ethan moved to the center of the roof, Gunther and Unic at his side. From a distance, it looked like a pinprick floating up toward them, slowly growing as it ascended up to the rooftop.

"Strito sends us a message," Ethan said to himself.

"No doubt," Unic added. "Most likely terms for our surrender…"

"Do not even hint at such a thought," Gunther said, his voice rising. "And besides, you do not belong here, Unic. This is not a…"

"Enough!" Ethan shouted. "Prepare to intercept the message."

As the object came closer, it became clear it was indeed a roving carrier. A small flyable container used to send handwritten communications in certain sectors of the galaxy.

As the carrier accelerated toward the rooftop, Gunther drew his sword, holding it out over the edge. The carrier bolted forward. Clank! It latched onto the blade of the outstretched sword.

Bringing the sword close to him, Gunther removed the carrier. A soldier standing next to him ran a small explosive detector over the object and passed it back. "It's clean," the soldier said.

Without hesitation, Gunther went to open the cylindrical carrier.

"Do you think that message is for you?" Ethan asked, outraged that Gunther would dare to open it himself.

Gunther gritted his teeth, "I assume the message is for all of us."

Ethan held out his hand, his face was hardened with rage. "Give it to your Czar!"

Gunther flashed a wicked grin, "Of course…My lord!" He said defiantly, slapping the carrier down into Ethan's open hand.

Turning his back on Gunther, Ethan reached into the carrier and opened the folded document inside. It read:

Ethan Educai,

As per the order of the galactic commission which oversees this region and in compliance with the rules of warfare, I am offering this opportunity for a peaceful resolution to this conflict. I am issuing a full cease-fire in accordance with the regulations of combat. This cease fire will expire one hour after you read this. I have a settlement of terms that will spare the lives of many. Whatever you may think of me, it is not my desire to see all your people die.

Come to the front gates alone, unarmed and you will be escorted to me. As far as your safety is concerned, inform your council that I am no fool. I have no wish to kill an unarmed man. I am also quite aware that it would be in violation of all ethical boundaries set forth by the rules that govern warfare. You will be returned to your people unharmed after I present my

Much to Gunther's embarrassment, after reading it, Ethan handed the document to Unic. Reading it quickly, Unic then lifted his hooded face back to Ethan.

"Would you think me mad if I were to consider this?" Ethan asked solemnly.

"I would think no such thing," Unic answered calmly.

Ethan walked away from the front of the roof. Seeing the Acidel again, he approached them.

"What is he doing?" Gunther murmured.

"He is your Czar," Unic said, "He will do as he wishes. It is not for you to judge him."

"Mind your tongue," Gunther said, "I caution you, Unic…be very careful of your tone. And do not speak to me of making judgments. A man who has never lifted a hand in defense of his people has no right!"

"The venom in your voice does not warrant a response. I have nothing more to say to you."

Gunther seethed, feeling underappreciated and filling with rage. Unic and all his musings were irrelevant to Gunther in a time of war. Another comment and Gunther would have no compulsions about chopping off his head.

Ethan paced back and forth in front of the Acidel. Seeing Josef standing guard, he walked over to him, "I remember you well, young lad."

Josef's face flushed, "Yes, my lord…I am Josef."

"I may be old but I am not senile, not yet anyway. I know who you are…the boy courier…the young man who killed the queen."

"Yes, my lord…It was an order…"

"Be that as it may, you still murdered…and I forgave you, we all forgave you…"

"Yes, my lord…you did."

"So tell me young Josef. Why do you stand guard over these slaves?"

"Because I have been ordered to do so."

"And what have they done? Or more specifically…What have they done…to you?"

Josef stammered, "…They…they are Acidel…is that not enough?"

Ethan shrugged and waited. He wanted more of an answer but

none would come. Josef looked beyond his Czar into the distance, following the path he had been conditioned to obey. There would be no changing the minds of the misguided young. Not when these thoughts have been relentlessly hammered into their consciousness since birth.

Resigned to accept these things he had no control over, Ethan sadly walked away and motioned for Unic to join him.

Placing his hand upon Unic's shoulder, Ethan whispered, "I did not set this wheel in motion. But now I must see it to an end…If I do not return…You must see that Stritonoly lives on…"

"Even the brightest star will eventually turn to dust."

Ethan smiled, "…If that is what shall be…See that it is done in a manner befitting our honor…"

"I am only one man," Unic said, "But I will do as I am able."

"I know you will try," Ethan said, looking back at the Acidel. "…I know you will try."

Chapter 15

Accompanied by several soldiers, Ethan left the rooftop.

Barok cowered against the rear of the roof, cold and frightened, not ashamed by his nakedness, ashamed by his past. He would give anything to erase the last year of his life. But alas, he could not.

Sir Gunther strutted contemptuously over to the Acidel. "Give me your report," Gunther demanded, facing one of the older soldiers standing guard.

"They were taken into the forest," the soldier said, "We swabbed them down with the solution. They are prepped and ready."

"Any problems?"

"Nothing that wasn't dealt with, Sir."

"I see many beaten and weary Acidel here. Will they be able to follow our commands?"

"We will see to it that they do."

Gunther smiled, "Well done. Continue supervision until I give the order."

He didn't notice me at all, Barok thought. Ramsitt was right. My appearance must have changed after my transformation. Will Shroomy even know who I am?

Barok lifted his head and peered to the front of the line. There she was; shivering with her arms crossed, wounds bleeding freely. It was difficult to see her this way, but he forced himself to look at her. He could not bear to see her in such pain. He hoped she would look his way, see the love in his eyes, see the Acidel he once was.

It was not to be…She never looked at him.

His heart sank.

"Wait here," Ethan said to the soldiers escorting him.

Slamming the door behind him, Ethan threw his cape on the bed. He was alone, back in his chambers, needing a moment to compose his thoughts before making his way to meet with Strito. He knew; in spite of the assurances he had been given, this was a meeting he would not return from.

Hastily moving over to a small desk that sat caddy-cornered between two bookracks, Ethan sat, consumed by a sudden urge to cry. He wished he could, but the lump in his throat was solid, unmoving. He wanted so badly an opportunity to sob. To unleash the weight of this burden, escape from his thoughts and just weep. But as he sat there waiting for the tears to come, he realized his body would not allow him that luxury. There would be no reprieve from the destiny mapped out for him.

Pulling a single sheet of paper out of the top drawer of the desk, Ethan lifted his writing implement and wrote what he knew would be his final testimony.

I have lived a long life, my physical body has grown old, but it has lived far longer than I ever thought it would. As I write this, I am breaking inside. The kingdom trusted to my charge is about to collapse. My heart bleeds for the tragedy which is about to transpire. It is doubtful this letter will ever find kind hands, but in the unlikely event that it does, please know that while I accept my failure, I tried the best I could.

My life has been spent in the pursuit of a higher cause, an infinite knowledge. I have sought to answer the questions that have plagued man since the dawn of time. I admit it has been a futile effort. Now, as I anticipate the final moments of my life, I see, far too late, that I have squandered my existence. I have wasted time pursuing answers that are simply unattainable, and as I wait for my demise to come, I have nothing left to offer.

There is no way to stop the ticking of the clock. This day will end, as will all things, and no man will be the wiser. There will be no victor to this war, for there can never be a victor in a universe so torn apart by ignorance and sin. Some things that plague my nightmares will live with me throughout eternity. I can only hope that when my heart ceases to beat, I will be granted the comfort of forgetfulness from these days of agony.

In closing, I will say that I am sorry.

Sorry, for I am only a man…

The Czar of Stritonoly,
Ethan Educai

Carefully folding the document, Ethan stamped it with the official seal and slipped it back into the top drawer of the desk.

Walking over to his bathroom, Ethan stood for a long moment looking into the mirror above the sink. His once bright eyes had faded, any hint of optimism evaporated into despair.

It all dances away from me now, he thought. All that will be left is a memory of a place called Stritonoly, and perhaps a distant recollection of a weak and battered leader who could not save it.

Lifting his shirt, he stared at the wounds upon the chest. Several long, jagged scars stretched across his torso. The markings left there many years ago by the mighty Konig.

He had undeniable proof upon his body of a force more powerful than any other, and as he looked at the disfigurement upon his chest, he remembered the storm. He remembered driving the knife into Dmitri's skull. In addition, he remembered all too well the ensuing devastation that ravaged the planet.

However, he dismissed the notion that something otherworldly had dug his claws into him that day. And even though he knew what he saw, it would forever be kept hidden away in the deep recesses of his memory. It was the one thing he consciously refused to accept: Faith.

Now, as he faced his own annihilation, the questions continued to plague him. Could he ever allow his own freewill to be terminated? Could he stifle logic long enough to believe in an entity that no science could ever prove existed? He had tried so hard for so many years. And after being held in the grasp of the Mighty Konig, he thought his perception might change, that he would somehow acquire the faith he so desperately sought. But the misery of years piled up faster than his faith could withstand. And even though the physical reminder of these scars would stay with him until his dying day, he could never abandon the intellect, which always brought him to one conclusion; Konig was not real.

Chapter 16

"So now what?" Becki asked, brushing her hair as she waited inside a portable mini-tent behind the transport.

"Now, we wait," Chlochelle answered. He stood there at the opening of the orange tent, his back to Becki who was sitting comfortably, legs crossed. The tent was spattered with the reflection of the sun's rays as it leaked in through the flimsy material. Nothing was in the tent except for two chairs, one for Becki, the other, presumably for Ethan.

"You really think he'll come?" Chlochelle asked, staring out the open curtain which wafted gently in the breeze.

"Ethan will come," Becki said slowly, "But it won't matter."

"Why do you say that?"

"Ethan is a man filled with nobility, it makes me sick. He will choose death over a life of slavery. To him, it will be honorable."

"Even for his people?" Chlochelle asked. "No man has the right to condemn all his people to death."

Becki grinned, continuing to brush her long hair, "It all depends on a man's perspective, doesn't it? If a man truly believes what he is doing is just, he can rationalize anything. Such is the disgraceful state of the human mind."

Chlochelle slowly turned to face her. "Comments like that continue to amaze me. Your insight is not lost on me."

Becki stopped brushing. Sitting up tall in her chair, she blinked her almond green eyes, grinned from ear to ear and slowly licked her lips.

Chlochelle felt his heart race as he struggled to gain composure. The awkward movements and stilted manner in his stance became ever more apparent. His attraction to her was impossible to disguise. "Princess…I am quite aware of the vast knowledge you possess… especially when it comes to the psyche of men…And the obvious power you have over them."

"Them?" Becki asked, running the back of her hand over her cheekbone, then slowly bringing her tongue out to meet her finger. "…You are not talking about 'them'…Why don't you just say it…You want me."

"I have implied no such thing!"

"You didn't have to."

"I am simply saying that…I can clearly see what you're doing… what you have done…and…"

Becki lost her smile, "Choose your next words carefully. If you plan to insult me, you had best reconsider."

"I am not a fool, I would never speak to you out of turn," Chlochelle said. "Strito obviously has strong feelings for you. That alone makes you my ally…In no way do I wish for us to be enemies. My words were an observation of your acumen. I meant it as a compliment."

"…Then you still don't know who I am…or what I am capable of…I cannot be tricked by a shoddy attempt at flattery."

Annoyed, Chlochelle turned away from her, "Neither can I," he said. "I only hope we can be civil toward each other when this day is over. I can be of great service to you."

"I have no doubt of that," Becki smiled. "And when the time is right, you will serve me well." Then her voice became uncompromising. "Just know your place," she said firmly. "I will not share Strito with you or anyone…so it is in your best interest to always remember your place…And do not test me!" She laughed, her tone suddenly rising, "Of course, feel free to try," her voice now madly possessed, "I would love for you to try…go ahead, try, try, TRY! In fact, I have a wonderful idea. Form a coup to take me down if you like, better yet, why wait, kill me now…go ahead, plunge a dagger into my heart! Twist it into my stomach. Watch me go BLAH!!!…I am so worried! Oh no, the crazed Chlochelle might just do me in," She laughed maniacally. "You won't…Because you can't…You are a coward like the rest of them… Nothing can stop me, least of all you…silly little man!"

Chlochelle didn't move, refusing to make eye contact with her, he just stared from the tent. His worst thoughts about the instability of Princess Becki were true. She was clearly unhinged, her ramblings wild and delusional.

Becki combed her hair robotically. Her thoughts were drifting far way.

Then, a black gloved hand pushed the curtain at the front of the tent aside.

"Did I hear screaming?" Strito said, stepping inside.

Shocked by his sudden appearance, Chlochelle took a few steps backwards. He did nothing wrong, but that didn't stop him from feeling guilty. He felt as if Strito somehow knew he harbored a secret lust for Becki's physical beauty.

"Is something wrong?" Strito asked, looking at Chlochelle for an answer.

Becki smiled. "Were you worried about me?"

"I thought I heard shouting."

"There is absolutely nothing wrong," Becki said, "Chlochelle was kind enough to help me prepare. I became irate for a moment, I'm sorry. I cannot help but think that Ethan will not listen to me. It will upset me if he dooms all his people to death because of his arrogance. Chlochelle was kind enough to let me vent off some of my frustration. I'm quite fine now."

"You have me worried," Strito said. "Are you sure you're able to do this?"

"Very able…and I'm looking forward to it."

"That's good to hear," Strito said, "Because the time for preparation is over. Our men have intercepted him. He emerged from a side entrance just a minute ago. He is being led here now."

"Bring him to me," Becki smiled.

Chapter 17

I know these things because they have been with since my birth. It is not about faith, it is about a certainty I feel with every fiber of my being. While I do not know the complete history of my parents, I know that my father was a brave man in the end. I know that he witnessed the eventual collapse of humanity. In bondage, he could only watch as the humans blindly welcomed insanity. My father was an Acidel. I do not know much more than that. But I know he gave his life for me. And I know his name, they called him Barok.

~ Taken from the memoirs of Queen Shroomy;
Ruler of the Last World

GUNTHER PACED BACK and forth behind the bowman. He held his sword drawn at his side and was grumbling incoherently as he stomped his feet solidly. The bowman knelt with their bows ready, peering down onto the lawn.

It was evident from Gunther's stride that he was furious. His heartbeat raced frenetically, no longer in anticipation of a battle. Now, a rage filled him that grew with every passing second. Disgusted by the way Ethan so easily dismissed him, ignoring his advice in lieu of council from Unic. His mind rattled with images of a bloody demise for his Czar. He could taste Ethan's downfall and wanted only to be a part of it. It was clear to him that if Stritonoly was to be saved, he alone would be the one to do it.

"Sir Gunther," The oldest soldier supervising the Acidel said with some trepidation.

Gunther stopped pacing, "What!"

The soldier gulped. "It is time for the mid-day feeding of the Acidel."

Gunther shot a glare at the soldier. If his eyes were blades, they would have chopped his head into a billion tiny pieces.

"I presume," the soldier asked cautiously, "We will skip the feeding?"

"What do you think?" Gunther shouted. "Have any of us eaten today? Why should I care if the scum of our planet our fed? Get back to your station!"

"I'm sorry for disturbing you." The soldier turned red, retreating back to his guard.

"You will not feed them?" Unic asked, moving vigilantly toward Gunther.

"Do not speak to me, Unic. I have greater concerns."

Unic moved up close to Gunther, he whispered, "Even the condemned are given food privileges."

"Are you placing yourself in charge?" Gunther asked.

"I assume no such role here. But in the Czar's absence, I must insist we follow protocol."

"And I must insist you leave me alone. You are right about one thing, you have no role here. This is my war, and I will decide what's best. And it would be best for you to take your leave. Go pray, talk, council…or whatever it is you do. This is not a child's game Unic, stay out of my way."

"You have been ordered to do nothing until the Czar commands it. And if I choose to stay here…I will."

"Come with me," Gunther said, grabbing Unic by the arm and dragging him to the rear of the rooftop. "Clear a spot for me," Gunther demanded, as several Acidel scurried away from the edge.

"I demand you let go of me," Unic said, his voice trembling under the weight of absolute fear.

Gunther positioned Unic on the very edge of the rooftop. "Tell me what is going on. Where is the Czar?"

"The Czar will tell you when he is ready."

Pulling a jagged knife from his belt, Gunther held it under Unic's throat. "What did the message say? Tell me now or I shall cut you."

"I don't doubt that you would."

"Then tell me now!"

Unic swallowed hard, "Strito requests a meeting."

Gunther pressed the blade against Unic's throat. He sensed the soldiers were looking on. "Look away from us," Gunther screamed. "This is not your concern. This man is a traitor to our planet." The soldiers turned away.

Unic yelled, "Imperial soldiers, you must listen to me. Do not take orders from this man. He is not your Czar."

"I am their leader," Gunther said, "They will listen to my commands. You have forced me to take control over this battle. You have conspired against your own people by keeping me in the dark. Now tell me what you know before it's too late. When is this meeting?"

"You wish to stop it?"

"Just tell me!" Gunther screamed.

"The Czar has already left the citadel. He is to meet with Strito shortly."

"He has fled without even consulting me. And you dare to keep this from me?"

"This is not your business. The Czar has made up his mind what is to be done."

Addressing his men, Gunther shouted, "Master Unic is guilty of treason. He has hidden valuable information from me and has placed us all in harm's way."

"Search your souls," Unic pleaded. "If you follow Sir Gunther, you will be sentencing our planet to certain doom. You will meet your ruin on this day, as will your families and all those you love."

The imperial soldiers were stone-faced, staring straight ahead, Unic's words falling on deaf ears.

Gunther laughed, "They will never listen to you. You are a criminal. And according to imperial law, treason is punishable by death."

"So you will kill me?" Unic asked.

"No," Gunther said, slipping the knife back into his belt. "You have killed yourself."

With the back of his hand, Gunther swung wildly, striking Unic across the face with all his might. Unic tumbled backward, frantically grabbing for the edge of the roof to no avail. Unable to stop his momentum, his body flew off the roof sideways, his horrifying scream echoing out as he plummeted to his death.

Unic Heldar left the only world he had ever known, and turmoil gripped Stritonoly.

Chapter 18

Ethan was ushered into the tent as Becki looked on.

Two men, one on each shoulder, pushed Ethan down into the chair opposite Becki.

Except for the crown that adorned Ethan's head, he looked like the frail old man he had become. He wore a white ruffled shirt and solid black pants, no rings, no jewelry.

Strito stood behind him. Though the mask hid his face, it was evident to all, that if his face could be seen, there would be a broad smile upon it. After years of pursuit and planning, the Czar of Stritonoly was finally at his mercy.

"You wear my crown," Strito said. "That is quite a daring move on your part. I see you come to me with no cape, no royal ornamentation… just the crown. Should I take this as an insult? Are you trying to provoke me further?"

"Take it however you wish," Ethan said, staring at Becki, their eyes locked together. "Why is she here? I came unarmed and alone as you requested. I am prepared to meet with you as per the order of truce. Why do you mock me by having her present for this?"

Strito slowly moved around to face Ethan, "It is so ironic…Is it not? This conflict began when we took your beloved princess. A princess you could have cared less about, a princess you held under lock and key. It seems to be your way, enslaving those who mean the most to you. Yet, you felt the need to defend her. I would guess it was a foolish attempt at preserving your reputation…I suppose it makes no difference now."

"She is one of our own," Ethan said. "We defend our own, and let us not play games. She has nothing to do with this. You could have walked away with her many times…that was never your intent…But be that as it may, I am not here to debate what is past. Let us focus on this summit…Am I here to meet with you or not?"

Strito nodded to the two men behind Ethan. At once, they wrapped his body with a thick rope and tied him to the chair. Ethan's face fell flat, though he was not at all surprised by such an action. The slim chance that a negotiation would take place faded from his mind. He had hoped for an opportunity to engage Strito in a war of words, perhaps corner him with good sense and the wisdom of his years. It was too much to wish for and not to be.

"I'll take this," Strito said, removing the crown.

Then, with the anger he had suppressed for a lifetime, he threw it to the ground at Ethan's feet. "You dare to disgrace me this way?" Strito yelled. "You know you are defeated and you have the audacity to wear this in my presence?" Strito raised his leg and stomped down upon the crown, crushing it to pieces. Before Ethan could utter a sound, Strito lashed out with a furious punch to Ethan's jawbone.

"You are in the presence of the Mejasz," Strito said. "And if you live past this day, you will address me as such…Say it! I want to hear you say it! Call me the Mejasz! I am your master now!"

Ethan felt the ringing in his ears, the metallic taste of blood filling his mouth. Then, he was swatted upright as Strito landed another blow to his face, this time opening a wound under his eye.

"Have you no honor?" Ethan mumbled, spitting up blood. "You will have to kill me. I will never call you the Mejasz…you are no more than a common thief!"

Strito pulled out a small triangular blade. Twirling it between his thumb and forefinger it caught the reflection of light, and for a split second cast a terrorizing sheen.

Lunging toward Ethan, he held the blade an inch from his eyeball. "I am the rightful ruler of this planet," Strito whispered. "Today you will pay for the wrongs you have done. Your offenses are not forgiven. Not by me, not by anyone. I am here to exact justice for the centuries of sin you have committed." Then, with a flash of movement, Strito slashed Ethan's cheekbone, opening a wide gash.

As blood trickled down the side of his face, the revolting stains of ill-omened crimson covered Ethan's white beard and shirt.

And Becki smiled…

Chapter 19

"THE CZAR HAS forsaken us!" Gunther shouted, as he peered out onto the lawn. "You cannot deny you saw him. That was the Czar himself being led to meet with Strito. I would have doubted it also unless I saw it with my own eyes. He has betrayed us all, left us here with no instructions, no guidance. What kind of leader does such a thing?" Gunther waited a moment, looked around at the soldiers who were clearly on his side. "He is no longer our Czar. He is a coward that flees when he senses defeat. But I do not accept defeat. And I know in my heart you feel the same."

A long pause followed. All that could be heard was the shifting of the forest, the leaves bristling in the wind.

The faces of the men were uncompromising, toughened by many years of cynical instruction. They were born and bred as warriors, never to accept loss without a fight. Gunther was more than just their commander; he was one of them, family. They would die for him without hesitation.

Gunther shouted with all the bravado of a conquering king, "I have trained you, nurtured you, taken you in and treated you as my own blood. I will not allow you to suffer because of a weak and foolish man. From this moment on…I am your Czar."

Josef drew his sword and held it to the sky. "Long live the Czar," he shouted.

Like automated machines in an assembly line, the men held their weapons to the sky. "LONG LIVE THE CZAR!" they chanted as one.

Then, like a hand mightier than any manmade force, a mighty breeze throttled over the rooftop. With nature directing their course, several winged creatures rocketed through the sky toward the sun. Their immense wingspan created fleeting shadows, which passed ominously over the citadel. In that singular instance of time, the reign of power on Stritonoly had been transferred. There was no further need for explanation or diatribe. It was uncomplicated and unconditional. In the eyes of the men who stood witness, Gunther was now the Czar.

"My Lord," A soldier said, running up and standing at attention. "Strito's men have been out of formation for some time. Their weapons are not drawn."

"It could be a trap," Gunther said thoughtfully. "But it could also be the very chance we need."

"We know what must be done. I agree, it would be better to have avoided such an action, but it times of peril, we cannot choose the easiest path, only the right one. We are in no position to make moral issues our own hands. Leave that to the politicians and naysayers. Critics there will always be, do not let them sway you. It takes bravery unbeknownst to their cowardly hearts to take swift and decisive action when circumstances are not what they should be. We must defend our people…at all costs."

With all the resolve known to him, Gunther said, "I need at least one soldier to supervise the first wave of Acidel when they reach the lawn." In the brief silence that fell after Gunther's words, the realization set in. Be it just or not, the Acidel were about to be sent to their fiery deaths. His command sealed the fate of the tiny slave race. Though most of them were in the dark about their current situation, they were not senseless or stupid. Barok felt tears well up in his eyes, a dread chill course through him. It was obvious to all that the end was near.

Josef took a step forward, "Let it be me."

Gunther smiled, "You seek redemption still?"

"I seek to prove my loyalty," Josef said with conviction. "I am ready for this test. I will do you proud, My Lord."

Gunther walked up slowly to face Josef. "…So shall it be then. From what we know, Strito's men are not watching the rear of the citadel. They seem to have concentrated their efforts on a full frontal assault. Their stupidity in strategic warfare is baffling, but a tragic mistake on their part is a window of opportunity for us. I wish to keep us locked down so we will lower you from the roof with the first band of Acidel. We will set you down behind the citadel where no one is the wiser." Quickly, he swung his massive frame around and summoned a bowman. He pointed to a tree. "Hit that tree with your arrow," Gunther ordered.

The bowman tightened his grip, prepared an arrow, and immediately shot it toward a tree just beyond the rear of the citadel. The arrow struck dead center into the bark.

"Good," Gunther said, turning back to Josef. "When we are ready, this bowman will fire a single arrow into that tree. That will be your cue to lead the Acidel to the lawn. I don't care how you do it, or what you tell them, just get them as close to Strito's men as possible and then get yourself out of harm's way. When we shoot them in the back, the explosion will level Strito and his men, it will be devastating."

Josef tried to repress a smile but could not. He knew that his action would be seen as heroic. His mind overflowed with visions of a celebrated parade in his honor. He felt like a master painter erasing his past with one swift brushstroke.

"How many can you handle?" Gunther asked.

"I can take them all," Josef answered obnoxiously.

Gunther laughed, "Ah…The eager hand of youth. I will give you ten. Let's see how you do."

Josef grinned, "It will be an honor to take them to the lawn…I will lead them to the death they deserve."

Summoning several soldiers holding thick cords with harnesses attached, Gunther ordered, "Strap them up!"

Josef was harnessed first, as ten Acidel's, were hastily plucked from the pack, and readied. Wide-eyed and innocent, they formed a single line without complaint.

The first in the line was Shroomy, the last…Barok.

Chapter 20

ETHAN HUNG HIS head, blood everywhere. There was no feeling in his face anymore. He had grown numb to the pain. The agony, which cut him the deepest, was in his heart. He was forced to face the acceptance of his failure and the regret of an incomplete and possibly meaningless life.

Satisfied in seeing Ethan this way, Strito and his men left the tent. In the silence that followed, Becki sat face to face with her former mentor, waiting for him to look at her.

After some time, Ethan finally raised his head. "Are you happy?" Ethan asked. An expression of resignation sketched onto his badly beaten face.

Becki looked into Ethan's squinting eyes. A genuine sympathy unexpectedly consumed her. It frightened her because up until now, she had only felt hatred toward Ethan. Seeing him in this helpless state, she could not deny a feeling of pity for him. "This is not what I would have hoped for. But you had to know this would happen. Your time as the Czar has come to an end."

"It is no surprise to me…And now you will have your kingdom. Isn't that what you want?"

"There are many things I want. But ruling a kingdom is not one of them."

This is not going how I had planned, Becki thought. Why do I suddenly feel compassion for this man? Get it together Becki!

Ethan managed a half-grin. "Why do we do these things?" he asked, not expecting an answer. "Man has fought wars for all of existence… and why? It is only now at the end I see the madness and futility of it all. Nothing can be gained…much is lost."

Becki turned somber, her eyes penetrating Ethan's sensibilities. She seemed once more like the child he had once known. "Ethan…The time has come for you to surrender. You can save many lives today if you do, and I can save you…The Mejasz listens to me. I swear to you, it is not too late."

Ok, that was good, Becki thought. Now I'm back on track. I sounded quite convincing. He will listen to me, he has to. He must know there is no other choice.

"Who are you?" Ethan asked. "I'm going to die today, I know that for certain. But what I don't know is who you are? I thought I did… And once again, I was wrong."

Does he see through my doubt? Becki questioned herself. What is wrong with you, Becki? Snap out of this. This man is like all the rest, he means you nothing but harm. He is your enemy; they are all your enemies. Trust only yourself and never let them see what you're thinking. Now go and play your part! Speak to him!

"I am the little girl you taught. I am the woman who conspired to kill my own family. I am innocent and wise, vile and cunning. I am all these things."

Ethan smiled, "Nothing and no one is a singularity…you said that once."

Becki smiled back at him, "I remember…Was I wrong?"

"Hardly…"

"So you will surrender?"

"I will."

Becki stood, "You will? I knew you would!"

"I will…" Ethan continued, "I will never trust you, and I will never surrender."

Beep…Beep…Beep!

"What was that?" Becki asked, a look of sheer terror and panic washed over her.

"You heard me correctly," Ethan said, "I will never surrender!"

"Not that you idiot!" Becki yelled, "That sound…What was that sound?"

"I do not find your antics at all amusing. You heard what I said, now do what you have to do."

Did he not hear it? Becki thought, her mind whipping around like a tornado. I remember that sound. I heard it in the forest many years ago. Why does it come to haunt me again?

"Do not play with me, Ethan!" Becki screamed. "Where did that sound come from? Do not treat me like a child. Tell me you heard it also."

"I heard nothing."

"You are a liar! A vindictive, evil man and I hate you! I will always hate you!"

Becki's eyes grew wide with horror. Pull it together, she thought.

"I am sorry…" Becki said slowly. "Please understand the strain this situation puts me under. However, since you have agreed to surrender we can…"

"I have agreed to nothing!" Ethan shouted.

"You are a liar!" Becki screamed. "You just said you would surrender. I heard you say it."

"I said no such thing, and I never will. You are mad! Delusional! Nothing has changed. You may have fooled Strito but you cannot disguise yourself from me."

"Then you will die!" Becki said.

"We will all die," Ethan said solidly. "And you have made me realize something…I have no fear of death anymore…In this current state of man, I only fear living. Give me my death and you will give me my reward…I will be free from all that binds me."

I have no answer, Becki thought. I need to compose myself. Turn away from his stare and think. What was that beeping sound? How did it come to this? I was once a sweet little girl, and now I condemn the man who gave me knowledge to his death. I hold his fate in my hand. I have wished for this moment, but now that it is here…I don't know what to do. The naïve little girl in me returns and I am lost again.

"Blessed is our God," The priest said, "Always now and forever, and unto the ages of ages." Ethan and his son Richard bowed their heads. The elderly priest hunched over, his eyes closed, his voice melodramatic to a fault.

Rebecca felt the wetness of a spiritual ointment as the priest applied it to her forehead. "What the hell is that supposed to do?" she thought. "It's kinda late to save me? What's done is done. Even in my final moments I have to deal with the ridiculous traditions of man; absurd, inane and laughable. I may be a druggie, but I'm not stupid! I guess everyone forgot what a smartass I was before I started getting wasted all the time."

The priest began The Lord's Prayer, "Our Father, who art in heaven…"

Rebecca heard every word as the priest solemnly delivered these holy words. She had chanted it countless times when her family used to go mass regularly. While she knew the prayer well, she had no idea why she said it or what it was supposed to do, if anything. Her feeling about prayer had always been the same; it was a thing you did because someone told you to do it. She could never wrap her head around what meaning it could possibly have. And even though she knew she would soon leave this world, she couldn't bring herself to believe. It seemed so hypocritical to change her lifelong intuition on a whim that she might attain salvation at some other time.

When the prayer was finished, the priest turned the page of his beat-up leather bound prayer book and began reciting, "O Lord God Almighty, the Father of our Lord Jesus Christ, who willest that all men should be saved, and should come unto the knowledge of the truth; who desirest not the death of a sinner, but that she should turn again and live: We pray thee and implore thee, absolve thou the soul of Rebecca Brown, thy servant from every bond, and deliver her from every curse."

"So this how it ends," Rebecca thought. "I'm guessing this is the last rites. I've heard about this, I think I saw it in a movie once, this is the first I've ever heard them…yeah, and I suppose it'll be the last time I hear them also, ha-ha. Damn, they are so morbidly dreary and absolute. And yet, this is all so strange. I don't feel like I'm about to die. I mean…I know it's happening…but I feel nothing."

The priest continued on, "Pardon her transgressions, both of knowledge and of ignorance, both of deed and of word, which she hath committed from her youth up, and hath cleanly confessed or hath concealed, either through forgetfulness or through shame."

"I suppose I'm forgiven now," Rebecca thought. "Shit, if I knew it was gonna be that easy, I would have sinned a lot more! And I have to be a little pissed about the fact that I spent the first fifteen years of my life doing nothing but good. Damn, I was a straight 'A' student, kind to everyone, played the violin, and went to church. And what was it all for? It never took away the pain; it sure as hell didn't keep my mother alive. I'll never apologize for getting high as much as I did, at least I was happy."

The priest coughed, turned the page and continued, "Yea, O Lord who lovest mankind, give thou command, and she shall be released from the bonds of the flesh and of sin; and receive thou in peace the soul of this thy servant, Rebecca, and give it rest in the everlasting mansions, with thy Saints; through the grace of thine Only-begotten Son, our Lord, and God, and Saviour Jesus Christ: with whom also thou art blessed, together with thine all-holy, and good, and life-giving Spirit, now, and ever, and unto ages of ages. Amen."

She couldn't put her finger on it, but she was fascinated by a warm sensation consuming her senses. "Is this the feeling of death approaching?" She asked herself. "I'm guessing no. More than likely, it's that last jolt of morphine kicking in. I don't suppose death would feel this peaceful. Although, I have no reference point to make any judgments…I've never died before…well, at least as far as I can remember I haven't. It's weird; I fear nothing…"

A powerful and hypnotic state of tranquility crept into her consciousness, and though her eyes had been shut tight since the accident, she could see the room clearly. Her father and brother were on her left side. The priest, holding a small prayer book, stood at the foot of the bed.

And then there was that sound.

It was the sound that tracked her down no matter where she went. The sound that echoed into every corner of every world she ever knew. The sound that refused to let go, even when her mind had long ago taken leave. The beep…beep…beeping of the heart monitor pounded into her brain like a jackhammer.

Beep…beep…beep…

Relentless in its detached emotional timbre.

Beep…beep…beep

Incessant and all-consuming in its eventual finality.

"Do you hear me?" Shroomy asked.

"I hear you."

"I want you to listen to me carefully," Shroomy said into Rebecca's brain. "Your heart monitor has been shut off for some time now,"

"Then why do I still hear it," Rebecca answered.

"Because it's inside you," Shroomy said softly. "And yes, it is a heartbeat you hear. It is the child that lives inside you."

"Then this child will die with me?" Rebecca asked.

"Not if you give her to me," Shroomy whispered. "Will you give her to me?"

"Yes."

The sound was the constant reminder that life still existed within every cavernous shell of flesh of bone. And Rebecca heard the sound, for the sound was always there. Even before the accident, even before her childhood, even before her first breath, the sound was always there…And though she was trillions of miles away, Becki heard it too…

Chapter 22

THE ARROW HIT the tree dead center just as Gunther said it would.

Seeing the arrow crunch into the bark, Josef felt a chill of exhilaration. "Now is the time," He said under his breath.

The ten Acidel under Josef's supervision squatted down next to him. Pushed up against the back wall of the citadel, they shivered as a cold wind began to pick up in the late afternoon. Several clouds had formed menacing patches over the citadel in the last hour and the sun was beginning to fade.

Josef had thought up several elaborate lies to tell the Acidel so they would go out onto the lawn when he ordered, but he soon realized it was unnecessary. The Acidel were conditioned to trust the orders of their masters, whatever they were. Josef took pride in the misery that would soon be inflicted upon these innocent victims, savoring his assignment with the gluttony of a rabid beast.

Moving swiftly, Josef led the naked Acidel past the lifeless body of Unic Heldar and ran with them to the side wall. They moved cautiously to the front of the building, slowing to a stop as they reached the bulky corner of the citadel. Peeking his head out, Josef saw the lawn clearly, the transport in the distance, Strito's men scattered about. Looking to the front gates, he saw the cage still covered in a black curtain, he paid it no heed. There was nothing to fear for Josef, once the Acidel were sent out to the lawn, he would retreat quickly. He only regretted the fact that he wouldn't see the enormous explosion Gunther had bragged about.

Turning his back to the lawn, Josef faced the Acidel, "When I give you the command, run as fast as you can to the men in black." He could have stopped there, but he felt compelled to say more, feeling the need to add his own dramatic flair to what he felt was his defining moment. "These men you run to, they are your friends. When you reach them, they will give you further instructions. Your life is about to change little ones. I am about to give you your freedom."

Barok stood tall amidst the pack of Acidel, cringing as he listened to the lies oozing from Josef's lips. Shroomy; dehydrated, beaten, and barely conscious, could hardly see what was in front of her let alone notice her former mate. Death was upon them and Barok would never have a chance to tell Shroomy he was sorry. The truth of what was about to happen bore into him like shattering glass.

There is nothing more I can do, Barok thought. I have tried in vain. All is indeed lost. I am the cause of this nightmare. May my name be cursed forever.

Josef had his back to them now.

Then…

He staggered.

Barok looked on with curiosity as Josef grabbed the side of his head. He was squeezing his temples with great force as he dropped his sword and stumbled over his own feet. First, he fell to his knees; then the weight of his body threw him forward. Methodically and with significant force, Josef started slamming his head into the muddy ground.

"What's…this…pain?" Josef mumbled, salivating freely as he continued to ram his forehead straight down into the surface. "Make…it…stop!" he begged, but the Acidel did nothing. They looked on in confusion as Josef rocked his body back and forth.

Then, his torso violently convulsed.

He vomited.

Then again…

This is our chance! Barok thought. Thank you Konig. I will not fail you.

"Come with me Acidel," Barok said, "I have no doubt this is a message from our divine one. Konig is providing us a chance for escape. He is giving us this opportunity. Let me take you to freedom. Follow me!"

The Acidel turned and ran away from Josef who lay face down in his own vomit. With a broad smile on his face, Barok led them scurrying back along the side wall from which they came.

Then, Barok froze in his steps.

Stepping out from behind the rear of the citadel, Ramsitt smiled. "Going sssssssomewhere? I knew you would betray me!"

Backing up as Ramsitt advanced, Barok pleaded, "Ramsitt, I was just coming to get you…we were on our way…"

"SSSSSSSilence," Ramsitt shouted. "You had your chance. Now it is my turn. Konig will not save you, no one will! No cosmic force brought that soldier to his knees. That pathetic excuse for a man is suffering from my telepathic grasp alone. And I will see to it that he dies a slow and agonizing death. As for you…"

"Please, Ramsitt…I was on my way…I swear it."

"And you lie to me! You are truly not an Acidel anymore. For an

Acidel could not lie to me with such ease. I know now why the pond of transformation could not accept you fully. There is human in you! And just like man, you have become a plague on all things. But do not worry, it will all be over soon. You will never poison another after today. When the day is through, only the spideron will roam this planet."

Ramsitt arched his body up, his wide frame casting a shadow onto the Acidel. As his tentacles lifted above him, Barok could hear the rest of the spideron tribe turning the corner to join their leader, hissing in anticipation of a kill.

They were trapped.

With nothing left to lose, Barok shouted the only words that would come to him "Acidel! Run! Run to the lawn!"

Chapter 23

The indisputable truth is that man cherished warfare. Whether it was a learned behavioral hindrance or a deep seeded compulsion for discord, is not known. Whatever the reason, they ultimately could not be tamed. Undeniably, this was the root of their demise.
~ Taken from the memoirs of Queen Shroomy;
Ruler of the Last World

"YOU ARE NOTHING!" Strito screamed.

Using the edge of his blade he cut Ethan loose from the chair, grabbed his blood-soaked shirt and ferociously lifted him up to face him. "Look at me!" Strito demanded. "I am the Mejasz. Your time is over; your people will die today, all of them! Your stubbornness is unforgivable."

"He will not surrender," Becki said in a monotone expressionless voice. Meticulously brushing her hair, she stared past them into the distance. Lost in a trance of her own, Strito accepted that she had become useless in this situation.

With the back of his hand, Strito struck Ethan across the face, blood spraying out and spattering the floor. "I offer you an opportunity to save the lives of your people and you defy me?"

Ethan looked at Strito, his face now a carpet of crimson and without sensation. "You are indeed a madman to think I would ever trust you."

"Even when you have no choice? You know of our body armor, you cannot win!"

"But I have a choice…And I would rather see my people die instantly."

Strito became even more incensed. He gripped Ethan's shirt and pulled him closer. "How could a leader say such a thing?"

"If I admit defeat, it is obvious what will happen."

"You assume too much. You assume you know me…you do not!"

"Surrender will give the very hand of evil a victory. That is something I will never do. I will not sentence my people to a living death. I will not be responsible for your heinous crimes."

"Stritonoly has enslaved the weak for centuries. How dare you speak to me of moral dignity? You are stupid man, and a hypocrite!"

"Use whatever words you like to defile me. I will never surrender."

"So you would have them die!" Strito yelled. "What is wrong with you?"

"I do not need to justify my actions to a man like you," Ethan said, a hint of a smile beginning to form. "I knew my life was over when I came to meet you. But I take pride in knowing this; I will die as the last Czar of Stritonoly. And I will die with honor."

"You are wrong again," Strito said, holding up his blade to meet Ethan's neck. "Upon your death, I will assume power. You will be nothing but an afterthought."

Ethan only smiled, "You will never see the throne. You will never be accepted…If you think otherwise, then you have proven your foolishness beyond any doubt."

Chlochelle stormed into the tent. "Acidel on the lawn!" he shouted.

"What are you talking about?" Strito asked.

"There is a small group of Acidel moving toward our men," Chlochelle said.

Ethan hung his head. Oh Gunther, he thought. What have you done…what have you done…

"Obviously some sort of rouse on your part," Strito said to Ethan. "My patience is at an end!"

Then, with one swift slash, Strito cut through Ethan's neck.

Becki looked on in disbelief as Ethan fell to the ground clutching his throat. His heartbroken, tear-filled eyes met Becki's for an instant. Then he shivered and fell forward into a pool of his own blood.

Ethan Educai was dead.

Chapter 24

A HUGE GOLDEN cauldron filled with flammable liquid had been rolled out onto the rooftop. Imperial soldiers dipped bulky rags into the fluid and hastily wrapped the rags around dozens of arrows. Several bowmen were already kneeling at the edge of the roof, prepped with their arrows aimed. The sopping rags were fully saturated with the viscous liquid. They clung to the arrowheads, ready to be set ablaze.

"Let us start with just one," Gunther smiled, watching as the Acidel sprinted toward Strito's men. "Enjoy this day, my friends. You are all about to take part in a glorious triumph. After today, no one in the galaxy will have the courage to meddle in our affairs ever again. We are on the verge of creating an immortal dynasty."

Placing his hand upon his best marksmen's shoulder, Gunther said, "Discharge your weapon on my command."

An imperial soldier moved toward Gunther with a blazing torch. He bent down in front of the selected bowman. Gunther nodded and the soldier immediately lit the rag attached to the end of the arrow. It instantly sent off a smoldering orange flame and a cloud of intense smoke.

On the lawn, Barok panted as he ran with all his might. As he approached Strito's men, he saw them raise their laser guns, rapidly moving into offensive positions. He stopped and turned. Shroomy was not far behind, struggling to keep pace as she staggered forward.

Gunther smirked, a malicious and uncaring grin cast over his scarred face. A lifetime of suppression under the command of others had been lifted, now he was the one in charge. He shouted with the pride of a newly appointed leader on the cusp of greatness. "Fire!" he yelled, sheer joy in his bellowing tone.

The bowman stretched back his bow, squinted in the direction of the Acidel, unhinged his fingers from the grip, and fired.

"No!" Barok screamed, as he saw the arrow being launched from the roof. Shroomy stopped running when she heard his voice. "Barok!" She said, "It cannot be!"

The arrow scorched a fiery trail straight toward Shroomy's head.

Everything was in slow motion, action ceased to exist. Barok's senses heightened as he ran toward his only love, his mate, and eternal partner. The arrow flared through the wind, shooting smoke and ash in a blistering streak.

Barok could hear his heart pounding as he ran faster than he ever thought he was able. He pumped his tiny fists as hard as he could, his legs hurdling to the fore with leaps not befitting an Acidel, desperate in this last ditch effort to save his Shroomy.

The arrow approached with abandon lifelessness, intent on only one thing, the termination of anything in its path.

Shroomy saw Barok running toward her, but her attention swayed when she detected the roar of the flaming arrow. She looked away from him, still in shock that he was alive. Then her eyes met the flames. She watched as the arrow accelerated and was now only several feet from her forehead.

With every ounce of energy known to him, Barok threw his body forward, lunging himself at Shroomy.

The arrow hit!

Barok grabbed for his shoulder that was now on fire. He stumbled and crashed to the ground. The arrow struck him in the middle of the back as fire rapidly consumed him. Shroomy screamed as the flames scorched down Barok's back, searing into his flesh, white blood gushing from the wound. She kicked the arrow loose from him, rolled him over backwards in an attempt to use the lawn to extinguish the blaze. Thick black smoke billowed up and encased them both in a blur of scorching cinders.

"They mean to kill us," one of the naked Acidel shouted, "We must flee!" With a flurry of little hands and feet, the remaining Acidel scattered, running for the forest.

"Where is the explosion?" The bowman who fired the arrow asked. "Sir Gunther! There was no explosion! What is happening?"

Gunther's face turned pale, his eyes locked on the failed attempt.

Grabbing the soldier closest to him, he screamed, "You told me they were all swabbed down with the solution! What have you done to us?"

"There were all swabbed down", the soldier stammered, "I swear to you, we prepped every one of them just as you ordered."

And yes, they were all swabbed down with the solution, all except for Barok. He infiltrated the line of Acidel after the soldiers had already prepared them. No one knew.

As the smoke subsided, Shroomy turned Barok face up, cradling his charred body in her chubby arms.

"I love you," Barok said with tears in his eyes. "Please forgive me for all I've done."

Shroomy cried, her tears falling onto Barok. "I will always love you,"

Shroomy said. "Close your eyes, my love, you are forgiven. This life is at an end, but our love will go on for the rest of time. We will always be together."

As Barok began to wheeze his final breaths, Shroomy leaned close to him and whispered, "I carry our daughter inside me. I have the faith that she will live on. Konig will protect her."

With his last words, Barok said, "I know he will…"

ETHAN BROWN FELT as if someone had cut his throat. He gasped for breath as soon as the heart monitor stopped beeping.

Then, the tears flowed.

The priest made a sign of the cross at the foot of the bed and stepped back. Ethan took one last look at his daughter, then turned and left the room.

Richard was more stoic, his cheeks were wet from the tears he cried, but now, there were no more tears left in him. The elderly priest put his hand on Richard's shoulder as they slowly walked out of the room.

Ethan stood in the empty waiting area across the hall from his daughter's room. After the priest left, Richard waited a long while before deciding he would go in and see his father, at least to say goodbye, if nothing more.

"Hey," Richard mumbled, standing in the doorway of the dreary waiting area.

"It's over," Ethan said, wiping his eyes with a handkerchief. "First my wife…now…my baby girl…And my son hates me…"

Richard resisted the urge to accuse his father of laying a guilt trip on him. He swallowed hard and moved closer to his dad. "I can't lie to you…I don't know how I feel about you, and I don't know if I'll ever forgive you for being drunk when mom died…But I don't hate you…I never hated you."

Ethan looked up, his blue eyes staring through a large glass window, that faced his daughter's room. Two nurses were going in and out, preparing the body for removal from the floor. "I have failed in so many ways," Ethan sobbed.

Silence.

"Do you remember my confirmation?" Richard asked.

Ethan looked at his son. "Your confirmation? Yes, of course I do."

"I can't believe I'm telling you this…but…Do you remember the name I choose?"

"Yes…You picked Joseph."

Richard smiled, happy that he remembered. "Do you know why?"

Ethan thought for a moment, then said, "I don't know…I assumed because he was Jesus' father."

"I wanted to pick Ethan…but I thought that might be too gay," Richard laughed awkwardly. "I picked Joseph because he was like the ultimate father to me back then. I mean, to be the father of Jesus Christ, that's some pretty cool shit…I could never believe that crap they told us in church. You know, that Jesus had a father named God but I would never see him until I died, seemed like a lot of bullshit to me…But I thought, I do wanna be like my dad…and if I don't pick Ethan, I'll pick Joseph…I guess it was a way of being like you…Back then…well…There were times I thought you were pretty cool." He laughed again. "I even made mom and Becki call me Joseph for a while. It's kinda funny cause when I was going through that phase, I was a real prick."

Ethan smiled, "I do remember that."

They both looked at the floor as silence absorbed them.

"So…" Ethan said, "You really wanted to be like me?"

"Once…yeah."

Ethan felt another rush of tears coming, but choked it back long enough to say, "I'm proud of you, Richard…I'm sorry I screwed things up."

"I guess we all screw up," Richard said. "Sooner or later…We all screw up…"

Chapter 26

Strito walked out of the tent with Chlochelle and Becki at his side. Emerging from behind the transport, he was now ready to join his men. He laughed upon seeing the few remaining Acidel scatter and run for the forest. "What do you make of this nonsense?" He asked Chlochelle.

"They just fired an arrow at one of them," Chlochelle said. "Two of them appear to be lying there dead. I have no idea why they would want to kill them. Perhaps they sense defeat and they wish to kill the Acidel off before we can take control over them. I don't understand it at all."

"As far as we know, the Acidel are inside the citadel?" Strito asked.

"Yes, as far as we know."

"I am at a loss for their mindless strategies," Strito said. "Order the men to shoot torches into every window, we will smoke them out."

"And when they come out?" Chlochelle asked. "What shall we do then?"

"We will fire at will!" Strito said with authority. "Of course, let us try to save at least a few Acidel; we could certainly use them for labor after this is over."

"I am so happy," Becki said robotically. "Strito…you are the Mejasz, the savior. I am so very pleased to share in your victory."

Chlochelle hung his head, as Strito stood proud.

"Finally," Strito said, "I can remove my mask. I have done what I said I would do. The prophecy has been fulfilled." He turned to Chlochelle, "Go now to the men and give them my orders. I cannot wait to watch the citadel burn."

Chlochelle ran toward the men, shouting commands. Strito's men immediately lit huge fiery torches and proceeded to throw them into every window. Some of them loaded the torches into oversized laser guns and shot them straight into the walls of the citadel.

Instantly, white smoke billowed out from the first floor windows. Flames of orangey-red licked up the walls, spreading vigorously.

Strito turned to Becki, "I am the Mejasz," he said, "I have waited for this day my entire life. And now, you shall be the first to see my face."

He reached for the side of his mask. With one swift tear, he ripped it from his head. He stood there, exposed for the very first time, a handsome but ordinary looking man with long brown hair and hazel eyes.

"You are more beautiful than I could have ever imagined," Becki said. "We will rule this planet together for many years, and it will be my honor to bear you many offspring. Please, my love…Let me kiss you."

"Of course," Strito smiled.

She pressed her body against his, her lips gently caressing his cheeks before coming to meet his lips. Strito's body stiffened as this long awaited moment of passion consumed his every sense.

Then, she reached for his beltline, removed his laser gun, and stepped back.

"What are you doing?" Strito laughed.

Becki said nothing, her face a chasm of iniquity and malevolence.

Holding the laser gun up, she fired it straight into Strito's face, his head exploding instantly. Brain matter and skull blew apart, dispersing into a miasma of gore. His headless body slumped over and crashed to the ground. Becki turned and ran, retreating behind the transport for cover.

On the rooftop, pandemonium ensued. Imperial soldiers stood helpless with swords that would do nothing against this enemy. Their faces filled with a mixture of anger and sorrow as they watched the smoke rising up all around them.

Furious, Gunther paced back and forth, thinking desperately for a solution, some way out of this nightmare. His demeanor had turned even more cold and arrogant, facing a certain defeat he refused to accept.

Peering out through the smoke, he could see Barok and Shroomy on the lawn. Barok was lifeless, but Shroomy was moving, her hand gently stroking Barok's forehead.

Strito's men marched forward, closing in on the fiery citadel. Their laughter grew louder as they reveled in the sight of the burning wreckage.

Gunther grabbed a bowman, commandeered his bow, and threw him to the floor. Readying an arrow, he screamed, "Light this arrow for me, someone light it now!"

A soldier quickly came forward with a torch and set the end of his arrow to flame.

"Get an Acidel!" Gunther screamed at his soldiers. "Do it now!"

Two soldiers picked a small, frightened Acidel from the rear of the rooftop and marched him toward Gunther.

"Lift this creature up," Gunther ordered. "On my command, throw this filth to the lawn."

The Acidel began to struggle with the death grip the soldiers had on him. It was to no avail as they lifted him with ease above their heads and waited for Gunther to bark out the terrible words, "Now, throw him now!"

The soldiers lunged forward with every bit of strength they had. The screaming Acidel propelled out from over the rooftop. With his arms and legs frantic in motion, the Acidel fell from the height as his wails of terror intensified.

Setting his sights for the falling and helpless Acidel, Gunther pulled back on the bow and shot his flaming arrow in his leathery back.

Just before the Acidel hit the ground, he exploded into a billion pieces of guts and gore. Gigantic red flames flew in every direction, scorching the front of the citadel and setting the lawn ablaze. Over a dozen of Strito's men crumbled to their knees, consumed by the overpowering inferno. They screamed as their body armor melted and then disintegrated under the tremendous heat of the fire. Their flesh left bare as they burned alive.

Gunther smiled as he prepared another arrow. Through the dense flames and smoke he could still see Shroomy. He lit his arrow, readied it and shot it directly for her forehead.

Suddenly, there was a forceful rumble as the cage below ripped into pieces. A giant claw quickly shot up and intercepted the arrow with ease, snapping it in two. Then, the beast that was Konig rose up and stood before Gunther. Taller than the citadel itself, Konig flashed his red eyes onto the rooftop. His hairy features, jagged teeth, and muscular enormity frightened even the most hard-edged warrior.

"This madness ends now," Konig said, his thunderous voice echoing out all over the planet.

Gunther clutched his head as a screeching sound suddenly reverberated into his brain. A high-pitched, vociferous chaos pounded through his being. He knew immediately what the pain was. He had experienced it once before.

Spideron!

Dozens and dozens of spideron had scaled the wall. Presently, they converged on the roof, overwhelming the soldiers with fright and bewilderment. They pounced on soldiers and bowman alike, slicing their heads off with their tentacles, callous in their lethal assault.

As Gunther fell backwards, he felt his body rock. His large frame started to spasm with an uncontrolled ferocity.

"SSSSSSSSSSir Gunther," Ramsitt said, standing over him. "We meet again."

With all the fury of the combative creature he was, Ramsitt tore into Gunther's chest with his teeth. Gunther's body shook viciously. Unstoppable in his ruthless attack, Ramsitt ripped Gunther's heart out and spit it next to his now dead body.

Konig watched with disdain as the massacre continued. The violence he witnessed only intensified his determination to see his mission through.

Raising his red eyes to the horizon, he saw the setting sun. Using all the power bestowed upon him from the reflection, which ruled all things, he called upon the sun to finish this war once and for all. From the center of his hand, Konig launched a single red beam of light toward the center of the sun. Immediately, the nuclear forces inside the sun came to a halt. Darkness fell upon the land. Then, the stars in the sky joined planets of all shapes and sizes as they danced on the canvas of the black sky. They raced off in every direction, rolling recklessly out of orbit. A thousand detonations blistered white light throughout the galaxy as stars and planets smashed into each other.

Now, finally, it was done. As the memories of a trillion years stirred through him, Konig summoned the galaxy to implode into itself.

The burning cinder of Stritonoly rocketed through the sky; dreadful and merciless as it approached the nova that was once the sun. Then, with the power of a cosmic wrath unquenchable and unforgiving, Stritonoly blasted apart. This was the end of time and space, and it liquefied everything. The shockwave of the final explosion brought about finality to all things everywhere.

And then… the universe vanished into nothingness.

EPILOGUE

There are two forces that can never be slayed; absolute good and pure evil. The powers of these combatants lie beyond the realm of any natural order. They are compelled to create conflict beyond infinity.
~Taken from the memoirs of Queen Shroomy;
Ruler of the Last World

Konig floated in the cataleptic void. Stritonoly had been leveled by the dominance of his rage. In conclusion, the universe was finally exposed for every crime and inequity ever committed. In the eyes of the mighty reflection, justice had been done.

Before Konig could return home, there was one more task to complete. He blew his breath across the emptiness. A giant grazing land appeared, exquisite and lush in breathtaking splendor, full of potential for life, far from the reach of sin and wickedness.

"This is your home," Konig said, as he placed the child of Barok and Shroomy down upon the grass. "You are the only survivor. I have saved you in an act of my own freewill. I will name you after your mother. Your name will be Shroomy and you will be the queen of this place one day. This place will be known to all as the Last World. The journey before you will not be easy, but as I did for your parents, I will protect you in times of hardship."

"She is my child too," Becki said, standing in the distance with her dress torn. Her blood-soaked face was expressionless. "I have fooled you yet again," she said, as a sly grin began to form. "By keeping this little one alive, you have acted on your own freewill. You have disobeyed the mighty reflection. It is only a matter of time now. I will ultimately win this battle, as I always do. You cannot keep me away from her forever, and it has been proven time and again, you cannot kill me."

"I do not need to kill you," Konig said. "You have fooled no one. Everything has occurred exactly as it should."

Becki laughed, "Is this a veiled attempt at humor? It is obvious what has happened. I sought destruction and I succeeded."

She smiled triumphantly, "You have failed again."

"Nothing has ended. This is only the beginning."

"The beginning of the end. I will never stop! NEVER!"

"And neither will I," Konig said. "I cannot kill you, but I will banish you from this land. Remember this as well, I will be watching. I am always watching."

"Do as you must," Becki said, "In the end, whatever you choose to do will matter not. If it is my desire to return, I will find a way. When I do, I will take what is mine."

"Be gone from here!" Konig shouted.

In an instant, the mightiest of winds whipped around Becki's body. She bent and twisted in a frenzy of hail and debris. Amid the relentless storm that encased her, she cried out a bitter and demented shrill.

Then there was quiet.

After that, she was gone.

...and the blind man said, "Whether he be a sinner or no, I do not know.

All I know is that once I was blind and now I see."

THE END